It was a long way to Trevarnon, two miles or more, and over stiles. She had walked that way many times to see her sister on her day off, but the path had never seemed so long. Brambles clawed her hems, and tall nettles slashed at her knees, and long before she had reached Trevarnon gates she was tousled, hot and panting.

She had wits enough to pull herself together. She stopped to retie the ribbon-ends which dangled to her neck, and pulled the 'stickle-back' grasses from her skirts, but her dark curls tumbled hopelessly about her ears, and the dust on her boots was impossible to cure. And this would be the first time she'd gone up to the house!

She looked up at the forbidding granite walls which fenced the grounds, the grey slate of the roof, glimpsed through the trees which screened it from the town. It seemed to glower back at her.

Well, there was no help for it. She steeled herself and began to walk resolutely up the drive.

Rosemary Aitken is a specialist in English Language and has written several bestselling text books. Her short stories have been published in a number of women's magazines and have been read on BBC radio. She has also written two prize-winning plays. Born in Cornwall, Rosemary Aitken now lives in Cheltenham.

BY THE SAME AUTHOR

The Tinner's Daughter

THE GIRL FROM PENVARRIS

Rosemary Aitken

ORION

An Orion paperback
First published in Great Britain by Orion in 1995
This paperback edition published in 1996 by Orion Books Ltd,
Orion House, 5 Upper St Martin's Lane, London WC2H 9EA

Reissued 1997

A CIP catalogue record for this book is available
from the British Library.

Printed and bound in Great Britain by
Clays Ltd, St Ives plc

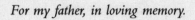
For my father, in loving memory.

PART ONE : 1899–1900

CHAPTER ONE

Katie's girlhood finished abruptly one spring day just before she was thirteen. It was also the day she met George Trevarnon for the first time.

It began happily enough. A blue May day, the sky mackereled with cloud, with the sun tweaking at sea-pinks in the hedges. A day to get out of bed early, when Father and the boys got up, so that Katie had been down the dusty lane, and up over the granite stile to Crowdie's farm, where drops of dew rainbowed the daisies, and was back with the milk almost before Mother had time to set the breakfast kettle sizzling on the hob.

When she returned, the house was all abustle. Davy Warren, her father, humming to himself as he shaved in front of a triangular corner of mirror propped over the kitchen sink. Tom, coming in with the firewood, at nineteen already a head taller than his father. Seventeen-year-old Jimmy, trundling back from the well with a barrel-cart full of water, he and his brother as like as two toby jugs on a shelf. Mother, busy as ever, packing the morsel-bags with a bit of lunch for the three workers, and filling the metal water-flasks they wore at their necks in the mine.

Even Willie, who, at six years old, had no chores to do, was tempted out of bed by the sun, and came out for breakfast before the men had gone. One of those rare mornings, when there was time to sit together around the table in the cosy darkness of the little kitchen, drinking their hot sweet tea.

'Pity Meg and Fanny aren't here,' Mother said, wielding the teapot, almost as if she had read Katie's thoughts.

'Well, you'll have your wish soon enough,' Davy said, 'with Meg's wedding Saturday. Fanny's got the afternoon off for it, and Meg'll be back home tomorrow, so you'll have your whole brood around you!' He put down his cup. 'Now, we'd best be away out, that tin won't mine itself.'

And the men were gone, leaving the house suddenly quiet. Mother cut thick slices of new bread for Katie and Willie to spread with blackcurrant jam, and eat on the steps in the sun. Then it was time for them, too, to go. Carrie Tremble, in plaits and petticoats, came in from next door, and they were off, into the dusty dark of Penvarris schoolroom. It was too good a day to spend inside, Katie felt, even when you were a good scholar, and Miss Bevan lifted up your flat-seams and your sums for Carrie and the others to see.

Even on the way home, the day seemed as contented and ordinary as ever. They had stopped, as they often did, beside the little stream that trickled across their path. Katie had made a leaf-boat for each of them, and they watched them float away, through the little rocks and eddies, towards the distant sparkle of the sea.

'Look at mine,' Willie said proudly, tugging at her pinafore. 'It's still afloat! Where will it go?'

'Who knows,' said Katie. 'It could stop here. It could go miles and miles across the sea and . . . .' She broke off.

'Go on!' Willie urged. 'What about it?'

'Not now.' Katie jumped up, her button boots springing on the tussocky sea-grass. 'Whatever's this?'

It was Mrs Lane, from number nine, clambering towards them. Her great moon-face was scarlet with the effort, and thin grey hair was straggling from its bun. She wore her best shawl, all anyhow, on top of her baking pinny.

'Katie Warren? That you, is it?' She lumbered up. 'You best get on home. Your mother's been took bad.'

Katie stared. Mother? She had been fine when they left this morning, putting out their bits of pasty for lunch, and singing 'I am just a sinner saved by grace' as she went down to the hens.

'Her time's come on her,' the woman said. 'Well, don't just stand there, get on 'ome. You'll be wanted.'

Still Katie hesitated. 'Is she bad?'

'Bad enough,' Mrs Lane said. 'Willie and Carrie, you come along of me, and we'll see can we find some dandelion leaves for that old donkey.'

4

And then Katie realised that her Mother was bad, too bad for Willie to go home right away, and she picked up her skirts and began to run. Her mind moved faster even than her feet. That baby wasn't due yet, not for another month or more. She hoped it lived, for Mother's sake. The last two had died, and since Jack died of the diphtheria her mother had wanted another son 'to make up' – for all she had six living children already.

Up over the gate by Crowdie's farm, and then it was downhill all the way to the Terrace, the single row of cottages huddled in the valley, defiant against the wind. Already she could see the neighbours clustered outside the house. They'd be bringing bits and pieces, a bit of brawn 'to build 'ee up a bit', barley soup, 'a drop of butter'. All her young life Katie had seen this, once every two years, regular as clockwork when another new baby arrived in the house.

Then she saw something else, and her mouth went dry. A pony and trap. That meant the doctor. Her mother *was* bad then. Really bad. Generally she just had Carrie's mother in from next door, like all the women did. If it was the doctor she must be bad.

Katie could feel tears in her eyes. It hadn't crossed her mind to be worried about Mother. She knew the stories, of course. You couldn't grow up in the Terrace without knowing the stories. All the girls told them, frightening each other, when they thought there was no-one listening, though they only half understood the words. Mrs Boas who had four sons and died of a 'flux' with the fifth. Rose Trembath, who had a terrible time with her daughter, and died of a fever after. Mrs Goodbody, who still boasted of how her Edwin came wrong-side first, and she bent the brass bedposts with the strength of it.

Mind, Edwin was sixteen now; and Mrs Goodbody was there in the street, standing with the neighbours outside the house and sipping tea, and no doubt telling anyone about it who would listen. But that wasn't Mother, Katie told herself. Mother was strong. Up and cheerful in a week or two, and herself again in six.

Yet they had called the doctor to her. That was a bad sign. Doctors cost money, and you didn't call them if you didn't have to.

Suddenly, from the house, there came a single scream of raw anguish. Katie froze. That couldn't be Mother, that awful animal cry. She braced herself, but there was no other sound. Round the door, even the neighbours fell silent.

'Mother!' Katie launched herself down the street. The women stood back to let her past, and she heard their murmured 'Here she is, the lamb!'

5

Father was in the hallway. She had never seen him like this before. He was in his working clothes, all red from the dust of the mine. He'd never even been to the 'dry' to change them before he came home. Only his face and hands were washed and when he looked up at Katie, his eyes seemed unnaturally white in his brown face, with the reddened cloth of his scarf and skullcap all round.

'Father?'

He stretched out a hand and took hers. Then the door of the bedroom upstairs opened. He gripped her hand so hard that tears came to her eyes, but he wasn't even thinking about it. The Doctor gestured with his head and Father went upstairs, dragging, like a wounded thing.

'Katie?' Mrs Tremble, Carrie's mother, presiding over Mother's kitchen, in a den of steam. 'There's no good standing there, my handsome, come and let me give you some tea.'

Katie shook her head. She had turned into some kind of statue, stuck there in the hall. After a minute or two Father came down.

'There's two babies,' he said. His voice didn't sound like his own. 'One's dead. The other might manage.' His eyes were filled with tears.

'And Mother?'

'She's still with us, Katie my love, but it's a question how long.' He ran an arm over his face, leaving long streaks of red dust. He didn't know, or care. 'She's asking for Fanny. D'you go up to Trevarnon and say she's wanted.'

Katie looked up the silent stairs at the bedroom door, and at Mrs Tremble in the kitchen. 'Can't I . . . ?'

He shook his head. 'Nothing you can do here, my handsome, except wait. Nor me either.' He shook his head again. 'Great animal I am, doing this to her.'

Katie looked at him, waiting for him to explain. He didn't.

'Well, get on then,' he said. 'Meg will be back before so long.' The moment between them was over.

She went back into the street. The women were still there, in shawls and pinnies, looking anxious: everyone loved Mother. They looked at her, hoping for news, but she shook her head, too full for speech.

'Poor lamb,' Mrs Goodbody said, pushing something into her hand. 'Here. A piece of saffron for 'ee.'

Katie sank her teeth into the warm yellow flesh of the bun. It tasted of spice and baking, and suddenly she was crying as she began to run.

It was a long way to Trevarnon, two miles or more, and over stiles. She had walked that way many times to see her sister on her day off, but the path had never seemed so long. Brambles clawed her hems, and tall nettles slashed at her knees, and long before she had reached Trevarnon gates she was tousled, hot and panting.

She had wits enough to pull herself together. She stopped to retie the ribbon-ends which dangled to her neck, and pulled the 'stickle-back' grasses from her skirts, but her dark curls tumbled hopelessly about her ears, and the dust on her boots was impossible to cure. And this would be the first time she'd gone up to the house!

She looked up at the forbidding granite walls which fenced the grounds, the grey slate of the roof, glimpsed through the trees which screened it from the town. It seemed to glower back at her.

Well, there was no help for it. She steeled herself and began to walk resolutely up the drive.

George was riding Coral, the chestnut mare. She was Robert's horse, and like all Robert's animals she was inclined to be nervous and skittish. Robert used the lash too much.

It was no good challenging him over it, George knew; he might feel the touch of the riding-crop around his own legs. Or perhaps Robert would simply smile that infuriating, superior smile of his, and make one of his clever remarks. 'Horses are like women, George, they have to know who's master. Perhaps you'll find that out, one of these days.' You could never tell with Robert.

Like today. Blister had gone lame, and Robert had suggested that George ride Coral instead. He could be like that, as casually kind as he was casually cruel. George had taken the horse out at once, of course, before Robert had time to change his mind, and it had been a fine ride. She was a big horse, and made light of ditches that Blister would have baulked at. Mama would have had a real fit of the vapours if she had seen their progress this afternoon. And Papa, locked away in his office with his port and his papers? It was hard to know. He might have been pleased.

It would be wise not to tell Robert. Not because of the risks – Robert enjoyed a risk – but because he would not welcome the idea of his younger brother doing what he did not do himself. And Robert did not much enjoy country riding these days – he preferred balls, and gambling and dinner parties and girls. Especially girls. He was only three years older than George, but women did seem to find him

7

irresistible, probably because he was showy and handsome instead of fair and slight like his brother. Even Mama idolised him.

Well, whatever else, George was pleased with himself. It had been an exhilarating ride. He was just cantering back down the avenue, with an idea of stabling Coral and then ringing for tea and muffins, when he saw the girl.

She was small and skinny, no more than thirteen or so. George, who at seventeen was starting to notice these things, could see that her breasts were just beginning to bud under the coarse frock and apron. A child, not much more.

She had not seen him, although he was nearly parallel to her. She was marching up the carriage drive with small determined strides, as though bent on some important purpose. What was she doing here? Come to sell pegs or heather? Probably not. She was clean enough, though her hair was tangled, and her skirts dishevelled. Pretty too, in a pinched sort of way, and too tidy for a gypsy. Still, she couldn't come stumping in here as though it were a public place. He cantered out onto the drive and confronted her.

'You there! Who are you? What are you doing here?'

She raised a startled face to his. She seemed even smaller now he was close, especially as he was a long way above her. He knew he looked well, sitting tall and proud in the saddle, with the reins looped carelessly over his hands, and he was ridiculously pleased to see admiration in her eyes. They were deep and blue. She had been crying, he noticed.

'What is it? What do you want?' he asked, more gently now.

The girl spoke. Her voice was a surprise, low for a girl. With the soft Cornish burr it was oddly attractive. 'I've come for our Fanny, sir. It's Mother, she's been taken bad and she's asking.'

So that was it. No wonder there were tears on her face. He felt guilty for having been so abrupt, and he turned the horse to a walk and wheeled beside her. 'And you are?' he said.

She glanced up at him again between dark lashes, obviously reassured by his gentler tone. 'Katie Warren, sir.'

'I'm George,' he said, 'George Trevarnon.' On an impulse, he leant over the horse's neck and held out his hand. She shook it solemnly. 'Fanny?' he went on. 'That's the housemaid, isn't it?' He knew the girl slightly. Fair haired, with a good figure and a pair of saucy eyes which she flaunted at Robert. Anything less like this sister would be hard to imagine.

Katie nodded, trotting along beside the horse. 'Where will I find her, Mr George? Only, Mother's proper poorly, and I'd hate for us to be too late.' They were at the house now, and she was gazing at the great square granite front as though it had been built expressly to keep her out. He looked at it for a moment, seeing it with new eyes. The imposing door with its twin flights of granite steps, the rows of handsome windows, blanked off here and there to escape the window tax of a hundred years before – how formidable it must seem.

He swung down from the mare. 'Wait, and I'll take you in.' He led Coral round to the stables and gave her to the boy. Normally he would never leave a horse unattended, but this was a special occasion, he told himself. In any case, Robert himself always left the stableboy to groom her.

'This way.' He clattered down the stone steps into the courtyard and hammered on the back door. It was not often he came to the servants' entrance, and Cook's face, when she opened the door, was a study. 'Where's Fanny?' he said, smiling at Cook's bafflement. 'Her sister's come to fetch her. There's illness at home.'

Cook found her voice. 'She's upstairs with Madam. Shall I go?'

'No need. We'll go ourselves. Come, Katie.' And he led the way out of the kitchen and up the stairs, pushing open the green baize door at the top. 'This way.'

But Katie had stopped. She was gazing open-mouthed around her, at the wide reception hall he had always taken for granted, at the chandelier, the statue at the foot of the stairs, the stuffed animals in their cases, and the pictures and ornaments which crammed the walls.

She obviously felt out of place here, but what should he do with her? 'This way,' he repeated, and held open the door of the drawing room. 'I know you're in a hurry. You wait in here. I'll find Fanny.'

Mama was in the music room. The shades were drawn and she was sitting back on the chaise-longue with a bottle of sal volatile in one hand and a fan in the other. The girl, Fanny, was setting the tea-table, to Mama's usual plaintive dissatisfaction.

'No, girl, no. Can't you put that down quietly? You clatter so.'

'Mama?'

She put down the fan and stretched out a hand to him. 'George, where have you been? I've had such a head all afternoon, and no-one to see to me but this wretched girl. I've been beside myself with boredom.'

He sat down beside her, and she gave him a wan smile. Like Robert,

9

she was transformed by her smile, so that one forgave her anything – even sitting here in a darkened room on a sunny afternoon with a fashionable 'headache'. Poor Mama, perhaps it was genuine, brought on by forcing her stocky frame into those ridiculous tight-waisted fashions – Papa was always saying so. He took her square, ringed fingers in his own.

'I've been riding, Mama. Robert lent me Coral.'

'He shouldn't have done so. She's too big a horse for you, George. Are you coming to have tea with me now?'

'In a moment. But first, I've come to fetch Fanny. Her sister is here. Her mother is ill and she's wanted at home.'

His mother looked at him blankly. 'But George, I can't spare her. I'm shut up in this room with a splitting head. Who is going to look after me?'

George tried not to look at the little maid, whose face had turned as white as her cap. 'Don't be absurd, Mama. Of course you can manage perfectly well. For one thing, I'm here. And for another thing, there's Daisy. I'm sure she could manage on her own upstairs.'

'That's just it, George, this head is all Daisy's doing. She's given her notice. Says she's marrying some fellow from the mine and they're going to America next month, if you please. Fine thing, when girls think nothing of throwing up a good situation at five minutes' notice. I've sent her packing. So you see, I can't spare Fanny today.' Mama could be spiteful sometimes. That must be where Robert got it from.

George set his jaw. He knew better than to lose his temper. Instead, he played his trump card. 'Oh, I think you could manage for a day or two, Mama. Mrs Selwood would lend you a maid. Shall I see what Papa thinks?'

He saw the lines harden in her face. 'Oh, your father will side with you, of course. He always does. What does he care about my health?' She turned to Fanny. 'All right then, go on home. But you'll work your half-day next week, in lieu.'

Fanny nodded. 'Thank you, Madam.'

'Your sister is in the drawing room,' George said, holding open the door. But she wasn't. Katie was still standing in the open doorway. Her face was flushed, and her fists were clenched tight. She must have heard every word. Suddenly he was angry too. He unbolted the front door. Fanny hesitated, but Katie was through it in a shot and down the steps to the carriage drive. After a second, Fanny followed her.

He pulled the door shut again. As he did so he glimpsed Katie looking at him. Her face was ravaged, but she was smiling. Her lips moved: 'Thank you.' She made no sound, but he read the words.

'George!' His mother's voice was querulous. 'You didn't let that girl out of the front door? What are you thinking of? And in her uniform too!'

He went back into the music room. 'Mama,' he said, the memory of the girl's face giving him sudden courage. 'Fanny goes out of that door every morning to clean the step. I think we can let her out of it once in a way, when her mother may be dying. If it were you ill, I should want to get home as soon as may be.'

His mother smiled. 'Perhaps you're right, George. Now, why don't you ring down for some muffins? Cook has made some, and the kitchen girl can bring them up.'

He went over and pulled the tasselled bell-rope. He hoped the maid would say nothing about him coming in through the kitchens. Mama would not approve of that.

Later, he would go back and see to Coral.

The big door shut behind them and the two girls started off down the drive. Fanny was fussing with buttons and strings.

'Come on then,' Katie said.

'I'm coming.' Fanny freed herself from apron and cap. 'There now!' She bundled them into a pocket and, holding out a hand to Katie, began to hurry so fast that Katie had to run to keep up with her. Back down the drive, past the place where that good-looking Mr George on a horse had stopped and been so kind to her, and back into the lane.

'Now tell me,' Fanny said, as soon as they were fairly over the stile and onto the field-path, 'what's to do with Mother?'

Katie told her, gasping for breath as she ran.

'Oh my dear life,' said Fanny, and together they hurried home as quickly as they could.

The little crowd gathered around the door had gone, and as they flung open the door Katie was encouraged to hear the sound of voices in the kitchen, and from upstairs the thin, feeble wail of a child.

'Here's Fanny come,' she called, and Father came out, washed and tidied now, and smiling, although his face was still strained and anxious.

He forgot himself so far as to plant a kiss on both their foreheads, as though they were tiny children again, but when he spoke his voice was as gruff as ever.

'Will you hold your noise, Katie Warren? Your Mother's trying to sleep.'

'She's all right?' Fanny asked.

'Holding on,' Father said soberly, and Katie knew that it was not yet over. 'They've taken the dead one for burying, but the other child is sucking. Tom's gone into Penzance for a bottle. Doctor says your Mother hasn't the strength to feed her.'

'Her? It's a girl, then?'

'Yes, a girl. As well it was, too. A boy would have killed her.'

'What are you going to call her?' Fanny was hanging her things on the hallstand.

'Hadn't thought,' Father said. 'Your mother only wanted "Jack" for a boy.'

'Call it Rosa,' Katie suggested, thinking of Rose Trembath across the way, who died of the childbirth fever. Rose had been very good to her and taught her to knit.

'Why not?' said Father. 'It's as good a name as any, and your mother was always some fond of roses. Go on up then, Fanny, but see you don't wake your mother if she's sleeping. You too, Katie. Just for a minute, mind. Doctor says she's got to rest.'

Mother was lying so still in the darkened room that she might have been dead rather than sleeping, but the creak of the floorboards roused her. She stretched out a hand to each of the girls, and murmured, 'You've come, my lovers,' in a voice which did not sound like her own. Katie felt the faint squeeze of her fingertips before Mother slipped back into a kind of semi-sleep. The girls had only time to glimpse the tiny wrinkled baby in the wooden crib before Father came and shooed them downstairs.

Mrs Tremble was still in the kitchen, and she had a pot of tea at the ready. 'Come on, drink this,' she said. 'There'll be a power to do in a while when Meg comes.'

Katie sipped her tea, but she could taste the salt of tears.

'Well,' Mrs Tremble said, covering the silence, 'how are you liking it up at Trevarnon, Fanny?'

'It's all right,' said Fanny.

'That Mrs Trevarnon,' Katie burst out, 'I thought she wasn't going to let you come.'

Carrie's mother pursed her lips. 'Great besom! Never think to hear her carry on that she started out a farmer's daughter over to St Ives.'

Katie was so astonished that she put down her cup. 'She never was?'

12

'True as I'm here,' Mrs Tremble said. 'And Mr Trevarnon was a Mine Captain once, down Botallack. Started out a tribute-worker like your father. Had a lot of luck with his tin-seams, mind. Though a lot of it wasn't luck, I dare say. I've heard folk say he had the best eye for a tin-seam in the mine, one time. Came to be a shift-leader and up to Captain.'

'Well, I never heard that!' Fanny cried. 'How did he come to get Trevarnon House then? Never got that on Captain's wages!'

Mrs Tremble laughed. 'No, course not, you great lummock. Went to Africa mining, didn't he? Came back with his pockets full of gold.' She sat down at the table, warming to her tale. 'Well, when he come home his health was bad, so he never went back in the mine. He went out to St Ives and lived on the farm, givin' old Mr Coombes a hand. But all the time he was looking out for a big house to buy. Then Trevarnon House came on the market. Called Lower Penvarris in them days. It was part of the Penvarris estate, but that was all sold off when old man Penvarris died.'

'And Mr Trevarnon just bought it?' It had never occurred to Katie that you could just buy houses. She had always supposed that you were born to them, like Lord Falmouth or Mr Poldair, and other folk rented them, as Father did.

'They do say he turned up at the sale in a smock, would you believe, and they wouldn't take him serious till they had sight of his gold. He changed the name and all, but then he never lived in it for a year or two. He went back off to Africa, had a woman out there they say, but nothing came of it, 'cause he came back and married the Coombes girl, though she was half his age. And there she is to this day, putting on airs and thinking herself high and mighty!'

Fanny made a face. 'So she does, too! Always copying the Selwoods and worrying about being invited to the best houses. Still trying to prove she's as good as they are, from what you say. Funny thing, I wonder I never heard that before.'

Carrie's mother poured them each another cup of tea. 'I'm surprised Cook never told you.'

'She's new.' Fanny said. 'They're mostly new, up to Trevarnon. Perhaps that's why. Mrs Trevarnon doesn't want people up there who remember where she sprang from.' She smiled. 'Won't they say something when I tell them?'

'Well, it just shows you, money talks!' Mrs Tremble said. 'That story was the talk of Penwith, one time. Mind, I expect Mrs

Trevarnon tried to forget it, and what with Mr Trevarnon becoming an adventurer and buying shares in Penvarris mine, and being on the Council and all, I suppose you don't hear about it like you did. Besides, it was twenty years ago or more, and some folks thought the world of Mr Trevarnon. Good miner, he was, and a decent man by all accounts.'

'Still is, if you ever see him,' Fanny said, 'though he's getting on a bit now. Must be sixty if he's a day. But he's shut up most of the time with a bottle and his books.'

'Well, he's got something to drink about,' Carrie's mother said, to Katie's surprise. The Trembles were strict Methodist, like themselves. 'He went out to Africa with his brother, but he died after like half of them do.'

'Poor soul,' said Katie. She knew about the 'African Disease', the dreaded phthisis that miners developed, in which the dust ate into your lungs so that you either died young, or lingered into a crippled old age, racked and coughing. 'That young Mr George seems nice,' she went on, to change the subject.

'You want to see Mr Robert,' Fanny said, with a faint lift of her eyebrows. 'Keep you awake nights, he would, he's that handsome.'

'You watch your tongue, my lady,' their neighbour warned her, setting to with the breadknife on one of Mother's new loaves, 'or you'll be giving Katie the wrong ideas – you shooting up like a young tree and turning out such a looker. You're too old for that sort of talk, and that's a fact. Now give me a hand here to get some raw-fry on for your tea. There's a power to do before your sister Meg arrives tomorrow, poor lamb. Some fine wedding she'll have with your mother in this state. Though it'll do her good to see Meg, I'll be bound.'

Then Tom came in with the bottle, and they were all too busy to talk.

CHAPTER TWO

Everyone was pleased to see Meg. She arrived from Truro on the last train, and the three boys went off to Penzance to fetch her in Crowdie's cart, borrowed for the purpose. Old Man Crowdie had been rather sweet on Mother when she was a girl, and though they'd both been married for twenty-odd years, he still 'looked out for her', as he said. He always gave her a drop of milk extra, and sent down the pudding skins when he killed a pig, for Mother to stuff with pastry and boil until the filling was fragrant with pork. Father would grumble and fret, but Katie could tell he was secretly proud of Mother's looks, and he wasn't above borrowing Crowdie's cart for special occasions, like tonight.

The boys seemed to be gone for ever, and Katie had already lit the oil-lamp in the kitchen, and was putting a candle in the candlestick to be taken up to Mother, when the clatter of horse's hooves sounded on the street.

'They're come,' Father said, knocking out his pipe on the hearth. He went into the hall and Katie heard his: 'You're here then?'

Then Meg's voice, between laughing and crying, 'Oh, we've had such a time. Some poor fellow with a cart lost a wheel on the road, and overturned into a ditch and his horse took fright, and Tom and Jimmy had to stop and help him, and all the time I was worrying about getting home because the boys told me about Mother. How is she now, then?'

'Fanny's up there with her now – she and Katie have been taking turns all the night,' Father said, as if he hadn't been there himself for hours too. 'Are you going straight up, or will we make you some supper? You must be half-starved.'

'I could eat a pig before you had time to kill 'un,' Meg agreed, 'but I'll see Mother first. Where's Katie to?'

'I'm here,' Katie said, coming forward to give her sister a hug, and they went up together.

Mother was lying back on the pillows in the great brass bed, and in the candlelight her face was as pale as the counterpane Great-Grandmother Warren had made as a wedding present. 'Crot-cheting,' Mother called it, but to Katie it always looked like lace, it was so fine and delicate. It was precious too, put on for special days like Christmas and Penvarris Feast, and carefully packed away until the next time in a special box under the bed. It was hardly ever washed, because it had to be squeezed by hand which took dozens of trips to the well, and took days to dry, hung over the big apple trees in the sunshine while Mother fretted over every puff of cloud, in case it should rain and it was all to do again.

But there it was now, spread over Mother, giving off a faint smell of camphor and lavender. Mother's hands were on top of it, and when she saw Meg, she lifted her arms to welcome her. She looked terribly tired, as if holding her hands out was almost too much for her, but she smiled weakly as she said, 'Well, hello Meg, my handsome. Come to see your little sister, have you?'

The baby was in the crib. Katie thought it was quite the ugliest thing she had ever seen, small and crumpled and purple with a round face like a pig. William had been a much handsomer baby. All the same, Meg seemed delighted with it, cooing and smiling, and saying 'What are you called, my beauty?' in a silly high-pitched voice.

'Rosa,' Mother said. 'Katie chose it.' And then her eyelids fluttered closed, and Katie had a moment of panic.

'She's drifted off again,' Father said. 'She'll sleep happier now we're all here. Come down and have a bite of supper, Meg, before your sides meet where your stomach used to be.'

So they went down to the kitchen, and Katie put a pilchard in the pan, while the boys brought in Meg's things from the door. There was a box, and a basket, and a long packet, and a woven frail full of goose-eggs which had somehow come home intact, and last of all came Willie lugging Meg's sewing machine, in a case which was nearly as big as she was.

'Don't know why she had to bring that,' Tom said with a wink. 'Weighs a ton!'

Meg, setting herself a place at table, paused with the fork in her hand. 'Mind your lip, Tom Warren! You'll be glad enough of a new shirt for the wedding, I'll be bound.' Meg had been apprenticed to a dressmaker, in Truro; Father had found the premium somehow, and she had served a year as a beginner and a second as an improver, so she could turn a seam with the best of them.

'He's only fooling,' Father said, and laughed, so that Katie's heart lifted as she tossed the salted fish in the pan, and fried it slowly in butter till it was soft and flavoursome.

After supper there were gifts for everyone. Mrs Lomas, the dressmaker, was fond of Meg, and sorry to see her go. Even in these first two years, when Meg had worked for nothing but her keep, Mrs Lomas always sent her home at Christmas with a little something in her pocket, and now she had excelled herself with a whole week's wages. There were goose eggs for everyone as a 'change' from the chickens they raised themselves. Father was particularly fond of their strange, strong flavour. 'Proper job,' he said.

There were beads for Fanny and Katie, and a length of beautiful cotton saved for 'the baby' when it was born, and which would come in handy now. There were collar studs for the boys and Father, and for Mother a bottle of proper scent from Truro market – violet, which she loved. Besides all that, Mrs Lomas had sent the end of a bolt of shirting: enough, Meg said, to make shirts for Dad and Tom for the wedding, and new fronts for Jimmy and Willie, which was nearly as good. And there were any number of ribbon-ends for Mother and Katie to trim their dresses and bonnets, enough to leave some for Fanny, who wouldn't be at the wedding because she was working Saturday.

Mrs Tremble came in again 'to see how things were', and stopped to admire. 'My word, Meg,' she said, 'all this fuss for a wedding. When me and Seth got married I just pinned a bunch of violets on my Sunday dress, and we went to work after. New shirts and ribbons! Anyone would think it was a funeral.' Then she blushed and stammered, and you could see she was thinking about Mother, and wishing she had bitten her tongue out.

But otherwise it was a successful evening. Rosa took some food, with Mrs Tremble's help, and everyone went to bed far too late. It was comforting, Katie thought, to slip into bed between Meg and Fanny like old times, although they took up more room than William, who was only small, and anyway slept at the bottom. Tonight he had gone into the boys' room, where he ought to have been all along, Father said – he was getting too old to share with Katie. There were only the three bedrooms upstairs and the two rooms down, so poor Father was on the front-room settee by the fire, so as not to disturb Mother.

Twice in the night Katie heard Rosa's thin wail, but it was first Meg and then Fanny who climbed silently from bed to tiptoe down to the kitchen and warm the milk. It was already set in a saucepan, watered as Doctor said, and with a little sugar and weak tea added on Mrs Tremble's advice, 'to give it a bit of substance'. The faint crying ceased, and Katie snuggled down into the warm hollow of the bed. Tomorrow Fanny would be back at Trevarnon, and Saturday Meg would be married and gone. If Mother wasn't better, Katie thought, it would be her turn then.

Tonight, however, she could sleep.

Davy Warren slept badly. The settee was hard after the sagging mattress of his own bed, and the baby's fretting woke him. Besides, he was troubled. Not for himself, although he would have to rise at five with a ten-hour shift to face, but for his wife, lying tired and quiet in the great bed upstairs.

'Rest,' the doctor had said. 'Complete rest.' Hard enough to do at the best of times, but with a young baby in the house, and three men to feed, and Meg getting married, and William to see to . . . He stirred uneasily. Mrs Tremble was good, always was, and she would come in for a few days sure as eggs, but you couldn't rely on other people for ever. Perhaps they could manage, him and the boys and Katie. He'd have to keep Katie from school for a week or two, and then perhaps Maggie would be on her feet again, and life would go on. Perhaps after all he wouldn't need to send for Lally.

Lally! For all she was his sister, the thought of her drove sleep from him. Lally with her prim, tight lips, and her sour ways. Lally in her black dress like coffin shrouds, and her hair scraped back into a tight bun, as though one loose wisp would entice the devil. Lally pinched and worn by years of looking after their own parents, until now that they were dead, she was left thin and dry and withered like a corn-husk, with all the warmth sucked out of her. Lally, who flayed cobwebs as though they were demons, and turned washday to purgatory. He thought of Lally in his warm, untidy house, and shuddered. Perhaps after all, it wouldn't come to that.

At last the grey half-light broadened into morning, and the girls came down into the kitchen. Meg began coaxing the unwilling fire,

18

Katie set to work slicing bread, and Fanny sat down with Rosa in her arms, trying to coax the child to drink.

Davy felt a sudden unreasoning anger towards the small red bundle that was the curse of all his woes. 'Bloody kid,' he murmured, so unlike himself that his daughters stared at him. But it was himself that he swore at, remembering a time, many times, when Maggie had turned away from him, muttering that she was 'too tired tonight', and he had insisted.

Outside the window, Willie went past, dragging the water-barrel on its wheeled frame.

'Where's Willie to?' Davy asked, to break the silence.

'I've sent him to the well,' Meg said. 'He'll have to start sometime.'

'I'll help him,' said Davy and went out slamming the door.

The cool beauty of the morning raised his spirits, as always. The grass shone with tiny multi-coloured lanterns of dew, and the distant sea glinted and sighed.

'Come on, Willie.' Davy seized the barrel. 'We'll see how quick we can fill 'un.'

When they got back, the kitchen was alive with warmth and chatter. Mrs Tremble was there, with Carrie and his own girls. Together they had charmed life out of the embers, and the fire was alight, with the kettle hissing and the goose eggs tapping merrily in the saucepan. Tom was chopping wood – he could hear the rhythmic fall of the axe, while Jimmy saw to the hens and Willie scampered off again, down to Crowdie's for the milk.

'Now,' Mrs Tremble said, as Davy sat down to the golden glory of his egg, 'you know your own business best, Davy Warren, but there's one or two things have to be settled around here, with poor Maggie being took bad.'

Davy lowered his head and murmured a word of thanks then dipped buttery bread into the yolk. It was good. 'Well?' he asked.

'Well, there's my eldest niece down number thirty-one for a start,' Mrs Tremble said. 'She had her baby a month ago, and she's got milk enough for two. Do your Rosa more good than that tea muck.'

Davy put down his spoon to protest, but she was too quick for him.

'She'd be glad of a few eggs and a few of they onions you've got coming on, so you'd be doing each other a favour.'

Davy nodded slowly. 'Yes. Could be. Until Maggie gets her own milk come in.'

Mrs Tremble looked at him sharply, but made no comment.

Instead she ran on, 'Carrie here can see Willie to school for a day or two, and Katie can stay and help me here for a bit. You're out of bread, and you could do with some more seed-cake, so I'll do a bit of baking in any case, and Katie'll see how. And we'll boil up that bit of ham for Saturday.'

From the corner of his eye Davy could see Katie's startled face. She could cook a meal, of course, but only Maggie had ever stirred up the cakes and set the dough in the bread-kettle. He avoided his daughter's gaze.

'Yes, maybe so. You're a good neighbour, Cissie Tremble.'

The woman flushed and scowled. 'How you do go on, Davy Warren.' But she was pleased. 'Here, take this egg up to your wife, while I set you something in your morsel-bag.'

He handed her the drawstring pouch, made from the soft stuff of a flour bag, and his eyes misted as he thought of Maggie stitching it patiently by the fire. He took the egg and tea up without another word.

Maggie was awake, just. Her eyelids looked blue against the whiteness of her skin. She smiled wanly.

He put down the tray and sat down beside her on the bed, taking her hands. 'You get better, you hear?' He squeezed her fingers with his blunt ones, and added on impulse: 'I think a lot of 'ee, Maggie Warren.'

He felt the faint pressure of her fingers in return. 'Don't you worry about me, you great lummox. It's me should be fretting about you, down in that mine. You're getting too old for it, Davy, look what happened to Titus Goodbody.'

'That was five years ago, Maggie,' he urged gently. How could he make her understand? She only saw the forbidding face of the mine, the pall of musty smoke and the clatter of the whims and stamps at the minehead, the lonely chimneys of the ventilation stacks, the dust and noise and smell of it. He loved the underground world. He loved the strange dark beauty of it, the fascination of tracing a good seam, the satisfaction of a clean stope, well-cut. He had tried to explain it – how killas rock was clean, somehow, and dry, sprinkling you with red dust without filling your lungs with grit like granite did, or choking you half to death with gases like the coal mines. She still thought of mines as black, and wet and dank. 'Five years or more. And Titus would never have fallen if he'd roped himself to his partner. That's what a pare is for. And I'm fitter'n most of them, a long way.'

It was no good. She said nothing more, but he hadn't convinced her. He could see by the way she lay back and closed her eyes.

'Eat your breakfast now,' he said. He gave her the tray and crept downstairs.

The boys were ready, their morsel-bags stuffed under their shirts, and their water-flasks slung around their necks. Smart as paint, he thought. Down the mine since they were twelve, underground at fourteen and already skilled men. He was proud of them. Good thing they had thought to bring his proper clothes home last night. He'd have looked a sight beside them, going off in his canvas trousers. He picked up the package in which he had tied his working pants, and knotted his scarf around his neck.

'I want to go down and get some more clay for the candles,' he said, shaking his clay tin. It meant an extra walk, but it was worth it. The damp earth at the tin-workings made the best clay. The minerals in the earth baked like pottery in the heat of the mine, and held the candle to the felt tull on your head as well as any candlestick. 'Are we off then?'

And, flanked by his sons, he set off into the early morning sunshine.

Katie watched them go. First father and the boys, then Fanny, who had to be back by eight, and finally Carrie and Willie. It was odd to see them set off without her. She stood at the door and watched them all the way to the stile, as she had often seen Mother do.

When she turned back into the house it seemed empty, though Mother, Rosa, Meg and Mrs Tremble were still there.

It wasn't the first time she'd been kept home, of course. Every year at apple-picking, and once or twice on washday when the weather was bad; and the time they all had measles and sat together, hot and spotty, by the fire and tried not to read because it was bad for your eyes. And when Jack had diphtheria, of course.

But that was different. Then everyone was off together. Not like this, watching Willie and Carrie walk away and staying behind herself. She shook herself. Most girls she knew had finished school at twelve or even earlier. It was only this year the new Parliament Act had come in and raised the leaving age to thirteen. If it hadn't been for Father she'd have stopped long ago, for good. She could never have nursed her dream of being a teacher, then.

'Lend a hand here, Katie my lover,' Meg's voice summoned her from the kitchen. 'We need a drop more hot from the kettle on these crocks.'

'Coming,' Katie called, and soon she was too busy for regrets. There was the house to clean, and the eggs to fetch, and the baking to set on Mrs Tremble's instructions. Neighbours called by with tidbits for Mother, and Mrs Tremble's niece came, roly-poly and laughing with her own fat baby in her arms, to feed Rosa, so the kettle was never off the hearth. Meg sat at the window and the sewing-machine whirred.

'Did her a power of good, the lambkin.' Mrs Tremble's niece came in buttoning her blouse. 'Better than that old tea. And I've got your mother's tray outside.'

'Did she eat anything?' Mrs Tremble's voice was sharp.

The niece shook her head, but said nothing. Katie caught the look which the two women exchanged, and she turned back to the potatoes which she was peeling into a bucket. It seemed as if the knife was slicing pieces off her heart. Mother had to get better. Had to. It was impossible to imagine the house without Mother's singing, her scolding, her infectious laugh. There was Meg's wedding, and Tom courting, and the new baby. And there was school. Katie couldn't bear to think about it. More than anything she wanted to be a pupil teacher. Maybe even, if she could save up enough, go to Truro and train properly like Miss Bevan. She was a good enough scholar, everyone said so. Father would have let her stay on, she was sure of it, even when she was thirteen. He was like that with his girls. Meg had had her apprenticeship, and Fanny could have done, if she had wanted.

'People want a skill,' he used to say. 'Even women. You never know when you're going to be left, and then a skill can keep you out of the workhouse.' There was quite an argument when Fanny wanted to go straight into service!

If anything happened to Mother, though, what would happen then? Somebody would have to mind the house. Katie had a sudden vision of herself, stuck in the house, thin and miserable like Aunt Lally. She dug out a potato eye savagely. How could she think like that, with Mother lying so ill upstairs?

'Cat got your tongue, Katie?' Meg asked. 'Mrs Tremble's talking to you.'

'Only thing is, I thought I heard someone at the door,' Mrs Tremble said. 'And my hands are all over flour.'

'I'll go,' said Katie, glad to leave the mountain of potatoes. She went out into the hall. Whoever would come knocking? Neighbours would come round the back, or shout and let themselves in. The doctor, maybe? She opened the door.

She recognised the horse first. 'Mr George!' Her voice was alarmed. Had something happened to Fanny?

She need not have worried. He smiled again, that slow gentle smile as though he were pleased to see her, and fumbled in his saddle-bag.

'Mother sent these,' he said, 'for the invalid.'

She stood like an idiot, clutching the grapes, unable to find words.

'I thought you might be at school,' he went on, 'but Fanny said they were keeping you at home.'

She nodded wordlessly. For an awkward moment they looked at each other in silence, and then he said, 'Well, I mustn't keep you. I hope your mother improves. Good afternoon.' Then he was trotting away down the stony street. He didn't look back.

Katie gazed at him, and then at the grapes in her hands. 'Mother sent these,' he had said. She remembered Mrs Trevarnon's petulant voice the afternoon before. 'You're some nice young man, George Trevarnon,' she said softly as he turned the corner back into the lane, 'but you aren't half a liar!'

She went back into the house and the smell of baking engulfed her.

CHAPTER THREE

George was cursing himself for a fool. Not for the grapes – nobody would grudge him a few grapes when the hothouse was full of them – but for his stupidity in taking them to the house.

It was such a miserable little house, for one thing: one of a row of miserable little houses, all exactly the same, except for the numbers on the doors. He'd caused a sensation, no doubt, by asking at the wrong one first, and then being watched all the way down the terrace by women twitching their curtains, or just standing on their front steps with their arms folded, brazenly staring. The news would be all over the street by now.

She hadn't even said thank you. Just stood there in that grubby apron, with brown smudges on her face and hands, staring at him like a frightened rabbit. What on earth had possessed him?

He had wanted to make up, somehow, for his mother's rudeness, and also, if he was honest with himself, to see the girl again. Though heaven knew why – she was scarcely more than a child! Was he getting like Robert, chasing after the servant girls? The thought disgusted him.

He was by no means in a good temper when he reached the stables, and when he found Robert flirting with the fat kitchen-maid, who had come out with some slops for the animals, his mood worsened. He swung out of the saddle and flung the reins towards his brother.

'Here,' he said, 'exercise your own horse in future.' He stamped off towards the house, conscious that for the second time in two days he hadn't groomed the horse.

Behind him, Robert whistled for the stable-boy, and ran to catch him up.

'Hey, steady on old man. What's eating you?'

George did not slacken his stride, but Robert was undeterred. 'It's not like you to turn down a ride on Coral. What happened? Did she throw you?'

George glowered. 'Of course not!'

Robert laughed. 'Well, don't take offence! It must be something. If I didn't know you better I'd suspect a woman.'

George said nothing, but he coloured in spite of himself. His brother, of course, noticed at once.

'By Jove, I believe it is! Well, don't keep it to yourself, old lad. Anyone I know? Or am I a pleasure yet in store?'

'You,' George said savagely, 'can keep your clever remarks for kitchen-maids. Don't you ever think of anything else?'

His brother gave a little knowing laugh. 'Occasionally. Money, food, drink, horses! But they're not half as interesting, old boy. As you seem to be finding out!'

George stamped past him and up the steps into the house. That was a mistake. Robert would only gloat. He shut himself gloomily away with a book for the rest of the day, and only came down in time for dinner. Even then, he was aware of Robert's meaningful looks, so, finding himself seated next to Caroline Selwood, a distant cousin whom Robert rather admired, he devoted himself to being assiduously charming to her.

She was seventeen, with a pretty, silly face, a simpering laugh, and no conversation, but she was flattered by his attentions. Her eyes sparkled like the little brooch which she wore on a band of black velvet on her throat, and her cheeks flushed pinker than the frothy silk of her dinner gown. With her fair hair in ringlets at her neck, she was decidedly attractive. Robert clearly thought so too, and was obviously rather put out at his brother's success, because he talked too much and too loudly, and drank far too much wine.

After dinner, when the ladies had retired, Papa called for the port and began a discussion with Major Selwood about Penvarris Mine.

'You have shares in it, don't you Selwood?'

Selwood grunted. 'Got out of mining years ago. Don't know why you keep on, Trevarnon. Always something to spend the venturer's money on. First there was the water laid on for the men to wash when they came up from underground, then it was hot steam pipes for them to dry their working clothes. And the purser tells me there's somebody now wanting to install moving belts to take the ore to the

25

stamps. It's everything for the miner these days, and nothing for the poor shareholder. They'll be looking for fresh subscriptions again before the year is out, you can depend on it.'

George watched his father. It was true – there had already been a call for new capital, but Papa would never part with the mine shares lightly. His heart was still in the business. It had been Papa, in part, who was responsible for the new washing facilities installed for the men, and this steam-driven conveyor belt was his idea – only one other mine could boast one. He had talked about it to George more than once.

But Robert was bored with all this talk of business. He leaned over under the pretence of passing the decanter. 'Quite the little ladies' man, aren't we?' His voice was mocking, but not unfriendly. 'Bet you a guinea she partners me at cards.'

'You can partner Coral for all I care,' George said sulkily.

'Hmm.' Robert pretended to consider this. 'Coral's probably a better player, but her nose is too long!'

George laughed in spite of himself. He was in a better humour by the time they joined the ladies.

In fact, there were to be no cards this evening. Mama pleaded a headache, and they all trooped into the music room instead. Caroline played the piano, without any particular talent, and sang a song or two in a thin pleasant voice, while her mother glowed with pride. Mama rallied enough to sing her favourite ballad in the thrilling contralto which was her party piece, while Papa looked embarrassed and Robert yawned and fidgeted.

'You might have won your bet,' Robert murmured as the guests were leaving. 'Pity we didn't invite Coral, she could have sung!'

George laughed again. He could never be angry with Robert for long.

All the same, he was not happy when, going to bed, he met his brother on the front stairs talking to Fanny. She had been up with the warming bottles, and he had trapped her in the turn of the stairs and was leaning towards her, his face dark and alive in the shadows. One hand was tracing the blonde curls on her forehead. He stepped back quickly as George came up, and the girl scuttled past him and down the staircase. She looked flushed and flustered, but not displeased.

Robert fell into step beside George, and climbed the rest of the flight as if nothing had happened.

'Pretty girl,' he said, cheerfully nonchalant. 'Too young, of course, but damned pretty. Lots of these miners' girls are.'

'Don't swear,' George said, and went to his room without another word. He felt obscurely guilty.

Davy Warren was feeling guilty too. Guilty, but relieved. Everything was all right – this time!

He went over the day again in his mind. There had been no premonitions. Going down the ladders at Penvarris, himself and Tom and Jimmy, with Eddie and Ted Goodbody, all singing away as they always did. Beautiful acoustics down the ladder shaft, and he loved to hear it, everyone taking their part, like they did in the Chapel choir. 'Rock of Ages'. Something beautiful.

Eddie grumbled as always. 'Don't know why they can't put in a man-engine, like they did down to Botallack, save all this walk!'

And his father, 'Save your breath to cool your porridge. Just get on down.'

Down to the sixteenth level, where the air was so warm that your canvas trousers clemmed to your legs and the sweat ran down into the leather 'slowgs' on your feet. The men on the twentieth used to boast that they could take their boots off and pour the water out of them, though the pit was as dry as a bone, under the sea and all as it was.

Then along the tunnel to their stope, and down the ladders. Overhand stoping, the kind Maggie didn't like, where each man stood on a step of rock, and drilled inwards towards the centre of the stope, laying charges that he could set off as he left, so that each day the step moved further and further from the roof and from the sides of the stope. Only, of course, the higher the stope the greater the fall, both for the man on the step and for the rocks above him.

They were careful, mind. The Goodbodys had lost a cousin five years ago: standing unroped too close to the edge of an adit, he missed his footing and fell forty feet. It taught you to be careful, not only with ropes, but in other ways. Watching your step carefully in the flickering light of the candle. Never moving the felt tull from your head, even when sweat and dust streamed into your eyes. Always watering the drill holes for fear of sparks which might set off the charges before time.

So it was today, working with Tom. Careful, methodical drilling. First the centre hole, then the easers, then the knee and shoulder holes. Then the charges, cut, measured and set so that the mined rock would collapse by degrees, always with a hole to fall into, so that it didn't jam and trap the unexploded charge for some other seamer to drill into and blow himself to kingdom come. Always careful.

Until Davy tripped. Caught his foot on a shovel-end and stumbled, dropping his pick with a clatter. Half a second, no more. But in that time the metal struck a spark from the dry rock, and a fuse caught.

'Get out!' Tom's voice. The boy was already halfway up the ladder, the rope tightening around Davy's waist. He scrambled after his son.

They rolled into the tunnel above as the explosion came, a great muffled roar. They flattened themselves against the wall as the blast rushed past them like a wall of heat, extinguishing the candles. They groped forward in the blackness, while below them the slow thick fumes of the blasting rose and twisted in a choking cloud out through the ladder-hole. In seconds, it seemed, they were stumbling and gasping, falling onto their knees coughing and fighting for breath, and then a kind of green fog came through the darkness to wrap lungs and brain in suffocating mist. As the fog took him, Davy heard the faint sound of voices. He tried to answer, but the mist filled his throat and eyes and blackness overcame him.

When he opened his eyes he was lying in the clean air at the pithead, with Tom beside him. They'd brought them up on the whim, and a crowd of anxious faces bent over them.

'You all right, Davy my son?' It was the captain from the counthouse.

Davy nodded. His head felt full of hot brass knobs, and his voice, when he spoke was hoarse and strained. 'Tom?'

'He'll do. Didn't half give us a fright, you two. Good job they charges wasn't laid up in the rock, or you'd have had half the stope down. They've cleared 'un all now. Got the safety men down. You lie down till you feel a bit more like, and then knock off.'

Davy shut his eyes again until breathing was easier. 'No damage,' he said, but of course there was half a day's pay lost, and there were the wasted charges to pay for. They'd cost wages too, to others besides themselves.

Noah Trembath came over, too, his young face strained and anxious. 'All right are you, Mr Warren? Only my Dad will be asking.' Davy found the strength to smile. Young Noah was sweet on Fanny, though she pretended not to notice. He was a good boy, Davy thought, and a hard worker, Fanny could do a lot worse. Besides, Harry Trembath had worked with Davy underground for years.

'You tell Harry that it'd take more than a bit of a bang to stop a Warren,' he said, with a lightness he did not feel.

Later he and Tom were well enough to eat a bit of their crowst, and the Counthouse Captain came out with some hot tea. That was like him. 'Good captains make good mines' people said, and if that was true Penvarris should have been the best mine in Penwith, instead of struggling to keep itself open.

It was only two, but he didn't go home. Instead, he went with the boys to the clifftop and sat watching the sea until the shift ended.

'No need to tell your mother,' he said. 'She'll only worry.'

Tom nodded, and they went to the 'dry' and changed into their clean things, and went home as if nothing had happened. But Davy couldn't sleep.

If they'd lost Tom it would have been the end of Maggie. She worried about them so. He'd get a job on the surface, 'come up to grass', first time one came vacant.

Thank goodness nothing else had happened to spoil Meg's wedding.

Saturday was fine and cool with a sharp wind blowing in from the sea. Father and the boys had been working 'doublers' on Friday – staying on for the evening shift so as to be free on Saturday morning. In the new shirts and fronts that Meg had made for them, and their Sunday suits, and with their good boots polished till they shone, the three of them looked as smart as paint, Katie thought. Even Billy Polkinghorne, the groom, who worked at the mine, and lived at the other end of the Terrace, and who would doubtless have bought a new second-hand suit specially for the day, could not look any smarter.

Meg herself was a picture in a brown shot suit with a lace fichu – quite as pretty as the picture of the Princess Royal which Katie had seen in a shop in Penzance. She had a wide hat with feathers, and knitted cotton gloves. By the time she had pinned a rose to her collar and cut a bunch of yellow roses to carry, everyone agreed she was the prettiest bride in the Terrace for many a year.

Katie's Sunday dress was trimmed with new ribbons, and she had picked pink rosebuds for her own collar and hat. Willie wore his velvet jacket that Aunt Lally had given him (made from old curtains, Mother said, but it didn't signify – Willie looked as smart as gentry in that coat) and Rosa had the cotton piece made into a handsome dress.

Fanny was having to work back to make up her time, and

Mother, paler than ever against her pillows, could not join the fashion show.

'First one to fly the nest,' she said, in a voice that sounded less and less like herself. 'Always wanted to see you girls married and settled, with children of your own. Not that everyone can expect to be as lucky as me. And now I shan't be there to see it.'

'Never you mind, Mother,' Meg said, 'Billy and I will be back after the service to see you before you can say "knife", and we're not leaving for London until the last train, you know.'

'I wish you weren't going at all, Meg,' said Katie, as they went downstairs. 'What you want to go to America for, I'd like to know?'

'It's Billy wants to go,' Meg said. 'Tell you the truth, Katie, I'm afraid of my life of that great boat trip. But they do say there's a lot of money for Cornishmen in America – copper, and tin – gold even. All sorts of miners are doing it, and coming back with no end of money.'

'Or not coming back at all,' Katie sighed, remembering one or two couples they had known.

'Don't 'ee fret, Katie,' Meg put her hands on her sister's shoulders. 'This place'll always be home to us, so long as there's family. It's just Billy thinks there's more chances in America.'

'Billy's right,' said Tom, coming into the kitchen. 'There isn't a lot doing in the mines here no more. There's been lay-offs all kind of places, with the price of tin being what it is. I've heard tell they're talking of closing Wheal Henry, things are so bad. Who's going to put money down the mines these days, and there's no end of improvements wants doing down most of them. Even Penvarris, those stamps want replacing. In America now, there's plenty of chances for those as don't object to a bit of work. I wouldn't mind going there myself.'

'You wouldn't!' Katie was horrified.

'I would too, and so would Jimmy, if it wasn't for Mother. She wouldn't like for us to be away like that, especially with Meg gone. But, oh yes, America's the place. No doubt about it. Noah Trembath is talking about going too. Given up hope of Fanny ever looking at him, I think.'

Katie was still thinking about that as they set off to the Chapel; Meg on Father's arm, picking her way carefully so as not to dirty her best boots; Jimmy and Tom looking solemn and strained in their Sunday suits, just a little too tight in the chest and too constricting at the collar; and last of all Katie with Rosa in her arms, and Willie, his velvet coat already dusty, capering beside her.

As the little procession passed the neighbours came out onto their doorsteps to gape and wave and call good wishes. One or two, like the Goodbodys and the Trembles, who were good enough friends to 'drop in after', fell in behind them, and by the time they reached the chapel there was quite a little congregation gathered. Old Granny Goodbody was standing on the steps telling everybody who would listen how in her young day nobody could get married in the chapel, and how young people today didn't know they were born, and what was the world coming to.

Billy Polkinghorne was there already, looking pink-skinned and scrubbed. He was in the choir, and so were Father and the boys, so there was some singing in the hymns. It didn't take more than a few minutes, and they were out again in the May sunshine, and Meg was Mrs Polkinghorne.

One or two of Billy's mates had come over from St Just to throw rice and rose-petals, although their minister didn't like it, and then everyone wanted to kiss the bride, and they all went back to the Terrace for tea.

There was proper ham, and cream that Crowdie had brought in, and blackcurrant tarts that Katie and Mrs Tremble had made, and saffron and heavy cake. 'Just like a Sunday School treat,' Carrie said, and really it was. There must have been forty people crammed into the little house, with food and tea for them all, though Mrs Tremble and the Goodbodys had to go home to fetch extra cups and glasses. For more than an hour they stood and sat and gossiped and cried, until it was time to drink the health of the happy couple in the raspberry cordial which Mother had made specially for the occasion from an old Methodist recipe.

Then Crowdie's cart was pressed into service again, and Meg and Billy climbed up on it with Freddy Goodbody, who was going to London to catch the same boat, and the cases were fetched and dropped and labelled 'Polkinghorne, New York' in white paint. Mrs Tremble gave Meg a tablecloth for her hope chest, and Meg had to put it in her hatbox because all the cases were packed and sealed. At last they were off, with Tom driving the cart, and Crowdie's dogs chasing at the wheels.

Katie came back into the house.

'You and Carrie set the kettle on,' Mrs Tremble said, 'and I'll take a drop up to your mother. She's had a busy day, bless her, and she'll be glad of it.'

It was true. Mother had been very tired all day.

Katie set the tray carefully, putting on it tiny tidbits of treats to try and tempt Mother's appetite, and Mrs Tremble took it upstairs. Carrie's cousin came in to feed Rosa, and as Katie went to wash the extra cup, she suddenly saw the wooden case of Meg's precious machine tucked behind the cupboard, where it had been put out of the way.

'She's forgotten her machine!' Everyone turned and stared. 'Look! Here it is, all labelled and strapped up and she's gone and left it.'

'Well it's too late now,' Carrie said. 'She'll have to do without.'

Katie's father looked grim. 'Perhaps they have them in America. They cost a power of money, mind. She'll be some disappointed about that.'

There was a general murmur of agreement. Mrs Tremble came into the room, and Katie was just about to tell her about the machine when she saw the woman's face.

Everyone stopped. Mrs Tremble put down the tray like a woman in a dream. Then she turned to Father. 'Davy, my handsome,' she said. 'She's gone!'

CHAPTER FOUR

Lally came on the morning of the funeral. She sat beside Katie in chapel, and was at her side as the procession made its way to the nonconformist graveyard, led by the band. Katie was aware of her aunt, a thin rigid figure in stiff pleats of black bombazine, worn unfashionably short, topped by a monstrous black coal-scuttle of a hat, smothered in ruffles and ribbons. She looked, Katie thought, like a collapsed old umbrella in a bonnet.

The procession stopped. Father and the two older boys went forward with Crowdie, who had insisted on being the fourth pall-bearer. Together they lifted the coffin from the funeral cart, and slid it into the ground on its four black ropes.

Fanny, who had the day off, and was carrying Rosa, wept openly. Willie buried his head in Katie's skirt. Tom and Jimmy bit their lips, while Father stood ashen-faced, and blew his nose a lot into his best white handkerchief. Even Mrs Tremble was crying.

Katie herself was too dazed for tears. Carrie came and squeezed her hand, but the day seemed to be happening to somebody else.

She was in the same daze as she walked home. She helped Fanny to change and settle Rosa, fetched water for the kettle, and handed ham and cake as though she were steam-driven, like a machine.

There was one awkward moment, when Mrs Tremble went to refill the kettle and was shouldered aside by Lally. 'Mind out of my kitchen.'

Mrs Tremble was going to say something, but she caught Father's eye and sat down again, scarlet-faced. Only she put her arm around Katie and gave her a quick hug, so for the first time that day she felt a little comforted.

Even so, Mrs Tremble was the last to leave. As she was going she asked suddenly, 'Where's the child to sleep?' She nodded towards Katie.

'Shall have to have the sofa,' Father said slowly, as though he had just thought about it. 'Fanny's back up to Trevarnon by eight . . .'

'She can come to us,' Mrs Tremble offered. 'Carrie'll be glad to have her.'

'It won't be . . .' began Lally, with a disapproving frown, but Father was too quick for her.

'That's good of 'ee, Cissie Tremble. It's been a hard day for all of us.'

'After supper then,' Carrie's mother said, smiling at Katie. 'See you then, my lover.'

When she had gone, Lally thumped the kettle on the hob with a clatter. ' 'Tisn't fitting,' she sniffed. 'Family should be together, a night like this. Katie could share with me, this one time, if she has to.'

Katie felt her skin grow cold. It would be like sharing the bed with a yard-broom. She was ready to say 'The sofa's fine' when Father forestalled her.

'The family isn't together, Lal. Meg's away tossing on the ocean the Lord knows where, and Fanny's back out before dark. The child could do with her sisters, and Carrie's the next best thing. I can see to the baby this once – there's only the one feed in the night.'

Lally poked the fire savagely. 'You spoil that child, Davy Warren. All this nonsense about staying on at school, too. If you hadn't been so soft with her she'd have left long ago. Great girl like her, time she had her feet under someone else's table. As for that baby, I daresay I can manage. I don't know why you have that great clumsy niece of Cissie Tremble's here to see after her, I'm sure. It isn't decent.'

'Lally,' Father said, his voice dangerously quiet. 'I'll see after my children the way I see fit. If you're coming here it will have to be to help, not hinder.'

Lally sniffed again, and began slapping butter on the bread, but she said nothing. Katie felt a surge of relief. At least she was to go to Carrie's tonight; that was something. For the rest, she'd have to worry about it later.

After supper, which was a miserable affair, Katie went out into the hall while Fanny put on her bonnet and shawl.

'I'll be here, Sunday,' Fanny said, in a low voice. 'Never you fret, Katie. You'll be all right, you'll see.'

'I wish Lally didn't have to come,' Katie said.

Fanny adjusted her ribbons. 'Look Katie, I know you want to be a pupil teacher and all, but if it doesn't happen, I mean, if . . .'

Katie nodded.

'There's a job up at Trevarnon. Daisy's gone, and they haven't found another girl yet. Mrs Selwood has sent one of her maids, but it won't do for ever. The girl's only trained as a parlour maid, and she has got no idea when it comes to looking after clothes and that. What Mrs Trevarnon wants is a general upstairs maid like me.'

'What's the difference?' Katie wanted to know.

Fanny smiled. 'It's a fancy name for turning your hand to anything,' she said. 'Apart from the kitchen and the dairy and the laundry, of course. Some of the big houses have parlour maids, and ladies' maids, and tweeny maids and all sorts, and a woman for the scrubbing – let alone footmen and butlers. Up to Trevarnon there was just me and Daisy upstairs, and Mr Tibbs, valet for the gentlemen – and he's the coachman's son, so he lives in the coachhouse.'

'I thought Trevarnon *was* a big house,' Katie said, remembering the huge hall and the rich rooms she had glimpsed in her brief visit.

'So it is, come to that,' Fanny agreed. 'Mrs Trevarnon would have a dozen more indoor staff if she had her way. But Mr Trevarnon doesn't believe in putting on airs. Anyway, like I say, the job'll be vacant. We had a relative of Cook's come up after it, but she was a great coarse piece with feet like a carthorse, and Mrs Trevarnon wants someone fit to be seen upstairs. They haven't said no, exactly, but you could see they weren't keen – especially Mr Robert! I could put in a word for you if you're willing, but it'd have to be sharpish. There's crowds of girls would be glad of the place.'

Katie could only gaze at her sister dumbly.

'I didn't say about it with Lally listening. She'd have had you up there before you could say "knife". I know you wanted to stay on at school and all, but Lally'll never let you be – she'll keep on at Father, you'll see, until he'd do anything to get a bit of peace. No, you think about it, my handsome. I'd be there, and we could have some rare old times.'

'Katie!' Lally's voice from the kitchen. 'Are you going to stay there gossiping all the night? There's crocks to be washed and beds to be seen to.'

Fanny reached out and gave her sister a quick embarrassed hug, whispered, 'You think about what I said,' and was gone. Katie turned back into the kitchen and started to clear away.

It was late when she got to Carrie's, but there was cocoa waiting. Mrs Tremble came in and brushed Katie's hair, the way Mother used to.

'Now you get some sleep, my lamb,' she said, as Katie snuggled down beside Carrie in the little wooden bed. 'There's always a place for you here, my love, and don't you forget it.'

And then, at last, Katie wept. It was her thirteenth birthday.

Lally couldn't sleep. The bed was lumpy, for one thing. The mattresses probably hadn't been turned properly, and the house was noisy. If it wasn't Davy turning and tossing in the room next door, it was the boys shuffling and coughing in the one opposite. Besides, every nerve in her body was on edge waiting for the baby to wake.

It was a pity, of course it was. She had nothing against Maggie Warren, she'd been a good wife to Davy, although she was always a flibberty thing. And she was no age, really. Thirty-eight, nine was it? But what did people expect, breeding like animals? Indecent, that's what it was. Hard to imagine good Christian folk behaving like that. The thought of it made her flesh crawl.

Yet women got married every day. That Fanny would be next. You could see it in the way she moved, all flounce and flirt. She wanted watching, that one. Though Davy wouldn't have a word against any of his girls. And as for Katie! The spit of her mother she was, the same blue eyes and tumbling curls. She'd be another Maggie before you knew it, with men half-killing themselves over her, and she never noticing.

Sooner she got a steady situation the better, and none of this education nonsense. That was no job for a woman. What was it the Bible said about virtuous women: 'Her candle goeth not out by night. She layeth her hands to the spindle, and her hands hold the distaff. She looketh well to the ways of her household, and eateth not the bread of idleness.' Nothing there about going to Truro and getting ideas above yourself. And she was forward, that child. Always a ready answer, and spoiled something terrible.

Lally turned her head on the pillow and sighed. The pillowcases weren't starched either. There was a lot to do. Not that she wasn't looking forward to it, in a way. She'd had lodgers in since her parents died, to help meet the rent, but they were casual people, came and went, and some of them not the kind you'd choose to share a house with. Travelling dentists, a couple of apprentices; once, by accident, an acrobat doing a turn at the Town Hall. No, it would be nice to have a proper family again, and a routine, and to have things to yourself. That William seemed a nice enough boy, if a bit wilful, and the older boys were much like her own brothers when they were young. Thank goodness she'd been the only girl.

And then there was Rosa. Lally wasn't at all sure about that. The idea of a baby seemed too primitive somehow, especially with that great clumping girl coming in with her soaking blouse to feed it. Disgusting, that was. At least all she herself had to do was to warm up the milkfeed standing ready on the side.

As if on cue, the baby started to whine.

Lally swung her bony legs out of the bed, and wrapped her shawl around her. The nightlight still flickered by the bed, and she picked it up and tiptoed downstairs.

The child was in the cradle in the corner of the warm kitchen. Lally put off the moment as long as possible by poking the embers, lighting the lamp, and washing her hands in the scullery before putting the milk to warm in a saucepan of water. The wail rose to a cry.

'Hush.' Lally moved to the cot. The child looked so small and fragile it would break. It stopped crying and looked up at her with wide, unfocused eyes. Lally began to rock the cradle, nervously at first, and then, as a tiny fist closed on one of her fingers she felt an odd tightening in her throat. Poor motherless little thing.

The child began whimpering again. 'She's hungry,' Lally thought, but the milk was not warm enough yet. Lally wrapped a blanket around the little form, and lifted the baby into her arms, rocking her awkwardly to and fro. 'Hush, my lovely, hush. You'll wake your father,' she whispered.

The child looked up, wondering at her voice, and on some impulse Lally began to sing – the first song that came into her head.

When Davy, roused by the crying, came into the kitchen, Lally was sitting on the stool by the hearth, cradling Rosa and crooning 'Fight the Good Fight' in a high cracked voice. She did not know that she was smiling.

The next day was purgatory. Katie went home first thing, before breakfast, although her mouth fairly watered at the plate of eggs Mrs Tremble would have pressed on her. Even then, she was too late to suit Lally.

'Where have you been, child? I'm here waiting for water and firewood too.'

'Tom gets the firewood,' Katie said in surprise.

'And don't you answer me back! If I want firewood, I want firewood. I suppose you don't expect me to fetch it myself, at my age?'

So Katie went. When Tom came down a few minutes later and went to the door as usual, Lally stopped him.

'Where are you off to, Tom Warren? And me with your breakfast ready to spoil?' She was cooking pilchards, and their strong smell filled the kitchen.

'You'll want wood,' Tom said.

'You've got your work to go to,' Lally retorted. 'Katie and me can manage.'

It was the same with the water. Willie was ready to set off with the barrel, but he was 'too little by half', and it was Katie who dragged it to the well and back, and fetched the milk, and collected the eggs. By the time Carrie came to collect Willie for school, Lally had all the mats hung over the line and Katie was sent to beat them with a carpet-beater.

She pretended the mats were Lally, and laid into them with a will.

'My life,' Carrie said, 'we'll be calling you Cinderella like that girl in the story.'

Katie had to laugh, but it really did feel a bit like that. Except that Lally herself never stopped working either. Day after day she scrubbed and polished and grumbled and swept. By the end of the week Katie felt that there wasn't a thing in the house that hadn't been washed or polished, and some of them twice! The bedding was airing in the garden, every drawer had been tidied and relined, and Lally was making plans for a great washday on Monday.

'These things need a good boiling,' she said, looking at Mother's pillowslips. 'Goodness knows how long since they were done properly.'

Katie glared at her in resentment. 'Don't you talk about my mother like that.'

'You hold your wicked tongue, Katie Warren! I never said a word about your mother!'

Which was true, but you didn't have to say the words to give the meaning. It was like the things she gave Katie to do. Mostly she found fault with them, but sometimes she just sighed and tossed her head and did the job again, whatever it was.

One or two neighbours came by 'to see if there's anything I can do for 'ee', but Lally soon saw them off. Only Mrs Tremble persisted.

'Lally Warren, I've been a friend of this family for sixteen years, and I'm not stopping now for the likes of you. Either you take this bit of saffron I've made the children for their tea, or I'll talk to Davy on the way home and tell him you wouldn't have it. Folk round here think a lot of Davy, and he won't thank you for turning them aside.'

Lally sniffed. 'I won't be beholden!' But she stood back and let Carrie's mother into the kitchen, while Katie made her a cup of tea.

'Have you finished with them rags, Katie?' Lally wanted to know. Katie had been given a box of her old clothes which Lally had found at the back of a cupboard, and was tearing them for dusters.

'Oh, leave the child be a minute, do!' Mrs Tremble said, not unkindly. 'There's more to life than work, work, work. Now look, Carrie and Willie will be home in a minute, and Davy'll be here before you know it, so what say you let Katie come in to me for a bit, and she can help Carrie with her homework, and then they can go down and meet their fathers. Give her a bit of company, and you a bit of peace and quiet.'

Lally looked thunderous, but Katie said, 'Just wait while I finish these rags, and I'll be right over.' And that was the end of it. Katie had never worked so hard in her life. Lally insisted that she did the potatoes too, but she flew at them until they were done, then washed her hands and face and ran next door before Lally changed her mind.

The Trembles' kitchen seemed warmer and cosier than ever before. There was tea waiting, and Mrs Tremble had made a heavy-cake. Katie sank into a chair and bit into the delicious warmth of the 'morsel'. 'Mmm!'

'How are you getting on with that Lally, then?'

Katie was too full of jam to say anything, but she raised her eyes to heaven.

'She's got a good heart, really,' Mrs Tremble said, sitting down opposite her and biting great chunks from her own slice. 'She only means to do her best, but she's never had young people around her. She hasn't had much of a life, poor soul.'

Katie scowled. 'Well, she doesn't have to spoil mine!'

'You'll have to be patient, my lover. She'll find her feet in a month or two.'

But somehow she didn't. Not though the spring blossomed into summer, and summer ripened into fall.

Sundays were worst. Lally's Sundays had always been a legend, even when Grandfather was alive, and the family had gone over, twice, to see him. Cheerless rooms that were colder than ever because it was a sin to fetch coals on the Sabbath. Cold meat, cold potatoes, cold pickles and tasteless lemonade because it was forbidden to cook on Sunday. And sitting, stiff and silent in the chilly kitchen, waiting for the clock to point to three o'clock when it would be time for the long walk home, and a chance to skip and sing and pick daisies in the half-light. Mother would scold and fret, 'Mind your best clothes, and don't dance like a heathen – it's Sunday!' but there would be a smile in her voice, and she would join in the singing with the rest of them, holding her soprano part while Father pom-pommed in the bass. Once, as they were snatching a warm cup of tea before going out again to evening chapel, Mother said 'That Lally! It's enough to drive you to Bedlam. Do you know she won't even let your poor father have his bit of book! A sin to read on Sunday! A sin to make a man a decent bit of dinner! It's a sin to carry on like she does, if you ask me!'

But now there was no escape at three. No escape ever. Only week after week of polishing and scrubbing, and Sunday after Sunday of cold potatoes. Father would never fight Lally over that – not if it was in the Bible. Only Lally did agree now to leave the fire stoked up on a Saturday, so the milk was warm for Rosa.

More than once, as the weeks wore on, Katie thought of Mother's cheerful soprano doing the twiddly bits in 'Washed in the blood of the Lamb' while she buttered the toast, and tears stung her eyes.

There was no school for Katie. Time and again she raised it, but there was always some reason why she could not be spared, though there was no difficulty in managing without her when it was a question of lifting potatoes, or picking apples, or picking stones up from behind the plough for Crowdie and coming home with a few coppers in her pockets.

Only two things livened Katie's life. Often of a morning, struggling home with the water barrel, she met George Trevarnon happening by on his horse, and he always stopped to bid her good day.

'He's sweet on you,' Carrie teased, and Katie would blush and flounce her curls, but secretly she looked forward to those few kindly words in the mornings, and the brightness of his smile. Without that, and her afternoon visit to Carrie's, life would have been miserable indeed.

'I believe that Lally's got a down on me,' she said, one October afternoon, when she was sitting in the twilight of the Trembles' kitchen under the pretext of helping Carrie with her stitching.

Mrs Tremble poured a cup of steaming cocoa. ' 'Tisn't that, my love. It's just she was brought up to think that women are there to serve their menfolk, and that good looks are sinful.' She carved a thick slice of new gingerbread. 'Besides, I sometimes think you remind her of herself – you make her think what her life might have been.'

Carrie looked up from her sewing. 'It's some shame you never got to be a pupil-teacher, Katie. It was never the same at school without you. I shall miss you, too, when I go to take up this situation.' Carrie had left school herself now, and had found a position as a kitchen maid. It was her cotton uniform which she was hemming.

Katie took a delicious bite. She missed her mother's cooking sorely: Lally's cakes were as flat and sour as Lally herself. Indeed the loss of her mother seemed to be sharper with every passing day. 'Yes,' she said slowly, 'I don't know how I shall manage without you, Carrie. I've half a mind to do what Fanny says and go up Trevarnon.'

'How's that then?'

Katie told her all about it. 'They're wanting an upstairs maid. The other one left. They had a relation of the Cook's up there for a month or two, but she didn't really suit, and they turned her off last week. Fanny says they are looking for someone again. Mrs Trevarnon might be hard, but she can't be so bad as Lally. At least I'd be paid. And, I don't know, home doesn't seem like home no more. All the life has gone out of it somehow. And I'll never get back to school now. I wish Father would have stood up for me.'

Mrs Tremble gave her a quick look. 'Your Father's tried to do what's right, Katie. But she's given him a hard time over you, no doubt of that, and he has needed her help for that dear child. I know it would be a disappointment for you, but you might do worse than go up there with Fanny. It might make things easier for your Father, too – he's got another little one to keep now, and Meg's money isn't coming in. He might be glad of a few shillings extra. Lally isn't the manager your mother was, for all her spring-cleaning.'

Katie hadn't thought about that. She said, very soberly, 'You think so?'

'Why don't you go up and meet your father, and talk to him about it. See what he says? But think about it carefully. Don't go rushing into things.'

'I will,' Katie promised, and she did, even when Willie came home

41

and wanted her help with his reckoning. She thought about Lally and Sunday, and Father scrimping and saving, about Fanny and a great staircase and a chandelier, and about a young man with a gentle smile leaning down from a big brown horse. By the time she met Father she had made up her mind. With his permission, she'd go to Trevarnon, if they'd have her.

CHAPTER FIVE

Davy was astonished to find his daughter waiting for him in the fading daylight, and even more astonished when he heard what she had to say.

'Well, I never did! What's brought this on, all at once, then?' Davy said, and then with sudden understanding, 'It's that Lally! I swear, she'd drive a saint to perdition. What's she been saying to you, my handsome? I know you always wanted to stay on at school, and I know we haven't managed that, but we'll find you an apprenticeship, so long as I've got two pence to rub together, if that's what you've a mind to.'

Katie looked at him, so like Maggie it made his heart ache. 'That's just the trouble. It isn't just what Lally thinks – though goodness knows she'd keep on till we were sick of the sound of it – but it would cost. I never thought about that so much, but with Meg gone, and now Mother, and a new baby, and Lally and all . . . It's like Mrs Tremble said, you might be glad of a bit extra.'

'So you've been talking about it to half the village already, have you?' He was touched. It was like her to think of the money. There was no getting round it, things were not easy – there had been the doctor to pay, for one thing, and the funeral costs to meet. He'd had a pound or two in the club and there'd been a whip-round on the shift, but Lally was no manager, and there wasn't a halfpenny left to spare. Already there had been days with dandelion and sorrel in the salad, and the blackberries gathered from the hedges had not been a pleasure this year, but a stark necessity.

He didn't like to think of the child giving up her dream like this – but

43

what with Lally, and one thing and another, if Cissie Tremble thought it was a good idea, it probably was. So he said, dryly: 'Well, it's a bit late for me to say anything against it then, isn't it? The boys'll miss you, mind,' he added, meaning that he would.

She caught his arm. 'I won't go if you don't want, Father.'

'Don't be so soft! Of course you must go if you want to. And I'll have a word on the circuit, see if you can't do a bit of teaching at Sunday School. You'd like that, I daresay?'

She nodded, her eyes bright.

'Well, then. And like you say, my handsome, nothing's like it was any more, is it? I can see how it isn't easy for you with Lally after you like a bloodthirsty Indian.' He didn't add that Tom and Jimmy had been saying much the same thing earlier in the day, and talking of joining Meg in America. Then the wages coming in would be thin, indeed. Lally was driving his family away. But what could he do? Lally herself had been struggling to make ends meet. You couldn't see your sister in the workhouse, especially when you had a home to give her and a baby wanting minding.

He squeezed Katie's hand. 'Well, if you're set on this, you'd better look sharp about it. Plenty of girls will be after a place at Trevarnon if there's one going begging.'

'What shall I do? Just turn up there and say I heard there was a place vacant?'

'You could do worse. They'll likely tell you to come back another time, but at least they'll know you're willing. Put on your best bonnet and apron mind, and try to make your hair look something like. Oh, and Katie . . .'

'Yes?'

'I shouldn't say anything to Lally about where you're going, just yet. Just say I've sent you an errand.'

For a moment their eyes met in perfect understanding, and then she was off in an unladylike flurry of skirts. He caught up with Tom and Jimmy and strolled home with them.

Lally was furious. 'That Katie!' she greeted him as soon as he opened the door. 'Here's me needing water for your tea, and she just puts on her bonnet and out the door without so much as a by-your-leave.'

'Yes,' Davy said. 'I sent her.'

'You make a rod for your own back. I've always said it, and I always will: you indulge that child.'

Davy hung up his scarf behind the door and looked at her. 'Lally,' he said, as gently as he could, 'let's have a bit of hush. It's been a hard day.'

Lally's mouth opened, then shut again. Davy went to the pitcher and had ladled milk into a cup before she said in a martyred tone, 'Well, I've only come here to help, but I know my place. I won't say another word about it.'

'Yes,' Davy said. 'That would be best.' He sipped his milk deliberately and she glowered at him, knowing he'd caught her in her own trap. She was bursting to say more, but she held her tongue, and contented herself with slamming tripe into the frying pan and beating the daylights out of the fire with the poker.

Later, as they sat uncomfortably round the table, Willie asked suddenly, 'Where's our Katie to? It's late.'

Davy saw Tom give his brother a kick under the table, and pile three of Lally's slices of bread into one.

'You'd better ask your father,' Lally said. '*I* don't know, I'm sure. And if you want your bread cut thicker, young man, you only have to ask! Though if you ask me, she ought to be out looking for a situation, great girl like that, instead of gallivanting about the countryside at mealtimes like a pagan.'

'That's all right, then.' Katie's voice surprised them all. She had come in so silently no one had heard her. 'Because that's just what I have been doing. I've been up to Trevarnon.'

Lally looked at Davy, but he only said: 'And?'

'I saw Mrs Trevarnon,' Katie said. 'She wasn't keen at first, with me being Fanny's sister, but Mr Trevarnon came in and said that good servants were like good horses, better from a stable you know.'

'And what did you say to that?' asked Davy, a little anxiously. He knew his daughter and her quick tongue.

Katie grinned. 'Oh, it was all right. I could see he was only trying to help. So then she asked if I was strong and healthy, and I said yes, and there you are. They've given me this uniform to alter,' Katie unwrapped the bundle she was carrying, 'until the sewing woman can make me a new one. I start first thing in the morning.'

Lally's expression did not change, but she got up from the table. 'And I suppose you'll be expecting me to help you to alter it? Well, sit down, girl, do, while I fetch you some supper. And you needn't think you can keep me awake tossing all the night, so you can go next door again if your father says so.'

Really, Davy thought, his sister had the oddest way of showing that she was pleased.

It had been a busy day. George had spent the afternoon with Papa, looking at the ticketing prices for black tin. There would have to be better markets to justify the new expenditure, so the mine purser said; no point in pouring good money after bad. Otherwise there would be lay-offs. George had thought of Katie's earnest face as she tugged the heavy water-barrel from the well each morning. Only he and his father, it seemed, could imagine what those lay-offs would mean to the men and the families concerned.

He was glad to turn to the open air, and a brisk ride on Blister before the sun went down on the autumn evening. He was up in the top field with the stable-boy when Robert cantered up on Coral.

'Fancy a gallop out, George old man? It's a splendid evening.'

George looked longingly at the fields melting into the golden glow of sunset, but he shook his head doubtfully. 'No,' he said. 'We've had enough for one day, haven't we, old fellow?' The horse nuzzled up to him.

'Great God!' Robert said with a laugh. 'That's a horse you've got there, not a blasted ballerina! Still, more fool you. When you've got a good horse, ride it, that's what I say. I've been out at the steeplechase today and it's given me an appetite for it. Come on, girl!'

He wheeled and galloped down the rise. For a moment George couldn't believe his eyes. Surely he wasn't going to set the horse at that gate? Not at that angle, on that uneven ground?

Yes, he was! George thrust Blister's reins at the stable-boy and set off at a run, shouting 'Take it square!', but it was too late. Robert was already swerving awkwardly towards the gate, and George flinched as he saw him dig in his heels and thrash at Coral's rump with his whip. 'She'll baulk!' he muttered, and sure enough the mare stopped abruptly, braced her legs and lowered her head. Robert tumbled over her ears in an undignified heap. George winced inwardly – Robert wouldn't like that, especially not in front of the stable-boy.

'Are you all right?' he shouted, but Robert was already struggling to his feet, while Coral retreated, baring her teeth and whinnying.

'Damned horse,' Robert said, brushing at the dusty stains on his riding breeches. 'Starts at the least damn thing.'

'It wasn't the horse's fault,' George said. He took Coral's bridle and patted her nose. 'You should have taken it square.'

'Full of advice, aren't we? I suppose you think you could do better?'

George turned away. Robert was in one of his difficult moods.

'Bet you couldn't,' Robert persisted. 'Come on! I mean it. A wager. A private steeplechase. I'll bet you the damned horse itself you can't jump that gate!'

'Oh, don't be stupid,' George said. 'Anyway, what have I got to wager with?'

'Blister!' said Robert. 'Coral against Blister. Come on, man, you can't say any fairer than that.' He was calming down. Already the bet was more important than the quarrel. Robert could never resist a wager.

'That settles it,' George said. 'I wouldn't risk losing Blister.' Robert smiled, and he added doubtfully, 'I wish you wouldn't let your friend Gillard keep talking you into going to these races. It's all very well for him, a few guineas is nothing to him. But you gamble too much, Robert. One of these days you'll bet more than you can afford to lose.'

It was a mistake. Robert rounded on him. 'All right, Goody Two-shoes. I don't need a lecture. I know why you won't bet. You couldn't do it!'

Couldn't he though? Suddenly George was as furious as his brother. He leapt into the saddle and cantered Coral towards the gate. Robert had to move backwards out of his way. The gate looked enormous, and for an awful moment George thought she wouldn't make it, but he urged her on, and suddenly they were up and over, clear and clean. George reined her in and slipped down out of the saddle.

'Lucky I wouldn't bet,' he said.

A dangerous red had risen to Robert's cheeks. 'Keep the bloody thing, anyway!' he muttered. 'Wretched animal made me wrench my ankle. Are you going to help me in, or are you going to stand there moralising all night?'

George did not feel as victorious as he expected. The whole thing seemed suddenly rather silly. He had been showing off every bit as much as Robert had. 'Are you really hurt?' he asked.

'Well, my leg is swelling like a balloon,' Robert said savagely. 'If that qualifies as being hurt. I shan't be able to wear boots again for a week.'

'We'd better get back to the house and get off the one you're wearing,' George said. 'Here, lean on me.'

Robert did so with a bad grace, and they set off, leaving the horses to the stable-boy.

47

'At least,' George said, wanting to make amends, 'you'll cut an interesting figure for Caroline Selwood at lunch tomorrow. You know what romantic nonsense she talks about the cavalry! She'll call you the "fallen wounded" and you'll be the hero of the hour.' Robert could often be won over by a little gentle flattery.

He was now. 'You might be right, old man,' Robert said. 'Though I thought you were making quite a play for her yourself.'

George smiled. 'I couldn't compete with you.'

'You don't get the practice,' Robert said.

'If you mean flirting with the maids, I'm not sure I want to practise,' George retorted. 'Anyway, when would I have a chance? They spend all their time flirting with you.'

Robert laughed, the quarrel forgotten. 'Tell you what, old man, tomorrow you'll be able to have a little maid all to yourself. Nice little thing. Hasn't got Fanny's figure of course, not yet, but she's presentable enough. Make a change after that dreadful lumpy cousin of Cook's. Thank heaven Mama finally got rid of her. This girl heard about the job and turned up this afternoon. Mama appointed her at once.'

'Really?' George was glad to hear it. Mama's irritation about the staff had made life at Trevarnon very stressful recently. 'How did she hear about it?'

'Some young sister of Fanny's, apparently,' Robert said carelessly. 'Kathy, Katie, something like that.' George felt his skin prickle, but Robert was oblivious. 'Mother wasn't keen at first, having two maids from one family and no experience either, but father talked her round. The girl seems quick-witted and willing enough, and at least she's presentable, as I said. So there you are, old man, problem solved. Practise all you like!'

George said sullenly, 'Don't be obscene!'

'Hey, steady on!' Robert protested. 'You nearly had me over, jerking away like that! What do you mean, "obscene"?'

'Well,' said George, aware that he had said more than he had intended, 'If she's younger than Fanny she can't be more than fourteen.'

'Thirteen and a half, she told mother,' Robert said. 'But you can't judge these girls by our standards. Married at fourteen, half of them, and three children at their skirt-tails by the time they're your age. Look at this one now.'

'This one' was Fanny, come out with stale crumbs for the hens.

When she saw Robert her face flushed, and she dropped her package and came over in a fluster.

'Why, Mr Robert! Whatever have you gone and done?'

'A riding accident,' Robert said, in a voice which suggested heroism. 'Fanny, can you fetch me Papa's stick, and get Tibbs to send some hot water to my room? On second thoughts, bring it yourself. Perhaps you can help me bathe it?'

Fanny's cheeks burned a little brighter. 'Right away, Mr Robert,' she said, and was gone.

'You see,' Robert preened. 'I'll lay you a guinea I can have her before the year's out.'

George shrugged him off angrily. He was going to reply, but Fanny was back with the stick. Robert took it in his left hand and put his right arm around her shoulders.

'I think I can walk,' he said, 'with Fanny's help.' He took two steps, and then stopped, drawing her closer to him. 'There,' he said, 'that's better. See you at dinner, George. And remember what I said, old man. A guinea.' He gave George one of his wicked leers. 'Two guineas says both of them!'

And leaning much more heavily on the girl than he needed, he limped into the house.

Katie was up at Trevarnon well before time, but Fanny was already waiting for her in the courtyard.

'She's here,' she called, seizing Katie's basket and leading the way inside.

Cook poked her head out of the kitchen door. 'You'd best take her up to her room and help her get sorted, and then make a start upstairs.' She nodded at Katie. 'Hello, m'dear, pleased to meet you. I can't stop now. We're all at sixes and sevens today. Mr Robert hurt his foot riding yesterday, and Mrs Trevarnon's taken to bed with her nerves, and there's company for lunch, so nothing'll be right for the day. You come down for a bit of breakfast later, and we'll have a proper talk. You see after her, Fanny, and show her what to do.'

Fanny led the way up more stairs than Katie had ever seen in her life. They seemed to go on for ever. She was quite breathless by the time they reached the top, and Fanny threw open a little door under the eaves.

'This is yours,' she said, dumping the basket on the bed. 'Mine's across the landing. Now let's get you into your uniform sharpish, or

Mrs Trevarnon'll be creating something chronic. In here, is it?' She started to rummage through the basket.

There wasn't much to search through. Some clean underlinen, a second-best blouse and boots and a Sunday dress, half a dozen trinkets, and a Bible. All Katie's possessions carefully packed in Mother's old frail.

The uniform was at the bottom. Lally had made a good job of it, with the aid of Meg's machine, and though it was still too wide at the waist, and too long in the sleeve ('to allow for growing' Lally said) it came somewhere near fitting. Fanny tweaked it straight, and Katie tied on the apron and cap which had been set ready on the bed.

'How do I look?' she asked, trying to see herself in the mottled mirror propped on the dressing chest.

'My dear life,' Fanny said, 'you'll have to do something with that hair. It's sticking out like a chimney-brush under that cap. You'll have to put it up, that's all.'

'I don't know how!' Katie wailed. 'I've never put my hair up.'

'Well, time to start,' Fanny said. 'You're a grown-up now, aren't you? Come here while I show you.' Fanny dashed into her own room and returned with a mouthful of hairpins. Five minutes later Katie's curls were subdued into some sort of order under her cap. 'There,' Fanny said. 'That'll have to do. Come on now, we'd best make a start, before there's the devil to pay.'

There was a lot to do. Grates to clean and set, tables to polish, ornaments to dust, carpets to sprinkle with tealeaves and sweep clean with a brush. Then Fanny went off to set breakfast on the buffet for the family and 'dress Madam', leaving Katie to air the beds and turn the pillows and clean the warming-pans while the Trevarnons ate. When the beds were made they went down to the kitchen.

'There's a power to do,' Cook said, hoisting a huge kettle onto the range. 'Manage all right, can you m'dear?'

Katie thought about Lally and smiled. 'Yes,' she said.

'Only there's nothing to you,' Cook went on, presiding over a table on which were set more shapes and sizes of knives and saucepans than Katie could possibly have imagined. She was more housekeeper than cook, Fanny said, because although Mrs Trevarnon pretended to make the decisions, it was Cook who wrote the menus and the shopping lists, and Mrs Trevarnon just said, 'Very well, Cook. Carry on.' All the same, Mrs Trevarnon called the woman 'Cook', so everyone else did too.

'Nothing to you at all,' she repeated. 'Ruby here'd make two of you.' Ruby was the kitchen-maid, a big stumpy girl with red hands and face and a scowl as broad as her hips. 'And it's no good you knitting socks with your eyebrows, Ruby, you wouldn't have liked working upstairs anyhow, so say hello to Katie like a good girl while I see if I can find these two a bit of breakfast left from upstairs.'

Ruby grunted.

'It's good of Mrs Trevarnon to let us have this.' Katie looked in disbelief at the piece of sausage, the end of bacon and the mushrooms set before her. 'Proper feast, this is.'

'You can thank Mrs Selwood for that,' Cook said firmly. 'She told Mrs Trevarnon she always gave the servants the leavings, and of course Mrs Trevarnon couldn't be outdone, so she said the same. Besides, what she doesn't see, she doesn't miss. Now come on, Ruby, and lend a hand to these carrots and help me with this here custard. You two had better change your aprons and set for lunch.'

Katie had never imagined there could be so much china in one family. It took them twenty minutes in the dining room just to put it on the table, and then all the knives and forks to be arranged in the right order, and glasses and flowers and little silver trays of sweets. All the time they were working Fanny was giving instructions about where to stand and what to do during lunch. There were a million things to remember.

'You just pass things today,' Fanny said, when they had finished the table. 'And don't try to serve out. But collect up the plates after. Stand the proper side, mind, and don't pile them up or scrape things off them. Just copy me and Tibbs. Stand back, look. Here they all come. Wait while they sit down, and then I'll ring for the soup.'

The party came into the dining-room. There was Mrs Trevarnon, looking much grander than she had done at Katie's interview, leaning on the arm of a thin grey-haired man with a moustache, who turned out to be Major Selwood. Mr Trevarnon was there too, even more red-faced than yesterday, accompanying Mrs Selwood. Then Robert, limping heavily on a stick with one foot in a slipper, followed by a young woman in a beautiful dress. And giving her his arm, George.

Katie felt her cheeks glow. He looked towards her and gave her the tiniest of smiles.

After that she might as well have been invisible. He never glanced at her again as she passed and carried, walking carefully so as not to upset the soup or spoil the perfection of Cook's custard.

The talk at the table was all about Robert's accident, and then it turned to the trouble in Africa.

'Got a friend on Kitchener's staff,' Major Selwood said. 'Served with him in the Sudan. He's been saying for years that there would be serious trouble in Africa next. Doesn't surprise me. Been enough trouble in the Transvaal already. Damn Boers. Your neck of the woods, eh Trevarnon?'

'Leave me out of this,' George's father said sharply. Too sharply, Katie thought. 'I'm not a military man.'

'Knew the country though, in your time? Plenty of scope for cavalry out there. I hear half the country is signing up. Train full of volunteers went out from Redruth yesterday. What do you say, young Robert?'

'Ask George,' Robert said sullenly. 'He's such an almighty horseman.'

George said nothing.

Caroline clapped her hands and opened her eyes wide at her cousin, as if she were six, Katie thought. 'Oh do, George! You'd look so dashing in that uniform, and with all those splendid horses. I should so like to see you a soldier.'

George turned crimson, but he smiled as he said, 'Ah, but is that because you have a fancy to see me in uniform, or a fancy to see me half a world away?'

Now it was Caroline's turn to blush and stammer. Katie could see that George had handled the situation nicely.

Major Selwood said, 'Well, you think about it all the same. There are worse careers for a young man with his way to make. I could pull a few strings for you. The St Ives farm won't keep you in this style, and with the price of tin what it is you might be glad of another string to your bow.'

So the conversation turned to mining. Black tin had fallen, whatever that might mean, and the mine-owners were being asked for more money to buy new equipment. It was Penvarris mine they were talking of, and George glanced towards Katie uneasily. She was so busy listening that Fanny had to give her a little poke to remind her to pass the pears to Miss Selwood.

'How could you be such a gummock!' Fanny scolded when the lunch party had gone out to take the air in the garden. 'Standing there with your ears flapping. It's just as well it was Miss Selwood and not Mrs Trevarnon you were handing to, or there'd have been something said, I can tell you. Not everybody is so easy-going.'

'I thought she was rather silly,' Katie said.

Fanny was mortified. 'You can't talk like that about folk upstairs!' Then she giggled. 'True though, isn't it? She's pretty, mind.'

Robert thought so, in any case, Katie thought to herself. She had seen the way his eyes followed his cousin all through the meal. But she didn't say so. Anyway, Fanny wasn't expecting an answer.

'Come on then,' she said. 'We can't stand here gossiping all day. There's too much to do.'

In fact, there was less to do than usual. The family were going to a Charity Supper and Dance in Penzance with the Selwoods, so after the dining-room was cleared and the tea served, and Fanny had cleaned Mrs Trevarnon's silk dress with dry breadcrumbs, and then helped her into it, while Katie carried water for the gentlemen and made up the fires, there were only the beds to warm and Mr Robert's supper to see to.

'I can manage now,' Fanny said, as they finished their supper. 'You get up to your room. There'll be twice the job tomorrow. Oh, and here's your treat.' She took out a packet from her apron. 'Carrie got it for you at the fair last week. Told me to save it for a treat tonight.'

Katie took the little package and went upstairs with her candle. The staircase seemed very dark and shadowy, and the house was eerily silent. In the bare little room she undressed carefully, said her prayers, and setting the candle beside her, climbed into bed. Only then did she unwrap the parcel.

It was a gingerbread doll, a fairing cake, with currant eyes and an icing apron. When she was a child she and Carrie had always loved a fairing doll. She didn't eat it but sat looking at it for a long time.

At last, she blew out the candle and tried to sleep.

CHAPTER SIX

There was so much to learn, the next few weeks fairly flew. The correct way to pass tea and scones, the secret of polishing silver without fingerprints, how to dust a chandelier. Katie was fitted out with her proper uniforms, print for mornings and a new black for later, and very smart she felt. 'It'll be stopped out of your wages, mind,' Fanny warned, but it couldn't be helped.

Father was as good as his word, and arranged things so that after two o'clock chapel Katie did a bit of teaching at Sunday School. Ruby's mother (even wider than her daughter) came 'for her letters', seeing she had worked on the Bal as a girl and never gone to school. 'Da could'n afford to send we,' she said. Ruby even forgave Katie for working upstairs when she heard.

Katie told Willie about it over tea – cheerless cold potato and pickle – in the kitchen at the Terrace, which had suddenly grown very small and cramped.

'That teacher of yours wants to see you,' Lally said. She had kept a small fire in 'for the child's sake', but she wouldn't have the kettle set on it in the Sabbath.

'Miss Bevan? Whatever for?'

'Don't ask me, I'm sure,' Lally said, taking Rosa on her knee. 'You'd best go down there your next half day.'

'I went bird scaring today for Crowdie,' Willie said, proud to be among the wage-earners.

Katie felt like a child again herself as she knocked on the door of the teacher's cottage the following Wednesday.

Miss Bevan greeted her with delight. 'My dear girl. Sit down while I put the kettle on and find a bit of seedcake.'

The room smelt of linen, and there was a flat-iron on the hearth. Katie was rather surprised to find evidence of such human activities, but she summoned her manners and tried to sip her tea daintily, as she had seen Miss Selwood do.

'Now then,' Miss Bevan said. 'I've got a little something for you. A sort of prize. Carrie got the Standard Five Prize, seeing you didn't finish your year, but you were always such a good scholar I thought you deserved to have something. So here you are. A special prize from me to you.'

Katie took the book delightedly. She didn't know if it was polite to look inside, but she had a quick peep. *A Tale of Two Cities* by Charles Dickens. Even a short glance was enough to show her that it was a proper book, with a story, not like the *Moral Thoughts* she'd won as an attendance prize last year.

'Thank you!' she said. Her mouth was rather full of cake, but she remembered her manners and gulped it down in a lump before she went on. 'That's some good of you, Miss Bevan.'

'My pleasure, Katie. And remember, if there is ever anything I can do to help, just ask. Now, how are you liking your station, my dear?'

Katie found herself telling Miss Bevan all about it – the daily chores, the grand lunches and dinners, the dark echoing landing at the top of the stairs where Fanny said there were ghosts, and the strange, delicious food which sometimes found its way down to the kitchen table.

'It sounds as though there are some things about it that you enjoy,' Miss Bevan said.

'Oh yes,' Katie said, thinking of a certain young man who sometimes smiled at her. 'Well,' she added, jumping to her feet in a scatter of crumbs, and hoping Miss Bevan would not notice the brightness of her cheeks, 'I'll have to go, or I'll be behind my time. Mrs Trevarnon doesn't like it if I'm out after seven.'

There were lots of things, in fact, which Mrs Trevarnon didn't like. Singing in the kitchen, slouching in the dining-room, clattering on the stairs. Katie sometimes wondered if there was anything Mrs Trevarnon *did* like. And then, by chance, she discovered something.

It was a sewing day, and the sewing-woman was in the linen-room mending. Katie was on the landing outside shifting from one foot to the other, waiting for the servants' sheets which were to be turned 'sides to middle' and resewn. The job was taking much longer than expected and there were other jobs to do, but Katie dared not leave without the linen. Mrs Trevarnon would want to inspect it personally before the woman was paid.

Katie stretched and fidgeted. Then, remembering the precious book in her petticoat pocket, she edged down the landing towards the light, and opened the pages.

'Well, girl! What are you doing?' Mrs Trevarnon had come through the baize door at her back. Katie tried to hide the book and gave a little bob.

'I'm waiting for the linen, ma'am, like you said. Only it's taking such a time.'

'And what's that you've got there? Give it to me.' Mrs Trevarnon stretched out a hand for the book. Katie handed it over unwillingly. 'Now, go and see to your duties. I'll inspect the linen here. I want to speak to the woman about altering my green silk in any case.'

Katie went. Through the rest of the week she kept hoping that Mrs Trevarnon would give her a good telling-off and return the book, but nothing was said. At last, on Friday, when she carried up the coals for Mrs Trevarnon's fire, she took her courage in both hands.

'Mrs Trevarnon, ma'am. I'm sorry you found me reading on duty, and it shan't happen again, but I should be ever so grateful to have my book back, if I could, ma'am. It was a present – well, a prize.'

Mrs Trevarnon opened a drawer and took out the book. She riffled through the pages. 'That's a long story for a girl to read. Do you like reading, then, girl?'

'Yes ma'am. Course I do. When I have a book.'

'Don't be insolent, child. I mean reading aloud. There's a book there beside my bed. Let's hear you. And look sharp about it.'

Katie fetched the book and opened it at the marked page. It was a poor thing, she thought, full of 'fies' and 'las', but she did her best, with different voices for all the characters. Mrs Trevarnon seemed to have gone to sleep, but the minute there was a pause her eyes snapped open. 'Well, don't stop there, child. Read till I tell you.'

Katie had finished the chapter before Mrs Trevarnon spoke again. 'Well, girl, if you want to read, you can read to me in the mornings when you've finished your chores. You can start tomorrow. Now you may go.'

'Can I take my book?' Katie asked, seizing it.

'Oh, very well! But don't let me catch you with it again.'

Katie fled.

'I don't know why you think you got off lightly,' Fanny said when she heard. 'You'll end up reading to her in your hour off. Daisy used to have to and she told me she hated it.'

But Katie didn't mind. It wasn't long before they'd finished the book. Mrs Trevarnon sent her to the library downstairs to find another. George was writing letters at the desk.

Katie hesitated. In all the weeks she had been at the house it was the first time she had found herself really alone with him. Then she found her tongue. 'Excuse me, Mr George, Mrs Trevarnon's sent me for a book.' And then, lest he misunderstand, 'To read to her.'

He got up. 'She's got you doing that, has she? She isn't a good reader herself, but she does like a story. Must be a bore.'

'Oh no,' Katie said. 'I like to read. Only thing is, I don't know what to take her.'

He selected a book from the shelf. 'Try this. She'll enjoy that.' He smiled down at her. 'And would you like a book for yourself, since you "like to read"?'

'Oh, I couldn't!' Katie said, taken aback. 'Anyway, I got one. Look.' She lifted her apron aside and took her prize from the pocket of her frock.

'You can if I say so.' He took the book and opened it with care. 'What's this? "Katherine Warren. For Reading and Good Scholarship." A prize? No wonder you're so proud of it. What does Mama say about this?'

'She said she wasn't to catch me on duty with it again,' Katie said, and forgetting herself in her alarm she added, 'So don't you go telling her.'

He laughed, holding the book just out of her reach. 'Supposing I did, Katherine Warren, good reader and good scholar, what then?'

'Oh, please, Mr George,' she began, and realised with a glow of relief that he was teasing her, like Tom did. With sudden wickedness she met his eyes. 'Or I'd have to speak to her myself, wouldn't I? I never did thank her for those grapes.'

George laughed aloud, and pressed her nose with one forefinger. 'I won't tell if you don't! Now, get along before she starts ringing for you.' He gave her back the prize, and added seriously, 'And I mean it. If you want a book, just ask me.'

'Thank you,' she whispered, adding as she closed the door, 'Mr Grapes.'

57

She could hear him laughing all the way down the hall.

Robert came down the main staircase, twirling his cane. He didn't need it now – it was months since that confounded business with the horse, but it looked well. It had a gold handle, and he could lean on it interestingly if there was a pretty girl nearby to notice.

There was a pretty girl nearby now. That little maid was coming out of the library, all pink and glowing. And from inside the room, laughter. George! Robert limped dramatically down the stairs and thrust open the door. She didn't glance at him. He'd have to see about that!

'That's an evil laugh, old man!' he said, as lightly as he could. George, who was sitting at the desk, coloured like a woman. Pretty as a girl, Robert thought contemptuously, with that blond hair and slim figure. Women were beginning to find him attractive. Robert straightened the fashionable tweed jacket over his own wide shoulders, and said, more harshly than he meant, 'Been charming the maids, have we?'

'She's a trick, that one,' George said with warmth.

Smitten was he? The girl was pretty enough, certainly, although Robert preferred women with a bit more flesh on their bones. Still, he made a mental note to look out for her again. He liked a bit of a challenge, and he was damned if George was going to get all the fun. She would be a challenge too, if her sister was anything to go by. It had taken months of patience to get anywhere near her. And here was the younger one all of a flutter over George. He would have to look to his laurels.

But this was not the moment to quarrel. Robert was quite capable of biding his time. He said, with a cheerful smile, 'Fact is, old man, I was thinking of taking a spin over to the Selwoods this afternoon, if you'd care to come along.'

George grinned. 'And risk my neck in that new pony-trap of yours? Not likely! You drive like a demon!'

Cheeky puppy! Did he guess that Robert's refusal to ride Coral was not so much because of a damaged ankle, but because he resented having looked so foolish?

'Besides,' George went on, 'I don't care to spend the whole of a fine afternoon goggling at the Major's guns.'

'Oh, come on, there's a good fellow.' Robert said. George could never resist an appeal to his better nature. 'Old man Selwood made a point of inviting us both, and it would be forward of me to go alone. Besides, he likes to talk to you.'

'Likes to lecture me about joining the army,' George said, with some spirit. 'Hasn't stopped since this South African business came to a head.'

'I should have thought,' Robert carefully did not look at him, 'it might rather have appealed to you. Queen and Country and all that.' A lot of things would be easier with George away. Caroline Selwood, for instance.

George shook his head. 'Had to shoot a horse once. Didn't care for it.' He smiled. 'More your cup of tea, surely? Guns and derring-do?'

Robert laughed. 'Not me, old man. I'd rather sit in the conservatory and drink tea with Caroline Selwood. That is, if you'll come with me. Now, what about it?'

'Oh, very well.'

'After lunch, then. I've been summoned to see Papa.' He made a little face. 'Another dressing-down over my gambling, no doubt. I've been unlucky, that's all. By the law of averages I'm certain to win sometime.'

'I wouldn't bet on it,' George said.

Robert laughed, but he couldn't resist a parting shot. 'I'll win those two guineas from you, see if I don't. Both those maids in a twelvemonth! Well, I'll go and get this lecture over. I could tell you what he's going to say by heart, by this time.'

But he was wrong. The moment he opened the study door he knew it. Papa was not sitting at his desk, looking severe. He was standing at the window, looking white and strained. Robert felt his bravado fade.

'Sit down, my boy.'

Robert sat down. It was years since his father had called him 'my boy'.

'Been gambling again, I hear?' Robert almost relaxed, but his father went on, 'More than two hundred guineas. That was a small fortune when I was your age. Still is, to most folk.'

Robert opened his mouth to say something, then looked at Papa and shut it again.

'Well, it's come to a head. I was tempted to make this decision anyway, but this latest foolishness has confirmed it. I have altered my will, Robert. No, don't say anything. Hear me out. I haven't disinherited you. I have just tried to prevent you gambling away this house and everything in it.'

Robert's mouth opened again, but this time he was too surprised to say anything.

'Your mother will have a life interest in the house if she survives me, but after that it will go to George, and the land around it. You, Robert, will have the St Ives farm and the fields at Lower Trevarnon. There is a farmhouse, but I shall have a new house built for you, more in keeping with your tastes. Don't look so stricken, Robert, you won't be a pauper. It was your mother's land, and there is a good living to be made, even if the tenant stays. And there is the Penvarris mining stock. That comes to you next year when you come of age. You may take the farm then, too, if you choose, and there is also a substantial sum of money to be divided evenly between you.'

Robert felt himself breathe out. Perhaps after all life might be just tolerable. A farm, a house, income, capital. A man might do worse, though he would be expected to take an interest in that dreary mine. And if Papa paid the debts . . . But his father had not finished.

'Your share of the money I am settling on you immediately. It is yours absolutely. You may do with it as you please, including settling those gambling debts. But be warned, Robert, when that money goes, there is no more. Our fortune was made with mining money, a once in a lifetime find. You behave like a man with half the acres of England behind him. And, remember, you will be responsible for your own expenses, once your house is built. I do not mean to be cruel, Robert – having the farm to manage may even help to steady you – but I have taken legal advice and this seems the fairest way to see that you do not cripple my estate for ever. Now, you may go.'

Robert turned to the door, but his father called him back. 'One last thing. I have said nothing of this to George, or your mother. As far as they know, this is simply a birthday settlement for you. If I discover that they have learned differently, I shall know whom to blame, and while I live it still lies within my power to leave Coombe Farm to anyone I wish.'

Robert nodded. He did not trust himself to speak. He resisted the temptation to slam the door, but on the stairs he gave way to fury, slashing the cane against his boot so hard that it snapped. He flung the pieces down the stairway with a clatter.

George came out of the library. 'Anything up?'

Robert forced his face into a smile. 'Broke my cane. Careless of me.'

'What was the lecture about?'

He kept his voice steady. 'Oh, the usual. And he's going to settle some money on me for my birthday.'

George whistled. 'Lucky man. Don't spend it all at once. After lunch then.' And he was gone.

Robert gazed after him. Resentment boiled. That damned brother of his. Always his father's favourite. Would to God he would go to the confounded war and get himself killed. But no! George would stay here, fascinating everyone. Even the bloody horses preferred him. And he would inherit Trevarnon. Well, George should be taken down a peg or two – he would see to it.

Robert could hardly eat his lunch for the bile in his throat, and through the long afternoon he had to watch while Major Selwood praised George's horsemanship, and Caroline simpered. He drove home like a demon, almost upsetting the trap.

Christmas came and went in a frenzy. Katie thought she had never been so busy. So much food and drink to prepare, so many people to serve, such quantities of decorations to dust and hang and dust again, that the child in a manger seemed to have been quite forgotten, Katie felt. No holiday at all for those below stairs, and it was almost New Year before Mr George found her one day in the library and slipped a little package into her hand.

'For you,' he said. 'A sort of late Christmas. It's another story by Mr Dickens – a special Christmas one about good spirits. But it is a secret. Just between ourselves.'

She tried to thank him, but she was smiling too broadly, and in the afternoon she was still floating on a cloud. So much so that Fanny said to her, as they were laying for tea, 'Oh lend a hand here, do, and stop standing about grinning like one half-baked. Whatever has got into you today?'

And Katie, longing to say it to someone said, 'I've been talking to Mr George. Some nice, he is.'

'Yes,' Fanny agreed absently, polishing the knives as she laid them. 'And Mr Robert, too. Those eyes.'

'Thought it was Noah Trembath you were walking out with,' Katie said.

Fanny snorted. 'Noah! He's gone to America.'

'I know that,' Katie said, 'but I thought you were writing, and all.'

'What's the use?' Fanny said. 'Anyway, Noah'll never amount to anything. Be a miner all his life. Mr Robert now, he's a real gentleman. You should hear him talk. Charm the apples off the trees, he would. Said I was prettier than Lily Langtry.'

'Who's she when she's home?' Katie asked, but then Cook sent up the cakes in the dumb-waiter, and she only half heard the answer.

There was something up with Mr Robert though. You could sense it. A sort of brooding unhappiness. Not that he couldn't be charming when he tried, and he always had a smile for Katie and Fanny when they met on the stairs. But there was something amiss.

She encountered him one morning when she went to clear the breakfast, staring through the window with such a scowl of anger and despair that she checked at the doorway. She stole a quick glance at the garden, but there was nothing to be seen but the bare trees, and the grey clouds, and Mr George stopping on the way into the house to chat to one of the gardeners.

Mr Robert looked up at her. 'Well, Katie?'

She flushed, and busied herself with the plates. 'I'm sorry sir, only you looked so . . . unhappy.'

He came over to her then, and tipped her face in his hand. 'Did I, Katie? I'm sorry. Money troubles, I'm afraid! Now, give me a smile and cheer my day.'

There was a movement at the door, and Mr George came in. Katie flushed deeper scarlet, and moved away sharply. She gathered up her plates and scuttled out of the room, giving Mr George a shy smile, but he did not return it.

She turned the corner and leant there against the wall, embarrassed and flustered. The next words reached her loud and clear.

'I wish you'd leave that child alone!' That was Mr George's voice.

'Me?' Mr Robert sounded mocking. 'My dear fellow, it's you she needs to beware of. I'm not in danger of losing her her position. What do you suppose Papa would say if he saw you mooning after her like a love-sick puppy? And smuggling Christmas presents to her on the sly – you needn't try to deny it, for Fanny saw it in her room! He'd have her out of the house in a jiffy, and you in the regiment in half the time, and well you know it. When I invited you to flirt with the housemaids, I never intended this.'

So Mr Robert had 'invited him to flirt', had he? Katie felt her cheeks burn, although she could hardly believe her ears. But in any case she began to avoid Mr George whenever possible. The idea of him being sent away, or of her losing her own position, haunted her.

Mr George did try to seek her out. 'Katie,' he said, a few days later, when he found her dusting the blue drawing-room. 'Have you been avoiding me?'

She dropped her eyes, colouring.

'Katie!' He looked at her with concern. 'It's that Robert, isn't it? What has he been saying to you?'

'Nothing, sir.' She refused to meet his eyes. 'If you'll excuse me, I've work to do.'

He stood back, looking surprised and puzzled, to let her pass.

But it was Epiphany which brought matters to a head. It had been a trying day. Peter Gillard had visited, declaring that since it was Twelfth Night he was to be Lord of Misrule, and he and Robert had turned the house topsy-turvy with their tricks – raw eggs instead of boiled on the buffet, and setting every bell in the house ringing, so that poor Tibbs had spent half the day being summoned upstairs, only to find the room empty.

Eventually Mr Gillard and Mr Robert had shut themselves in the billiard room, but not before they had hung decorations out of the window on the ivy. Fanny and Tibbs had got most of them down with the aid of a step-ladder, but it was almost midnight and there was still one paper chain dangling out of reach.

Katie finished serving supper and went out onto the drive.

'Oh, darn it,' Fanny said, looking up at the bit of chain. 'We've got to get it down for Twelfth Night, and Tibbs has gone with the carriage now, to fetch Mr Trevarnon home. Can't get the ladder near enough because of the steps. I wonder can I fetch it down with a feather duster?'

There was a laugh behind them in the darkness. It was Mr Robert, smelling of cologne and whisky. 'Defeated you, have we? There now, and I have two guineas riding on it with Peter Gillard! I was sure you resourceful girls would find a way to have it down.'

Katie shot him a glance. He was smiling, more cheerful than she had seen him in days. She measured the distance in her mind. 'I might reach it,' she said, suddenly taking the challenge. 'If I were to stand on the railings, Fanny – you'll have to steady me . . .'

Fanny laughed. 'Typical Katie. Always was up a tree as a child. But don't you go doing that, Katie, you might fall.'

'No,' Robert said laughing. 'I'll lift you up myself. We've got five minutes to midnight – we'll do it yet. Quickly – I can hear Gillard coming. I'll have his money yet. Fanny, get the feather duster!'

Fanny ran round to the kitchen, and Katie, seized by his mood, put one foot on the railings, and hoisted herself upwards, tucking up her skirts like a hoyden. Mr Robert caught her by the legs and held her steady, chuckling.

'One more inch!' she called, and he lifted her bodily. She made a wild lunge for the paper chain, caught it, and fell backwards into his arms, so that they both collapsed laughing onto the grass.

'All right?' Robert was saying, lightly, when a dark figure came towards them across the grass.

'You lost your bet!' Robert called gaily. Katie would have added something, but the words died on her lips. It was Mr George.

He stood for a moment, looking down at them, his face white and angry in the moonlight. 'What's all this?' he said, in a strained voice. 'Or shouldn't I ask?'

Robert's arm tightened around her waist, and she could feel a laugh rising in him. 'As I say, you lost your wager. George didn't believe you would do it, but you did, didn't you?'

Katie felt suddenly flustered. Whatever must they look like? She got to her feet and straightened her crumpled skirts. 'It was nothing, Mr George. Just a bit of fun, with it being Twelfth Night. It was only to win Mr Robert his two guineas. And it was easy, really. I'm not as little as you think!'

Robert said, his voice laughing, 'So, bad luck, George old man, afraid that's two guineas you owe me.'

For a moment she thought Mr George was going to hit him, but he only said 'You bastard,' very quietly. 'Did you think of Katie, or only of yourself?'

He had been alarmed for her safety. Katie turned scarlet. 'I know what you're thinking, Mr George,' she said quickly, 'but it was nothing, truly. I've done worse before and come to no harm.'

'Katie,' he said urgently, 'come inside. I must speak to you alone.'

Robert stood up, and put his arm around her. 'Are you going to go with him, Katie?' She could feel his laughter, and in the moonlight his eyes were gleaming, in that devil-take-all way he had. There was some game going on, she could sense it. What was he playing at? Her mind raced.

And then memory stirred. Of course, that conversation she had overheard in the hallway between the two brothers – what was it Mr Robert had said? 'Papa would turn her off and send you to the regiment in half the time if he could see you . . .' Was that what Mr

Robert had in mind? A report to Papa? Or to his mother – she would believe his every word!

Well, if that was his little game she would not oblige him. She would not be party to his little traps. She would not allow herself to be alone with Mr George, and there would be nothing for anyone to tell Mr Trevarnon. 'I'm sorry, Mr George,' she said, flushing crimson, 'but anything you have to say to me you can say in front of Mr Robert. I have nothing to say to you in private.'

She could sense his hurt and bewilderment even in the darkness. George turned away coldly, and went slowly back towards the house.

'What did I tell you, George?' Mr Robert called, and his voice was triumphant. 'Here – where are you going? Come back!'

But Mr George did not come back. His brother laughed. 'Ah, Katie, you have served him a sorry trick without knowing it! Poor fellow. But it serves him right! He's too serious by half! We'll let him lick his wounds tonight but we will tell him tomorrow that it was only the chains you were chasing.'

But in the morning, there was no sign of Mr George. Not the next day, or the next. Mrs Trevarnon took to her bed, and her husband went out in the carriage and returned, white-faced. Even Mr Robert looked concerned. At last there was a telegram. Mr George had taken the commission that Major Selwood had spoken of, and joined the First Cornwall and Devon Horse. He was going to Africa.

In all the time she worked at Trevarnon, Katie never saw him again.

PART TWO : 1902

CHAPTER SEVEN

Katie awoke from a dream of a young man on a horse. It was already May, but the morning was cold and it was dark in the little bedroom. She pulled her shoulders back into the warm nest of the bedclothes for a moment, and then got out of bed and poured herself a basin of washing water from the enamel ewer on the washstand.

In the two and a half years she had been at Trevarnon she had learned to wash and dress quickly, and a few minutes later she was walking down the stairs in her uniform and cap, her skin still in a stinging glow from her wash. She pulled back the bolts, lifted the catch and pushed open the heavy door into the yard.

A thick grey mist was frowning in from the sea, wrapping everything in cobwebs of damp. The grey granite of the house loomed out of it, and grey trees dripped over grey walls onto the wet cobbles. Katie emptied her basin hurriedly, but she was shivering, and glad to get into the welcoming warmth of the kitchen.

'Ah, there you are, Katie!' Cook was already at work, and the first pots were hissing on the stove. 'It's some raw this morning, and no mistake. Sit down girl, do, and have a bite of something warm inside you. You look half perished.' She took a fresh loaf as she spoke and sliced off a generous inch of new bread. 'There now,' she broke it into rough cubes and poured hot water onto it from the kettle. 'You wrap yourself around that before you go upstairs. You won't have a minute to yourselves this morning, I'll be bound.'

Katie took the bowl and sprinkled sugar and a dipper of milk over the fragrant mixture. 'Mrs Trevarnon never will trust Ruby with the best dinner service, so Fanny and me were washing dishes till past midnight,' she said, 'but there's still the rooms to get straight before the family come down.' She took a hasty spoonful of the bread and milk, glad of its delicious comforting warmth.

'There'll be more of that too, with this new King,' Cook said, pouring tea into a thick cup and pushing it towards her. 'They say London's full of it. Great dinner parties and I don't know what. Wasn't like that in the poor Queen's time. And when it comes to this here coronation, our feet won't touch the ground – you mark my words.' She sniffed. 'Though why we should suddenly have parties just because they have them up London beats me.'

Ruby had come in with a bucket of coal for the scuttle, and she gave her cackling laugh. ' 'Tisn't the folks up London. It's Mrs Selwood had two dozen to a dinner Sunday gone,' she said, 'so the missus had to go one better, didn't she? Jump off Land's End, she would, to show Mrs Selwood a trick!'

'You mind your lip, my girl,' Cook said. 'You'll have a clip round the earhole talking like that. You go and get those eggs in from the dairy, and look sharp about it.' But Katie could see the smile in Cook's eyes even as she scolded.

Katie blew on her cup to cool it. 'Where's Fanny to?' she said, to change the subject.

'Upstairs,' Cook said, 'working.' But there was something in her tone which made Katie look at her in surprise.

'Doesn't she want any breakfast? That's the third time this week. 'Tisn't like Fanny to be off her food. Whatever's got into her?'

Ruby stopped at the door with the eggbasket on her arm, and snorted with laughter. 'That's a good one, that is, "What's got into her"! I reckon you want to ask Mr Robert that! Just mind he don't try to show you!'

'Ruby!' Cook's voice was sharp.

'Well, 'tisn't any secret, is it? What else would she be doin', off down to Mr Robert's new house, near every free afternoon? 'Tisn't even finished building yet. "Showing her the ropes" he says. More than ropes he showed her, I'll be bound.'

This time Cook did aim a cuff at her, but Ruby was too quick. The kitchen door slammed shut and she was gone. Cook turned to Katie, 'Don't you mind her, Katie. Fanny's troubles aren't any laughing matter, I know.'

Katie stopped, her spoon halfway to her mouth. Fanny's troubles! She gazed at Cook. She couldn't mean that! But Cook was busying herself unnecessarily with the bacon flitch. That was exactly what she meant. Katie put her spoon down and pushed the bowl away. Fanny! It wasn't possible.

But of course it was more than possible, it was likely. Ruby was right. All those hours Fanny had spent down at Lower Trevarnon, even though no one was living there yet. And these last few weeks, Fanny had begun to look so tired and ill.

Katie caught Cook's eye. 'You think . . . ?'

Cook looked away and started chopping mushrooms with great attention. 'My dear Katie, I'm not saying a word. If she hasn't said anything to you there's likely no truth in it, anyhow.'

But Katie knew better. She pushed back her chair and went upstairs without another word. Fanny was in the dining-room, on her hands and knees, sweeping the grate. Her eyes were red-ringed, and her cheeks were unnaturally bright. She looked up as Katie came in.

'You're here then? I was beginning to think you were never coming.' She poked savagely at the firebricks.

Katie said nothing.

After a moment Fanny went on, 'Well, don't stand there all day watching other folks work. I've got things to do, if you haven't.' Her shoulders were stiff, but her voice trembled as though she had been crying.

Katie said gently, 'Why didn't you tell me?'

And then the tears did come. Fanny dropped the brush and ashpan into the hearth and buried her head in her hands. When she looked up her face was smudged with tears and soot. 'Oh, Katie,' she sobbed, 'I'm that scared I don't know where to put myself. I tried taking castor oil – they say that'll do it sometimes, but it's no good.'

'Have you told Mr Robert?'

Fanny started to cry again. 'No. It won't do no good anyhow – he'll just turn me out without a character. Oh, Katie – whyever didn't I take Noah Trembath when he wrote and asked me? Now I've gone and lost you your job too, I shouldn't wonder.'

'Yes,' Katie said. It was unlikely that Mrs Trevarnon would keep her on now. Why couldn't Fanny have been contented with the faithful Noah, writing every month from California?

'What are we going to do?' wailed Fanny.

Katie picked up the broom. 'Well first,' she said, 'we're going to

71

set this room to rights. After that, we'll see.' She was surprised to find that her voice was calm.

In her mind she was making frantic plans. Tomorrow was her day off. She would go and see her father and Lally. They'd have to tell Robert and Mrs Trevarnon, too, but she held no hopes for that. If only Mr George were here. He might have listened. But he was far away. There was nothing here but the cold unforgiving mist creeping at the windows.

She lifted her broom and began to sweep.

George shifted a little in the saddle. He was hot, and dirty, and tired and hungry. His shoulders ached and his legs chafed in his boots. He had been riding since six, and though the African sun had lost the venomous heat of a few months before, it was still strong enough to sting the skin and make the cloth of his uniform stick to his back in a clammy mass.

It was all a long, long way from home, from cliffs and fields and gentle grey granite. A long way from other rides, when he had waited by the well to see a pretty young miner's daughter and her barrel-cart. But he would not think of that.

He reined in, took his water bottle from his belt and allowed himself a long slow drink. The water at least was clear, fresh from Headquarters that morning, not like the muddy brackish stuff they had been forced to draw from the ditches more than once in the early days of the war. It was a wonder they hadn't all died of fever.

The horse beneath him gave a little whinny. She was as tired as he was, more tired perhaps, and he had no drink for her. He patted her, giving her a moment to draw breath while he scoured the country with his field-glasses. Nothing.

That was the trouble with this country. Great acres of nothingness. Scarcely even a tree or a bush to break the monotony. Only, far away to the west, a plume of smoke rising lazily into the air. Another Boer farmstead was burning. This, once, perhaps had been part of that farm, but nothing of it remained. All the stock pillaged or eaten, all the crops hidden or destroyed. Nothing now but this parched stony earth, and in the leaden sky the great ugly birds of prey which wheeled and waited.

Yet, George knew, that emptiness could be an illusion. Any of those rocks might conceal a Boer guerilla fighter, with a Mauser already trained to fire: any stunted bush might hide a dispossessed farmer, hungry for revenge. And, he realised suddenly, on the horizon the storm clouds were clustering: not grey, but a dull angry orange. There would be a storm tonight. George had been in Africa long enough to fear such storms. Lightning that tore the sky apart with ragged ribbons of light, thunder that rocked a man's ribs, and rain that fell in a deluge of savage drops that stung the skin, drenched tents and bedding, and invaded your very boots. He must get to the blockhouse before the rain came.

It should be in sight, by this time. Already he had been riding an hour longer than he had calculated. He adjusted the glasses and searched more urgently. And then he saw it. There, surely? Four or five miles away, a giant rock that was not a rock but an ugly round building? Then, once he had found it, he could make out the gleam of sun on the iron roof, the dark smudge that would be a tangle of barbed wire, ditches and walls.

'Come on, girl,' he urged the horse, and she moved forward again. Tired as they were, he coaxed her into a trot. But as he rode, his eyes still swept the horizon, and he kept a hand free for the Lee Enfield rifle which he carried at his saddle.

Even then, the horse sensed them first. He saw her ears prick, and felt her falter slightly. Only then did he see the distant dust, and the dark specks against the veldt which meant a band of riders, moving fast. Despite the heat, his sweat ran cold. Boer commandos? Some bands of them still scoured the country, and there were rumours of how they treated prisoners. But out here, in the open, so close to the blockhouse? At this stage in the war, it was unlikely. In any case, on a tired horse, he could not outrun them. Slowly, his hand tightening on his gun, he rode to meet them.

He would shoot, if necessary. There was no doubt about that. He had done so in the past. One dreadful night when he was with the Devons after Captain Bolitho was hit, and five of his comrades lay dying of cold and wounds in the passes outside Pretoria, he had pulled that trigger to dreadful effect. One young Boer had fallen grotesquely backwards across his horse. The other had slumped forwards in the act of aiming his Mauser. George had got through to get help, and stretchers, but those two faces still haunted his dreams.

The horsemen were closing now, recognisable forms against the endless veldt, and as they came nearer George saw, with a rush of relief, the familiar slouch hats and long-stirrup style of the Transvaal Volunteers. Australians, half of them. He pressed on to meet them, and as they cantered up, he offered a salute.

'Captain George Trevarnon, 1st Devon and Cornwall Horse, on attachment to Lord Kitchener. Message for the officer commanding.' He felt in his pocket for the despatch.

'Letter for you, Harry,' said one of the men.

George stiffened. The informal discipline of the Volunteers was legendary, but that was no way to address an officer. But the man they called Harry seemed not to mind.

'Captain Harry Leadbetter,' he said. He did not salute, but brought his horse up close and offered a huge sunburned hand. 'Welcome to Hell, Trevarnon. Nothing here but boulders and Boers.' He opened the despatch, read it and nodded briefly. 'New disposition orders. None too soon either, for my liking. Now, Trevarnon, you could do with a rest, and your horse with you. We'll get you back to the blockhouse, and find you a meal. You're in luck – Lefty here managed to liberate a cow or two from a Boer farm this afternoon, and some potatoes to go with it, so we'll have a fine feast. I daresay we can find something for that horse of yours, too. Meanwhile, tell us about these talks at Vereeniging. Will de Wet surrender, do you think? The Boers round here aren't ready to give up yet. We haven't had a pitched engagement for months, but they're still at it. Blowing up bridges, picking off supply trains. Even had them break through the block-house defences to steal the horses.'

Lefty gave him a lopsided grin. 'Bloody Boers wanted them back!'

Harry smiled. 'Yes, you can't altogether blame them. Starving, half of them. We've taken prisoners with scarcely a coat to their backs. And still fighting. Still, that's enough of that, come on inside and let's see if there's anything left that's fit to drink. We might as well have it if the war looks likely to be over any day. Leave your horse with Lefty – he's the best stableman left alive this side of the Murrumbidgi, since Breaker Morand was shot.'

George had met Morand, the tough, brave horseman with the pen of a poet.

'Shot?'

'Executed.' Harry Leadbetter said. 'Accused of shooting prisoners. As if it was better to starve them to death.' He swung down from his horse. 'Bloody stupid war. Come on in, out of the rain. You can take back my answer tomorrow.'

They went into the blockhouse. Above them the sky opened in a blazing zigzag of light, and the first drops of rain began to fall, heavy as tears, leaving deep spreading circles of damp in the dust.

It was still raining as Katie opened the field gate and let herself into the back of the Terrace. Father's potatoes were just showing, and the hens clucked peevishly in their enclosure, but only a few bedraggled buds showed where Mother's herbs and flowers had blossomed. Katie hurried up the muddy path and opened the door into the kitchen.

A cloud of warm steam rushed out to meet her.

'Come on in, Katie, do!' Lally called. 'And shut that door before the child runs out under the horses.'

There wasn't a horse in the paddock, but Katie shut the door obediently and peered through the damp mist of the kitchen. Every inch of the room seemed to be hung with washing. Lines of wet garments criss-crossed the ceiling, and every chair had been pressed into service as a makeshift clothes-horse. Father's socks steamed on a string in front of the hearth, giving off a smell of hot wet wool.

'Put the kettle on,' Lally said. She was sitting by the window, its panes wetter inside than out, with Meg's sewing machine on the table. She had been hemming dusters, made from an outgrown shirt of Willie's, and a neat pile of them lay beside her. 'Take off your shawl and dry yourself. You'll be soaked through, I'll be bound.'

The idea of anything drying in this steam-bath made Katie smile, but she took off her wet shawl gladly and draped it over the stool. The kettle was by the hearth, cold, so that Rosa should not scald herself while Lally's back was turned. Katie set it on the hob, and sat close to the fire, where her clothes began to steam with everything else.

Rosa toddled over on her sturdy little legs, holding out a rag doll for Katie to admire. 'Lalla made,' she said solemnly. She was a solemn child, with big blue eyes and yellow curls, and a little round face that seldom smiled.

Katie took the doll. It was not a beautiful toy. Lally had made it from a sleeve of the shirt, with a rough circle for a face, and the body a simple bag stuffed with rags.

She thought back to the washing days of her own childhood, when the boys had been at home, and the kitchen was always full of life and laughter. She remembered the little line set at her own height, and how her own tiny ribbons had been washed and starched and gaily hung on it with giant pegs almost as soon as she could walk. Baking days when tiny hands helped to cut uncertain circles from greying pastry, to be cooked with as much care as anything on Mrs Trevarnon's table.

And she looked at Rosa – scoured and scrubbed to within an inch of her life, kept to one end of the kitchen for fear of falling into the fire. 'Who's a lucky girl then?' she said. But she had her own answer to the question.

Soon the kettle was boiling. Katie busied herself with the tea things, but her mind was racing. She could imagine what Lally would say when she heard, but someone had to tell her. Then at leaast Fanny could perhaps come home. She bided her time, waiting for a suitable moment.

Lally was talking about Willie. He was 'doing them proud' at school, and looking forward to joining his father down the mine in a few years. Not that Davy expected to be 'down the mine' for much longer; he was still promising to take a surface job when one came vacant.

'Mind, it'll take a rock-fall to make him do it,' Lally said, putting aside the last of her dusters. 'But I keep telling him, he could go in the sorting sheds feeding the stanning machines. They're looking for men, now they've put in those new machines. He wouldn't get the money he used to, but we don't need it like we did, what with a bit coming in regularly from Tom and Jimmy in America, and you and Fanny sending home every week.'

It was now or never. 'Well,' Katie said, 'I wanted to talk to you about that.'

Perhaps something in her voice betrayed more than the words, because Lally whirled to face her. 'And what's that supposed to mean?' she demanded. 'Fallen out with Mrs Trevarnon, have you? Too much to say, that's your trouble, my girl. Well, if that tongue of yours has let you into hot water, you talk yourself out of it again, that's all. You go back and tell Mrs Trevarnon you're sorry. She won't get help like you again, and she knows it.' Lally was allowed to criticise, Katie thought, but Mrs Trevarnon wasn't. She opened her mouth to speak, but Lally hadn't finished. 'Here,' Lally cut a jam pasty into rough pieces. 'Have a piece of this, but don't go eating it all. I want some for your father's tea when he comes.'

Katie tucked her piece into her kerchief. She had no appetite for eating. 'It isn't me,' she said. 'It's Fanny.'

'Fanny?' Lally tucked one of the new dusters around Rosa's neck to keep the pinny clean, and handed her a piece of pasty. 'What's she gone and done? Breaking the china, is it?'

'It's not that.' Katie didn't know how to go on.

'What is it, then?' Lally began pouring tea. Katie got up to help her, and when she turned back Rosa was stuffing the last piece of pasty into her mouth.

'Naughty girl!' she said sharply. 'That was for daddy and Lally!'

Lally turned round. 'Don't you raise your hand to that child. And there's no need to talk so sharp! It's only a bit of tea. It's all right, my lover, Lalla'll make another. Now, let's hear all this about Fanny, or is this another of your silly games?'

'It's no game,' Katie said. 'Fanny's going to have a baby.'

There was a dreadful silence. Lally put down her cup and folded her arms and lips. 'Well that's it, then,' she said. 'I'm not having her back in this house, and you can tell her that from me. Bringing shame on your poor father like that!'

'But what about Fanny?' Katie asked.

'What about her?' Lally retorted. 'If thine eye offend thee, pluck it out. Well, plucked out she shall be. There's a home for you, of course, Katie – I daresay Mrs Trevarnon won't want hair nor hide of either of you. But Fanny can take her wicked self somewhere else.'

'But where's she to go?'

'She should have thought of that sooner,' said Lally. 'I daresay the workhouse will have her. She can't come here, bringing scandal on the household. With a child in the house and all.'

'I wonder what Father will say,' Katie said.

'Oh no doubt you can wind him round your little finger like you always do, Katie Warren, but I'll tell you one thing. If Fanny comes here, I leave. I won't share the same roof as that child of Satan. So you can think about that before you talk to your father.'

Lally meant it, that was obvious. Katie pushed away her cup and plate and stood up. She went to the settle and threw her damp shawl over her shoulders. 'Bye, Rosa.' She knelt to give the child a kiss. 'You be a good girl to Lalla and do what she says, you hear?'

'Where are you going?' Lally said. 'You can't just go off like that with nowhere to go.'

'If Fanny can, I can. I can't just desert her now. If she can't come home, I shan't either. So don't be looking out for our bit of money from now on, we'll be needing it ourselves. Perhaps you'll even think twice now about nagging poor father into taking a stannery job.'

'But where will you go?' Lally stood twisting the jammy duster in her hands.

'I don't know. Truro. Redruth. Somewhere.' She opened the door and stepped into the cool air. A fine rain was still falling.

She walked back up the hill away from the street, and the enormity of what she had done struck her. From here on she had no home, and probably no job. Lally had meant what she said – it was no good trying to get word to Father. Lally would only leave, and stir up a scandal. Perhaps, sometime, after the baby was born . . .

She stopped at the stile and looked back for a moment, tears in her eyes.

Then she turned her back and walked resolutely on.

CHAPTER EIGHT

Robert sauntered up the avenue, cursing at the puddles and slapping at his leg with his whipstock. He was not in the best of tempers. That bet with Peter Gillard had been a mistake. How was he to get hold of sixty guineas?

It was no good applying to Papa. He'd hardly been able to persuade him over such worthy causes as furnishings for the new house. And there was precious little in the kitty. There had been seed-potatoes and feed bills to pay for the farm at St Ives, and the mine shares were costing money in spite of the price of tin. Wanting yet more new subscriptions from the shareholders. What did the wretched place want with new winding gear anyway?

And now that fool of a man in Newlyn had refused point blank to give him more than twenty guineas for the pony and trap. It was worth more than that, and they both knew it, but he'd had no choice. And he was still forty guineas short. It was a mess, that's what it was. And this confounded weather didn't help.

His scowl lifted a little when he saw Fanny waiting for him at the turn of the drive. She had no business to be there, of course. He'd have to speak to her about it. Pretty girl. Willing too. And waiting for him in the rain like this did make a man feel attractive. All the same, it wouldn't do. You couldn't allow yourself to be followed about by the servants. He composed his face to issue a stern rebuke.

But whatever was the matter with the girl? The rain had reduced her hair to tatters, and her face was all lumpy and red with tears. He sighed. The child had been getting very intense recently. No, certainly, he would have to extricate himself from this. Gently, of course, very gently. Pity. Still, there was that pretty red-haired maid up at the Selwoods'. Or Caroline herself, come to that. She had become very attached to his company now that George was away.

Of course. It was so simple when one thought of it. Caroline. She was the only child of the house, and the Selwoods had money, plenty of money. Robert thought with pleasure of the big house with its rolling grounds and well-stocked stables. She was a pleasant enough girl, and not one to interfere with her husband's running of things. And marriage need not be too limiting. Why had he never thought seriously of Caroline before?

But would she have him? Yes, almost certainly she would. Caroline's ambition was to be mistress of her own household, and her father would be unlikely to raise serious objections. Thank God for Lower Trevarnon – it was almost finished, and it gave a man a certain cachet. He might even be able to delay the actual marriage. The simple prospect of a Selwood connection would unloose his mother's purse-strings, if not Papa's.

He was so pleased with this solution that his manner to Fanny was more magnanimous than he had intended. 'Hello, curly-head,' he said. 'You shouldn't be out waiting for me like this. You've got work to do.'

'Oh Mr Robert, I had to talk to you.'

He smiled, but made a mental note to put a stop to this as soon as possible. He owed it to Caroline, he told himself, and felt a little glow of moral pride at his own self-sacrifice. 'Well, what is it, Fan?'

What she told him made him draw back in horror. Well, if this wasn't the most accursed luck! There was no real problem about the girl of course, but if Papa got wind of this there'd be nothing forthcoming, he could be sure of that. Irresponsibility, he'd call it. And what would Mama say?

He said it for her. 'It isn't mine, is it Fan? How can I possibly be sure of that?' He saw her terrified stare. 'It's no good looking at me like that – it could be anybody's, pretty girl like you!'

She refused to be comforted. 'There's never been anybody but you, Mr Robert. You know that. And you promised you'd look after me, that's what you said.' She was snivelling now.

'Well, you won't be able to stay,' he said. 'My mother will never stand for it. You'll have to go, and your sister with you.' The thought of Katie was sobering. She had spirit, and he could see her making sure that Papa knew all about this. And Caroline Selwood too. That would cut the purse-strings with a vengeance.

'I'll kill myself,' Fanny moaned, half to herself.

Dear God, anything but that. There would be no holding Katie then. 'Now you listen to me, young Fan,' he said, putting his hand on her shoulder. She looked up at him doubtfully. Odd how he could have once found her so attractive. Now he forced himself to draw her towards him.

'I said I'd look after you, and I will. Here.' His hand went to his pocket and he drew out two of the guineas. 'Look. There's five weeks' wages apiece.' He dropped them into her hand, and closed her fingers over them. 'And there's another one of those for you, if you and your sister are out of Trevarnon by tonight.' Mama would create a scene, he thought to himself, but Caroline might be persuaded to part with her maid for a day or two. And that would give him an excuse to visit and talk to her Papa.

'I'll have to see Mrs Trevarnon.'

'You leave that to me,' he said. 'She'll have to be told, of course, and you won't expect her to give you a character, after this. But you meant a lot to me, little Fan. I said I'd look after you, and I have. Now, there's a train at six thirty-two – and a guinea waiting for you if you and your sister are on it.'

He watched her trail slowly up towards the house, and skirt around to the back. Then he squared his shoulders and went in to face his mother. As he walked upstairs he was preparing his line. 'Dallying with a man in the avenue, and when pressed she admitted she was expecting a child. And her sister no better. Dismissed the pair of them at once.'

Mama's scene was no worse than he had feared, and it was with a lighter heart that he went to see Caroline. She was in the conservatory reading.

'Mr Trevarnon, what brings you here?' There was a colour in her cheeks which was most attractive. He began to warm to his task.

'Miss Selwood . . . Caroline . . .' Her blush deepened. Deuced pretty girl. And money too. A man could do a lot worse. He said, with real feeling: 'I came today, to speak to your father. May I hope that, should he consent, you would give me encouragement?'

She was delighted. You could read it in her face, in the way she stammered, 'Why, Robert, Mr Trevarnon. You are too flattering!'

He took her hands, emboldened. 'I may ask him, then?'

She hung her head, but murmured, 'Yes, you may.'

He wondered about kissing her, but decided against it. She was not a servant after all, and there was nothing official between them yet. All the same, he felt emboldened to ask about the red-headed maid. Caroline was charming about it, and even Major Selwood was more encouraging than he had hoped.

When he got back from the Selwoods', the Warren girls had gone. And he hadn't given Fanny that guinea. Oh well, he reflected, it was too late now. Besides, when he had made that promise, he was a free man. Now, he was as good as betrothed, and one couldn't expect an engaged man to make gifts of money to other women.

He felt almost light-hearted as he rang for Tibbs to help him change for dinner.

Katie was amazed, on turning the corner of the avenue, to find Fanny waiting for her by the gate in her best apron and shawl.

'Whatever are you doing out here at this hour, with dinner to be seen to and everything?' She spoke before she noticed the tangle of parcels and baskets leaning against the wall. 'Oh, my lor,' she said with sudden realisation. 'You've told her. Whatever did she say? Give you your notice?'

She didn't really have to ask. Fanny's forlorn face and the jumble of packages told her everything.

'It isn't just me, Katie,' Fanny said, gesturing to Katie's own basket with the others. 'You've got your marching orders, and all.' She started to cry. 'I'm some sorry, my lover. You'd best go home to Lally. I'm going to catch the train to Truro, half past six. I've been thinking about it all afternoon, and I reckon that's best.'

'Truro?' Katie echoed. 'Whatever will you do in Truro?'

'I thought I might go and see Mrs Lomas. She was some fond of Meg and she might do something for me. If not, I suppose I'll have to go cap in hand to Lally. Otherwise, there's always the workhouse.' Fanny's voice broke on the last word.

Katie sighed. 'Well,' she said, 'this is a pickle and no mistake. I didn't expect us to be on the streets this very day. And there's no hoping for anything from the Terrace.' She told Fanny the events of the afternoon. 'So,' she finished, her voice sharper than she intended, 'if we're going to get on that train of yours we'd best get moving. Though how you hope to manage the fare all the way to Truro I'll never know.'

'They gave us five weeks' wages,' Fanny said. 'A guinea apiece. More'n I thought.'

'Mrs Trevarnon did that?' Katie stared at her sister. Fanny made no reply. 'I see. Well, we can count ourselves lucky you spoke to Mr Robert, I suppose.' It was lucky, she told herself fiercely. Her feet were squelching in her boots from her hike across wet fields, and her shoulders ached with the damp of her clothes. She had been longing for the warmth of Trevarnon kitchen after the confrontation with Lally, and Cook's 'Monday tea' of cooked vegetables left over from the dining room served with the scrapings of the gravy, hot and savoury from the pan. And instead, here she was, wet with the drizzle of rain counting herself lucky to have five weeks' wages and nowhere to go. What had she done to deserve this? She felt furious with her sister, who was standing beside her sobbing, long miserable sobs into the tail of her shawl.

'Oh for heaven's sake, Fanny,' she exclaimed sharply. 'Don't make the day any wetter'n it was.' She picked up her basket, and one of the brown paper packages. 'And come along, do.' She set off back down the avenue, not looking around until she heard footsteps. Fanny was beside her with her basket and the other two bundles, still sniffing tearfully from time to time.

Katie said nothing as they turned down the long slow hill into the town. Across the grey roofs and the curling smoke of the chimneys, the sea gleamed, coldly grey in the late afternoon light. Katie gazed at it for a long time. In all her life she had never lived far out of sight of the open sea. Until now.

She hitched up her parcels and marched into the station. Everything was bustle. Women in smart gowns and fur tippets picked their way to first-class carriages, accompanied by languid young gentlemen in tweeds, or little dogs on ornamental leads. Fat women, in coats too tight at the stomach, stomped through the puddles to sell flowers or hevvacake. Boys hollered headlines. And everywhere uniformed railwaymen carried bags, or fluttered flags, or moved about with oil and hammers at the wheels of great steaming trains.

Fanny stopped and looked around nervously, and even Katie hesitated, but the hands of the great clock were already showing half past the hour. There was scarcely time to buy a ticket and ask directions from a surly and bewhiskered railway clerk before they flung themselves into a third-class carriage. They squeezed into a seat beside a stout woman with an umbrella, bestowed their baggage as best they might, even as the train began to get up steam ready for departure.

Fanny leapt up and looked out of the window, so restless that Katie said sharply, 'Oh, do sit down, Fanny. You're like a cat on a furnace, jumping up and down like that. I don't know what you expect to see. Did you think Mr Robert would come and see you off?'

'Oh, leave me be, do!' her sister said, sitting down and gazing sullenly out of the window.

There was a whistle, and a shout, and a flag, and the train, which had been hissing to itself like an angry animal, began huffing out great coughs of smoke which shook the carriage. There was a lurch, and they were moving.

'There now,' Katie said, settling herself on the hard seat. 'We're away.'

But Fanny was still staring out, with a face as white as chalk. Through the rain streaked window and the billowing smoke Katie could see the huddle of grey houses blur into the grey of the sea, and the familiar profile of the Mount loomed, passed and faded from sight. The world seemed suddenly very large and strange.

'Never been further than Penzance before,' she said to Fanny. 'I know Meg's done it scores of times.'

But Fanny didn't move. It was a long time before she spoke.

'He never came,' she said, in a trembling voice. And that was all Katie could get out of her for most of the journey.

On the veldt it was still raining. The rain drummed down on the iron roof of the Transvaal blockhouse with a ferocity which roused George from sleep. He lay still for a moment, blinking into the darkness, listening to the rhythmical rapping of the drops.

In the last two and a half years he had learned to sleep anywhere. Sometimes under stars with a horse for company, sometimes in ditches or sodden tents, sometimes in fresh linen at staff headquarters. Once or twice under a cart on a battlefield with mortar fire rumbling around him. No, it was not the discomfort of a straw palliasse on the rough floor of a blockhouse which made him watchful now.

Something was amiss.

A flash of lightning split the room like midsummer. In its sudden light he glimpsed his gun leaning against the wall, and his folded jacket and boots. Beside him other men were stirring. And something else. A movement, a silhouette, stealthy beyond the grille of the window.

He rolled over, stretching a hand for boots and gun. But already the alarm was sounding. Trumpets and voices. 'Boers!' someone shouted. 'Broken into the compound after the horses.'

A shot rang out. Another. A sharp cry and horses neighing. George picked up his rifle and ran out with Lefty into a confused hubbub in the corridor.

Leadbetter was already there with a dozen men, kneeling beside a rifle port, his gun aimed. 'Get down!' he shouted. 'The bloody place is crawling with Boers. Cut the wire and come in under cover of the storm. They may have grenades. You can't see fifty paces when this rain sets in.'

George slid down to kneel beside him. The rattle of fire and confused shouting was drowned in a roar of thunder that rattled the doorframes. 'We'll try a sally in a minute,' Leadbetter said, 'but mind how you fire. There's guards of mine out there.'

The main door was being eased open. A man swung a lantern, and was fired at for his pains. The lamp shattered as a Boer bullet hit the glass. The quiet, a terrible watchful silence. Only the whinny of a horse and the stinging patter of the rain. George scanned the darkness, but there was nothing to see but the impenetrable blackness and the rain. The waiting was oppressing all of them. George could hear his heart thump.

A man started forward, but Leadbetter stretched out a hand to hold him back. 'Wait for the light!' he hissed.

Then it came, brilliant, blinding – doubly unexpected because they were waiting for it. And a dozen men, ragged outlines in battered hats, scattered across the compound, caught like figures in a magic lantern slide. Some astride, bareback; others frozen in the very act of slipping a snaffle over the animal's head. All armed.

A split second, no more, then the darkness, blacker than before. The image of the scattered men seemed to dance a moment before George's eyes. Then, from behind him a rifle cracked, and bedlam was loose.

A scream, shots, shouts. Men ran forward carrying lanterns, their shadows dancing in the slanting rain. The Boers scattering, riding, firing, driving horses that shied and snorted and thundered past in a flurry of hooves and mud.

Cameos reached him from the flickering light. An old Boer with a grizzled beard, clutching a bleeding arm with a hand that still clutched the reins. Leadbetter kneeling in the teeming rain, load, fire, load. A horse rearing as a bullet caught its leg, and careering madly in circles.

A lad in outsized trousers racing for the wire in a hail of fire, but stopping to retrieve his hat.

Then the sky seemed to boom into thunder, and the Boers made a sudden dash, eight or ten of them together, towards the great jagged hole they had cut in the wire, urging the horses they rode and driving others.

One of Leadbetter's men let fly with his rifle and a horse fell, snorting and shrieking. Its rider, a dim shape in the glow of the lanterns, dropped to one knee behind it and began to crawl backwards, using the horse as cover, rifle cocked.

Another sheet of lightning. For an instant horse and man were caught, pinned in the light. The young Boer crouched over his Mauser, the horse contorted, its back leg twisted under him, lips pulled back over its teeth in agony.

And then darkness. But George had seen enough. He would know that horse anywhere. It had been given to him by a laughing man called Harry Morand when his own horse was killed at Pietermaritzburg, and he had named it as he had named all his horses in this accursed war.

'Blister!' he shouted, and started out of the blockhouse.

'Get down, Trevarnon,' he half-heard Leadbetter's call, but he already had his rifle raised. Years of hunting rabbits with Robert on the moors had given him a deadly eye. He aimed, and fired, and the horse fell back, mercifully dead.

'Trevarnon!' Leadbetter shouted again, and out of the darkness the Mauser spat. Again. And again.

The first bullet caught George in the hand. It was too dark to see, but he felt his rifle fly out of his grasp, and found himself staring stupidly at the glimmer of his fingers as he felt the warm stickiness travel across his palm and up his sleeve.

And then there was a sharp punch, and a fire in his thigh. He tried to step forward out of the pain, but the ground was melting under his feet, and the rain was falling green around him as he toppled forward onto the wet stone. It rose up to swallow him in soft black mist.

CHAPTER NINE

'Truro! Change for Falmouth!' the man called, and they clambered down, in a flurry of baggage, and made their way out onto the street. The sun was setting, and a chill little wind fretted the grass opposite the station, where a terrace of new houses had been begun.

The town would soon be all the way up the hill, Katie thought, looking down on the cluster of granite-grey buildings stretching away into the valley. Or city; rather. There were the towers of the great church that they were making into a cathedral, almost completed now. And far to the left, the edge of the wooden viaduct. Meg had often talked about that. Katie thanked her stars she hadn't gone further than Truro on the train – the thought of crossing that high narrow bridge made her knees quake.

Everything in Truro seemed to be stretching upward – trees and gas lamps and chimneys and telegraph poles, and was that the mast of a ship she could see, moored on the hidden river?

Fanny brought her down to earth. 'My lor,' she said, 'some steep, isn't it? And look at all those streets. However are we going to find Mrs Lomas before it gets dark, in all that lot?' She glanced wistfully towards the hansom cabs drawn up at the station entrance.

Katie shook her head. 'We've got feet,' she said, 'and tongues in our heads. Fore Street, off Princes Street. I've heard Meg say a hundred times. Someone's bound to know.' Though there was little chance now of finding the place before the shop closed, she thought to herself. Even in Truro the shops would shut at lighting-up time.

'I know who'll know,' Fanny said, and was off, bold as brass to the entrance to the goods yard, where a man with a big horse was manoeuvring his cart out through the narrow gate. When he spoke it was in a voice that carried across the street.

'Princes Street. I'm going there myself. You and your friend can ride on the shafts if you've a mind.'

Fanny was already climbing aboard, but Katie drew back. As the cart came into sight she recognised it as a brewer's dray, with barrels of beer lashed down to its curved bed. The Methodist training of a lifetime rebelled.

'Well, what are you waiting for, I shan't eat you!' the man shouted. There was no help for it. They had to find Mrs Lomas as soon as possible. Katie came doubtfully forward and scrambled up opposite Fanny. It seemed to her that simple action took her further from home than all the trains in Christendom.

'Hold tight down Richmond Hill!' the man called, and they had need to. The road was so steep and the dray so heavy that even that great horse had to sit back with his haunches half on the ground to stop the cart running away with him. The cart lurched and rumbled, the beer in the barrels sloshed menacingly, and the carter sweated and swore. Katie didn't open her eyes until they were safely on flat ground once more.

They turned into a handsome street of broad pavements and fine granite buildings, many of them three or four storeys high. Even at this hour the town was busy with cabs and carts, and horses and bicycles; but the boys were already putting up the shutters, although the lamp-lighter had not yet begun his round.

'We'll be too late, after all this,' Fanny wailed. 'Though goodness alone knows what Mrs Lomas can do for us, anyhow, this time of night.'

That was true too. Somehow, getting to Mrs Lomas had seemed to offer a solution to their problem, but whether the woman would help them, or why she should, they had never stopped to reflect. Katie began to feel the rising of real panic. It might be the workhouse yet.

The man turned out of the wide street into a narrower one. 'Well,' he said, 'this is Princes Street, and Fore Street's that next turning. I'm going to the public round the corner, myself, but I'll let you down here. And mind you don't lose those packages, walking around Truro in the dark.' He hesitated. 'The public is always looking for quick girls, if you're wanting work.'

'Do come on, Fanny,' Katie said hastily, as they thanked him. You could never tell what Fanny would take it into her head to do next. 'Mrs Lomas will be closing.'

Fanny was looking thoughtfully after the dray, but she picked up her packages and followed Katie into Fore Street. Mrs Lomas, in fact, was not difficult to find. There was a large window, full of bonnets and hoods, and a notice in curly lettering: *Mrs E Lomas, dressmaker and milliner of Quality. Haberdashery and Drapery goods supplied.*

Through the window they could see a figure in a black skirt and apron, winding lace onto a reel at the heavy counter, and encouraged, they tried the door. It opened, causing a little bell to ring. The figure looked up.

She was not much more than a girl, dwarfed by the bolts of material and the riot of wool, ribbons, buttons and packets of pins, stacked round her on every side.

'Mrs Lomas?' asked Katie, knowing that it wasn't.

'She's upstairs, madam,' the girl said, as though Katie were a grand lady about to spend five shillings on a pair of gloves. 'What name shall I say?'

'Say we're Meg Warren's sisters,' Katie said, and they were shown up.

Mrs Lomas herself was a large bombazine-clad lady, with combs in her greying hair, and scissors hanging at her belt. She had a forceful look, and the steel glasses on her nose did nothing to soften her expression, but Katie remembered the little acts of kindness to Meg, and persevered.

'It's like this,' she began, and out it all tumbled – they had no job, no home and Fanny was expecting, though they could sew, Katie said. Mrs Lomas ignored this.

'And what shall we call you?' she said to Fanny.

'Fanny, ma'am.'

Mrs Lomas' expression did not change. 'No, the other name. You're not calling yourself Warren, I should hope? A widow without a husband might have some call on our charity . . . and I should buy yourself a ring too, my dear, without delay, if it's only a curtain ring.'

Fanny gaped, but Katie understood. Mrs Lomas was giving them some firm advice. She gave her sister a little poke with her basket, and Fanny stammered, 'Oh . . . uh . . . Trembath.'

Katie sent up a little mental apology to poor Noah, and Mrs Lomas said, 'Well, I'm glad we've sorted that out. Now, I'd like to help you for Meg's sake. But I can't. I might have taken one of you as a beginner, but that's no earthly use. Even if I waived the fee, you want to be earning a few shillings, not learning a trade for nothing but your keep.' Katie's heart sank, but Mrs Lomas went on, 'I do know a woman with a room to rent. It's not a mansion, but it's a respectable house, clean and dry, and the woman's honest. Here,' she scribbled something on a piece of paper. 'Go to this address and tell her I sent you. And if you come again, come up the back way, not through the shop!'

They were dismissed. Fanny was inclined to bewail their luck, but Katie knew that they had been shown a kindness. A respectable house, that was quite a lot, as she was beginning to realise. Without Mrs Lomas, they would have had little hope of it.

They found the house, after a dozen false turns, one of a row in a little muddy lane leading down to a small river. A boat was beached at the far end where the waters lapped, and from where a strong unpleasant smell rose. Something small and furry scuttled from the shadows and disappeared with a splash.

'Ugh!' Katie was ready to stop. 'Rats.'

This time it was Fanny who made the decision. 'Beggars can't be choosers.' She rapped on the front door.

It was opened a crack by a woman with a scrubbed anxious face, who held up a candle to see their faces in the deepening gloom; but at the name 'Lomas' they were admitted to a tall, gloomy hallway, heavy with the smell of cooking cabbage. The woman regarded them doubtfully. 'Two girls on your own, I don't know so much. Widow, are you?'

'Mr Trembath is in America,' Katie said carefully. 'He is hoping Fanny here will come out to join him by and by.' That much at least was the truth.

'I see.' The woman behind the candle looked as if she saw only too clearly. She hesitated. 'Well, if Mrs Lomas sent you, no doubt you'll do. Upstairs it is . . .' She led the way. 'The closet and tap are in the yard. You share them with me and the two shop-girls on the middle floor. Half a crown a week, and a penny a day for coals. Here's the room.'

It was a long, low attic under the eaves, with a table, two chairs and an iron bedstead with a mattress. There was a tiny fireplace with a trivet, brush and poker, a half-used candle in a candlestick, and an enamel bowl set under the skylight to catch the drips. There was a small shelved recess as a cupboard, otherwise the room was bare.

Katy looked around. It was a far cry even from their rooms at Trevarnon, but it was clean and dry, and a roof over their heads. 'We'll take it.'

'Three weeks in advance,' the woman said, and Katie knew that even the name of Lomas had not been enough to smooth their way completely. Katie counted out the nine and threepence, and the woman lit the candle from her own and disappeared.

Fanny spoke. 'My lor, Katie, whatever have I brought us to? We haven't so much as a kettle to boil ourselves a cup of tea. Or anything to drink it in.'

Or any tea, Katie reflected, but at that moment the woman returned with a bucket of coals and a few grudging spills of paper to light them with. Katie urged an unwilling fire from a handful of the lumps. Somehow its glow and meagre warmth made them both feel better and, blowing out the candle to conserve it, Katie suddenly remembered Lally's piece of jam pasty.

She took it out and broke it carefully in two. There was no more than a mouthful, but it was something. Then, suddenly weary, she flung herself down on the bed beside Fanny, wrapped herself in her shawl, and slept.

Davy came up from the shift and laid his sodden canvas trousers on the hot steam pipes of the dry. Well, that was that. Tomorrow they would be baked stiff with dust as they always were, but he would not be putting them on to go down the ladders with the others. He was a surface worker now.

The men were coming up to him, slapping his back and joshing him, 'Don't 'ee stay out in the light too long, Davy lad, you'll sprout up like a sunflower. That's how we miners keep so small.'

And he was smiling and joking back. 'You'll have to shift a sight more ore-stone now, Eddie Goodbody, if I'm working on the stanners.' But there was no smile in his heart. He knew what they were saying. 'Davy Warren has come to it at last.'

It had taken him long enough. Three years, near enough, since he had made his promise to Maggie, and what changes there had been since then: it was as if his luck had been buried with her.

His pare, for one thing. First his boys had gone, and then Noah Trembath, and now there was only him and Eddie and Harry, and a couple of new lads who couldn't tell tin from mica. And the mine itself was changing – all that new venture money, and they had lost the main lode. Only thin seams now, mined in narrow ends so far from the winze that the blasting smoke hung in the air for hours and the men breathed shallow. A new shaft sunk, that's what they wanted, further up where the killas met the granite, and new winzes to ventilate it. Then it would be like old times, when there were ten working shafts at Penvarris, not a single end where a candle would not burn. But the shareholders wouldn't stand for the expense.

There was tin down there, too. Davy was sure of it. He'd contracted for his pare to work towards it, week after weary week, in ends so narrow that the man mining had to work singlehanded, holding his boryer in one hand and beating it home with the other, changing hands only when his arms ached. But it was no good, they'd never hit the rich tin, and the air was so foul now that the only way was to dig out wider – tram after tram of useless stone. And less tin meant less pay. There had been a few lean months for all the tributers lately.

Even so, it was the accident with Harry Trembath which had made his mind up for him. Davy had known for a long time that Harry's eyes were failing, many times he had held his breath as Harry missed his footing on the wooden planking over an open shaft. But he had said nothing, knowing that Harry's heart, like his own, was in the stopes.

Until that day. Eddie Goodbody started it, bringing an empty tram-truck back from the 'grizzly', where he had tipped the stone down for sorting. He rode it back, like most of the trammers, using the slope of the track and his own weight, and giving two knocks on the pipes to warn the men ahead that he was coming. Davy was walking up the level with Harry Trembath when the knocks came, and he saw what happened.

Harry stepped off the track sharply – a man underground knew better than to stand in the path of a riding trammer – but instead of moving sideways into an entry, he made for a place where an old stope had been abandoned, and all but stepped fifty feet into the shaft below. Davy rushed forward, narrowly avoiding the rushing tram, seized Harry by the coat-collar, and after a struggle, hauled him to safety. It had been a near thing.

'It's my own fault, Davy, my handsome. I've known me eyes were going, but I've never said. I thought that was a clean level – never saw they timbers. Never saw the blooming hole. I hoped it wouldn't come to this, but I'll have to give'n up. If you weren't there I'd have fetched up in Australia.'

'What will you do, Harry? They need men up to ground.'

Harry shook his head. 'No. They wouldn't let me even near the stamps, eyes like mine – specially with they new stamp heads. They've fitted them to the old cams and there's a great hole now – a man could easy fall down there if he couldn't see for looking. No they'd have me sweeping up in the carpenter's shop – me, after a life underground. No, Davy, reckon I'll give it up altogether. My boys have sent me a bit of money from America, and I reckon I'll buy myself a bit of a cart or something, see if I can't make a living that way.'

'Not thinking of buying one of they retired pit ponies?' Davy asked. There were one or two, used for the heavy haulage on the wide levels, but Davy hated to think of the poor creatures, never seeing the light of day from the moment they were lowered down, blindfold, until they were retired.

Harry shook his head. 'Never fit for nothing when they do come up,' he said. 'Either frightened of their own shadows, or turn into little hellers, and give you a real run-around. No, I hear they're getting rid of one of the surface horses that isn't pulling his weight. More sense than us, Davy boy, we don't know when we're past it. Reckon I'll go see the mine captain tonight.'

But it wasn't only Harry, Davy thought. A tributer like himself was responsible for his pare. He should have said something to Harry long ago. Or stopped Eddie riding with the trammers. There was a long silence, and then he said, heavily, 'I'll go with you, Harry.' It was time to keep his promise to Maggie, and find a surface job.

So here he was, Davy Warren, a stannery man. He looked around the dry once more, and turned for home, his throat and eyes dry and swollen. At least, he thought grimly, it would please Lally.

'Well,' he said, thrusting open the door roughly. 'I've done it. I've come up to ground.'

But there was no reply. Willie, sitting at the table frowning at his books, did not look up. Lally finished rolling the linen for ironing, and turned to the stewpot without a word. Even Rosa climbed onto his knee in silence.

'Well,' Davy said at last, 'What's to do then?' No-one answered him. He clenched his teeth. It had been a hard enough day without this. 'What's to do?' he repeated, and then, struck by a sudden thought, 'Where's Katie? She's usually here, Monday.'

His sister turned, the ladle in her hand. She was shaking with emotion. Fear? Indignation? He could not tell. 'Been and gone and not coming back, so she says. Nor Fanny either.'

Something deep and deadly stirred in Davy. He set Rosa down gently and got to his feet. 'What?'

Lally told him, her voice quivering, her lips pursed and her ridiculous grey head bobbing in emphasis. 'I told her,' she said, 'she could stay away and good riddance too!'

Davy was not a violent man, but the blow which he struck on the table scattered Willie's books, and sent the milk-jug crashing to the floor. 'You said what?' His voice was a roar.

'I thought . . .' Lally began.

'You thought! You don't think enough, that's your trouble, woman. Two girls like that on their own in the world. Do you want to send them to the devil? I'm still their father and this is still my house. You didn't ask what *I* thought!'

He didn't stop to consider what he might have said himself.

'Willie!' The boy was picking up his books. 'Do you go over to Trevarnon now, my son, and give the girls a message to come see me as soon as they have a minute. Off quick, before it's too dark to see.'

Lally set his plate before him with an injured sniff. 'I made a bit of jam pasty for your tea, but Rosa had it.'

'If you spent one half the Christian charity on other folks you save for that child we'd be a bit happier round here,' Davy said. 'Rosa too . . . Now hold your hush woman, and wait while the boy comes back.'

It seemed a long, long wait, but Davy sat motionless until the door opened. Willie's face told its own story.

'They've gone, Father. That Ruby told me. Taken all their stuff. Mrs Trevarnon's in a proper taking, and there's a new girl up there from Selwoods. But they've gone. Nobody knows where to.'

Lally gave Davy a sideways glance, 'Maybe it's meant,' she said. 'Girl in her condition, scandalising the neighbourhood.'

This time his hands swept the cups and saucers from the tabletop, but when he spoke his voice was unnaturally calm. 'Lally Warren, talk sense or don't talk at all. You drove away my sons with your sharp tongue, and now you've driven away my daughters. You ever come between me and my children again, and so help me, I'll turn you on the parish, sister or not!'

He pushed back his chair. Lally stood looking helplessly at the shattered china. He pulled on his boots.

'Where are you going?' Lally ventured.

'Out!' And he was gone, out into the cool night air, down to the cliffs where the waters mourned and sighed for Maggie, and Fanny and Katie and the boys, and the happiness that was gone.

It was a long time before he went home. In the silent house he could hear Willie, weeping.

Over the next few days, Katie learned the meaning of despair. Buying the barest necessities had taken most of their resources, and no-one, it seemed, wanted a live-out maid without a character. Katie squandered precious pennies on a copy of the *Gazette*, but there was nothing in it for them. Worse, there was an article about a new-born baby washed up in the mud which brought Fanny to tears; and a report of a train blown up in Pretoria which cost Katie her sleep.

Wednesday was market day, and they earned a few pennies by walking out early in the countryside to find honeyfungus and primroses to bunch and sell, and there were enough broken and damaged mushrooms for their own tea. There was a large panful, but even with a twopenny loaf and dandelion tea it didn't seem enough. Katie was learning to be permanently hungry.

'If we were boys,' Katie said bitterly, mopping the last morsel of mushroom with her crust, 'we could earn a few coppers holding the horses. How much have we got left?'

'Three and elevenpence three-farthings,' Fanny said. 'That's a week's wages, near enough. And we made sixpence today with our flowers.'

And a long way that'll go, Katie thought, when we have another mouth to feed. And in two weeks' time there'll be the rent to pay. 'It's no good,' she said. 'We shall have to see can we find a job in the laundry when it opens.' It wasn't likely. They would want younger girls, who cost less. 'Or, I suppose, there's the workhouse.'

'Well, it doesn't have to be both of us,' Fanny said reasonably. 'You could live in. Or go to Mrs Lomas, come to that. She as good as said she'd have you in the workshop as a beginner. Or we could go to the public. The man said they wanted a girl there.'

Katie shook her head. 'We haven't come to that yet. Tomorrow I'll try knocking on doors. There must be work, if you know where to find it, and there's plenty of tradesmen and the like might be glad of general help.'

But it was late in the afternoon before she was rewarded. A woman in Boscawen Street wanted a sewing woman half a day a week. Three shillings a month, and tea provided. Katie was given a sheet to hem to 'see if she suited'. It took an hour to finish, but the woman seemed satisfied and the bargain was struck.

It was a start, she told herself. Besides, it had given her an idea. Where there was one opening, there might be others. Mrs Lomas might know. She hurried to Back Lane and up the stairs.

'Fanny!' She thrust open the door.

There was a fresh loaf on the table, a jug of buttermilk, and a pack of tea sweepings. Fanny knelt by the fire, stirring a pot from which rose the good smell of onions and bacon.

'I got a job,' she said, before Katie could speak. 'Three shillings a week, and tips. One of the customers gave me sixpence, so I got some butcher's scraps for a bit of supper.' She looked at Katie defiantly. 'I aren't going to be able to work long, so I might just as well do what I can now.'

Katie said nothing. Fanny must be working at the public house! She could not bring herself to speak the words. For a moment she thought of refusing the stew, but her hunger was too strong for her. 'I got a job too,' she said. By common consent nothing further was said about Fanny's place of work.

From then on, however, Katie's search for work redoubled. Mrs Lomas was polite, but not encouraging. She would 'ask around' she said. But when Katie arrived at Boscawen Street, as arranged, there was better news. The woman's cousin, farming outside Truro, wanted some plain sewing.

It was a long weary walk to St Clements, and a longer, wearier one home again, but now she had the promise of six shillings a month, and the woman had given her an egg besides, for her trouble.

It was almost a week before anything else came Katie's way. Fanny got her wages and spent half of it on flour, dripping, sugar and currants, and a twopenny jug with flowers on it because it caught her fancy.

'How can you do that, Fanny, when we're scraping for half-pennies?' Katie scolded, but Fanny only shrugged and said if she didn't buy it now she never would. 'We can't wait for ever for your sewing customers to come!'

Yet come they did, little by little. Katie was a good worker, and she began to have a small following. There were unexpected jobs, too. People who didn't often buy dresses were having things turned or trimmed for the Coronation teas. Katie found herself sewing until she dreamed of flatseams, and buttonholes danced before her eyes. Her fingers were raw, but she never willingly turned down work. The time was approaching when Fanny could not be earning outside, but sewing could be done at home, if there was work for two. And there would need to be, if they were to go on paying the rent.

But it was Mrs Lomas who gave Katie the commission which was to change her life. She had got into the habit of calling into the shop every Monday morning to buy thread and needles, and Mrs Lomas never failed to ask kindly after Fanny and herself.

This morning she came bustling down the backstairs to greet Katie, her mouth full of pins. There was a little waiting room at the back of the shop with a chair and table placed in it for the convenience of the occasional husband, or ladies waiting for fittings. Mrs Lomas pointed meanfully at the door.

'Me?' Katie said idiotically, and the woman gave an exasperated nod. Katie went in.

There was a man in the room. A big square man, in a tweed suit, with a bowler hat which he was twisting by the brim in his huge red hands. He reminded Katie of her father. When he spoke, his voice was educated.

'Are you the young lady . . . ?'

But he got no further. Mrs Lomas, minus her pins, swept into the room. This, she told Katie, was Arthur Olds, who lived in the street. He was an architect and builder, with his own company, and a very busy man. He needed someone for sewing, since his wife had died, and left him with a sickly child and only half a household of staff. 'And maybe to sit a bit with the child,' Mrs Lomas continued, 'to give the nursemaid an afternoon off once in a way. The child can't be left and Mr Olds has his business to run. I thought Katie might suit,' she finished, turning to the man. 'It's not our sort of work, and not everyone can turn their hand to a bit of this and that.'

'Two afternoons,' the man said. 'Shilling a week, if that suits.'

Katie could have kissed him. A shilling a week regular, that was handsome pay for a few hours.

'Only,' he said, 'I'd want you to start next week. Tuesday and Thursday, if you can manage that. I know it's the Coronation day, but the nursemaid has Thursday off and I'm due to be in the procession of guilds.'

Katie mentally juggled a few of her existing commissions. 'I can manage that,' she said.

He smiled. He had a nice smile. 'Then I'm sure I can manage to find an extra few pence for your pains. Number Twenty-three. Next Tuesday afternoon, then.' He offered a massive hand for Katie to shake.

Katie went home jubilant. For once they would throw caution to the winds. Those extra pence would buy a tin of peaches, or a morsel of pressed beef. She and Fanny would have a Coronation tea all of their own.

CHAPTER TEN

Workmen were busy putting up the street-bunting when Katie presented herself at Number Twenty-three. It was a big, forthright stone house, imposing enough to make her hesitate. Should she climb the steps to the polished front door, or go down the iron staircase into the area?

She was still hesitating when the front door was flung open, and a small black whirlwind accosted her from the steps.

'The sewing girl, are you? Come away with you then, do. I've been half the afternoon wondering after you.'

It was still a few minutes before her appointed hour, and Katie's cheeks blazed as she climbed the steps and was let into the hall. It was a strangely bare and cheerless house. Everything was polished and scrubbed, but there was not a flower, not a picture or a rug, nothing, as Mother would have said, to 'give the place a bit of life'.

The woman was already climbing the stairs to the sewing-room. She was no higher than Katie's shoulder, and no wider than a rake, but there was a kind of suppressed energy about her that made her seem much larger than she was. From the springy grey curls that bobbed under her frilly cap, to the neat buttoned boots, she seemed to be in continual motion. Even her eyes, which were shrewd and grey, flickered alarmingly as she looked Katie up and down.

'Well you look sturdy enough, I'll say that for you. No doubt with an appetite like an elephant. But can you sew, that's the question?'

'I think so, ma'am,' Katie said, finding her voice for the first time. 'If you tell me which of this I'm to work on.'

The table was stacked high with linen of every sort, pile upon pile of it, neatly ironed and starched.

'Bless my soul, girl, all of it!' the woman said. 'We've been without a sewing woman ever since the mistress died three years ago. The housemaid's worse than useless. More thumbs than fingers – and as for that nursemaid, you'd think she'd never fetched a stitch in her life. And with the child so ill, it's been boil boil boil the linen – no wonder it's falling apart.' She was on the move again as she spoke, drawing up the chair, opening the curtains wider, rearranging the folded sheets. 'Peabody's my name. The master calls me "Mrs" but I started as Peabody, and that's good enough for me. I don't hold with titles. You got a name, I suppose?'

'Katie, ma'am,' Katie said, wondering if she should have said 'Warren'.

'Dear God, hasn't the girl got ears? Peabody's the name, and I'll thank you to call me by it. Now, I'll let you get on, or you'll still be here Christmas.'

Katie took out her sewing things and picked up the first sheet. The woman was right, the hemming was washed thin and faulty in several places. She threaded her needle and began to sew. Peabody. She couldn't call the housekeeper 'Peabody'! What an extraordinary woman.

Her fingers were still flying an hour or more later when Mabel, the lumpy maid, came in with a tea-tray. It held a sturdy enamel mug of hot strong tea, two thick slices of bread and jam, and a slab of plain cake that would have fed Lally for a week. 'Peabody' was obviously providing for the elephant!

The girl caught Katie's smile. 'Typical Peabody,' she said. 'No frills.' Katie wondered that Mr Olds stood for it, and the girl seemed to read her thoughts. 'Suits the master though. Been with him years she has. Stayed with him when the mistress died of consumption, and through the child's sickness and all. Used to be a lot more staff, then. Two upstairs maids and a valet, to say nothing of the kitchen. Most of them gave notice, though, with diphtheria in the house.'

'But not you?' Katie asked.

'Oh, it was all right for me,' the girl said. 'My sister died of it years ago, so I wasn't likely to catch it. Proper carry-on it's been, though, baths of disinfectant outside doors, and wet sheets hanging every-where, and having to wash your hands with carbolic every time you went near Miss Eva's room. Still, that's over at last. Doctor says there's no danger now – that's how we've taken on sewing help again after all this time. Mind, that nurse is still here – poor Miss Eva's so delicate a good puff of wind would blow her away. But it's been a long time. Three years, give or take.'

That explained a great deal, Katie thought. The scrubbed look of everything in the house. The faint smell of carbolic and disinfectant which still lingered in the sheets. She felt a little sorry for Mr Olds, losing his wife and nearly his daughter too.

'Do you really call the housekeeper Peabody?' she said, pushing away the cake with a sigh. She dared not wrap it up and take it home under Mabel's eagle eye.

'Lord, yes,' the girl giggled. 'Won't be called "Mrs" on any account. Disappointed when she was young, my mother says. Even Miss Eva calls her Peabody. By the way, she'd like to see you before you go. Miss Eva that is. Stuck in her bed all day, but she likes to know what's coming and going, especially if you're going to sit with her sometimes. I'll take you up before you leave, but I'd better get on, now, or Peabody will be roasting me with the gammon.'

It was only six when Katie went upstairs with Mabel, and there were still hours of daylight left, but Eva's room was dim enough for the oil-light on the table to be already lit.

The nurse, a big raw-boned girl with red hair and an up-country accent, was stirring something into a tumbler with a long glass pestle and scolding as they entered. 'No, Eva, that's enough. There's only a page or two of the story left, and that can wait till tomorrow. I've your medicine to see to, I can't be reading to you now.'

Katie looked from her broad freckled face, to the thin pinched one on the pillows. The skin was pale, almost transparent, and there was no colour in lips or cheeks. The blonde hair might have been beautiful, but it lay lankly across the white forehead. One hand, so pale it was almost blue, lay on the counterpane, beside a coloured story book. Katie's heart melted.

'I'll finish the story, if you're too busy.' Ever afterwards she wondered at her own audacity, but the nurse seemed unsurprised.

'As you like. Might as well get to know the child if you're coming to sit with her Thursday. Only mind you don't make a rod for your own back.'

Katie took up the book and finished the tale. Eva lay back with a contented sigh.

'I'll read to you again on Thursday.'

'You'll miss all the excitement,' the nurse said, hovering with her concoction at the side of the bed. 'There's to be bands, and guns, and processions, and sports and even a bonfire with fireworks.'

'I wish I could see Father in his trade procession,' Eva said.

'Never mind, we'll have a good story,' Katie said.

All next day that tired little face haunted her thoughts, and she hurried home the next evening, quite eager for Coronation Day.

Fanny was sitting on the bed, letting out the darts in the front of her skirt. She leapt up when Katie came in.

'My dear life, Katie, there's such news! I saw Carrie Tremble in town – she's to be married to a clayworker up to St Austell and she was going up to see his people. And,' her face was fluushed, 'what do you think? Noah Trembath is home – asking for me, too. Carrie's going to tell him where I am, though she's not to say anything to Lally.'

Katie put down her basket with such force that the eggs almost toppled from their brown paper bag. 'Fanny!' Her voice was sharp. 'You can't go seeing Noah. Not in your condition. Whatever would you say to him? And you calling yourself Mrs Trembath, too!'

Fanny flushed and took up her sewing, but said nothing – until she saw Katie setting out the slices of pressed beef and eggs and jam. 'My life Katie, have you found shares in a gold mine, or what?'

'It's not for now, it's for our Coronation tea. Mr Olds promised me a few pennies extra for working tomorrow.'

Fanny gaped at her. 'Haven't you heard? The town crier's been crying it for hours. The poor King's got appendicitis. The Coronation's postponed!'

George came up from the bottom of a deep green pit into a nightmare. He was drowning. Someone was levering his lips apart and pouring liquid into his open mouth, and he could not struggle. He forced his eyes open.

The nightmare was true.

For a moment he gagged and spluttered, and a voice above him said, 'That's enough. He's coming round.'

The torment ceased, and his eyelids closed again, but very slowly he became aware of things. Light, coming from a long window. People walking, hurrying, whispering. The smell of soap and iodine, and the sweet, sickly smell of decay. A weight on his leg which burned and ached, and a thirst which tore at his throat and stomach. And under it all a lowing sound, rising and falling, like cattle in a market.

He tried to raise his head and fell back with a groan.

'Oh, you're back with us then, are you?' With an effort George made out the speaker, a shortish man in a field uniform whose face and arm were grotesque in bandages. He was sitting on the side of a neighbouring bed, looking at George from his one swollen eye.

George tried to reply, but managed only a moan.

'Well, hold your noise, or you'll be more trouble awake than asleep. I was here when they brought you off the train. Shouting and carrying on something cruel, you were. Many's the night I've had to lie here listening to you. Ten times worse than that lot, you were!' The lowing noise, George realised – it was men, in pain. 'Still,' the man went on, 'it's been a bit better the last few days. Beginning to think you were going to sleep forever. Your young lady will be pleased to find you've come round. Been here every day, asking after you.'

'Lady?' His lips formed the word, and his heart gave a little lurch. Katie couldn't be here, surely?

'You can hear me, then?' the man said. 'Didn't know if your mind had gone, like poor Samuels over there.' He gestured to a further bed, and George took in rows and rows of similar cots which filled the room. 'Yes, I don't know what you've done to deserve it. Her mother came in first, just a few days after the peace was signed. They've been good, some of the Boer women. Voluntaries – you know, giving comforts and that. And when she heard "Trevarnon", you'd have thought it was Kitchener himself the way she carried on. Insisted on seeing you, though you weren't any picture, I can tell you. And since then the daughter's been coming in. Attractive girl too. Fallen on your feet, you have, Trevarnon.'

He learnt a lot from the little lieutenant before the orderlies came and cursed at them to be quiet. They were in a hospital in Pretoria, brought down the line from Pietersburg. Through a mist George could dimly remember a journey of jolts and agony, stretchers and stations, but it was kinder to forget.

A doctor came to see him. 'You're a lucky man, Trevarnon. If you'd done this in the early part of the war we couldn't have helped you. Didn't have the hospitals then, or the supplies. But you're well off here. You've lost a lot of blood, but the fever's gone down, and the wound is clean. You'll always have one leg shorter than the other, but we'll have you on your feet again.'

But that was a long way off. His lower body was a mass of bandages, sticky and hot, which had to be changed, soaked off and torn agonisingly clear. The wound he glimpsed before the new dressing was bound on turned his stomach, and made the livid yellowing scar on his hand look trivial. He began to wish he could slip into unconsciousness again.

The girl came. She was as pretty as the lieutenant had said, big and blonde with blue eyes, a quick gentle smile, and a strange air of being at once unknown and oddly familiar.

It was strange to him, this meeting of enemies. Yet from the beginning they talked like old friends. He told her about Cornwall, the mines, the moors, the sea. She told him about her life in Pretoria with her widowed mother, and how they had had to leave it during the war because her mother was British born, but how their farm on the veldt had been burnt because they were Boers.

'It hasn't been easy,' the girl said. 'We sold some of the stock and more was raided. And my poor mother was neither fish nor fowl. Her father was British, came over for the goldmines in the sixties, and then bought land, but mine was a settler. My mother brazens it out, but I don't think the rifts will ever be healed.'

George nodded. 'It was good of her to visit.' He was propped on his pillows these days, and the world had stopped spinning.

'It's like her,' the girl said. 'Always does the unexpected. Like choosing my name.'

'Kernerwek Brunner,' he said, savouring the words. 'Is that a Boer name?'

She laughed, an unexpected laugh. 'And you a Cornishman! No! Brunner is Boer enough, but Kernerwek means Cornish. It *is* Cornish! Cornish for Cornish! My father was surprised, but he was a lot older than my mother, and I think he would have done anything for her. She has always loved all things Cornish, oh, ever since she was a little girl at the mines. I think it was the romance of the place – the way the men spoke of it – just like you do.'

George smiled. 'Mine's a Cornish name, too,' he said, looking for a bond between them.

Kernerwek nodded. 'I think that's why she picked you out. The hospital Volunteers each picked a name. She was the one who asked me to come and see you.'

'I'm glad she did,' George said softly.

She coloured and turned away. She was so pretty, the soft curve of her cheek framed against the sweep of her hair.

'Well,' she said, 'you must get well again soon, and then you shall meet her. There is a party for my birthday, in October. That's ten weeks. It will be spring by then, this terrible winter will be over, and you will be much better.'

George said gently, 'What would people say, your mother inviting an enemy soldier?'

She smiled. 'The war is over. Lots of society people are doing it. And mother wouldn't care. Anyway, she's half British herself. She'll invite you if I want you. I will talk to her myself.'

George smiled at her enthusiasm. She was older than he was by a year or two, but war had aged him. She was a girl, he was a man.

But he would go to her party. Dance, if his leg allowed it. Meet her mother and friends. And then? Who knew. There was nothing for him at Trevarnon now, and there were worse places than Africa, even in the aftermath of war, with sunshine and servants, and a girl who adored you.

For he had to face the fact. Kernerwek Brunner loved him.

June gave way to July. The rain, which had threatened the county show, and the ill-fated coronation parades, gave way to blue skies and warm sunshine. Katie, walking back from St Clements, had to stop to admire the view, the distant river glinting silver in the evening sunshine, framed by a sweet scented tangle of roses and honeysuckle which arched the path.

She stood for a moment to watch a ship, sails furled, battle up against the tide, pulled by a ferocious little steam-tug with smoke pouring from its funnel. Then she hurried on. There was work to be done.

She had started taking in sewing at home. Fanny could not go out for many more weeks. Already her waist was thickening, and both her skirts were let out to the limit. Clothes would soon be a problem, and not only for Fanny. There was the baby to think of, and Katie's own dresses were getting tight under the arms and too short at the hem. And then there were boots.

Katie sighed. The pile of sewing awaiting her at home was not enough to buy a length of long-cloth, let alone keep them all in bootleather, now Fanny had lost her wages.

She wondered for the hundredth time about hiring a sewing machine from Mrs Lomas. Mrs Lomas would give her good terms, and a machine would make light of the sewing, but they would have to find so much more work simply to pay the rental. And work was scarce. The Coronation would not produce orders a second time. People already had their dresses.

Yet could they afford not to have a machine? All the sewing women had them. Katie shook her head. Even Mrs Lomas would want paying in advance, and one week's hire would take all of their meagre savings.

Down the lane and into the town. The shops were half-shuttered, with boys in aprons raising canopies, and men in waistcoats taking in sacks and baskets from the shopfronts. Katie stopped to barter with the butcher for some ends of meat left over at the chopping block, and came away with a bagful for twopence. That would make a tasty stew.

'Well, I see you've some sense with your money, I'll say that for you.'

'Peabody!' Katie smiled at the little figure bustling in with elbows flying, a black cloak flung over the black dress, and the grey hair streaming out from its cap and pins as though a hurricane had struck.

'Come down for a bit of beef for Miss Eva,' Peabody said with a sniff. 'Nurse says she's to have a drop of beef tea for her supper. I ask you, beef tea at this time of night! Not that I begrudge Miss Eva, think the world of her I do, but that nurse, she's enough to make you lose your salvation. Comes down to the kitchen "I think we'll just have a little scrambled egg, this evening, cook", when you'd like to send up something a bit special for the child's appetite. Thinks she's gentry, that's her trouble. And when you do send up scrambled egg she wants beef tea. And no Mabel to send out for it. I don't know how she thinks I'll ever have the master's dinner on the table.'

Katie smiled in sympathy. She had watched Peabody make beef tea before, forcing raw meat through a hair sieve. It was a long, slow business.

'Still,' Peabody went on, before Katie had a chance to frame a word, 'won't be so long now to put up with her airs and graces. Doctor came today and said Miss Eva can start taking the air soon. Doesn't really need nursing so much as looking after. I told Mr Olds about that woman, nurse she may be to that child, companion she isn't.' Her hands were busy with her shawl and her parcels. 'I wonder you don't ask Mr Olds about sitting with the child a bit more. She's taken to you, with your reading and your stories and all that. He's said so himself.'

Katie flushed. There had been one embarrassing Thursday afternoon when Mr Olds had come in, to find her telling stories to Eva, as she had used to tell them to Carrie and Willie back at the Terrace, her sewing lying forgotten on her lap. He smiled, but when he handed over her wage packet that night he said, 'For sewing and story-telling,' and she had been careful to keep sewing ever since.

'No,' Peabody said, looking at her face, 'I mean it. He thinks the world of that child, and I'm sure you'd be a bit more company for her than that nurse. I don't mind telling him so! Now if I don't get this beef home Miss Eva will never get her tea!' And away she went in a fluster of packages. Just like the little tug she had watched earlier, Katie thought.

She walked home in a dream. Would Mr Olds really let her come and read to Miss Eva? Sick people did have companions. Mrs Selwood was always talking about some cousin of hers who'd had a companion for years. Miss Eva would need a proper governess though, wouldn't she? Or would she? Perhaps she could help her with her reading and her sums. Peabody thought she could, and what Peabody thought Mr Olds usually thought too. Katie smiled. She would speak to Mr Olds. It couldn't do any harm, she told herself. He could only say no.

Her head was still full of schemes as she turned into Back Lane, and she would hardly have glanced at the man who came out of one of the houses, if it were not for his clothes. He was jauntily dressed in a check suit, with brown and white shoes and a brown hat with a feather – like something out of a handbill, Katie thought. He had a thick moustache, and as she passed him he hesitated a moment and raised his hat. Katie stopped and watched him to the end of the street.

She was even more surprised to realise that the house he had come from was her own. Not only that, but Mrs Williams, anxious and faded as ever, was watching him go with an air of suppressed excitement.

'Evening, Mrs Williams,' Katie said as she went in. 'Visitors?'

'Oh, Miss Katie,' the woman said with a little giggle. 'As if you didn't know. That was Mr Trembath. Your Fanny's husband.'

'Noah!' It was true, Katie realised. Under the moustache and outlandish clothes, it was Noah. No wonder he had doffed his hat. And, close on the heels of that realisation, a second one. 'He came to see Fanny!'

'Course he did.' Mrs Williams was still smirking like a schoolgirl. 'Though I don't mind admitting, Miss Katie, when he first came here knocking I nearly didn't let him in. "I'm looking for Miss Warren and her sister" he said, polite as you like, though he was done up like a Christmas parcel even then. "My name's Trembath," he said, and then of course I realised. Well, I didn't know where to put myself. You see, I never really thought there *was* a Mr Trembath, Mrs Lomas or no Mrs Lomas.'

Katie opened her mouth to speak, but Mrs Williams was still apologising. 'No, I was wrong, and I don't mind admitting it. So if I've been a bit offhand with you both, I'm sorry. And I have to say, he's a nice boy, in spite of his looks, and that fond of your sister. It's a pleasure to see them together. It's a sorry shame he has to go back to America so soon. Still, it's been a nice few weeks for them, hasn't it? Shame he's always got to catch the train to Penzance just before you get home. I offered him a room here, but he said no, they're saving.'

'Weeks?' Katie found herself saying.

'Oh yes,' the woman said. 'End of June, was it? Anyway, like I say, I'm sorry to be so offhand. Anything I can do, you let me know. Now, I can smell my cabbage burning.'

But Katie's mind was not on cabbage as she climbed the stairs to the attic.

'Fanny!'

Fanny looked up from the potatoes she was peeling, with an innocent air.

'I've just seen Noah. And I spoke to Mrs Williams. Whatever has been going on? Having Noah visiting up here and all? How did he know you were here?'

Fanny flushed. 'Well,' she said, 'I wrote. But it was Mrs Williams let him in. Took him for my husband.'

'Well she would,' Katie said, 'seeing that's what you call yourself.'

She meant it as a rebuke, but Fanny said, 'Well, so I will be. He's asked me to marry him, when he comes home, and I've said yes.'

Katie stared. 'You mean it?' A rush of relief swept over her. If Fanny was married then their problems were over. The child would have a name. Fanny would be settled. She herself could make peace with Lally, start again, look for a living-in job. Maybe even – she dared not even think of the possibility of living-in as a companion for Eva. 'He doesn't mind about the child?'

Fanny didn't answer.

'You haven't told him,' Katie said, in sudden horror. 'You said you would marry him. You led him on, and you haven't told him.'

Fanny turned a tragic face towards her. 'I meant to, Katie, honestly I did. Only he was so pleased to see me, and I had to be sure he really wanted to marry me, and it would solve everything . . . I couldn't just tell him.'

'You'll tell him next time he comes,' Katie said firmly.

'There won't be a next time. I was going to tell you, Katie, really I was, only I was afraid you'd put a stop to it. And tonight he waited, he really waited, but you were later than usual, and he had to catch his train. And,' she finished miserably, 'he's going back to America tomorrow.'

'Then you'll write to him,' Katie said. 'You can't carry on like this. Whatever would the man say if he came back and found his wife-to-be with a child? I never heard the like!' She took up the knife and began to pare a swede.

But Fanny was holding the saucepan with a faraway look in her eyes.

'Yes,' she said at last. 'Yes, I promise. I'll write and tell him.'

She wrote the next day, but she didn't show Katie the letter.

CHAPTER ELEVEN

It was almost a fortnight before Katie plucked up the courage to speak to Mr Olds. Even then she might not have done so if it hadn't been for the baby-clothes.

Mrs Williams brought them up, as a kind of peace-offering, Katie guessed. There was a shawl, a robe and two bonnets. They had belonged to her daughter, Mrs Williams said. They were old, and much washed, but there was wear in them and Fanny was delighted. 'I only wish I had a bit of ribbon to trim them.'

There was ribbon from some of Miss Eva's pillowcases which had worn through with boiling and were past repair. Katie plucked up her courage and spoke to Peabody about it.

'Bless me girl, I'm sure Mr Olds won't grudge you a bit of ribbon if you ask him.'

But Mr Olds was adamant. It was out of the question. 'You can't use ribbon when it's been in a sickroom. Who knows what germs there might be on it? What did you want it for, anyway?'

Katie explained. Her sister was expecting and her 'man' (she chose the word carefully) was in America, so there wasn't the money for baby-clothes.

'My dear girl,' Mr Olds said, and the next Tuesday Mabel came to the sewing room with a little bundle of garments, tiny flannel vests, embroidered coats, small knitted gloves and baby nightdresses painstakingly pintucked and trimmed with lace.

'These were Miss Eva's,' Mabel said. 'Mr Olds said to give you them for your sister.'

It was so kindly done, and Fanny was so enchanted, that Katie found it hard to meet Mr Olds' eyes when he looked in on Eva on Thursday. She murmured her thanks.

'Well, they won't fit Eva now,' he said, and made her laugh. 'Now, if you would like any extra sewing to help make ends meet, you just let me know.'

Katie took a deep breath. 'Anything extra would be very helpful, sir, and I'm very grateful. Or, if you're willing, I could come and read to Eva a bit more, sometimes, if she isn't needing a nurse so much.'

Mr Olds looked from her to his daughter, his eyes twinkling. 'You'd like that, I daresay, the pair of you. And Peabody's been preaching it at me for a week or more. I can see I'm outvoted. Very well, young lady, you shall come another afternoon and read to Miss Eva.'

Later, as he gave her her wages, Katie said, 'Begging your pardon, sir, but about the reading. I'll only come if you want me. I mean, perhaps you'd rather Miss Eva read stories to herself.'

He looked tired, suddenly, sad and worn, and his voice was weary as he said, 'No. She's never been well enough, you see. She was always delicate – inherited weak lungs from her mother, and this diphtheria was almost the last straw. She never had schooling. Not strong enough to be taught.'

'Bless me, sir, I could teach her in no time.' The words were out before Katie could stop them.

But Mr Olds did not seem to mind. 'You think so? And who have you ever taught, young lady?'

'My brothers, sir, Willie and Jack, when he was alive, and I always helped Carrie with her reading and sums . . .' Somehow the little list brought back so many memories that Katie found her eyes filling with tears.

'Well then,' Mr Olds said. 'You come in and read to Eva an extra afternoon. Shilling a week. And, if the Doctor says so, you can try and help her learn herself. Don't you tire her, mind. And if it works out, well, we might see about increasing it. But mind you, if you're sewing, you're sewing, and if you're reading, you're reading. Whatever job it is, see you keep your mind on it.' She gazed at him in confusion, but he was smiling.

'Yes, Mr Olds,' Katie managed, but her heart was so light she had difficulty in walking sedately down the stairs. Once around the corner she skipped like a child, all the way home.

She was being paid to read, and to teach. She would succeed. She would try so hard that Eva would soon learn to read and Mr Olds would soon increase her hours.

She would. She would!

Robert was bored. Already. He had not been engaged above an hour and already he was stifling a yawn.

It was unreasonable, he knew it. The Selwoods had done him proud tonight. Anyone who was anyone was here, willing to attend a ball at the Selwoods' when they would never have come to Trevarnon. He could see Mama at the other end of the ballroom, delighted by so many introductions, so many new acquaintances. This would fill her social calendar for months. Papa was with her, nodding and smiling with the grim determination which he saved for what he called 'social junkets', a glass already in his hand.

His engagement had delighted the pair of them, and for once they had seemed united in their pleasure. Mama was enchanted by the idea of a closer link with her distant cousin, and an entrée into one of the oldest families in the country. Papa seemed pleased too, muttering about 'settling down' and 'showing responsibility'. Robert was rather pleased about that. Ever since George had gone to the Transvaal Papa had withdrawn into himself more than ever. It was more than the loss of George, Robert was sure; rather Papa seemed to be living more and more in the past, and becoming less and less contented with the present. Until this engagement.

Yes, it was a glittering occasion. Major Selwood had seemed genuinely proud when he made the official announcement. Caroline was looking radiant. He should have been the happiest man alive, especially since Papa had come out of his torpor sufficiently to discover hidden depths to his pockets and augmented the finances to the tune of a handsome amethyst necklace for the bride-to-be. Which was all very fine, Robert reflected, but it didn't put any cash in his own pocket.

Still, all he had to do was wait, and play the dutiful husband. It was that part of the exercise he was finding irksome, he thought with a wry smile. As an engaged man he was now bespoke, and although he could dance with all the prettiest girls he was already feeling his new status. He could not flirt with any of them, and they were impatient to be back in the arms of some more promising partner. As a prospective son-in-law there were more tedious formalities too. Any minute now he would be expected to lead out another of Caroline's horsefaced cousins, just as he had already danced with her mother and two of her aunts. And it was only eleven thirty.

He sighed. A man in his position could not even forget himself in champagne. Too many people would be looking askance and counting the glasses. He began to wish it was time to go home, where there would at least be Ruby, or if he was skilful, one of the new maids.

The orchestra struck up and he went to claim his partner. She was a dumpy girl with freckles and crooked teeth, and a high-pitched voice in which she kept up a commentary on the other guests.

'The St Aubens couple – doesn't she look well? I understand the King may be coming to visit them before the year is out. And Mrs Trengarrow – got up a Coronation Ball in June, spent a fortune and all for nothing, and then for the real Coronation last month her dance was a sorry affair.'

Robert muttered something in reply. The gossip irritated him, not so much because it was ill-bred, as because he had laid out a good deal of money for his own celebrations in June, only to have to rearrange them at even greater expense. The August Coronation had been a poor show by comparison. People were calling it a 'family affair', but what they meant was 'half the show at twice the cost'.

But his companion hadn't finished. 'And there's the Poldair girl,' she said, in a whisper that carried half across the ballroom. 'Striking girl, but I don't know if that dress is altogether suitable.'

This was a tantalising tidbit. Robert manoeuvred his partner so that he could get a clearer look at the young woman. Striking she certainly was, pale, auburn-haired, with a pair of dark eyes which shone with a kind of mad intense light. She held her head very high, and her movements were fierce, almost headstrong.

The dress was defiant too. Not the filmy, silky, lacy whites and pastels of the other young girls. Not even like his own partner's blue silk, shot with a blush of silver. It was a bold, deep emerald velvet, trimmed with rose, and cut low at the neck and deep at the waist, like the dress of some medieval princess.

She paused in the act of taking the glass which her father was handing her from a tray. Her eyes met Robert's. He smiled, meaningly, and she turned away but her cheeks had already flushed to match the roses on her gown.

'Trade money, of course,' the toothy cousin was saying, bringing him back to the present. 'But they cut a figure, don't they? Made a fortune out of saddlery in the Crimean War, and I believe they are invited quite everywhere. Which reminds me, what news of your gallant brother? Shall we expect him home soon?'

'George? He managed to stop a bullet in the leg, somewhere in the Transvaal, only a day or two before peace was signed. They've transferred him out of Pieterburg, but it was touch and go for a time. General Roberts is a friend of Selwood, as you know, and he wrote a personal letter. He's out of the woods now, but Mama is frightfully cut up about it.'

Mama was taking the floor as he spoke, on the arm of an elderly officer, but the cousin only said, 'It must be terrible for you all.'

Robert put on his anxious face. 'Very hard on Mama,' he said, for the hundredth time that month. 'Wondering if he would pull through.' Try as he would, he could not quite suppress the thought of the money that might have been available if George had not pulled through.

The music stopped and he was able to lead the cousin back to her companions. Morwenna Poldair was talking to Caroline. He straightened his shirtfront and ran a hand over his hair. Decidedly the evening was looking up.

He was smiling as he approached them. 'Excuse me, ladies.' He offered Caroline his arm. 'My dance, I think?' But he was looking deep into the burning eyes of Morwenna Poldair.

George was getting better, decidedly better. His daily airing in a wheelchair had given way to an outing with the aid of a stick and the arm of a nurse.

The first few steps had been agony, like walking on knives, but he had persevered, and as he gained strength his legs had learned how to hold him again. He walked with an ugly lumbering limp, but he was on his own feet. He would be out of hospital soon.

For what? He had to ask himself the question. For a return to Trevarnon, where the memories of an earlier life were waiting to haunt him? It was ironic really – the letter from Robert under his pillow which told him of the engagement, and the departure of the Warren sisters. 'Remember that foolish business when I bet them that they could not reach the decorations, and you assumed the worst? I felt badly about that at the time, when you went away before I could explain, but it must have been an omen after all. Got themselves in trouble in real earnest and we had to send them off without a character . . .' The vision of that night in Trevarnon had returned to haunt George's dreams. Could he bear to go back there, when the doctors pronounced him fit?

Most of his companions had already left. Some with grey faces had slipped away into darkness silently, like lamps in the night. Some, like poor Samuels, succumbed by inches, sweated and swore and stank. Others recovered enough to stumble out to a pension and an altered life. George was one of the lucky ones.

An officer from headquarters came to see him. George knew the man slightly; they had met before, knee-deep in a filthy ditch. Now the man's uniform was laundered and pressed, every button gleaming. The war was over. George had heard it a thousand times, but in that moment he felt it for the first time.

The man came to his bedside, ill at ease in a hospital ward; he spoke in a mumble. 'Bad show . . . sorry to see . . . rotten luck . . . make the best . . .' George half-listened to the platitudes. The next words, however, took him by surprise. 'Take your pension if you like, but told me to tell you there was a position in intelligence. Don't rush into a decision, but when you're out of here, you can join the mess while you think . . .'

He told Kernerwek. She was delighted. 'You must think about it, George. You'd love Africa, I know you would. There is so much space, so much freedom. The future is here, not in Europe.'

He looked at her wryly. 'A limping cripple? In the King's uniform? What sort of a soldier should I be?'

'They don't want you to fight,' she said, 'And anyway, you don't have to stay in the army. There are other things you could do.'

'Such as?' He gestured towards his shattered leg. 'Who wants half a man? And an ex-enemy too.'

She coloured. 'You know about animals. And there isn't enough stock in this country, after the war. They're going to need horse-breeders, buyers, people who know a good horse when they see one.' She did not mention her own mother's farm burned and empty on the veldt, but the knowledge of it hung between them in the silence. 'Anyway,' she said at last, 'what would you do in England?'

He had asked himself the same question. After the last three years, could he adapt himself to the tiny round that was Trevarnon? Mama striving to compete with the neighbours. Papa shutting himself away more and more. Robert all strut and swagger, with no more pressing interests than his debts and his women. He had grown a long way from all that. And the girl, Katie, what had become of her? Married to some mine-worker more than likely, with, as Robert had said, a child at her petticoats. He shook his head.

'Don't look sad, George,' Kernerwek said. 'Look, it's only a week or two until my party, and you will be out of hospital. And you have time to think.'

He smiled, and they talked of other things, but the problem nagged him. She was lovely, bright and gentle as spring, and in her company he felt content. But what future was there in this country for a man who had fought against it? And she did not stir him. The quickening of his flesh was reserved for his dreams of a girl, older now, with a mop of dark curls and quick laughing eyes.

He left the hospital at last. There were so few men, thirty at most, that they were talking of closing the ward and moving them elsewhere, perhaps to a civilian hospital. George was glad that he had escaped the punishing journey on stretchers, carts and trains.

He moved into headquarters. Here, too, there were only a few men, administrators and negotiators for the most part. Battles to them were not blood and noise and horses, but crosses on neat maps. George found himself spending more and more time in his quarters.

And Kernerwek was strangely silent. She had been convinced that her mother would want to meet George before the party, but no invitation was forthcoming, and now that he was in the garrison he could no longer expect her daily visits. He was surprised to find how much he missed them.

At last the invitation did arrive: Mrs Anna Brunner requested the pleasure of his company at a ball to celebrate the birthday of her daughter. He was not alone. Several officers had received them.

He went in a carriage, with one of the senior administrators and his family. He had taken care over his appearance, belt and buckles sparkling, and the army bootmaker had made him a special boot which minimised his limp. All the same he needed his stick, and his arrival reminded him, ironically, of Robert's riding accident and the fuss the ladies had made of him.

There was no such attention here. There were scores of pretty girls, but their eyes were for the dashing, dancing men in their uniforms, or the young society beaux from Pretoria, who were coming back to the town now that the peace was settled. There were other young men too, with gaunt faces and sunburned hands, who moved away when the British officers entered. His erstwhile enemies, George realised.

It was a magnificent room, low and white in the settler style, with fine furniture and flowers everywhere, the dazzling daffodils, which many of the Dutch still grew in the brief period before the scorching southern summer. But even in this setting the scars of war were evident; in the fine curtains damaged in the fighting and never replaced, in the dresses of the women, and the restraint of the food set on the dainty tables.

Yet everywhere there were servants. George thought with a smile of Trevarnon, and mother doing her best with a limited staff. Here there were almost as many servants as guests, so that before you were ready to sit down, a black footman had placed a chair at the ready, and a black maid was standing by with a table to place at your elbow. It was the first time he had been waited on by the unpaid 'kaffirs', as Kernerwek called them – the ones in the officers' mess were paid orderlies – and it troubled him, obscurely.

But he had little time to think about it. Anna Brunner was coming towards him. She must once have been beautiful. Now in her forties at least, she was still magnificent, red hair piled on her head, and her fine shoulders rising from a froth of deep blue lace that made her skin look smoother than ever. It was not white skin as an English lady's would be, but bronzed and shining. It was no wonder, George felt, struggling to his feet, that an older husband had indulged her. Even at her age, she turned the head of every man in the room.

By her side, Kernerwek. As blonde as her mother was auburn, pretty, gentle, and sweet. Yet tonight she looked troubled. She smiled at George.

'Captain Trevarnon,' Mrs Brunner said. 'I am so pleased you are able to be with us.' She held out a pair of strong, tanned hands, dazzling with rings, and the fingers which gripped his were warm, supportive.

He glanced at her in surprise, and found that her eyes were full of entreaty. He had meant to say a thousand things, but he stopped, confused. Kernerwek was right, this was not a woman to be cowed by opinion.

'Why, there is Captain Smith, Kernerwek,' her mother said. 'Do see that he is properly introduced.' Kernerwek moved away, and Mrs Brunner turned back to George.

'I am glad to see you so well recovered, Captain Trevarnon. I saw you, you know, when you were first brought to the hospital. Foolish of me – when I first heard the name – but when I saw you I knew you must be his son. Even then, his eyes, his hair – and now that you are recovered the likeness is remarkable.'

'You knew my father?' It was, of course, more than possible. Mining in the Transvaal. A successful gold mine.

She looked away, busying herself with her fan. 'Oh yes,' she said. 'There were a lot of Cornishmen in the Transvaal in those days. But that was long ago. Let us talk of the present.' The eyes met his again. 'Kernerwek now, such a pretty girl, don't you think? So like her father, too.'

He looked at Kernerwek again, now walking back across the ballroom with Captain Smith. He saw, as if for the first time, the blonde hair, the blue eyes, so like his own, the somehow familiar air. And with a cold sinking of the stomach, he understood.

'Was this your revenge?' he said, bitterly. 'It was cruel. To Kernerwek, too.'

She laid a hand on his arm. 'I did not intend this. When I learned of her feelings I tried to stop it. Believe me.'

'Does she know?' he whispered, and Anna Brunner had time to shake her head softly before Kernerwek arrived.

'Mama, Captain Smith.' And the evening swirled on.

He could not dance, and he did not choose to converse. He sat a little while, furious with despair, and left as soon as convention permitted.

'Make my excuses to Miss Brunner,' he said to her mother. 'I have no appetite for it.'

He was on the next ship home.

CHAPTER TWELVE

Davy closed the stannery door against the bite of the November wind, and set off up the mine-lane, finding his way by the white painted stones glimmering in the swiftly falling night. He would go to the dry and then wash and change as he always did, but he hated it, this mingling with the surface workers while the real work was going on far below under his feet.

The late shift had just gone down, but for the men on the vanners there was no night working, no working doublers either. His day was governed by the sun, when the men breaking the ore could see the rocks they smashed, and when the daylight failed the stamps too were silent.

It was tedious work, tending the belts which carried the crushed ore to the vanners, and the great buddles, twelve foot and more around, where the powdered rock was mixed with water so that the good tin sank and the waste water turned a sickly red which ran out to dye the sea for a mile around.

What skill was there in that? Judging the level perhaps, where to stop the flow to draw the second and third level tin, and leave the finest at the bottom. But for the most part the machines did it all, so that a man was reduced to a slave, watching the great sweeps skimming off the sludge or feeding the belts and the massive stamps, which devoured the ore like starving mechanical monsters.

Why had he ever made that promise? Why had he let despair drive him into taking a surface job? His head rang with the noise of the stamps and the thump of the engines and the hiss and rattle of the buddles.

Perhaps that was why he failed to hear the cart as it came up the lane behind him. The driver had to shout to him to stand clear.

'Come on past!' he called back, moving to the side.

'Davy Warren? I know that voice!' The cart lurched to a stop. Davy could just make out the hunched figure under the battered hat.

'Harry Trembath?'

'Come up on here and ride up to the dry, Davy lad, save wearing your legs to stumps.' He indicated a place beside him on a pile of sacks. 'Been down with a load of candles for the engine-house.'

Davy hoisted himself aboard.

'What are you doing now?' Harry Trembath wanted to know. Davy hadn't seen him since the day he had left the mine. He had done what he said he would do, moved to Penzance and now made a little living bringing small loads to and fro on the cart bought with money his sons had sent home from America. 'Happy on the surface, are you?'

Davy didn't answer. 'Heard from the boys?' he said instead.

Harry stopped the cart, to Davy's surprise. 'Yes,' he said and his voice was embarrassed. 'Had a letter from Noah last week. Glad I saw you, Davy, or I might have been up to the Terrace to find you.'

Davy stared at the dark figure blankly.

'If my boy has got your girl in trouble I'm some sorry, Davy – being previous with their wedding vows. But he's got a good heart, Noah, and he's always been fond of your Fanny.'

'Noah?' Davy broke in amazed. 'I didn't know he was home.'

'Been and gone back,' Harry said. 'Didn't tell me he was seeing her – young cub! Said to me he was going up to Truro all that time to have some gold assayed. Not a bit abashed, either. Wanted to marry her before this, he says, but she wouldn't have him. Now she'll have to.'

But Davy was following his own train of thought. 'Truro?'

'Well, Truro might have nothing to do with it, for all I know. Haven't she said where she is?' Harry sounded concerned. 'Didn't like to maybe, with that Lally in the house. I heard she turned the girls out long ago, for some call or another, though Mrs Tremble will have it that she just wanted to be head cow in her own byre.'

Davy nodded absently. It was like Cissie Tremble to stand up for the girls, but there was bound to be gossip, though with the girls away in service their absence had not caused too great a stir. He said gently, 'Ah, she knew about the child, Harry, but never stopped to ask whose child it was.'

'Wouldn't have made no difference, anyhow,' Harry said. 'A sin's a sin, stands to reason. But he will marry her, Davy, soon as he can get a ship home, and take her back with him, so he says. Or go to Australia – they're crying out for miners out there. Won't stop the child being base-born, I daresay, but if a man comes to a new country with his wife and child they don't ask too many questions.'

Davy said, 'It's as well her mother's not here to see it,' but in spite of himself his heart had lifted. Fanny was safe and well. And Katie? With her, no doubt. Already his mind was full of a thousand schemes. How could he find them?

'Got her address, have 'ee?' Davy wasn't quick at ciphering but he could read, and Willie would help him.

Harry shook his head. 'Noah'll have it,' he said. 'I'll get my girl to ask him when she writes. Now, you want to go into the dry and change, do you? I'll wait, if you're quick, and take you home on the cart. I promised some of them sacks to Mrs Goodbody.'

He eased the cart to a standstill and Davy swung down. What would Lally say to this, he wondered. He took his place in the line and washed the red dust and stone chippings from his face, hands and hair, and changed into his walking clothes. Make more trouble no doubt. Well, for once he would say nothing. But he might, he just might, have a word with Cissie Tremble. If anyone knew where Katie was, she and Carrie would.

He pulled his scarf on, wrapping his ears against the cold, but he was whistling as the cart lurched homeward through the wintry night.

It was getting colder. Surely it had never been as cold as this at the Terrace? More than once lately the water in the ewer had been covered in ice of a morning, and the women at the pump were remembering the great blizzard when the pump itself froze and people were boiling snow for their tea.

The penn'orth of coals did little to warm the place, either, and Katie was glad she had used the warmth of summer to hoard some of their firing. Even so, Fanny, confined to the house all day, wore woollen mittens and often blew on her fingers as she sewed. It was as well they had hired the machine with Katie's 'reading money': Fanny's hands were too numb with cold to do fine work. The little machine whirred late into the night, often by the light of the fire, for there was not a penny to spare.

The smallest things became important. Katie always contrived to bring home some of Peabody's bread and butter and a slice of cake for Fanny on her Mr Olds afternoons. Farmers' wives sometimes paid in potatoes and onions, and though Katie had to struggle home with the parcel she was always grateful, because the women gave her more than her sixpence would have bought. But without Fanny's wages there was never really enough to eat, and Katie could see her sister's cheeks getting thinner and thinner, even as her belly got larger. She began to lie awake at night worrying. The worst of the winter was yet to come, and soon there would be another mouth to feed.

In desperation Katie went into the church, threw herself onto her knees and prayed.

She had been in a church before. Mrs Trevarnon had insisted on the staff attending morning service when they were on duty, and today she was grateful. The tall dark building with its stained glass and faint, musty, candley smell was not as strange as it might once have been, though it was a far cry from the simple brass cross and wooden pews of the little chapel she had been raised to. But it was still the house of God, she told herself, and muttered her prayers with more courage. It gave her a strange sense of peace. With the need to work all hours, and Fanny's shame, to say nothing of her job in 'that place' (even now Katie could not bear to frame the words 'public house'), they had not been into a chapel since they left Penzance. Even today she had no time to linger.

She was disturbed, therefore, to see a man who had got up from a pew at the front of the church halt in the aisle and look towards her. He was waiting to speak to her, she felt sure. Going to ask her what she was doing in his church, more than likely. Or ask a lot of questions.

Confused, she got to her feet and moved towards the door. She did not look up as she hurried past the waiting figure. But he called after her.

'Katie?' It was Mr Olds. The Archbishop himself could not have covered her in more confusion. 'What are you doing here?'

What could she tell him? If she explained it would seem like begging, and she wasn't reduced to that yet.

'Saying a prayer for my sister, sir,' she said. That at least was true.

He smiled. 'You're a good lass, Katie.' He jammed his hat on his head, and wrapped his coat around him. 'I haven't seen you in church before.'

'No, sir, we were chapel at home.' She stopped, abashed. Now he would ask why she hadn't gone to the chapel here.

But instead he said softly. 'Yes, one does turn to prayer, doesn't one? I think I've come here every day since poor Mary died, and then when Eva took sick . . .'

Katie felt a rush of warmth for this man, so like her own father in his loss, and before she had thought she had reached out a comforting hand to his arm. It was a momentary touch, before she recollected herself and withdrew it, blushing and confused. 'Oh, I'm sorry, sir, whatever am I thinking of?'

He looked at her for a moment, and she was startled to see tears on his lashes. 'You were thinking of me, Katie, and I appreciate it. Just like you think of my girl, Eva. She's fond of you.'

Katie smiled, glad of the change of subject. 'I'm fond of her. She's a quick scholar, Mr Olds. She's learning to read ever so quick. In no time at all you won't be needing me to read to her.'

Mr Olds looked away, as if troubled, and when he went on it was in an altered tone. 'Yes, that was something I wanted to discuss with you, Katie. You do a lot of sewing work, don't you?'

'Yes sir.' Katie could not keep the dismay out of her voice. What had she said that for? Now he would think of getting a governess, or sending Eva to school. Still, she comforted herself, that couldn't be till next year. Or could it? His next words sent a chill to her heart.

'You've got a lot of work in the next three weeks or so, I've no doubt, with Christmas coming up?'

She heard herself say, through dry lips, 'Enough to manage, sir.'

'So you wouldn't have any extra time to spare?'

She could hardly believe her ears. 'Extra?'

He seemed to be avoiding her eyes. 'Well, it seems to have been a great success, and it would be good for Eva. The doctor said she could start to have a teacher a couple of days a week, and I wondered . . . I don't suppose it would be possible . . . ?'

She gazed at him, dumbstruck. He seemed to misinterpret her silence, because he went on, 'I would pay, of course. Two days a week, I could manage three and six. And your lunch, naturally.'

Katie was already making delighted calculations, three and six for her teaching, that covered the rent already, and she would still have four clear days for sewing. And two lunches a week meant less food to find. All this for work that was no work, because she loved it. She found herself nodding, almost too full for words.

She saw his face clear, and then he frowned again. 'And there's your sewing,' he said. 'I couldn't expect you to do that too, though you've done wonders with it. I'll send the rest of it out. Perhaps Mrs Lomas might know somebody.'

She was about to say 'I'll do it,' when inspiration struck, and she said slowly, 'I know someone, sir.' Two afternoons a week for Fanny would be a great security, and that way they did not even lose the income.

He nodded. 'I'll leave it to you, then. How soon can you start?'

She longed to say, 'This afternoon,' but it was impossible. This week there were too many clients, but with a little juggling . . . 'Monday, sir?'

He beamed. He was as pleased as she was. 'Well, are you walking my way?'

She hesitated and then shook her head. 'There's something I've got to do,' she said. She must slip back into the church to whisper her thanks.

He smiled. 'Monday, then.'

Katie lived through the next few days in a dream. How she didn't make mistakes in her sewing she would never know. Her mind was already busy with a thousand schemes for teaching Eva, memories of her own schooling, and little tricks she had developed to help Carrie and Willie.

But Monday did not go at all as she had hoped. On Sunday afternoon, Fanny suddenly turned pale and clapped a hand to her stomach.

'I'm all right,' she said when Katie asked. 'Something I ate.'

But as the day drew on it was clear that she was not all right. The pains grew sharper and longer, and by Monday morning Fanny was moaning in agony, clenching her fists until her palms bled, the sweat standing on her forehead and her face white as chalk.

Katie watched her in panic. She had stoked the fire, as she had seen Mrs Tremble do, and set the kettle to boil. There was a clean sheet set on the bed, and another – purchased from the pawnbroker and boiled for the purpose – torn into neat strips on the table. But beyond that Katie knew no more than Fanny, now sobbing in terror as well as torment. How animals were born she knew from her childhood. But how to help?

She wanted to go for Mrs Williams, but Fanny grasped her hand, imploring her to stay. Only when a great gush of blood and water burst out to flood the sheet Katie could bear it no longer. She opened the door and fled down the stairs.

Mrs Williams was standing in the hallway, gazing up as Katie came clattering down. 'What's the commotion?'

'It's Fanny,' Katie said. 'The baby's coming.'

Mrs Williams' pale eyes lit up. 'Have you lined a drawer or something to put it in?'

Katie shook her head. The arrival of the child had seemed somehow so remote. She hadn't thought of anywhere to put it.

Mrs Williams tutted. 'Well, I never did!' She was up the stairs in a moment. 'We'll have that clean sheet for a start, and you can line a drawer and make a cup of tea . . .' Her presence was reassuring, and Katie was grateful. Even Fanny seemed a little calmer. 'Now let's have a look . . .' Katie realised with surprise that the woman was enjoying herself.

'Now,' Mrs Williams said, 'you save your strength, Mrs Trembath. It's all going nicely, but it'll be a little while yet. Is there someone expecting you, young Katie?'

Katie's eyes opened in alarm. Of course. Her first day with Eva. She nodded.

'Well, you'd better get over and tell them you can't be there today. I'll sit with your sister while you go, and after you can come down and fetch me when things start to happen.'

Start to happen? It seemed to Katie, flinging on a shawl and bonnet and rushing down the street that things were happening already, and she was hot and flustered by the time she reached Fore Street. Whatever would Mr Olds say? She blurted out her apologies to a startled Peabody.

'Well, you get back to her!' Peabody said. 'I'll tell Mr Olds.'

Katie needed no second bidding. She was in Back Lane in no time, and into the house. For a moment she turned cold. There was the ominous silence that she remembered from the Terrace, and she fled up the stairs with her heart in her mouth. Then a groan from Fanny. She would never have believed a groan could have been such a welcome sound. She thrust open the bedroom door.

Fanny was lying back, half-covered, on the bed, gripping a piece of sheet which Mrs Williams had looped over the bedpost. Katie could see her thrown-back head, and the veins standing blue on the damp pale forehead.

'Come in do,' Mrs Williams said, 'And shut that draught. You're just in time. She's . . .'

But she was interrupted by a roar from Fanny, a long wailing roar that ended in a gasp. Mrs Williams darted forward and picked up something purple and wriggling. She dangled it from one hand and smacked it sharply. It gave a sharp, feeble cry.

Fanny was lying limp and gasping, but there was a slow smile on her strained face. Mrs Williams was winding a strip of sheet around the long rope-like cord which still attached mother and baby.

'Now you watch this, young Katie, and you won't be needing me so much another time.' She picked up Katie's scissors which had been standing in a bowl of hot water. 'There! Now,' she handed Katie the tiny squirming thing, 'you clean up your nephew while I see to your sister. And wrap him up warm before he catches his death.'

Katie obeyed. The little body was so small that she was half afraid it would break, but she managed to clean it and wrap it in Mrs Williams' little robe. Fanny stretched out her arms, and took the child to her breast.

Suddenly, there was a knock on the street door. Mrs Williams was still clucking round the room, bundling up linen and making tea, so Katie went down, half-glad of an excuse. Her hands were shaking with a mixture of fright, joy and relief.

Mr Olds came into the hall, twisting his hat in his hands. 'Mrs Lomas told me where to find you. Is there anything . . .' he began.

'It's a boy,' Katie said, feeling the tears streaming down her face.

'Don't cry,' he said, but she was trembling, and she stepped into his arms like a child.

England looked grey. George had never remembered it so grey. Sky, sea, stone, streets, even the people huddling against the misty rain. So grey, so strangely small and circumscribed after the great sprawling acres of the veldt.

He shifted uneasily in his seat. The carriage was comfortable, but the journey chafed him, even more in mind than body. He had been unprepared for the reception waiting for them at the dockside, bands and parades and children waving flags. A ship full of returning soldiers, hardly one of them unscarred. And then suddenly, this. No longer a wounded officer, merely a limping English gentleman with a stick, rattling towards Cornwall through the wet, tedious afternoon.

And then, unexpectedly, there it was. The curve of the bay, the Mount, the dear familiar huddle of the town. And as the train hissed to a halt in the busy bustle of the station he could already see Papa pacing the platform. Papa. His father, and Kernerwek's. With a sigh, he opened the carriage door and summoned a porter.

Papa saw him and smiled. George limped towards him, and before Papa could offer him an embrace, extended his hand. Papa grasped it warmly.

'Welcome home, my boy. It's good to see you. Your mother's invited some people for supper as a little celebration. Insisted, though I said you'd be tired, so she's kept it to ten. Ourselves and the Selwoods, Old Mrs Selwood, and some friend of Caroline's, made no end of money in the Crimea. I don't care for the fellow, he has no conversation, but your mother's cock-a-hoop over it. You know what she's like.'

George nodded. 'You said ten.'

'There's a daughter. Striking girl, but too pushy for my taste. Still, your mother likes her, and it balances the table.'

The girl had been invited for him, George realised, as they sat down to the meal. Morwenna Poldair. She was, as his father said, striking, but her bold eyes were not for him. It was Robert for whom she laughed, talked, sparkled. And Robert knew it. No one else seemed aware, least of all Caroline who prattled happily while Robert and Morwenna smiled towards her, and locked glances over her head.

George pleaded a pain in his leg and excused himself straight after dinner. Mama looked furious, but he no longer cared for social niceties. It was, after all, his homecoming.

His fire was lit and his bed turned down by a little redhaired maid, one of the three girls he had seen waiting at table. He shooed her away, and sat for a long time in the armchair staring into the fire and thinking.

Robert looked in on his way to bed. 'Still up, old man? Thought you'd gone off to get your beauty sleep. Caused no end of a stir – wounded soldier and all that, Caroline was quite smitten.'

George looked at his brother as if for the first time. He took in the handsome face, the careless eyes, the slack, sensuous lips. He thought of Caroline, of Morwenna, of that cruel trick he had played on Katie, and a little flicker of rage and disgust stirred in him.

'What happened to the Warren girls?' he said, as if Robert had never spoken.

His brother laughed, a suggestive, dismissive chuckle. 'Mama had to get rid of them,' he said lightly. 'Got themselves in cub.'

George got to his feet. 'Did they?'

'Yes,' Robert said lightly. 'They . . .'

George hit him.

Robert staggered back, his hand to his jaw. 'What was that for?'

'For Caroline. And Fanny. And Katie. You, wasn't it?'

He half expected a blow, but Robert just said, 'Don't be absurd. I'm going to bed.'

George couldn't sleep, that night or the next. Robert avoided him. George spent a morning with Mama who patted the sofa and pleaded with him to tell her about the war, and sent the maid for sal volatile when he was foolish enough to try. With Papa he was constrained.

At last he got out of the house and took the dog cart out. He intended to go to the farm, but he turned as if drawn by invisible threads to the Terrace and the well. It seemed unchanged from his first visit, three and a half years before.

This time he knew the door. A woman opened it, a tall fierce witch of a woman whose frown turned to a scowl when he gave his name and asked after the Warren girls.

'Trevarnon, are you? Some employers you turned out to be. Well, they're gone, and not coming back, and I'll thank you to do the same.' And she slammed the door.

George went slowly and painfully back to the cart. Served him right perhaps. What business had he to come here?

'Mister?' It was a girl, about sixteen, thin and graceless in a thick skirt and a coat two sizes too large. Her manner, though, was gentle, and she offered him a hesitant smile. He paused. 'I couldn't help hearing you talk to Lally. You're from Trevarnon?'

He nodded. 'George Trevarnon. I was asking after the Warren girls.' He made a swift decision. 'The second one especially,' he said, thinking of Fanny and Katie. He had forgotten, if he ever knew, the existence of Meg. 'I hear she may be in trouble.'

She gave him a sideways glance. 'Yes, it's true. That's why your family turned her off. Surprised you didn't know that – but you've been off at the war, haven't you? I remember Katie saying. I'm a friend of hers, Carrie Tremble my name is.'

'So, my brother was right.'

'Oh yes, she's having a baby, right enough, if she haven't had it already, but,' she glanced down the street, 'the father's coming back from America to marry her as soon as maybe and they're off to Australia. Lally don't know that though, at least not yet, so don't you go saying.'

128

'And what about the eldest girl?' George said through dry lips. It was polite to ask about Fanny.

The girl looked surprised. 'Married and living in America. Has been for a long time.' She hesitated, 'I shouldn't be talking to you perhaps, sir . . . that Lally'd scalp me if she knew. But I was a friend of Katie's . . .'

He nodded absently. 'Do you see her?'

'Not often, sir, on account of she's living in Truro, but with this wedding and everything I do see them sometimes . . .'

He took out a sovereign and pressed it into her hand. 'If you see her, give her that from me. Tell her to buy something for the baby. If not, I'm sure you can find a use for it.'

He drove off before she could say more, feeling as empty and desolate as the moors. He went to the farm and tried to take an interest in winter broccoli.

That evening he apologised to Robert for his outburst. Robert was surprisingly forgiving about it, but nothing was ever quite the same again.

PART THREE : 1902–1903

CHAPTER THIRTEEN

It was a strange Christmas. Fanny was too taken up with Nicholas and her sewing to think of anything else, and it was left to Katie to make what she could of the season.

Even Katie's heart wasn't in it. At home Christmas had always been a family time, and even the last years at Trevarnon there had been a bustle and rush, with Cook in a frenzy of gravy and giblets, and Ruby eyeing the best brandy set aside to light the pudding. This year there would just be the two sisters and Nicholas, and the little attic room had never seemed so bleak.

All the same, she did her best. She went for a walk the Sunday before Christmas, and came back with her arms full of green branches from the hedgerows and a barrel hoop she had found in the stream. She sat down at the table and wound the greenery into a circle, as she had seen her mother do, decked it with ribbon and mistletoe and hoisted it to the ceiling where it dangled incongruously among the drying baby clothes.

Fanny was delighted, but Katie eyed it sadly. Mother had always had oranges and sugarplums hanging from the hoop, strung by cotton, to be plucked and eaten on Christmas day, but there was no money now for such treats. Still, there were the filiberts harvested from the hedges on autumn afternoons, and fresh pippins and new eggs and a big thick slice of cooked pork from one of the farms. There was even an extra sixpence set aside in the box on the mantelpiece for a tin of pineapple for Christmas tea. It was as festive as she could make it.

Fanny was no help. There was Nicholas, of course, but she was in a strange and secretive mood altogether – bundling away her sewing whenever Katie came into the room, and avoiding any questions with an irritating smile. Katie would have suspected her of sewing for her own wedding, if she hadn't glimpsed the material – a great length of grey woollen suiting, which Fanny could never have afforded, and would not have chosen if she could.

Katie put the thought out of her mind. She did not like to dwell on the idea of Fanny's marriage. It would be so lonely without her. And there was the money. How could she continue to live here and teach Eva once Fanny had gone?

Still, that was a problem for another day. Today it was Christmas Eve, a damp chill morning, with mist that hung in dismal clouds, and rolled at the windows from the evil-smelling river at the end of the lane. Katie got out of bed quietly, so as not to wake Fanny – Nicholas had woken more than once to be fed. She dressed quickly, stirred the fire to warm the room and heated the kettle for a drop of tea. It was late – her own sleep had been disturbed – and she had scarcely time to swallow a crust of bread before the clock was striking eight and it was time for her to go.

She folded a piece of newspaper into her boots, where they were letting in water, laced them on, and wrapped her shawl around her to keep the damp from the faded skirt and blouse. There were four packets on the mantelshelf, offcuts from Mrs Lomas, hemmed to handkerchiefs for the folk at Number Twenty-three Fore Street. She dropped them into her frail. One for Peabody, one for Mabel, one with a lace corner for Eva, and another, larger one. For a moment she hesitated. She would never have dared offer a gift to the Trevarnons. Then, with a swift movement she swept it, too, into the basket. It would be accepted, as it was given, with gratitude.

Then she went to the box where their carefully hoarded savings were kept. She would buy the pineapple on the way home, and maybe even a few sweetmeats. Being Christmas Eve, she was working only until midday.

The box was empty.

Katie stared, unable to believe her eyes. In the bed Fanny slept on, her face untroubled.

'Fanny!' Katie's voice was sharp. 'What have you done with that sixpence?'

But Fanny did not stir, and with a sigh, Katie turned away closing the door softly behind her.

The chill of the morning seemed to have seeped into her heart. What had Fanny used the money for? Extra coals perhaps? Or milk? No, they had enough for their needs. Some frippery, more likely.

She felt angry and depressed as she walked through the streets. They were decorated for Christmas, with bold letters on the shopfronts, and the shopkeepers sporting holly in their hair or on their apron-strings. The toy-shop window had a mechanical Father Christmas endlessly lifting a parcel under a gaslamp tricked out to look like a lantern. But Katie hardly noticed.

She was still frowning when she got to Number Twenty-three. Mabel saw her coming and flung open the door.

'You're to come downstairs first.' And Katie was ushered into the spicy warmth of the kitchen.

The room was alive with breakfast, but Peabody was already stacking buns onto a cooling rack in delicious clouds of fruity steam. It was a striking contrast to the scene Katie had just left, and she hesitated.

'Well, come on in then,' Peabody said, 'and don't stand there looking like a wet week. Eva's dying to see you, and Mr Olds is looking for you too, but I won't have it said that anyone set foot in this house of a Christmas Eve without a morsel of figgy pudding. Here!' The steaming cake was thrust into Katie's hand, and she bit into it. It was the taste of childhood, sweet and spiced, and speckled with fruit. Katie blinked back the tears and could hardly voice her thanks.

'Get along with you, and a merry Christmas,' Peabody said, scowling happily. 'And mind you come down before you go, you hear?'

Katie went upstairs, cheered in spite of herself by the warmth of her welcome. To her surprise the drawing room door was open, a blazing fire was in the hearth, and Eva herself, painfully thin but glowing with excitement, was sitting propped with cushions in one of the big fireside chairs.

'Katie! Doctor says I can get up for an hour or two. And I'm to come down for dinner tomorrow, and Father says I can watch you dress the tree.'

Dress the tree? Yes, there it was in a big bucket in the corner of the room. Not a gigantic tree, like the one at Trevarnon, which was so high it had to stand in the stairwell; but a good sturdy tree, six feet or more. And at its foot, a box in which Katie could see a dusty pile of little ornaments.

'Well now, Katie, are you up to the job?' It was Mr Olds, coming in with his hands full of paperchains. 'I shall never manage on my own.' And he handed her the end of a chain, and went to the tree as though it were the most natural thing in the world.

There was no teaching that morning. Instead Katie was busy with scores of little candles in iron holders, miniature rocking horses and drummer boys, bells and bugles. There were scarlet ribbons, and then a dozen tiny boxes, each to be filled with a dragee from the box of sugared almonds on the table, and hung among the boughs. Last of all, there was an angel, no bigger than Katie's hand, which Mr Olds had to wire to the top of the tree by standing on a footstool, and even then it hung sideways, as though it were trying to fly. It was a wonderful tree.

Eva was enchanted. Mabel and Peabody were called up to admire it, and then Eva was so tired that she had to be carried to bed by Mr Olds. Mabel and Katie helped her undress and she was asleep before they left the room.

Mr Olds was in the drawing room when they came down.

'Katie!' She went in. Her heart was thumping. She had been embarrassed by his presence ever since the day when Nicholas was born, and she had run so precipitately into his arms. He had never alluded to it again, but it seemed to her that since then he looked at her with different eyes.

He was looking at her now. She felt her cheeks flame.

'Thank you for helping me with the tree.'

'I'm paid to help.' It sounded ungracious, and she said hastily, 'Eva loved it.'

He smiled, 'She's making good progress. Largely thanks to you, I think. And this new doctor, go-ahead ideas he's got. Says she should go out for a bit, as soon as the weather improves. She'll need more attendance then.' He looked at her, that special searching look, again. 'You will – won't you – come to us full time? Live-in?'

'Oh, I couldn't!' The words were out in an instant, though it was hard to say why not. She had been half-planning to find a live-in post when Fanny went. There was no reason why she should not come to Number Twenty-three. Unless . . . But she said, 'It wouldn't be right.'

He seemed to read her thoughts. 'Eva is fond of you, Katie. We all are.' He turned away as if he were changing the subject. 'I haven't decorated a tree since my wife died. We used to do it together. I didn't think I could face it again. But you made it easy.'

She coloured again. 'We did it for Eva.'

'Of course,' he said gravely. 'For Eva. But this . . .' his voice was suddenly hearty, 'is for you. A Christmas box.' He dived behind the ottoman and reappeared with a huge parcel. Katie staggered under the weight of it. 'Not now,' he said. 'Tomorrow.' He dived again, and came up with two more parcels, for Peabody and Mabel. 'They shall have theirs under the tree.'

It was so unexpected, so different from the Trevarnon Christmas, that she could only blush and stammer. At Trevarnon it was so cold, so formal, lining up on Christmas morning to shake hands and curtsey, while Mr Trevarnon called your name, and the mistress handed you your half-crown in an envelope, and the material for your year's uniform. This was so hearty, so unforced, that she was brave enough to burrow in her basket and bring out her little packages to be laid reverently under the tree.

Then she must go downstairs. There was a notebook from Mabel, and a slab of fresh seedcake which Peabody had baked with Mr Olds' connivance, and a package from Eva containing a handstitched bookmark. Katie could scarcely carry her bundles and basket, and Mr Olds insisted on walking part of the way with her to carry her packages, as though she was gentry.

'You are very good,' she said as they parted.

How good, she realised the next day, when the package was opened. A fur monkey for Nicholas, a box of figs, and a whole new uniform. A double gift, as she realised, recognising the fine woollen cloth, for it was Fanny who had secretly been given the commission for the sewing, not only for Katie's own uniform, but for Peabody's and Mabel's as well.

'I do believe Mr Olds is sweet on you, Katie,' Fanny said, as they sat on the bed and opened the bulging brown-paper parcel, tied up with string and sealing wax. 'Whoever heard of giving skirt, blouse and cape, all ready-made, and new boots too.'

'Nonsense!' Katie said firmly. 'He's done the same for us all. I saw the parcels.' But she knew in her heart of hearts that Fanny spoke the truth.

And a few minutes later, when Fanny produced not only a tin of pineapple purchased with her own profits, but also a copy of Mr Kipling's *Just So Stories* 'to read aloud to Eva' the mystery of the missing sixpence was solved. A strange Christmas, but a happy one.

George was chafing. He had been chafing ever since he got back from Africa. After the excitement, the danger, the strange and different circumstances of war, life at Trevarnon seemed empty and tame.

He tried to interest himself in the farm, and spent hours with the farm manager discussing the merits of seed potatoes. The man was civil and patient, but the place had run successfully for two years without George, and he could not persuade himself that he was indispensable now. There were matters at the mine calling for attention, but that was Robert's affair these days, and Robert was entirely intent on his new house and his fiancée, when he wasn't flirting with Morwenna Poldair. Papa had retired into himself more than ever – which was perhaps just as well. George feared the day Papa would ask one question too many about life in Africa . . .

The wound in his leg meant that George could no longer even gallop out his frustrations on horseback, as he would once have done. Instead he was obliged to submit to the social routine. Morning calls with Mama, dinners and dances. Especially, he noted, dinners and dances at households with eligible daughters. More and more, he was chafing.

Particularly he was chafing at this New Year house party. He was used, by now, to being a kind of social passport. As a wounded veteran and officer he found himself accepted at county houses where Mama and Robert were ecstatic about being asked. 'The best circles,' Mama had said triumphantly, and Papa didn't care as long as there was good food, and there was plenty of that. But George suspected that this invitation to the Poldair house was Morwenna's doing, and had more to do with Robert's dark eyes than with anyone's social standing.

Perhaps, he thought morosely, it was all very well for the London folk who had come down on the train expressly to spend four days with the Poldairs. It was all new to them. But for people who lived only twenty miles distant it was all very familiar, without the advantages of your own interests and possessions.

For it seemed to George that there was nothing to do at Goldmarten. Except eat. They seemed to devote the whole day to it.

It began at eight thirty, with tea and toast sent up with the shaving-water. Then there was breakfast, hours of it, porridge and fish and omelette and kedgeree and cold meats and scones and jam and out-of-season fresh nectarines from God-knows-where. There was scarcely time to make a damp sortie to the gardens or the church before it was time to change for luncheon. And what a luncheon. Ptarmigan and champagne, cold meats and salads, and of course soup or sorbet and a dessert or two to stave off starvation.

A brief break for bridge or billards, and then tea in the drawing room, with egg sandwiches and cucumber sandwiches and five kinds of cake.

This year it was too wet to walk it off in the garden (all the fault of Mr Marconi and his radio signals, so everyone said) so in the afternoons Morwenna arranged an amusement, music or charade, while the older generation exchanged small-talk or slumbered in the library.

Then it was time to dress for dinner, and eat again. Course after course of it, soup and fish and game and beef and sorbets and puddings and cheeses and fruit, all set before them as though food were a novelty soon to go out of fashion.

An hour or two of music and dancing, in which George could not join, and then midnight brought supper, spirits for the gentlemen and Vichy water or fruited punch for the ladies. And when they rolled bloated to bed, there was the night tray on the bedside table, with a sustaining stock of sandwiches and fruit.

There had always been a good table at Trevarnon and in the officers' mess, but George had never seen so much food in one place. It was enough for an army. In fact, he could remember days in the field, especially in the last month of the African war, when a single cow and a sack of rotting potatoes would have to be enough for an army. He thought back to the Brunner's party, the dozens of servants, the shortage of good food. All this plenty seemed somehow disconcerting.

Even so, he might have enjoyed himself if it had not been for Robert and Morwenna. Their behaviour hovered permanently just this side of indiscretion. Eyes that locked over the luncheon table. Hands that brushed at cards. Dances that lingered a little too long and too close. Caroline affected not to notice, but became more and more withdrawn, and from time to time Morwenna flirted openly with Peter Gillard, who was escorting her, and diverted public attention. But George was acutely aware of it.

So was Robert, evidently. There was that tell-tale spot of crimson in his cheeks, that extra sparkle in his eyes. He had always loved a gamble, a little flirtation with danger, and George could see that he was enjoying this one. So when Morwenna tricked herself out for a charade in scarlet petticoats, and hooped her skirt up to show her ankles like a Parisienne guttersnipe to represent 'Revolution', George did not clap as readily as the rest.

'You are a curmudgeon, George,' Morwenna said, throwing herself down in the chair beside him. 'I'm sure I thought that was the greatest fun. Didn't you, Robert?'

And Robert smiled and glowed and gazed at Morwenna, while Caroline acted out her charade, something dull and demure about milkmaids, in a long white smock.

If it was not Morwenna, it was Peter Gillard and his talk of motorcars. He had an obsession about them. He had seen one, he said, on the road to Plymouth. 'No horses, you know, and travelling at such a clip. I stopped and spoke to the automobilist and he offered to take me for a spin. Twenty miles an hour is nothing to these machines, and the modern ones are so comfortable, with hoods, so that one can venture even in the rain. When the weather is better, and the roads are dry again, I swear I shall have one for myself. There are several in the county already. It would be quite practical, you know, to set off from Penzance after breakfast, go to Truro, and be back again for lunch, if you had a good run of it and no mishaps.'

'Such fun!' Morwenna said, tearing her eyes away from Robert for a moment. 'You absolutely must come again for my birthday weekend in March, all of you. Peter shall bring his car and take us all for a spin, if he has found one by then.'

'A motorcar?' Robert said. 'Now that would be something.'

'You're not thinking of one too, are you, Trevarnon?' asked Peter Gillard.

'Not me. A married man's got too much responsibility,' Robert said with a laugh, but George had seen the gleam in his brother's eye. Robert wanted a motorcar as much as he wanted Morwenna.

'I tell you, Lally,' Davy said, pouring warm water into a basin to bathe his chapped hands, 'I heard it from Noah's father. Coming home he is, as soon as ever he can find a ship, and they are to be married and go to Australia. Poor Fanny. I wonder is the child born yet?'

Lally sniffed. 'Poor Fanny, indeed! Poor child more like. Brought up by a couple of heathens and living the Lord knows where.' She might have said more, but Davy's look silenced her. She turned away, and skewered the eyes out of the potatoes like a demon tormenting sinners.

Davy said nothing, but went back to the kettle. It was boiling now, and he added the steaming water to the bowl, sprinkled the balsam into it, and bent forward, gulping in great lungfuls of the fragrant steam. Lally put down the knife and came over with a towelling cloth.

'My dear life, Davy, put this over your head and get the benefit. You'll catch your death one of these days. It's all this standing out in the rain gossiping to Henry Trembath for hours – and all for folk who are no better than they should be. Noah Trembath, indeed. Some tale that is, this late in the day.'

Davy took a last deep breath, and pushed the bowl away. 'I've known it three months or more,' he said evenly.

Lally whirled round to gaze at him, her triumph vanished. 'You knew, and never told me?'

He stood up and put on his coat and scarf. 'I did.'

She was still staring. 'Why didn't you say?'

He was lacing his boots as he spoke. 'Because there's times, Lally, when I think your tongue, for all its Christian prating, has got a devil in it. And when my daughter comes home, married, with my grandchild, she'll be welcome in my house. And I'll thank you to make her so.'

Lally pulled her lips together and said, 'Well, I know my duty, I suppose, even if I'm to be called names for it. But I don't know why she'd come home now, suddenly, when she's stayed away all these months.'

He said slowly, 'Because I'm going to write to her and ask her to. And I know what you're going to say, Lally Warren, so save your breath to cool your pasty. Harry had a letter back from Noah, with Fanny's address, so young Willie can write the letter for me. He can cipher better than I can these days, or you either. And if I know my Fanny, she'll come, so you'd better make up your mind to it.' He jammed on his hat.

His sister said, dully, 'Where are you off? I was going to make you some more blackcurrant cordial for that cough.' She gestured towards the jam standing ready in the cup, with its precious slice of lemon already in it. 'I'm just waiting for this kettle to boil to pour over.'

Davy grunted. 'I'll have it when I come back. I'm going to see Carrie for this address. Should have done it long ago. And when Rosa wakes up I'm going to take her down Crowdie's to get the milk.'

Lally put down the swede she was slicing and wiped her hands on her pinny. 'It's the middle of winter,' she said, with a spark of her old defiance. 'It's dark. You know it is – that's how you come to be home this time of day. Besides, it's like Greenland out there. You want the child to catch your cold? Isn't it enough to have you coughing your heart out?'

'You'll turn her into a mollycoddle, afraid of her own shadow. You can't wrap the girl in cotton-wool the rest of her life!' But he did not persist, and when he went out he did not go to Carrie's. Instead he walked up over the stiles to meet Willie, clambering home with the water-barrel, and they went together to Crowdie's. He asked Willie about the letter, and the boy glowed with pride and pleasure.

Davy felt his heart lift. 'Come on, my son,' he said, giving Willie a playful punch. 'Race you to the tree.'

He was still a good runner, but he let himself be beaten, and the child's clear laughter, ringing in the dusk, was more medicine than all the balsam and blackcurrant in the world.

CHAPTER FOURTEEN

The March wind was more lion than lamb, as Mother would have said. Too cold today to take Eva out in the invalid carriage to the Waterfall Gardens, to watch the early ducklings swimming on the Leats. The poor child would miss her 'walk', which she dearly loved after so many years of being confined to the sick-room. Peabody fretted and fumed and said she would 'catch her death', but Mr Olds' doctor was full of revolutionary ideas about fresh air, saying it was the latest thing, and was even going to be used in curing consumption.

Today, though, Peabody would have her way. The wind was strong enough to bend the daffodils half double, and the waxy pink flowers of the 'came-earliers' were battered and bruised brown. Even Katie's new grey cape could not keep out the chill.

She glanced down the street, half expecting to see Mr Olds. Since Christmas Eve she had several times encountered him in the street on the way to and fro between Number Twenty-three and his office down on the Quay, and he had walked her a little on the way. She had put it down to coincidence, until Peabody's meaning glances, and Mabel's giggling glee had convinced her of the truth.

This morning there was no sign of him. Secretly, that was a relief. Mr Olds was a kind man, like her father, which was why she had turned to him so naturally in distress. But he must not suppose there was anything more. It wouldn't be seemly. She must find some way of letting him know that she preferred to walk home alone.

She stepped out across the road, dodging the street-cleaner on his cart, who stopped sprinkling water to let her past. She lifted up her hem from the wet cobbles and turned towards Princes Street.

As she passed the 'Iron Duke' she averted her eyes, as she always did. It was bad enough, she thought, that men had to have these things built in public places, without having them stuck in the middle of the road and decorated with wrought iron, like something to be proud of. She had said as much to Fanny once, but Fanny just laughed and said she wished they'd build things like that for women too. Really, having Nicholas hadn't made Fanny any more ladylike!

All the same, Katie could never walk past without dreading she might meet the butcher, or the baker's boy, or worst of all Mr Olds, coming from behind the iron screen. She turned her head away and examined the passing carts and coaches with elaborate interest.

There was a brougham trotting past, the coachman sitting bolt upright on his box, immaculate in his dark green coat and black top hat, his whip held motionless and upright in his right hand. The cab slowed for a moment as it passed her, and she saw into it clearly. Two men were inside, squeezed into the narrow interior, both laughing uproariously. One of them looked at her appreciatively, and murmured something to his companion. He turned, leaned forward, and Katie found herself looking into the bold, laughing eyes of Robert Trevarnon.

She saw recognition dawn.

Confused, she dropped her eyes and stepped back, and the brougham moved off. She turned and hurried away, but even as she did she heard the trotting hooves slow to a stop, and heard the coachman's 'Whoa there!' and his grunt as he clambered down to open the carriage door.

She did not look back, but hastened on, skirts flying. Two women with baskets stepped back in alarm as she hustled past them, and the telegraph boy was almost startled off his bicycle. She did not slacken speed until she had put the warm bulk of the baker's horse between herself and the brougham, by skirting round the edge of the breadcart as the animal ambled gently along its accustomed route, stopping of its own accord at every customer's door.

'Katie!' Her own name made her jump, but it was only Mr Olds coming out of the tobacconist, a sheaf of building plans in one hand as usual, to fall into step beside her.

Secure in his presence, she stole a look behind her. Robert and his companion were standing in the roadway laughing. For an awful moment she thought they might call after her, but they looked from her to her employer, and began to walk back to the brougham, still waiting up past the 'Iron Duke'.

'Those two bothering you, are they?' Mr Olds said, following the direction of her glance.

She flushed. 'It's nothing. An old friend of Fanny's, that's all.'

'Well, any trouble, you come to me,' Mr Olds said. He took her elbow protectively with his free hand, and she made no attempt to withdraw it. Nothing was said, that day or any other, about being happy to walk alone.

That night she went home by a different route.

Robert stood for a moment beside the brougham, watching the retreating figure.

'I tell you, Gillard, I know her. Used to be a maid of ours.' He swung himself up into the carriage beside his friend.

'Doesn't seem very pleased to see you!' Gillard said.

'You can see why,' Robert said lightly. 'An assignation, no less.' He glanced at Gillard's face and could not resist the temptation to add, 'She was pleased enough to see me once.'

Gillard chuckled. 'More than once, I daresay.'

Robert was gratified. He enjoyed his reputation as a lady's man and 'regular fellow'. He laughed. 'Pity my brother wasn't here to see her. Always had a soft spot for her, I fancy.'

'Admiring from a distance while you moved in, eh?' Gillard said. 'Sounds like George. Though I must say I admire his taste. Damned pretty girl, that. Where is he, by the way? Thought he was invited to Goldmarten with us this weekend?'

Robert made a face. 'So he was. The Poldairs made a point of asking both of us, with it being Morwenna's birthday. No. Some damn-fool scheme about going up to Plymouth to see the rest of the Regiment come home. You know what these army types are like. Regiment first, last and always. Rather be out there fighting the Boers, than here at home with a bit of comfort. Missing a damned good weekend, that's all I can say.'

'Well, I shan't mourn him for one,' Gillard said. 'We'd never have come out to see this motor if George was of the party.' He leaned forward and tapped the little glass window. 'Drive on coachman. Hendra Farm. You know where it is, don't you? Smart as you can!' And the brougham jolted on.

It was stuffy in the tiny carriage, and Robert, accustomed to an open carriage or Papa's large four-in-hand, felt a little queasy. He had drunk too much port, perhaps, the night before – it was always a temptation at house parties, and at the Poldair party, more than most. He wished, at least, he had eaten a little breakfast.

'Shall you go to Fowey, next month?' he said. He had found that conversation distracted him from the lurching of the cab.

'I should say so! There's a black filly running that I mean to back. I've got five guineas on her. What do you say, Trevarnon?'

Robert laughed. 'I never wager on an empty stomach,' he said, but he could not suppress a sigh. The truth was that he could not lay his hands on five guineas if he'd a mind to. These first two months of running his own establishment at Lower Trevarnon had cost a fortune: food and drink had run away with his allowance, staff were a confounded expense, and being betrothed had meant a whole series of presents for Caroline. He had contrived to get himself invited elsewhere for as much of the time as possible, but even that entailed tipping the servants, and the hospitality would have to be returned in due course. After he was married, he told himself. And he'd have to settle to it soon. Selwood was getting restless: the marriage could not be delayed for much longer. He looked through the window at the coachman's shining buttons with increasing gloom.

'Cheer up, old man,' Gillard said. 'Almost there! We'll have time to look at this famous automobile and be back before the ladies have finished their kedgeree. I'm determined to have it, you know, if it will serve at all. Morwenna is quite ravished by the idea. The women are mad for motor-men, you know. I wonder you don't think of getting one yourself, Trevarnon.'

'Give me a horse, any time,' Robert said. Two hundred pounds, a motor-car might cost.

'Oh, your coachman could drive it, if you haven't a mind to,' Gillard said, rubbing salt into the wound. Robert affected a double dog-cart which he drove himself. He had never ceased to regret his pony.

He was saved from having to reply when the brougham turned sharply at a gate. 'Hendra Farm,' Robert said, and they jolted down the drive.

The moment he saw the automobile he was lost. It stood in the harness-room, sparkling in the dark blue livery with red-painted wheels. It looked so smart and modern, oddly short without the shafts for the horses, only the double loops of the springs projecting forward over the wheels. It had an open cabin with a polished bench and a little gate to climb into a separate seat behind the driver. Robert had never seen a motorcar close to before, and he watched in fascination as the farmer tinkered with this and that, fussed over the engine, poured water here and petroleum there from a series of cans strapped to the runningboard, and finally swung the heavy handle a dozen or so more times. The engine coughed suddenly into life, and as suddenly, died again.

Gillard was looking unimpressed. 'I say, you know, I daresay horses are a lot more reliable. Or maybe one ought to think of having a brand new machine. There must be a reason for selling this one, after all.'

'I'm buying a larger automobile, Mr Gillard,' the farmer said, sweating at the handle again. 'This one doesn't suit my wife. But it climbs hills and everything. Good as a coach. Just a little more adjustment, and then I can give you any trial you like. Almost brand new. It's a snip at a hundred guineas.'

But Gillard had lost interest. 'No, I don't think so. I saw a fellow with that new de Dion in Plymouth last month. Hood and leather seats. Think I'll have them drive it down. Better a new machine in the long run.' He was already climbing back into the brougham. 'Come on, Trevarnon.'

Robert was still staring at the motorcar. Where could a man get a hundred guineas?

'Come on, man,' Gillard said again. 'The ladies will have eaten all the muffins and be wanting us to escort them around the park.'

'Coming!' said Robert unwillingly. 'Though I'll bet you five shillings the ladies haven't missed us yet.'

'Thought you never wagered before breakfast,' Gillard said. 'But I'll take your money.'

He did too, because when they returned Caroline was looking for them, woefully, in the music-room. Robert had to listen to her play for almost an hour before she was placated. Morwenna joined them, and leaned over the piano, turning the pages.

The men went out after rabbits in the afternoon, and the ladies went riding. Morwenna scandalised the Selwoods by dressing in the new 'rational dress', a skirt divided like a man's trousers, and a coat cut like a hunting jacket.

'Much more modest,' she said. But there was nothing modest in the way she threw her leg over the saddle and rode her horse astride, like a man. Caroline, sitting sidesaddle in her riding dress, looked demure and dowdy beside her.

Why, Robert asked himself, had he ever been fool enough to get trapped into an engagement with Caroline when the world held Morwenna? Morwenna, whose very presence set his flesh aflame. Morwenna, who could buy and sell the Selwoods a dozen times over?

Images haunted him all afternoon, and he didn't down a single rabbit. Morwenna in her masculine dress, with her shining hair flying loose around her face, or beside the piano, allowing her wrap to slip an inch too far from her beautiful shoulders, turning the pages for Caroline and smiling only for him. The gleaming blue of the automobile, its steering wheel set like a dinnerplate atop its column, promising a whole new world. And most surprising of all, the grey-clad figure of Katie Warren, smart and slim, hastening away from him in a Truro street.

George sat down in the railway carriage with a sigh. Was it wrong of him, perhaps, to be making this trip? Certainly Mama thought so.

'George, how can you be so rude? Turning down a houseparty at the Poldairs', and Morwenna's birthday, too. Whatever will people think of us?'

'Oh, they'll understand,' he found himself saying. 'The last of the Regiment coming home and all that. I ought to be there. Didn't you read about the reception they gave the *Doll* when she came in last month? Hundreds of volunteers turned out to meet her, and most of the returned officers from the Regiment. It'll be the same this time. Dozens of people are going up for it. There's to be a proper reception; parades and banquets and speeches by the mayor. I expect there'll be a list of those attending published in the papers.'

That was cunning. Mama's ambition was to find her name in one of the society guest-lists printed in *The Times*. He pressed his advantage. 'Anyway,' he went on, 'Robert and Caroline have gone to the Poldairs'. I won't be missed. With this leg I can't dance, and I've been so dratted restless since I came home that I'm no asset.'

'Let him be,' Papa had said, when he heard of it. 'Chap should see his own regiment home if he wants to. He's not a child, Nellie.'

'Don't call me Nellie,' Mama retorted, and there the matter rested.

So here he was, on his way to Plymouth, while Robert and the others ate and drank and flirted at Goldmarten. Well, he was well out of it. He sat back as the train pulled out of the station.

Out of the station, round the curve into Mounts Bay. The storms had heaped the sand with wrack, deep slimy piles of weed, higher than a man's knee. The men were already at work, pitching the slippery fronds onto the carts for fertilizer, while their patient horses snorted and twitched.

Past Marazion town, where the sea, still fretted by the gales, rose into long angry rollers, which crashed in white fury against the rocks below. The carriage window was stained with salt by the flying spray.

It would be strange, seeing his old comrades again. It seemed a world away, the veldt, the war, Kernerwek. His mind ran on a thousand memories.

'Truro!' the voice said, and a new set of associations began. Katie. George felt a quickening of his pulse. 'She's living in Truro,' the girl in the Terrace had said.

Was she still here, somewhere, out there in that sprawl of houses and churches and inns? He even looked for her as the train crossed the stone arches of the brand-new viaduct, but he could see nothing beyond a blur of stone and a web of scaffolding on the top of the new cathedral. It would be finished soon. He might come up for the ceremony. The Prince of Wales was coming. Would Katie be there, somewhere among the watching crowds? Had she ever received the money he had sent?

'Odd thing,' said the clergyman opposite, misinterpreting his interest in the scene. 'They've left the pillars from the old wooden bridge they took down last year. Never move them now, you'll see. Still be there in a hundred years.'

George smiled agreement, but said nothing. He was not in the mood for conversation. He was still lost in his thoughts when the train pulled into Plymouth.

He had been here before, of course. Embarking for Africa, and even before that, once or twice as a boy. Even so, it didn't seem familiar. He left the train, commissioned a cab to take his luggage to the hotel, and walked slowly through the streets. There were crowds gathering and he had difficulty making his way to the dockside, but people gave way when they saw his stick, and he was there in time to see the ship edge gently into her berth. A great cheer went up as the heavy ropes were thrown ashore, and the last survivors of the First Devon and Cornwall Horse were home from the war.

The men came down the gangplank. Most marched, some limped. One or two had to be helped, leaning on the shoulders of comrades. There was no sign of the horses. There were one or two familiar faces from the hospital at Pietersburg, but there were some missing. Some who would never come home again. George sighed.

'Cheer up, man,' said a burly fellow at his side. 'Blooming heroes, they are. Give them a welcome home.' George smiled politely, and moved on into the crowd.

Everything was a-bustle. It was exactly as he had told Mama. There were bands at the dockside, and parades on the Hoe, and speeches and toasts and children waving flags. There was a banquet, to which he obtained an invitation, and he found himself with three young returning officers whom he slightly knew. They talked his language, knew the land he knew, but he was apart, no longer one of them. Still, they made him welcome, talked over old battles, drank the health of old friends in a bottle of port, and old horses in a second, third and fourth.

'I say, Trevarnon,' said a familiar voice. George looked up. Perhaps it was the port, but he couldn't place the handsome, slightly familiar Captain in front of him. 'Smith. Met you at the Brunner party. Hoped I'd see you here. Promised the Brunner girl I'd find you somehow. Stunning girl, wasn't she? Pity she was a blasted Boer. Engaged to one of Kruger's men I hear, and gone back to the farm now. Anyhow, she's sent a package for you. I was going to send it on through the Regiment, but as long as you're here I might as well look it out for you straight away. Let me know where you're messing, and I'll get it sent over first thing in the morning.'

'Good lord, Trevarnon,' one of his dinner companions said, when Smith had gone, 'you're a dark one. Have a girl in Pietersburg, did you? Lucky man! I wonder you ever came home!'

George gave him a wan smile, and soon afterwards pleaded a pain in his leg and said goodnight.

CHAPTER FIFTEEN

Katie told Fanny of her encounter as soon as she got home. 'Who do you think I saw today?' she said, ducking under the lines of wet baby-linen to set her parcel of sprats on the table.

Fanny looked up from sewing something in sprigged mustard muslin. 'I don't know, who? And don't holler, Katie, I've just got Nicholas to sleep.'

Katie untied her cape. 'Robert Trevarnon.' She cast a sidelong glance at her sister. 'Stopped his brougham and got out. I'm sure he recognised me.'

Fanny didn't look up, only her cheeks flamed a little redder. 'Well, if he's come to look for me, he's come too late. Noah'll be here on Friday, and Monday I'll be married and gone.'

Katie nodded, tossing the fish into the frying pan. 'Wasn't looking for you, I doubt. Still, funny to see him here.'

Fanny didn't answer, and after a minute she said, holding up her sewing for inspection, 'What do you think of this? Saw it in uncle's when I went to redeem the jug.' Fanny's flowered jug had seen the inside of the pawnbroker's very often in the last few months.

Katie looked at the work. 'You're never going to wear that? Muslin in March? You'll perish!'

Fanny laughed. 'Oh, I must have something pretty for the wedding. And I've got that plaid skirt from the tallyman. I'll change into that before I go and see Father. I'm some glad he got Willie to write – it won't seem so bad, leaving, somehow.'

Katie tossed the sprats and said, 'You mind you do change, now. You can just hear what Lally would have to say if she saw you gallivanting about in muslin at this time of the year, wedding or not. "Vanity, vanity sayeth the preacher." And don't you go telling her you've been buying from the tallyman, either. Never buy what you can't afford, that's her motto. Hello, who's this?'

It was Carrie, pushing open the door. 'Hello Katie, hello Fan. I smelt the frying, so I knew you were here. Mrs Williams let me in.'

'I'll set on some tea,' Katie said, 'and you'll stop and have some sprats? There's enough for three.'

'No,' Carrie said, 'I got to catch the train. Got to be back by nine. It's my half-day off, see. Only been up to St Austell for the afternoon to see Ernie. Hardly worth it, neither. Takes me half the day to get there, and the other half to get back. And now I've missed the early train, so I shan't see the inside of the shops in Penzance this week. Still, while I was here, I thought I'd stop by and see the baby, and wish you well, Fanny. I'm working Monday, so I shan't be able to come and see you away. Banns are up, though. Saw them last week when I went to see about posting ours. It's to be our wedding in three weeks.'

So then there were more congratulations, and Carrie was invited to admire the bride's wedding outfit. 'Woman must have been a giant,' Fanny said. 'The skirt was that big. A bit of skimping and I can cut a jacket from the piece I've taken out, and have a two piece costume, like you see them with in the papers.'

'You'll be having a trousseau, next,' said Carrie. 'Buy something with that guinea, did you?'

'Guinea?' Katie asked, almost dropping the frying pan. 'What guinea?'

'The guinea George Trevarnon sent,' Carrie said. 'I gave it to Fanny last time I was here. Don't look like that, Katie. It was hers. For her and the baby, he said.'

Katie began to concentrate very hard on serving the sprats. 'And you never told me, Fanny!'

Fanny coloured. 'Well, I owed the tallyman two weeks on the skirt, and I wanted a nightgown, and a new longcoat for Nicholas. Besides, I thought you might be upset, seeing he sent it to me and not to you. Mind you, it's my belief he found out Mr Robert owed me a guinea he never paid, and winkled it out of him somehow. Can't see why he'd send it me else.'

'Whatever are you on about, now, Fanny?' Katie said carefully. 'What do you mean, Mr Robert owed you a guinea?'

Fanny told her the story.

152

'You mean to say you let him dismiss us without even a word to Mrs Trevarnon? Whatever possessed you, Fanny? The Lord knows what tales he told about the pair of us!'

Fanny turned a sullen red. 'Well, it's no good you creating, Katie, it's too late now. And it's clear Mr George isn't holding anything against us, or he wouldn't have sent that guinea.'

'I suppose so,' Katie said. 'It was like him to think of it.' And, she thought to herself, it was a delicate way of letting her know he had not forgotten them. 'I wish you'd told me. We might have written to thank him.'

'Wouldn't have done no good,' said Fanny. 'Anyway, it's not too late. You could write to him now if you want.'

'Post is closed,' Katie objected, but the thought of writing to George brought the colour to her cheeks.

'I've got to walk past Trevarnon to get home,' Carrie said. 'I could deliver'n if you want.'

Katie took a page of her Christmas notebook and wrote. It was a short careful letter thanking Mr Trevarnon for his gift of money for the baby. She wrote it in her best copperplate hand, and signed it 'sincerely, Katie and Fanny Warren'. Then, after a moment's thought, she added their address. She did not expect an answer, but one could always hope.

George's rooms were in a small hotel not far from the Hoe. It was comfortable and clean, and had long associations with the army and navy, so that it had more of the atmosphere of a mess than of a lodging house. The guests were almost entirely retired officers, many of whom were also here to greet the Regiment, and most of the staff had served the flag at one time, so there was a pleasant military air to the dining-hall and the bars. There were deep, buttoned chairs in brown leather and copies of the London papers in the smoking room, and severe regimental counterpanes on the brass bedsteads.

Even the bathroom smelt familiarly of Macassar oil and bay-rum, just like the one at Regimental HQ in Pietersburg; although here the water was drawn for you from a modern gas geyser over the bath, which spouted steam like a bad tempered dragon, not hauled in and heated laboriously by sweating orderlies and kaffirs.

Breakfast was equally forthright and masculine: mushrooms, toast, kidneys and bacon, and tea, Indian and strong, was brought on a sturdy silver tray – not served in half a dozen fiddling china pots with beribboned labels denoting 'ginger', 'China' or 'Earl Grey' as it would have been at the Poldairs'.

George was beginning to enjoy himself. He had a serious conversation with a retired major about the problems in Serbia, discussed the future of horse-rearing in the Transvaal with a cavalry officer who had just returned, and then settled into a window seat with a good brandy and a copy of *The Times*. He had not admitted to himself how much he had missed regimental life.

The package arrived a little before lunch.

Its arrival startled him; he had succeeded in lulling himself into forgetting it. But when the boy arrived with it on a silver salver, he found that his hands were shaking as he took it and broke open the seals.

She had not written a great deal. Just a short note with grief and bewilderment in every word. And three photographs. One of himself, with his regiment, looking proud and youthful beside his horse. A study of herself, taken perhaps for her birthday and tinted by hand in the studio, the dress, the blonde hair and blue eyes picked out in gentle colours which gave the portrait extraordinary life.

The last photograph was not a formal likeness. It had been taken by some enthusiast setting up his equipment in a field, and it was some moments before George could identify the figures in the photograph. Two women, their hair loosely tied back under wide headscarves, were bent under the weight of sheaves of rough grass, tied with coarse rope and carried slantwise across their shoulders. The hands that held the rope looked chafed and torn, and the women's faces were worn with effort.

George turned the photograph over. On the back Kernerwek had written: *As you can see, we have gone back to the farm. It is hard to find feed for the horses, where everything was burned, but we manage.*

He looked at the print again. Yes, it was Kernerwek, and her mother, all the joy gone from face and figure, scratching a living in that despoiled land. One of Kruger's men, Smith had said.

George sat for a long time staring at nothing. He was thinking about the women at Trevarnon. Caroline, silly and simpering, showing off her small talent for pretty, simple tunes on the pianoforte. Her mother and his own snacking on sandwiches before a dinner party so as not to overeat and spoil their reputation as 'ladies', or the perfection of their swanlike figure so painfully achieved by their stays. Morwenna, headstrong and tempestuous, so accustomed to her own way that she

154

did not stop to consider that any other way might exist. Which of them, he wondered, would submit their manicured hands to sharp straw to keep a farm alive, or stop a horse from starving?

The lunch bell summoned him and he folded his photographs carefully back into their wrapping. But his mood did not leave him, and that afternoon he wired Trevarnon. He would be staying in Plymouth for at least a week, the telegram explained. He had received sad news of an old friend.

A hundred guineas. The thought had been uppermost in Robert's mind all night, ever since his return from Goldmarten. How the blazes could a man raise a hundred guineas?

He dressed moodily, found fault with the temperature of the shaving water, pronounced his tea too strong and his collars too starched, cursed his valet and altogether came down to breakfast in such a bad temper that the little housemaid, overanxious to please, dropped the spoon and scattered sugar on the breakfast table. He left his bacon untasted and went out of the house scowling. Nothing about the place pleased him, although it had been built to his design.

He slammed the gate behind him and, spurning the dog-cart, set off to walk up the lane to his parents' house. He generally went to Trevarnon on Mondays. His mother liked to see him and he was sure of a good lunch which cost him nothing beyond Papa's strictures on his extravagance, and Mama's enquiries about the likely date of weddings.

This morning, though, even his visit home was soured. There was this wretched business of the mine. The Captains were talking about sinking a new shaft further inland, because the present lode was not bearing up, and the purser was for taking a party of venturers down the mine for an inspection. Robert shuddered. A dark, dirty uncomfortable journey down a stinking wet hole in the ground – he would never have entertained the idea for a moment. And then Papa had heard about it and was positively seized with enthusiasm.

Robert had tried to talk him out of it. 'Oh, don't be absurd Papa, you haven't been down a mine for half a century. It's only nostalgia – you were glad enough to get away from it once.'

But Papa had proved remarkably determined. 'I'd like to see it again.' All Mama's headaches and cajoling could not move him a jot. 'Nonsense, Nellie – some of the biggest names in the county will be there – the whole visit is about raising more capital from the shareholders.'

Robert scowled. 'Well, they needn't think they can raise a subscription from me,' he said sourly. Dear God, a man could not be expected to spend money he didn't have on a mine he didn't want, when he was at his wits' end to buy an automobile!

And that was his undoing, because his father said, unexpectedly, 'Well, I might be prepared to meet the subscription call myself, if you take the invitation. You might take me as a guest, I suppose?'

So there he was, driven to it, and the prospect did not improve his mood. He stumped up the drive to the house, and Tibbs let him in.

He was early. His impatience had brought him here half an hour before he was looked for, and his parents were both engaged. Papa was in the library with the estate manager, while his mother was upstairs having an altercation with the sewing-woman about the state of the hemming on the best bolstercase. Robert could hear her raised voice from the sewing-room.

There was nothing to do but kick his heels in the drawing-room. Cook sent up tea and scones, which he ate with relish, having had no breakfast; and he glanced at the papers, but still his parents did not come.

He went to the window and looked down idly at the two gardeners, one trimming the lawn below him, the other behind the wall in the rock-garden, weeding the path. He scowled. The solitary garden-boy at Lower Trevarnon was a tow-headed youth, related to the cook, whose willingness was only matched by his inability to distinguish a daffodil from a dandelion.

Robert stifled a yawn. There was not even George to talk to, since according to Cook he had taken it into his head to lengthen his stay in Plymouth. What the devil did he want to do that for? It would have been fun to tell George about the houseparty at Goldmarten. The fellow took himself so seriously now, with his dreary talk about Africa and farming and politics. It was a positive pleasure to scandalise him with bits of gossip about the London doings of Lily Langtry, or even the local ones of Morwenna Poldair.

He wandered into the hall. He could still hear voices from sewing-room and library. There was a tray on the table with the morning's post. He ruffled through it idly. A pink sealed letter for Mama, an envelope *For the attention of J. Trevarnon Esquire* in the distinctive copperplate hand of the bank, and whatever was this? An unsealed note, in poor ink on cheap folded paper, addressed to George of all people.

He flicked it open with a forefinger. Katie and Fanny Warren. A gift for the baby. There was a baby, then? His baby, if Fanny was to be believed. He felt a momentary irritation. What was George doing sending money to his baby? None of George's bloody business.

Still, as he had said to Peter Gillard, George had always had a soft spot for that younger one, Katie or whatever she was called. But sending her money? What would Papa say if he heard about that?

There was an address, too. Back Lane, Truro. So that was where they were. He saw again in his mind's eye the neat figure in the grey skirt and cape. Evidently they hadn't ended in the workhouse, as he had half-supposed. Presumably not, if George was sending money.

'Robert!' Mama was calling from the top of the stairs. He slid the letter into his pocket and went forward to meet her. 'You should have sent Elsie to fetch me. I've had such a time with that wretched woman and her hemming. Now, have you had tea? And how was Goldmarten? Come and sit in the drawing-room and tell me all about it. Who was there? Caroline, of course – did I mention they were calling for lunch? Major Selwood wants to speak to you afterwards, I fancy. But who else was at the Poldairs'? Shall we see the list in the papers?'

He sat down beside her and told her about the houseparty. It was gratifying to give her the details. Biarritz ginger biscuits for tea? Because the King was partial to them, and anyone who was anyone had them set by 'in case'? And where could they be had? Only in France? And would dear Morwenna be prevailed on to send some, if the Poldairs went abroad this year? And on, and on.

Presently Papa arrived, and the Selwoods, and it was time for luncheon. It was a fair lunch – Mama always had Cook prepare something special for the Selwoods – lobster bisque, with game pie and cold meats to follow, and profiteroles and a good selection of fruits and cheeses. All the same, after the weekend, it seemed depressing fare.

Caroline seemed to share his mood. She was withdrawn and melancholy.

'You're very quiet,' he murmured over the dessert. Mama was telling Mrs Selwood the tragedy of the bolstercase, and Papa and Major Selwood were discussing Captain Scott's exploits in the Antarctic.

Caroline looked at him with her big puppy eyes. 'Are you regretting your engagement, Robert?'

He glanced around, but her voice was so soft that no-one else had heard. 'Of course not,' he said, in genuine horror. Dear God, if she should slip through his fingers now! Papa would never forgive him, and what would he do for money then? 'Why do you say such a thing? Dearest?' he added quickly.

She gave him that childlike, shy smile. 'Only, you know, you must find me dull by contrast to Morwenna. I haven't her sparkle, and I can't have it, although I try.'

He gave a little laugh, trying to sound casual. 'Morwenna? She's charming, of course. A fellow can't help liking her – but as an acquaintance, that's all. He doesn't want that in a wife.' There was truth in that. Morwenna might be sitting on a fortune, but she would never be compliant enough to leave money matters to a husband. He pressed Caroline's elbow under cover of the table. 'Morwenna's style is all very well for a weekend party, but a man needs more . . .' he hunted for a word '. . . sensibility in a wife.' She was weakening, and he pursued the advantage. 'How could you suppose such a thing?'

'It's only,' she said hesitantly, 'that you never seem to want to set a date for the wedding. And . . .' she dropped her eyes. 'You'll think me a silly thing, but last night I broke the clasp on my amethyst necklace I had for my engagement. It felt like an omen.'

'My silly girl,' he said, keeping his voice caressing. A plan was forming in his brain. 'You give me that necklace and I'll take it to Truro myself. I know a man there will fix it stronger than ever before. How's that for an omen?' That necklace ought to raise twenty pounds at the pawnbroker, and if that filly of Gillard's came in at Fowey there would be enough to replace the clasp, redeem the necklace, and buy the motorcar into the bargain. There might even be a profit.

'And the wedding?' asked Caroline doubtfully.

'Don't be a little donkey,' he said gently. 'I want the wedding as much as you do. We can't get married in Lent, can we, and we must have fine weather for your finery. What do you say to the end of June?'

'A June wedding!' Caroline said, loudly enough to draw the attention of the whole table.

'Or July,' said Robert, but it was too late. Major Selwood was already calling for a calendar, and Mama was insisting on champagne.

The ladies spent the afternoon in the library planning a wedding list. Caroline was radiant, and there was still the depressing prospect of the mine visit, but at least the next day Robert had the necklace in his pocket.

CHAPTER SIXTEEN

The day of Fanny's wedding dawned bright and clear. Katie had been given the morning off, and Mr Olds himself came to the ceremony, and so did Mabel, though it was too cold for Eva, who had to stay at home with Peabody. Mrs Williams came. She was wild when she first found out that 'Mrs Trembath' was not yet Mrs Trembath after all, but she wore her best black coat, that she had had for her husband's funeral, and Harry Trembath, being his own master, drove all the way up in his cart in spite of his sight, to see his son wed and take the new family to Penzance after.

Mr Olds had been better than his word. Not only did he consent to be a witness, but he brought the curate from the church, who was a friend of his. The man couldn't marry them, of course, since Fanny and Noah were chapel, if they were anything, but he did say a prayer and gave them a blessing, and that made Katie feel a lot happier. It seemed as if they were properly married, then, and not just signing a legal contract like a miner's licence.

Noah was as proud as punch of the baby – almost as if it had been his own, Katie thought. Had been from the first time he set eyes on the child. He did say something, going into the registry, which disquieted her a little. 'Come on handsome, hasn't he, being early born?' Showed how much men knew about babies – Nicholas was a little late if anything! A little niggling doubt rose at the back of her mind. Surely Fanny had told him the truth when she wrote? But she put the thought firmly away. Of course she had – Fanny wouldn't deceive her. Anyway, Noah was happy, he was good to Fanny and she wasn't going to spoil their day.

Fanny wore her mustard muslin, and looked as good as a chocolate box, with her straw hat trimmed wth a yard of ruched ribbon, and a great bunch of violets pinned to it. There were goosebumps on her arms from the cold, Katie noticed, but you would never have guessed it to see Fanny smile. Noah was dressed to kill in his check suit and brown hat with a feather, and his father was nearly choking in his high collar and necktie. Altogether it was as pretty a wedding as Fanny could have hoped for. Even Nicholas, in Katie's arms, was as good as gold, and didn't cry once till it was over.

There was a proper wedding feast too. Mrs Williams had boiled a fruit cake, and Katie had managed a quarter pound of boiled beef, and what with pickles and a great threepenny loaf there was plenty for everyone – even Mrs Lomas, who stopped by to wish them well.

Then Fanny went into Mrs Williams' room and changed into her plaid skirt and best blouse, and tied her good shawl over. The muslin dress was wrapped in paper and string, and put into one of Fanny's three boxes to go on the cart. There were all her clothes and all the things for Nicholas, though most of the household goods were being left for Katie. Noah had insisted.

'I've seen it happen in America. Folks take stuff half across the world, and when they get there, they find most of it's broken and the rest isn't wanted. Katie'll be needing the pots and pans – she'll be hard enough pressed as it is without your money, Fanny, let alone having to buy cloam. No, we'll buy new when we get to New South Wales. I got money put by for that. And we shan't want for bedding. Feyther's given me a good eiderdown and a great piece of calico for sheeting. It's waiting for us at Penzance.'

That wasn't all, either. Mrs Lomas had a piece of pretty chintz for curtains or a bedspread or even a good cloth. Mrs Williams had looked out a pair of feather pillows, good as new. 'Can't break them, and they'll come in handy on your travels,' she said.

Noah did not escape without wedding china. Mr Olds had brought a pretty tea set, and Katie insisted that they take Fanny's flowered jug. Her private present to Fanny was folded away at the bottom of a box – two pairs of new drawers, proper soft knickers tied in at waist and cuff, and trimmed with a ruff of lace. They had been made, lovingly and secretly, from two of Peabody's 17lb flour bags, which were soft and fine, and looked and felt almost like butter-muslin when they were boiled long enough. Besides, when the cloth was boiled the blue stencil of the miller's mark became near enough invisible.

The boxes were handed up. Noah was going to drive back, to save his father's eyes, so he climbed into the driver's seat. Harry got up behind him on the boxes, still protesting that he could drive it blindfold. Noah spread a clean piece of sacking on the seat beside him to save Fanny's new skirt. Then she was up, and Nicholas was put into her arms.

'I can call you Mrs Trembath now, can't I, Mrs Trembath?' Mrs Williams said, and the cart lurched off.

'I'll write,' Fanny called, and she was still calling and waving as the cart turned the corner and they were gone.

Mrs Williams went back into the house, and Mabel and Mrs Lomas followed her. Katie stood looking at empty road. She could feel her eyes stinging, and presently Mr Olds came to stand beside her and put his hand protectively on her shoulder.

'You'll miss them.'

The kindness was too much and the tears began to flow. She turned her head away, but he held her to him with one hand and offered her a handkerchief with the other.

'Here,' he said. 'Dry your eyes.'

She obeyed.

'And you be careful with that handkerchief. Somebody very special gave it to me.'

It was the gift she had hemmed for him at Christmas. She glanced up at him but he avoided her eyes.

'It's good for Fanny that she found a good man,' he said, after a moment. 'I hope she'll be happy. You'll be lonely without them, Katie.'

The tears started again, and she buried her face in the rough warmth of his coat. He patted her shoulder and said awkwardly, still staring past her at the houses opposite, 'Perhaps you should think about getting wed yourself, Katie. I'd make you a good husband, if you'd have me. Eva needs a mother, and she's fond of you. No,' he said, as she was about to speak, 'don't give me an answer now. Give it a week or two without Fanny and see what you think. I know you were wondering about looking for a live-in post, and if that's what you decide, I'll help you find one.'

'But . . .'

'You could come to me,' he said gently. 'I even suggested it. But you said it yourself, Katie, it wouldn't do. I can hardly have you living in the house as a paid companion when I want you for my wife.

But, whatever you decide, I'll see that you're looked after. You know that?'

She nodded. 'I think . . .'

He shook his head. 'Not now. I've sprung this on you too sudden. Give yourself time to know how you feel.' He squeezed her shoulder for a moment, then let her go. 'And you'll always come to me in trouble. Promise?'

'Yes, Mr Olds.'

'Yes, Arthur,' he corrected softly.

She might have answered him, but Mrs Williams came out, offering tea. He shook his head, smiling, and left without another word.

That night the little attic room seemed achingly lonely and bare.

Lally looked around the front room with satisfaction. The floor had been swept and polished, and mats beaten to spotlessness, and the furniture dusted to within an inch of its life. There was even a bunch of daffodils stuck awkwardly in a handleless cup in the middle of the mantelpiece, and the whole room smelt of flowers, caustic soap and beeswax.

'Lal-lal.' Rosa came trundling in from the kitchen, dragging her rag-doll by one leg as usual. 'Rosa want cake.'

'Rosa's a greedy girl,' Lally said, stopping to stuff the wayward curls back under the ribbon from which they were escaping. 'Can't have cake until Aunty Fanny comes.'

Why she called Fanny 'Aunty' she didn't know. If anyone was 'Aunty' it was poor little Rosa here, with that girl bringing her baseborn child into the house, bold as you like. Still, Davy had insisted, and if Fanny was decently married now it was a Christian duty to forgive and forget, even if the wedding had come a little late in the day. And if anyone knew her duty it was Lally Warren. At least 'Aunty Fanny' had a respectable ring to it, and Fanny would be Mrs Trembath by this time, so the Warrens could hold their heads up in the Terrace tomorrow.

'Imagine that Noah being the father after all,' she said aloud.

Rosa said, 'Cake,' and Lally blushed at talking like that in front of the child.

There was cake. Lally had made a batch of saffron, and Rosa's favourite 'Trafalgar Squares', spiced and fruity bread pudding, sprinkled with nutmeg, and baked crisp and brown, to be eaten cold.

'Wait!' Lally said again, but Rosa's lip trembled dangerously, and

Lally, tutting, went into the kitchen and cut a fragment of the cooling cake. 'There now. And don't let your father catch you eating that when he comes home. And don't spill it on your best pinny, either.'

Rosa was tricked out in her best, a blue dress that had once been Katie's when she was small, cut down and altered. There were no tucks or flounces for lengthening; Lally had cut them away, because the fade showed where they had been let out. Instead a length of pink ribbon had been painstakingly inserted into waist and hem, and the dress reassembled around it, and embroidered with pink wool to match.

'You can't let the child play in that,' Mrs Tremble next door had said when she first saw it. 'It'll be a misery to wash.'

'I'll be the judge of that,' Lally had said, but the woman had proved to be right. The light ribbon showed every bit of dirt, and even on Sundays it was no end of a game keeping Rosa away from walls and floors, and today, what with the coalscuttle and the garden and the bootblacking no pinny invented was ever enough. Why the child could not sit still and look at a book she would never know. Still, she was a good girl, and Lally was proud of her. More than proud, she was that soft that once or twice when the child was crying, she had even taken Rosa in her arms and tried to comfort her with an awkward kiss.

But here it was, four o'clock and company expected, and Rosa was roaming the house looking for mischief.

'Now, miss,' Lally said, picking Rosa up and propping her in Davy's corner of the settle beside the fire, 'you be a good girl and sit still for Lally. Willie will be home from school directly, and your father will be back as soon as he can get off shift. I suppose it will be "Mr and Mrs Trembath" then and treating them like gentry. Well, they'll be better off in Australia, I daresay, where there aren't folks to know the half of it.'

Presently Willie came, and after he had taken off his cap and changed into his Sunday trousers, he sat and played cat's cradle with Rosa and told her stories to keep her amused.

'What's keeping your father?' Lally grumbled, a little later, when the teatable was set, and the hearth had been swept and the front-room fire lighted. 'He won't have a chance to make himself decent before they arrive, at this rate, and they can't stop here waiting. They've got to catch the evening train.' She would not admit, even to herself, how her own heart was fluttering at the thought of the visit.

There was a rattle of a cart in the Terrace, and a horse's hooves on the loose stones. 'They're here!' Willie shouted, forgetting his manners in the excitement and rushing to the door. 'Wherever's Father to?'

The day at the mine had never seemed so long. Davy had been too full of feeling to eat his bit of croust at lunchtime, though Lally made a much better pasty these days than she used to. True, she was still liable to put in bits of peas, or broccoli, which had no business to be in a pasty at all, and she was heavy-handed with the pastry, but she did her best and he was grateful.

He tried not to think about Maggie, and the tasty morsels she had always contrived for him. He had never guessed how much his wife had scrimped and saved and gone short to see that he had plenty, not until Lally came and showed him different.

How Maggie would have loved to see this day – Fanny married and the first grandson in the house. Meg had two girls, in America now, but he had never clapped eyes on them. The Atlantic ocean was too broad. And now Jimmy and Tom were both writing and talking of getting wed. It seemed sad that a man should never meet his daughters-in-law.

Perhaps after all he would take that money that Meg's husband Bill had offered. Then he could go and see for himself. That would be something to talk about after, wouldn't it? All the way to California. Might do that when Rosa was older. Good work for miners out there, they said, and decent pay for a skilled man. Enough to buy your own house, like Bill Polkinghorne and Meg had done, or travel the world like young Noah. Enough to visit his boys, too, even if they were a bit spread – they thought a lot of Cornish skills out there and he still wasn't too old to go back underground. Proper man's job instead of standing here tending machines like a factory apprentice.

He turned his attention to the belts again. The ore-stones rattled past him, on their way to the steam-driven crushers. He cast his eyes over them expertly, sizing up those with a good lode, shifting them to meet the stamps in an even flow, and now and again removing a dead stone of worthless rock.

'Today's the day, then?' Over the crash of the stamps, one of the men shouted cheerfully from the vanner. 'Nearly there, Davy lad. Only another tram or two.' He nodded through the open end of the shed to where the men worked outside with mallet and pickaxe. 'The breakers are knocking off any minute for the light.'

Davy glanced up at the hopper behind him, where the trams of broken stone were winched up the incline and the fines shovelled onto the belts. There was still a lot of stone to shift. He would have replied, but a fit of coughing prevented him.

'Some cough you've got there,' the man said, sticking his head around the side of the stamps. 'You all right, are 'ee?'

'Mind where you stand,' Davy said. 'That end kerbstone's been missing ever since they put in the new stamp-heads. Slip down there easy.' He had to raise his voice, even then, over the thunder of the stamps.

'You mind that cough,' the man returned.

' 'S nothing,' said Davy. 'Just a bit of a cold I picked up Christmas. Can't seem to shift it, no-how.'

'Ah,' the man said.

Davy turned away, nettled. ' 'S nothing,' he repeated, almost to himself. He had said nothing to anyone about the deep ache that had begun in his lungs, and the flecks of red in his spittle once or twice in the sleepless racking night.

The man would not leave it be. 'You want to get it seen to,' he said.

'Just a bad throat,' Davy said. 'I got me scarf on, see, keep me neck warm. Wool next to the skin, that's the job for a cold.' He pulled the end of it free and flapped it at the man from the vanner.

'Ah,' the man said again, and went back to his work.

Davy, irritated, did the same. 'Drat,' he said, half to himself. He had not paid attention to the stone coming in from the trammers. There was a great lump of dead rock already halfway up to the stamps. Looked like a lump from the tram-way. It must have slipped past the men breaking on the grizzly – the light was fading and their thoughts were halfway home, like his own. It would be under the crushers in a minute or two. They would break it, certainly – it would take more than a lump of granite to stop the stamps, and with the missing kerbstone it would easily go under, but it would be a slow business and the ore-stone would pile up behind. Have to stop the belts then, and there would be no end of a performance. Could be another half-hour, and he wanted to be sharp home tonight, with Fanny coming.

There was still time. The belt moved slowly, and it was still two feet from the stamps. Too heavy to lift, and he didn't have space now to put a bar in to lever it away, but it would roll, surely. He put his forearm on it and gave it an exploratory heave. It moved easily.

No problem. He grasped the stone and rolled it towards him. It fell jerkily, the weight coming all of a sudden, but Davy was no stranger to rock. He moved back and let it fall, and leaned over it again.

This time it would clear. But as he leaned away his scarf tightened, pinning him against the belt. He was caught, awkward, in the far pulley, and he struggled to free the end. Leaning as he was he couldn't bring his weight to bear, and the belt moved forward, tightening the scarf. The weight of the stone behind him piled up, pressing him forward.

He panicked now. The scarf was throttling him. He clawed at it gasping, trying to shout, but the cloth at his neck gagged the sound. He was pulled off his feet, across the belt. And all the time the stamps were pounding nearer. The missing kerbstone gaped beside him. And then he was falling sideways, his face still pinned to the belt. He was choking.

'Davy!' someone shouted, but they were too far away. He grasped wildly at the air while his lungs burst. Mercifully, blackness claimed him an instant before the stamps did.

CHAPTER SEVENTEEN

Fanny's homecoming was not at all what Lally had planned. Harry and Noah Trembath came in meekly enough, and sat in the front room with their hats on their knees, making conversation like proper visitors. But no sooner was Fanny through the door than she was off upstairs, hand in hand with Willie, to see a top he was whittling and admire his copy-book from school.

It was the same at tea. Fanny was up and down like a yoyo, fetching plates and kettles, and none of Lally's sniffing and glaring could prevent her. In the end Lally had to say, 'Sit still, Fanny do, and let yourself be waited on. You're supposed to be a guest.' Only then did the new Mrs Trembath consent to sit and eat her bread and cheese and Trafalgar Squares like a lady, instead of dancing about like a heathen.

Nicholas seemed quite a nice child, considering. He was a great, lumpy baby, of course, not a bit like little delicate Rosa when she was born, but she was bound to say he looked healthy enough, and he seemed contented. After all, it wasn't his fault if he was born the wrong side of wedlock. Willie was quite taken up with the idea of being an uncle, and carried the child about until it fell asleep, and Rosa was tickled to death to see a real baby in the cradle instead of her raggedy doll.

The men enjoyed the baking, and might have eaten it all, if Lally had not put some by on a plate for Davy. 'I can't understand how he isn't home,' she kept saying, every few minutes. 'He belongs to come before this.'

'Pity we had to start without him,' Fanny said for the third time. Her eyes had been straying to the door ever since they sat down.

'There's no help for it, Fan,' her husband said. 'We'll miss our ship if we're not on that train. He'll be here as soon as may be.'

'He wouldn't miss Fanny for the world!' Willie put in. 'He's been on about it all the week.'

'Hope nothing's happened to him on the way home,' Harry Trembath said, wiping his moustache politely on the back of his hand. He voiced everybody's thoughts. 'It's times like this you must be glad he's got a surface job. You'd be in some taking if he was this late up from underground.'

'Some problem with the machines, I've no doubt,' said Lally. 'Would happen today, of all days. They had a paddle split on a vanner a month or so back, and they were there all hours draining the tin right down to let the men get in and fix it.'

'We've got a few minutes yet,' Harry Trembath said, pulling his watch from his pocket and holding it inches from his face to see the time. 'If he hasn't come by then we'll stop by the mine on the way to the station, see if we can catch him there.'

There was a rattle at the door.

'That's him,' Fanny said, springing up. But it was Cissie Tremble who came into the room, whitefaced and shaken, with Eddie Goodbody behind her.

'Whatever is it?' Lally said, looking from one to the other.

Eddie cleared his throat, but it was Cissie who spoke. 'There's been an accident, down at the mine,' she said, after a moment. 'Eddie's just come running to tell us.' Eddie was still in his working clothes, his eyes white circles in a mask of red dust. 'I'm sorry, Fanny, your father would dearly have loved to be here, but they can't spare him yet.'

Lally, who had been holding her breath, gave a sigh of relief.

'There's scores of men down there,' Cissie went on, 'all trying to free whoever's trapped. Stopped the shift and all. I wonder you didn't hear the hooter.'

'Wasn't listening for it,' Lally said. 'Well, that explains it. I knew Davy would have been here if he could, but if there's a fall, of course they'll all be down there doing what they can. Let's hope it doesn't let the sea in like it did down Land's End a year or two back.'

Eddie was going to say something, but Cissie Tremble cut in. 'No, I haven't heard that, but it's a nasty business, from what I hear. It's some shame, Fanny, but there's no point in you waiting here. Could be hours yet.'

'We'll stop by on the way,' Fanny said.

'No,' Cissie said firmly. 'They'll be crowds there by this time, and you'll only be in the way. You'll never see him anyway. He'd rather think you were safe on your way. He meant to be here, Fanny, and that's the main thing.'

Fanny was shaken, but she'd lived too long beside a mine not to understand. 'Tell him to write,' she said. 'And give him my love and say how sorry we are to miss him, especially for this. Bound to be someone he knows, and all.'

Cissie nodded. 'He doesn't need telling, my dear, he knows how sorry you are, better than any of us,' she said gruffly.

'Well, I hope he isn't doing anything heroic,' Lally said suddenly. 'I know what Davy's like. Anyone he knows, he'll be the first one down. He's been mad for a chance to get back underground – there'll be no stopping him now.'

'Pity he weren't there, then,' Eddie said. Cissie glared at him, and he blew his nose loudly on the piece of rag from his pocket. The skin showed white against the dust where he had rubbed it.

'Well, what a thing,' Harry Trembath said.

'I'll help you get the horse,' Eddie offered. 'Leave it in the field, did you?'

'Only tethered to a tree,' Harry said, but he went out with Eddie. When they came back he looked tired and grey.

'You all right, Dad?' asked Noah.

'Blessed horse gave me a fright,' Harry said, and he would say no more.

'You drive the cart, Eddie,' Cissie said, 'and Willie, why don't you go too and see them off? Take Rosa, for a treat.'

'Not in her best dress. And it's getting dark!' Lally protested, but the children were already being bundled out and into the cart. Eddie hoisted them up, leaving rough red fingermarks on their clothes and hands.

'Make sure you write, mind. And see you make a good life for that child,' Cissie called, and the cart was gone, up the darkening street.

'Now, what's all this about?' Lally demanded. Cissie and Eddie had simply taken command for the last few minutes. Then she caught sight of Cissie's face. 'Oh, my lord,' she said, and her voice was high and wild. 'It's Davy, isn't it? And you let Fanny go and never said.'

'Better she went,' Cissie said, and there were tears in her eyes. 'Poor child. Some wedding day it would have been for her. Like Meg, it is, all over again.'

'He's hurt bad,' Lally said.

Cissie shook her head. 'You come and have a cup of tea. They're doing all they can. The children can stop with us tonight.'

'Dead?' Lally said, but she knew the answer. 'I'd better go down there.' It suddenly seemed very important to do something. 'They'll let me see him, bring him home.'

Cissie put a hand on her arm. 'There's nothing to see, Lal. He went under the stamps. Crushed to a pulp.'

Lally closed her eyes to shut out the pictures, and Cissie Tremble took her in her arms.

The letter was waiting for Katie when she got home on Wednesday night. She was late, because she had stopped to buy turnips on her way home, and she'd been fussy with them, planning to eat the greens as well as the roots, and make two meals of one.

Mrs Williams brought the letter up, and lingered by the doorway. You could tell she was curious, and no wonder – there wasn't much post to Back Lane as a rule.

It was Carrie's writing on the envelope. Katie would have known it anywhere, all loops and curls. It had driven Miss Bevan mad at school. But inside was a letter in a different hand, pointed and crabbed. It was short, more like a telegram than a letter.

'Your Father died. Funeral Friday. There is a bed for you here if you like. Fanny got off safe. Your affectionate aunt, Leila.'

The words hit her like an Atlantic roller, cold and sudden and savage. It must have shown on her face, because Mrs Williams let off hovering and came over to her, saying, 'What is it, my lover?'

Katie could only hold out the paper, dumbly. Her mind refused to function. All she could think was that she had never heard Lally called 'Leila'. It made the letter seem more remote than ever.

'My dear Katie,' Mrs Williams said, and then, as she replaced the note in the envelope. 'There's another letter here.'

It was from Carrie, three painstaking pages of it, and the ink had run, as though someone had wept tears on the page. Katie read it and reread it, feeling the horror of the story, but far off as though it was happening to someone else. A hundred pictures of her father flashed through her mind: Davy digging, Davy singing, Davy bringing home treats for Christmas and whittling whistles from broken twigs. But Davy dead was beyond her imagination. Her brain refused to comprehend it.

Mother says you can stay with us if you'd rather. Lally won't like it but it might be best. We've got the children anyway till after the funeral. Friday's my half-day, so I shan't have to get time off.

But I will, Katie thought. She was still too stunned to think properly, and she began to put on her bonnet and cape. She would go and see Mr Olds. He would be there, she knew. He had brought some of his drawings and plans to work on at home, as he sometimes did. He would know what to do.

'You can't go out this time of night,' Mrs Williams said. 'You come down and have some tea with me.'

Katie shook her head. 'I must let them know.'

'Well, if you must go, I'll walk with you,' Mrs Williams said. 'You're not fit to be out alone in this state, you'd be under someone's wheels before you noticed. Wait while I get my coat.'

She was back in a moment, buttoning it round her. It was an old-fashioned coat, smart, with a nipped waist and peplums and big leg-of-mutton sleeves, the one she had worn to the wedding. 'If you were a bit smaller Katie, you could borrow this for the funeral. Black looks decent, a time like this.'

It was kindly meant, and Katie managed a smile.

'Mind,' Mrs Williams said, 'your grey is nice.' She kept it up all the way into town, talking as if words were oil, and would soothe the pain.

All the same, Katie was glad of her company. She did not like the town at night. The friendly bustle of the day was gone, the gas lamps made pools of shadow beside the houses, and the blank shops lowered behind their silent shutters. Only a few food-shops stood open, where the women from the steam laundry and the tannery bickered and shrieked over the price of broken biscuits and bacon ends. They were raucous and rough, and more than one had a jug under her shawl ready to fill with beer or porter and take home for supper from the publics.

The publics were open. There were pools of light at the doorways, and as you passed there was the sound of loud music and laughter and the sweet, bitter smell of the beer; and now and then a shout and a scuffle, or a man staggering and singing would lurch out into the street and the noise would rise and die again as the door swung closed.

Katie drew her shawl about her, and walked close to Mrs Williams. She was glad when they got to Fore Street, and rang the bell at Number Twenty-three.

She should have realised that Mr Olds would be at dinner. Of course he would, this time of night. She hadn't stopped to think clearly before she set off on this errand, and she was filled with embarrassment when Mabel went in to the dining room and he came out of it, his napkin still in his hand.

'It's her father, sir.' Mrs Williams found words where Katie had none. 'There's been an accident at the mine, and they want her down Friday for the burying.'

'My poor Katie,' Mr Olds said.

'It's the end of the family,' Katie said, and suddenly she began to cry. Peabody was sent for, and a tray of tea, and Katie was ushered into the dining room before she knew where she was.

Peabody came, and declared that the child must eat. Mrs Williams was offered, but she had her own tea keeping warm over a saucepan, and she was sent home in a hansom. Katie was given a place at the table, and found herself with a plate of beef and onions and cabbage and carrots, and a rice pudding sent up specially from the kitchen. It was one of the best meals of her life, but she wasn't hungry, and it took Mr Olds and Peabody combined to persuade her to eat some of it; but finally she did, and she felt better after it.

'Now then,' Mr Olds said, when Peabody was satisfied, and the plates were removed. 'What about money for the train? Have you got enough?'

Katie had not thought of that problem, but she scarcely had time to. Mr Olds insisted on giving her a florin.

'Come in and teach Eva tomorrow if you want the company,' he said, 'but we shall know why, if not, and you are not to worry about it. Now, what are we to do with you tonight? There is a room here, if you want it, or would you rather have a cab?'

So much kindness brought the tears to her eyes again. 'I'm sorry, Mr Olds, I've put you to a lot of trouble.'

He smiled. 'But you promised. Come to me in trouble, I said, and so you have. You kept your promise and I'm pleased, Katie. It gives me hope that maybe you will turn to me if you want an anchor. But I don't want to press you tonight, it wouldn't be fair. Now what about that cab?'

He wouldn't take no for an answer, and she rode home like a lady.

Getting his hands on the necklace had been easy. The next step of the plan was proving confoundedly difficult.

He couldn't get away, for one thing. There seemed to be some plan of Mama's for every minute of the day: decisions about hymns and prayers and guest lists and entertainments and food and clothes. Especially about clothes.

And for another thing, there were his own misgivings. Supposing that Caroline – or even worse, her father – found out what he had done. He could say goodbye then to any hope of the Selwood fortunes, and you could be sure the whole county would hear about it, so there would be no other rich young woman to take Caroline's place.

That was why he had fixed on Truro. Easy to reach, yet far enough away for the Selwoods never to go there. And certainly not to the pawnbroker. No, Truro was safe enough.

It was convenient, too. Only a few miles from Hendra Farm; he could go up and take another look at the automobile, supposing that wretched farmer hadn't sold it by now. And there was always the delicious prospect of a meeting with Morwenna. More and more, he found, meeting Morwenna had become an addiction with him. And she seemed to share it. She could find some reason to come in from Goldmarten while he was in Truro. That sort of secret rendezvous was just the kind of adventure she relished. Besides, she was mad for motoring too.

He toyed for a moment with the idea of telling her about the necklace, but it was too dangerous, even with Morwenna. She would get too much pleasure from that kind of power over him. He would just tell her about the car. She wouldn't ask where he got the money. She came from the wrong kind of family. In Morwenna's world money was taken for granted.

He would buy the car. Provided, always provided, Gillard's wretched filly came in. But it would. He was sure it would. When Gillard backed a horse it always won, it was only when Robert bet against him that he lost his wagers. And if it was five to one there ought to be enough to buy the motorcar and redeem the necklace. So what was he waiting for?

Monday. First thing on Monday he would go to Truro. That would give him time to raise the money before the Fowey meeting, and it would be a good idea to get rid of the wretched necklace before Mama or somebody came across it and started asking questions.

He opened the box and held the amethysts to the light. They were nice stones, finely matched, and the setting was good. Oh yes, he should get his twenty guineas for that.

He slid the box into his back pocket. As he did so, his fingers touched paper. That wretched letter of George's. He'd forgotten about it, he should have taken it back before now – someone might have noticed that it was gone. Well, it was too late now. Better to put it in the fire and say nothing. He glanced at it again.

'The gift of money.' What was George up to? It was a worrying thought. It was no moment now to have his brother digging up the business of Fanny, and ruining everything.

Yet why else send money at this stage? Or was George a darker horse than anyone knew? Surely he couldn't have been supporting the Warren girls all along? But that younger one had been smartly dressed, someone was looking after her.

He pictured her in his mind's eye. She had certainly blossomed into a stunner. George had picked the better stayer, you had to hand him that. And she had spirit too, he remembered. Since he had known Morwenna, Robert had come to admire spirit in a woman.

Well, he had the letter now, and no-one else knew anything about it. As long as George stayed in Plymouth there was no threat. Besides, he thought suddenly, there was an address on the bottom of the note. Why add that, if George already knew where to find them? It was very disquieting.

He looked at it again. Back Lane. It would be possible to find it. Discreetly perhaps, just to see what was happening. He wouldn't have to talk to Fanny – although, who knows, she might even be glad to see him. He could pretend he had come about that money he had promised her, and never paid. He had always felt slightly uncomfortable about that. Perhaps he could call to deliver it, now he had the address. She could hardly object to that. Besides, he had always been able to charm Fanny.

And, if he was honest with himself, there would be a certain pleasure in seeing Katie Warren again. Yes, that settled it. If he could pawn the necklace for a reasonable sum, Fanny should have her guinea.

He folded the letter and put it back into his pocket. He was still smiling when he went downstairs.

CHAPTER EIGHTEEN

It rained on the day of the funeral. Katie took the early train to Penzance, but there was no one to meet her, and she had to take the horse-bus to St Just and walk the rest of the way to Penvarris Chapel, and even then she got soaked through.

The chapel was packed when she arrived. Most of the folk from the Terrace were there, and no end of people from the mine, underground as well as surface workers, and two of the captains, and men she recognised from the counthouse. Her father had been well-liked.

She hadn't had time to go to the Terrace, so she didn't have the chance to follow the coffin, but she saw it coming on Harry Trembath's cart, all draped in black and so heaped with flowers you might have thought it was a carnival float coming. There was Lally behind it, her face set hard as plaster, as though afraid it might crack and show the tears behind her eyes. Willie, with his cap rammed down hard over his ears, and his neck and nose blotched and red, trying to look manly. It tore Katie's heart to realise how much he had grown since she last saw him.

He caught her eye and she saw the sob rise in him. She gave him a little nod and fell in behind with Mrs Tremble and Carrie, walking with Rosa between them. The band was marching too, and the choir from St Just, or as many of them as could get the time, were bringing up the rear, and they lined the chapel while the coffin was brought in. They sang 'Abide With Me' with deep harmony, and Katie felt the lump in her throat. How often her father had sung that.

It was only a brief service, but there was plenty of feeling, and respect; even though Lally had to lean over and snatch Willie's cap off as the coffin passed. And then the long walk in the rain to lay Davy Warren beside his wife again, and Jack, and the children who never were. Willie threw in his handful of earth with Lally and Katie, but Rosa wouldn't and ran off, so Katie had to go after her.

There was baked ham back at the Terrace, and sandwiches and tea, but it was a cheerless funeral feast. Lally fetched and carried, spurning all offers of help, and turning aside any expressions of sympathy with a sharp 'We'll manage, thank you.'

The guests swallowed their sandwiches and left, until only Katie, Mrs Tremble and Carrie remained. Then Lally did consent to sit down in the front room and take a cup of tea herself, while the others washed up, but ten minutes later Katie found her still sitting perfectly motionless, like a waxwork, with only a little muscle working at the side of her mouth, with the tea stone cold and a little skin forming on the surface.

'Trouble is, Katie,' Mrs Tremble said, when she reported back to the kitchen, 'what's going to happen now? Lally would rather die than say so, but it was your father paid the rent. They won't turn them out overnight, and anyhow there's been a bit of a collection down at the mine, so there's enough for a week or two. But I don't know what's to become of them, Katie. An old woman and two small children and nothing coming in. I'll do what I can, of course, for your father's sake, but there is a limit. And Lally won't take charity.'

'I don't know,' Katie said. 'I could come home, I suppose.'

'Can't see how that would help,' Mrs Tremble said. 'You got work where you are, and a roof over your head. It would make more sense for Lally to come to you, if it came to the worse. Could do a bit of sewing like Fanny was doing, maybe. Carrie told me you have quite a little business up there.'

'I don't know so much,' Carrie said. 'She's got Meg's machine, I know, but Lally works that careful and methodical she'd never make enough to feed three of them, let alone give anything towards the rent. You and Fanny were hard pressed enough, and there was only two of you.'

'Anyhow,' said Katie, 'we'll have to see what Lally says. I can't see her ever wanting to move in with me.'

'Or you wanting her to,' Carrie said. 'It'd be like living with the Inquisition, especially when you've been used to your own place. Besides, you'd be falling all over each other in that attic, there'd never be room for four.'

There was a pause, and then Mrs Tremble offered, 'I might take Willie, while he's at school, if he'd do a bit about the place. I could do with a pair of willing hands, and with Carrie gone and my boys grown up there's room. But that Rosa's a fair handful. Does what she likes, and Lally lets her.'

It was a generous offer, and Katie said so. 'That's very kind . . .'

'What's very kind?' Lally's voice demanded from the doorway. 'You're too ready to take, Katie Warren. Always were. You've got your own two feet. Stand on them.'

'I was going to get the children to bed,' Mrs Tremble said. 'We agreed they were staying next door tonight.'

Lally sniffed. 'I can't see why, but if that's what they want I shan't stop them. Are you staying, Katie?'

'I got to get back to Truro,' Katie said. She suddenly felt the need to get away and think, though it tore her heart to leave Rosa and Willie alone with Lally, especially in this state of mind. She would have to think of something. 'I must get back,' she said again.

'Might be best,' Lally said. 'And go soon, if you're going. While the rain's stopped.'

'I'll walk with you,' Carrie said. 'I've to get back by nine. I'll just get those children off, and I'll be back.'

Lally started packing away the ham and cups without another word. Katie went to the hall and put on her damp cape and bonnet.

'Good night, Lally,' she said softly.

There was no response. On an impulse, Katie went over and planted a kiss on the dry, withered cheek. Lally went on stacking saucers on the shelf. She didn't look round.

'Don't worry, Lally. About me and Fanny. You did what you thought right. You looked after Father and Willie and Rosa. You did what you could. Nobody could do more than that.'

Silence.

Then Carrie called 'Coming, Katie?' from the door. Katie turned away. It was no use.

But as she closed the door a tiny sound made her glance behind her. Lally was still standing at the cupboard, her back stiff as a ramrod, arranging plates in a pile. But there were tears running down her face. Perhaps for the first time in her life, Lally Warren was crying.

Robert walked down River Street whistling. It had been a very auspicious beginning.

Twenty-seven guineas. Even now he could hardly believe it. He hadn't even had to haggle. The old fool in the pawn shop had taken the necklace and examined it through an eye piece, then he just peered over his little round spectacles and said mildly, 'Twenty-seven guineas. Twenty-one days to redeem. That is my offer. Will you take it?'

Would he? He might have accepted half as much. Twenty-one days was not long of course, but it was long enough. The Fowey meeting was two and a half weeks away. That gave him plenty of time. And if he gave Caroline her necklace within a month, so much the better. She was already fretting about having it in time for the wedding.

He had hoped to see Morwenna, but although he had dropped a hundred hints at the ball on Saturday, she had not responded. He had tried to get away from Caroline and speak to Morwenna alone, but his fiancée seemed to read his mind, and stayed so close to his side she seemed positively welded there. So he could look forward to no assignation.

But there was still the automobile. How was he to get to Hendra Farm? With twenty-seven guineas in his pocket, and the races at Fowey, the car was as good as his, provided that wretched farmer hadn't sold it to someone else in the meantime. He walked down to the collection of hansom cabs grouped at the bottom of Lemon Street. It might be a confoundedly expensive business, but lacking Peter Gillard and the brougham, it was pay a cabman or walk.

Or it might have been.

'Mr Trevarnon. Now this is a surprise!' It was Morwenna, driving a sulky, looking perter than the pony, in a deep blue costume and a hat with a peacock's feather. She pulled up beside him and he climbed awkwardly onto the rail. There was no room on the seat for two.

'I thought I should never find you,' she observed, flicking the tail of the reins against the animal's rump, so that the pony clattered on smartly, scattering a gaggle of shopping women and startling a cat from the pavement.

'What do you mean by that?' he said, clinging to his perch with both hands as the sulky danced madly over the bumps.

'Oh, don't be so absurd, Robert! You spent the whole of supper on Saturday night telling your wretched Caroline that you were to be in Truro this morning. Don't pretend that you didn't intend me to hear!' She shot him a sidelong glance. 'Though what jeweller you were visiting where I found you I'm sure I can't divine.'

Robert flushed. 'The necklace was only a device,' he said. 'I hoped to call on you, and go and see that car at Hendra.'

'A motor?' Morwenna looked at him, her eyes sparkling. 'You are a rip, Robert. Shall we do it then?'

She was astonishing, he thought, as the sulky bowled up the lanes out of the town. Astonishing in her beauty. Even more astonishing in her behaviour. She had come out on purpose to find him, and she drove the sulky with so much dash she threatened to dislodge him. The daring of it made his heart pound with excitement, although he was a little concerned about the figure he would cut, rattling up like this in a carriage driven by a woman, and as they came to the turning he offered to take the reins from her.

'What nonsense, Robert,' she said, snatching them away from him. 'I can't perch up where you are, like a monkey. Anyway you shouldn't manage the pony half so well as I do. And don't pout. There is room for only one sulky on this road.'

So he had to laugh, but he felt uneasy, as though in some obscure way she had bested him.

He forgot his chagrin, though, when they drew up and the farmer came out to meet them. He remembered Robert, or affected to, and was delighted to show them the motor-car. No, he hadn't sold it. It was a bad time of year, when the roads were so rough after the bad weather.

This time the engine did start. 'A loose wire, that's all it was,' he explained. 'You want to have a spin in her?'

Of course they did. It was amazing, the most astonishing thing that Robert had ever done. The freedom of horseback, and all the effortlessness of a train. It rattled and lurched on the bumps, of course, but no more than the sulky, and at the end of ten miles it was as tireless as when they set out.

'You could go to the other end of the county in this,' Robert said, raising his voice to be heard over the roar of the engine. The wind caught his words and whistled them away.

'Or Scotland,' Morwenna said. She was sitting with her head thrown back, one hand clutching her hat, her hair streaming in the wind and her cheeks crimson with excitement. 'You must buy it, Robert, I positively insist.'

He had come to that conclusion himself; anything to have her there beside him with that glow in her cheeks and that devil-may-care look in her eye. But until the Fowey races it simply wasn't possible. He shook his head, laughing. 'I've got to look at some others,' he said.

They turned a corner, and the road ran steeply downhill. There was a ridge in the road, where a steam had crossed it, and the front wheels ran into it. The car juddered to a stop and sank to its knees, the wheels folding out like wings on either side. Robert rose in the air and sank back, hard, against the seat.

'Dang it,' the farmer said, and got out to examine the damage. Robert was irritated, but Morwenna thought it hugely diverting.

'What a joke,' she said. 'Well there's no use standing here gaping. We'll be in the village,' she said to the farmer. 'You can pick us up when you get it moving.'

It was a charming village, with ducks and a green and a country inn where they sold good ale, and honest ginger wine. The landlord brought them bread, and they threw morsels to the ducks, and Robert fed some to Morwenna, and she pretended to be a duck and bit his finger. But her eyes were playing a different, more dangerous game, and by the time the farmer reappeared, with the motorcar hoisted onto a cart and pulled by a pair of horses, Robert's pulse was racing faster than any automobile.

When they got back to Hendra and the sulky, he thought of kissing her, but she drew away with a laugh and insisted that she must get back to Goldmarten. 'I was expected back hours ago,' she said with a smile, 'and Papa will be furious.'

But she didn't look the least concerned as she dropped him back in River Street and the sulky drew away.

All in all, it had been such an encouraging day that he simply had to find Back Lane. It wasn't difficult, and when he knocked on the door and the thin grey woman answered it, he knew that his luck had not deserted him. 'Fanny?' the woman said. 'No, she was married last week and gone to Australia with that child and his father. But Katie's here. Just come home from Mr Olds'. Who shall I say?'

'Tell her Mr Trevarnon,' Robert said, 'come in answer to her letter. Oh, it's perfectly all right,' he added, seeing the look in her eyes. 'I used to be her employer.' He gave her his most charming smile. 'Here,' he held out the letter, 'see for yourself.'

A moment later he was being ushered indoors.

Katie could not believe her ears. 'Mr George? Here?'

'Mr Trevarnon, in answer to your letter. That's what the gentleman said,' Mrs Williams repeated. She was in quite a flutter. 'Nice looking gentleman, too.'

'Yes,' Katie said, her cheeks flaming. 'Yes, he is. Yes. I'd be happy to see him.'

She looked around the room. It had never looked so poor and barren, but at least it was tidy and clean. For the thousandth time she blessed Mr Olds for her neat uniform and good stout boots. But it wasn't for Mr Olds that her heart was pounding and her mouth was suddenly dry.

There was a tap on the door.

'Come in,' she said, gripping her fingers against the chair until they showed white.

Her heart skipped a beat as the door opened, but when she saw the man who stood there it almost stopped altogether. *Robert* Trevarnon! She felt cold and sick. She tried to speak, but the words choked her.

'Surprised to see me?' He was coming towards her, smiling that confident, honeyed smile. She caught her breath.

'Don't be afraid, Katie.' He was laughing at her, looking her up and down with those casual, mocking eyes. She clasped herself defensively, as if she were suddenly stripped of her garments. 'What is there to be afraid of, a pretty girl like you?'

'What do you want?' Her voice was a croak.

He gave her a playful frown. 'That's not very friendly, is it, Katie? Not when I came to give Fanny something I owed her.' He took out a guinea and placed it on the table.

Suddenly she was furious. 'How dare you? How dare you come here! Haven't you done enough damage? Ruined Fanny's life, or would have if Noah hadn't married her. And what about me? Packed off like parcels, and what did you care what became of us? And now you have the nerve to come here, offering your guinea like a fairy in a pantomime. Where was that guinea when we were struggling to find clothes for our backs, or bread for our bellies?'

'Katie!' He put his hand on her arm to restrain her.

She snatched herself away. 'Don't touch me! How dare you touch me!'

He held his hands up, innocent. 'No, Katie, believe me. I didn't mean it to be like that. But I didn't know where you were. How could I send the money? And then George got this letter. I came, as soon as I saw it, but I seem to be too late.'

There was some justice in that. She gave a deep sigh. 'I suppose so, it was stupid of me to send it, I suppose, but Carrie said that she'd seen him down at the Terrace, and he'd sent some money . . .'

Why did that make him smile suddenly, in that self-satisfied way?

'You wanted to thank him and let him know where you were?' He picked up her hand and patted it. 'It was only natural.'

She snatched her hand away. 'What did he want to show it to you for?'

Robert shrugged. 'Perhaps he thought I should pay my debts.' He gazed at her with a sudden seriousness. It was worse than the teasing. 'He isn't here, you know, Katie – he's gone to Plymouth. Something about his wretched regiment, he says, but reading between the lines, I think there's a woman in the case. George is never happy these days unless he's thinking about Africa.'

It was foolish, the way that news made her blood run colder. What could George Trevarnon have ever been to her, or she to him? She attempted a smile. He took it as encouragement.

'I wanted to see you anyway, Katie.' His voice was urgent. 'Ever since I caught sight of you in town the other day. You were always a pretty girl, Katie, but now you're beautiful.'

He caught her arm again.

'Don't!' she said.

'Don't what?' He was closer, pinning her arms, pulling her towards him. 'Don't admire you? That's not possible, Katie. Your sister was pretty, but you are magnificent.' One of his hands caught her hair and pulled it back, so that her head went up and her face was tipped towards him. 'Don't kiss you?' She might have cried out, but his lips were on hers and he was kissing her roughly. 'Don't do that? Is that what you mean?'

She twisted her head, but the pain from her pinioned hair made her cry out. One of his hands slid across her shoulder and towards her breast. But the action released his grip and she tore one hand free and slapped him with all her force. Her fingers left four red imprints on his cheek. For a moment, her heart raced. What would he do to her now?

But he let her go, laughing.

'What a little minx it is!'

'Get out!' Her hair had tumbled from its pins and she felt pillaged and dishevelled. 'Get out or I'll scream the place down.' She was breathing hard.

He must have believed her, because he said, 'All right, Katie, I'll go. For now. But I'll come and see you again. I promise.'

'I'll tell everybody . . .' she said.

'Tell them what? That Fanny has my child? But she doesn't, does she, Katie? She's married the father. The lady downstairs told me. Or will you tell them that I came visiting? But I've got your letter, thanking Mr Trevarnon for his kindness and offering your address.' His voice was suddenly dangerous. 'So what are you going to tell them, Katie? Or shall I tell them – why I bring you a guinea when I call?'

It was a threat. Her reputation was her livelihood. She picked the coin up and flung it at him, but he swung out of the door and it clattered onto the floorboards. She heard his laughter all the way down the stairs.

She was shaking. She closed the door and leant against it with all her weight, but there were no returning footsteps, and after a long time she straightened up. She was sobbing as she moved the table against the door, and jammed the back of the chair under the handle. She could not eat, and though she tossed for hours in the darkness, she could not sleep.

She turned the problem over again and again in her mind, but she could find no solution. She had been dismissed with Fanny, without a character, but she had built a new life, slowly, block by block. And here was the same man, threatening to pull it down around her ears again, unless . . .

Tomorrow she would ask Mr Olds. He would know what to do. But already she knew what he would say. He had made his offer very clear already.

Was it fair, to turn to a man like that, when only short hours ago her pulse had raced and her spirit lifted at the very thought of someone else? Mr Olds was not George Trevarnon. No, her heart whispered, but he is not Robert Trevarnon, either. He is a good, kind, worthy man and you are a lucky woman that he has asked you.

In the morning she didn't go directly to Eva. Instead she went to the study door. He was at his desk, working on some papers. 'Mr Olds?'

He looked around, and when he saw her, stood up, smiling. 'Katie?' He saw her face, and held his hands out to her like a father. 'You've come to give me your answer?'

She took a deep breath. 'Yes, Arthur. I will be your wife.' And she ran forward into the safety of his arms.

PART FOUR : 1903

CHAPTER NINETEEN

Arthur – she must get used to calling him Arthur now – had applied for a special licence. There was no reason to wait, he argued, and after Robert Trevarnon's visit he was not happy to have her living in Back Lane a day longer than necessary – sensing her fear, although in fact she had said very little about it.

He found a little rooming-house in Lemon Street, 'dinner provided', and insisted on taking her there himself. Katie panicked when she saw the place – her meagre savings would never stretch to this. She had already paid Mrs Williams the week in advance and there was very little left, especially as, it seemed, she was not to teach Eva again until the wedding was over.

'It would put you in an awkward situation,' Arthur had said. 'Come and see us by all means, Eva would miss you dreadfully if you didn't, and so should I, but I can't employ you one week and marry you the next.'

But no Eva meant no money coming in, and in any case the rent here would have been beyond her. She waited until Arthur had left and then went to see the landlady.

'The rent?' the woman said. She was a thin, nervous soul with an anxious face like a rabbit. 'But my dear girl, it's all taken care of. Your fiancé has paid for everything.' The nose twitched. 'No, you make yourself at home.'

Katie, overcome by embarrassment, went back to her room, but it wasn't much like home. There was a carpet on the floor, not so thick as the carpet at Trevarnon, or even at Number Twenty-three, but a proper carpet, that went under the bed and everything, so you could stand on it without getting cold feet when you got up, and when you wanted to wash in the morning.

There was a real brass bedstead, with two pillows and fresh sheets and a quilted coverlet, and a soft mattress which swallowed you up when you lay down. The wardrobe was huge. Big enough to take all the clothes for everybody at the Terrace all at once, even supposing one lot wasn't in the wash. There was even a picture of three chubby children eating soup, and a text which said *God bless this house*.

Katie unpacked her possessions. They seemed swallowed up in those enormous cupboards and drawers, but she arranged them as best she could and went down for the 'dinner provided'. It wasn't an elaborate dinner, just a stew, but it was nourishing, there was plenty of it, and it was served to her. She hadn't been served like that since she was a child.

The evening, though, presented a problem. For the first time since she could remember, Katie had nothing to do. There was no sewing, no cleaning, no cooking, not even Fanny to talk to. She undressed and sat for a long time in the delicious comfort of the bed reading her *Just So Stories* and feeling like Lilly Langtry. But it was rather a guilty feeling.

It was the same in the morning. No water to fetch. It was brought, hot and steaming, to her room. She ate a few spoonfuls of porridge – she was still too full from the night before to eat any more – put on her cloak and walked to Fore Street, wondering how she would fill her day.

She need not have worried. Eva wanted an outing. She could get out of the invalid carriage now, when they reached the park, and walk around for a few minutes, and she hated to miss it. Katie had been anxious about what Eva would think of her news, but she need not have worried – Eva was delighted, and could talk of nothing else. When they got back Arthur was waiting.

'We must think about your wedding outfit,' he said with a smile. 'I'll take you shopping, a wedding present.'

'You've already paid for my lodging,' Katie protested.

He laughed down at her. 'That wasn't a present. That was a month's wages in lieu of notice.'

Dear Arthur. He knew how to give a present so that it was possible to accept. They went out together. On the steps he offered her his arm, and she felt oddly grown up as he took it and they set off into town.

Katie was not prepared for what happened next. She had expected to buy material, and perhaps a bonnet and gloves. Instead Arthur took her to an emporium, with shop-made costumes, ten and six apiece. Kate was appalled by such extravagance, but Arthur insisted that she choose one. She didn't know where to begin, so the assistant whisked her into the fitting room behind the little lace-curtained door, and helped her to try them on and model them for Arthur. Each time she stepped out she saw his eyes light up with pleasure. In the end she chose a blue one, with a little jacket and a stand-up collar, trimmed with a satin edge, because Arthur smiled most broadly when she came out in that.

It still seemed like a dream as the salesgirl put the money into the little brass canister and sent it whizzing across the wires to the cashier, while she wrapped the costume in tissue and placed it in a box to be carried away then and there. A brand new costume, chosen and paid for, just like that.

Then there were other shops. A hat to match, a beautiful deep blue with a big brim and a bunch of cherries, new gloves, and shoes – real shoes with a strap and a little heel, not boots.

And finally, there was a visit to Mrs Lomas. Arthur murmured instructions and then left her alone in the shop for this. Katie was taken into the upstairs room. She blushed scarlet as she stripped to her shift to be measured and fitted. In front of Mrs Lomas, too!

'He's spent no end of money,' she said, as Mrs Lomas laced her into a corset, taking her breath away. 'A quarter's wages, near enough. I could have made it for a fifth of the price. It doesn't seem right to take all this.'

'Hold still,' Mrs Lomas said, giving an extra tug to the laces. 'No, Katie, you enjoy it. Poor man's been on his own too long, it's a pleasure for him to have someone to buy for. You let him buy you some pretty things. There'll be time enough for sewing when you're married. Now, how does that feel?'

'Terrible,' Katie said wryly. 'If I'd known you had to be half-strangled to be married I wouldn't have said yes.'

Mrs Lomas laughed, but she let out the laces a little. 'You're not used to it, that's all, and with your little waist you hardly need it. Some of the ladies that come in here have to lace their corsets so tight they can't stand up quickly without feeling faint. But wait until we've finished, and then see what you think.'

She brought out a frou-frou skirt, a camisole with suspenders, lisle

189

stockings, and a pair of silky knickers with lace edging. Whatever would Lally say?

'Now try the costume,' Mrs Lomas said, and Katie could hardly believe the transformation. In the mirror was a beautiful, elegant lady in blue. The corset gave her a real figure, she swished as she walked, and the pretty shoes and stockings made her feet look two sizes smaller.

A proper Cinderella. Her own grey skirt and cape, which she had thought so smart, seemed drab by comparison, and she could hardly believe her fortune when Arthur came for her, and took her home in a cab, surrounded by parcels.

Only one thing marred her pleasure. She went down to the kitchen, full of glee, to share her pleasure with Peabody and Mabel. But Mabel didn't smile.

'I suppose you'll be all airs and graces now, and we'll have to call you "madam".'

'Of course not,' Katie said. But Peabody replied firmly, 'I should think so too! When Katie marries Mr Olds she's mistress of this house, and that's how you'll treat her. And don't look like that, Mabel Harris, you were tickled enough when Mr Olds was courting her. Deserves a bit of happiness, poor man, and Katie'll be a pleasure to work for, you'll see.'

'Don't be silly, Peabody,' Katie cried. 'You've run the house for years. I shan't interfere. And what we should do without Mabel, I don't know.'

It brought a smile to the girl's face, but as Katie went softly upstairs she felt that more than the kitchen door had closed behind her.

It *would* rain, the day of the races, just when a man needed to travel half way across the county. Peter Gillard came early, in the brougham.

'Ah, there you are, old man! Ready for a flutter on the fillies then? Should be a good day, in spite of the weather.'

Robert regarded him with a jaundiced eye. 'More amusing than yesterday, at all events!'

Gillard laughed. 'Ah, yes, you went to the mine, didn't you? What a confounded bore. I paid up, of course, one can hardly do less, but I cried off the visit. Thinking of selling my shares, anyway, if I can find a buyer. Prices are up at present, but there's no future in it. So, how did it go?'

Robert pulled a wry face. 'Oh, they'll have their new shaft, right enough. Pouring good money after bad. I should have let them knock the mine and good riddance, but Papa was enchanted.'

'Well,' Gillard said, 'you might tell a fellow more than that. Was it amusing?'

Amusing! The whole day had been purgatory. Robert's stomach contracted at the thought of it. Just going to the counthouse had been bad enough. The path was uneven, and he had stumbled like a fool, conspicuous in his elegant clothes, while the mine-captains, be-whiskered old fools in dusty waistcoats and important bowler hats, had strolled down the treacherous incline as though it were a carriage-drive.

Then an hour of shifting from one foot to the other while the purser spread out plans on the counthouse table, and the captains stabbed their fingers and droned on about seams and shafts and winding-engines. He might have dozed on his feet if it weren't for the noise – the incessant thump and clatter, hiss and groan of the machines – and the pall of damp air and dust that hung everywhere.

A tour of the mine shops, then – carpenter, blacksmith, rope-makers, even a barber – all tidied and swept especially for their visit, so Papa maintained. It was hard to see how. Robert could not imagine how they could possibly be any more filthy and shambolic than they were now.

And then, the moment he had been dreading. He did his best, even at this late stage, to talk his way out of it. He was fascinated by the streaming sheds, he must have another look – although in truth the puddles of slimy tin, the men shovelling up to their knees in sticky red mud, and the horrible corrugated jagging boards shaking to and fro filled him with disgust. But it was no good; the captains simply gave the party another quick tour of the sheds, and then it was underground.

It was everything Robert had feared. They went down on the whim, in a sort of huge bucket affair, to save the walk. Robert thought he would have preferred the ladders, and almost said so, until he saw the ladder-shaft, hundreds of feet of flimsy ladders poised over nothingness. And when they got out at last, and walked along the level, it was not much better. Filthy streams of water underfoot which ruined your boots, little outcrops of rock overhead which threatened to knock you senseless. Shadows and darkness, though Papa swore that the candles and hurricane lamps hung on the wall had been added for their benefit, and that the miners normally depended on the bunch of yellow tallow candles which hung from their buttonholes. And down here, a remarkable, unearthly quiet; echoing clanks, rumbles, voices, and occasionally a far-away 'boom' which someone said was the beat of the pumping engine, but Robert knew, in a cold and clammy sweat, was an explosion.

And then the final indignity, a trip back from the end of the level riding in the skip along the tramway. Robert was enthusiastic at first – anything rather than walk in these caverns of hell – but the first ten seconds changed his mind. The trammer in charge, scrubbed and polished for the occasion, like the skip itself, gave two loud thumps on the compression pipes, and set the thing in motion. The sensation of plunging helpless into the darkness at an increasing speed, with tons of rock over your head, threatening to engulf you at any minute, had haunted his sleep last night. Even now he could feel the prickle of sweat along his collar when he thought about it.

He looked up to find Gillard grinning at him. 'Well?'

Robert managed a shaky laugh. 'Not your cup of tea, old man. Not a woman in sight!'

Gillard laughed too. 'Well, we'd better look sharp, old man, or we'll be late. The Tregorrans are expecting us for lunch, you know.'

Robert glanced out of the window, and looked at the brougham doubtfully. The recollections of yesterday had turned his stomach, and the thought of travelling all the way to Fowey in that stuffy, swaying contrivance made him feel distinctly queasy. 'I made sure we were travelling in your motor,' he said, with as much indifference as he could muster, as he fastened the ruby tie pin which Caroline had given him for Christmas.

Gillard laughed. 'And so we should, if it weren't for this con-founded weather. Though you know, Trevarnon, you might not have liked it as well as you suppose. I took her out for a spin on Saturday, and we were just tootling along nicely when we came to a great pig in the road. Confounded animal wouldn't budge, of course. Tried to go round it and hit a rock. Broke the chain and had to pay to have the de Dion towed back to town. I was afraid Morwenna would fly into a sulk, but she thought it the greatest lark.'

'Morwenna?' Robert felt a short, sharp stab of jealousy. Despite his engagement to Caroline he had begun to think of Morwenna as his own, as if she would come to him by some divine right, and Gillard's words gave him an unpleasant jolt. It was unfair on a fellow, Robert felt, to be pulled between two worlds in this fashion. On the one side

Morwenna – all excitement, passion, adventure; on the other the dreary economic reality that bound him to Caroline, duty, and that dismal mine. It was hard to play the ladies' man and force a knowing smile. 'Morwenna, eh?'

Gillard laughed again. 'Yes, Trevarnon. She's a rip, that one. I don't mind telling you.' He gazed out of the window, and said nonchalantly, 'Tempted to follow your example, Trevarnon.'

'Example?' What had the man heard? Had their little adventure in the car somehow come to the ears of his acquaintance in Penzance? That could be damned awkward – Selwood would cut up about it, and Papa would withdraw that offer of meeting the mine subscription, venturer's visit or no.

But Gillard was looking at him mildly. 'Settle down. Marry. She's a damned handsome girl, Trevarnon. Your Caroline is pretty enough, I grant you, but there's something about Morwenna that makes a man's blood race, don't you know? Hey,' he added, glancing at Robert's face, 'steady on, old man. No disrespect to your Caroline. It's as well we don't all have the same tastes, or there'd be deuced few happy marriages.'

Robert collected himself enough to make some casual reply. He had been a fool to let his feelings show – it was as well Gillard had put such an interpretation on it – and would have to be more careful in future. All the same he was inwardly glowering, and his temper was not improved when he found that Gillard was proposing to take the train to Fowey. That would mean a fare, and first class too, in this company, and he had been quite counting on a free trip in Gillard's motor. Never mind, he comforted himself, if this filly came in he would have a motor of his own before the weekend was out.

It was such a relief to get out of the brougham and into the air and comfort of the railway carriage that he recovered some of his good humour, and was able to joke with Gillard about the horses and women they passed on the journey. When they came to change trains, the station master, who knew Gillard's family, came up himself to escort them to the new carriage, an attention which was flattering enough to make him feel quite lighthearted by the time they reached Tregorran.

Lunch was excellent, and the race-going party set out in high spirits in the Tregorrans' four-in-hand, with a well-stocked hamper perched up beside the coachman. It promised to be a good afternoon, despite the drizzle.

It was irksome, of course, not to be able to bet on most of the races, and there was not even a woman in the party. The Tregorran boys were friends of Gillard's, and Robert did not know them well. He was glad of it, because it enabled him to disguise his anxiety over the big race.

He managed it well. He had laid his twenty guineas as casually as any of them, and forced himself to glance away as the horses thundered up the field. The damp ground made them slow and Robert thought his heart would actually stop before the race was over. When he looked back the filly was running well, but there was a grey on her shoulder as they approached the winning post. It occurred to him, with a little cold shudder of realisation, that Gillard's filly might lose.

Gillard was watching, a resigned smile on his face. Robert's mouth went dry. It couldn't lose, it couldn't! And then, on the last furlong, the jockey urged the filly into a last frenzied effort. The black, by a nose.

Gillard slapped his hands in triumph. 'Good show, Trevarnon! What did I tell you, eh?' But Robert's hands were trembling, and he did not lay another bet the whole afternoon. He could not wait for the weekend to be over, but it was Easter and he would have to cool his heels until Tuesday at least.

But he had won, Papa had paid his subscription call, and that dreadful visit to the mine was over. Things were looking up. As he lay in bed that night he was already dreaming of the motor, and of a red-haired girl laughing beside him.

Lally came up for the wedding. Katie had not expected it, but Lally wrote back to say she was coming, and on the morning of the wedding there she was, a ramrod in black in a dreadful coalscuttle of a bonnet.

'Registry, indeed,' Lally sniffed, looking around the room in Lemon Street, 'and paying for you to be here. I never heard the like!' She glanced at the bed where the underwear was laid out ready to put on. 'And whatever have you got there, Katie Warren? You're never going to wear that! Just as well I left Rosa and Willie at home with Mrs Tremble. I'd have died of shame if they'd seen their sister wearing that!'

'They wouldn't see it, Lally,' Katie protested, unable to resist a smile. 'You wear it underneath!'

'Always did have a clever answer. I told your father so, many a time,' Lally said. 'Well, he never did see Fanny wed, and he won't see you neither, so you'll have to make do with me. But if I'd known what I was letting myself in for, I might have saved the fare.'

There was something in her voice which made Katie look at her suddenly. She hadn't realised before how much Lally was missing Davy. And the fare from Penzance could not have been easy to find. No wonder Lally had left the children at home. 'Thank you for coming, Lally. Arthur will be glad to meet you.'

'I should think so, I'm sure,' Lally said, but she seemed mollified, and went downstairs cheerfully enough while Katie changed.

She felt like a princess in a story book. Warm water, scented soap and hot fluffy towels to wash, and then every stitch she put on clean and new and pretty, from the inside out.

She looked around the room. Most of her possessions had already been packed into the large wooden box which Arthur had sent round, and she folded the skirt and blouse she had been wearing onto the top, and closed the lid. It was like closing a book at the end of a chapter. She twisted her hair into a knot, put on the hat and gloves, and went downstairs.

Lally glanced at her as she came into the hall, then looked away. Katie was hurt for a moment, until Lally turned and stared. 'My life, Katie, it's you! Whatever do you look like! Turn around and let me see you. Ideas above your station, you're getting, my girl. Mind, you clean up decent, I'll say that!'

From Lally that was high praise. The little landlady emerged from her burrow and exclaimed in delight, and so did one of the other guests. Then the cab arrived, as Arthur had promised. Lally, struck dumb by these 'goings-on', said nothing all the way to the registry.

The ceremony passed in a dream. Arthur's friend the curate was there again to give a blessing, and there was quite a little crowd of people outside the registry office and later gathered in the drawing room at Number Twenty-three.

Peabody had made sandwiches and salads and even baked a cake, and she moved around the room offering food and beaming at Katie as though she was personally responsible for her happiness. Mabel came and went with the teapot. Mrs Williams was there, and several of Katie's sewing customers, and a number of people she didn't know who were friends of Arthur's.

Mrs Lomas came up and said, 'And when you need anything for yourself or Eva, you will think of us, won't you, Mrs Olds?' which gave Katie quite a turn. It was the first time anyone had called her 'Mrs

Olds', and the idea of being a regular customer of Mrs Lomas was startling.

Eva was allowed down, though she had not been to the wedding for fear of catching a cold, and she was sitting on the end of the ottoman beside a tiny wizened woman in an old-fashioned hooped skirt, with a lace jabot and a kind of eyeglass on a stick.

'You must meet my aunt,' Arthur said, taking Katie's elbow and guiding her to where the old lady was. 'Aunt Beryl, this is Katie, my wife.'

Aunt Beryl pulled herself very upright and examined Katie through the eyeglass for several minutes in silence. Then she said. 'I suppose you know what you are doing, Arthur. The child is young enough to be your daughter. Still, what's done is done.' She turned to Katie. 'I hope you make him happy, child.'

And that was that. Arthur squeezed her arm and murmured 'Aunts can be difficult!' as he led Katie away, and she, recollecting herself, took him to meet Lally.

Lally was sitting on a narrow chair, very precise, with her arms hugged to her side and her knees together as though she was trying to take up as little room as possible.

'I don't know, I'm sure,' she said, as soon as Katie came close enough to hear. 'Curates and registry offices. Your poor mother will be turning in her grave. And all this carry-on. You know what the Bible says about treasure on earth.'

'But a virtuous woman is a prize above rubies,' Arthur said, which took her so much by surprise that she allowed herself to be coaxed into eating cake. He introduced her to Beryl, and Katie saw them half an hour later, still perched on the ottoman.

'They are quite happy,' Arthur said, 'agreeing about how deplorable it all is.' And made her laugh.

'I didn't know you had an aunt,' Katie said.

'She lives at Polruan,' Arthur said. 'She's the third life on a cottage my grandfather built.'

That meant nothing to Katie, and she might have asked him about it, but Arthur went on, 'How does your aunt manage?'

Katie told him.

'It was good of her to come,' Arthur said. 'It can't have been easy to manage the fare, in the circumstances.'

Then Arthur produced sherry and glasses. Katie was horrified. She had never tasted alcohol, and certainly never been present when it was offered to guests. And whatever would Lally and Aunt Beryl say?

But Aunt Beryl was already taking little ladylike sips, and complaining that it was 'too dry', whatever that might mean. Lally was watching her with a kind of horrified fascination, but she said nothing, and Peabody brought her a glass of cordial and one for Katie too.

There were toasts, and good wishes and farewells. Aunt Beryl sent for a cab, and Lally, perhaps because of the sherry, refused to share it and went stomping off in the direction of the station.

Arthur had booked a trip on the river ferry, the first time Katie had ever been on the water. For a whole hour they drifted past wooded slopes and sleepy villages, and then returned as the setting sun turned the ripples gold, and the steady pulse of the steam engine mingled with the late mournful calls of the birds.

Later there was dinner, and then bed. She had known what to expect, and she allowed him his due. He was awkward, but gentle and grateful, and afterwards, looking at his face as he slept on her breast in the moonlight she thought that it was a little thing, a small price to pay for making him happy.

CHAPTER TWENTY

Caroline was in the music room when George came in. He was surprised to see her. Lunch had been over for an hour and she and Robert had gone off together for a walk in the gardens. Certainly the weather was chill for April, but at least the day was fine and the spring flowers were making a wonderful show, carpets of late narcissi and bluebells under the trees in the park, and the rhododendrons and azaleas turning the avenue into a blaze of purple. Just the day for a lovers' stroll.

Yet here was Caroline, seated miserably at the piano, staring at nothing in particular. She wasn't even playing. She looked up sharply when George came in, and then sank back again with a little sigh.

George almost said, 'Where's Robert?' but he stopped himself in time. He knew where Robert was, and so did Caroline if she had any imagination, which he sometimes doubted. He was out in his precious motor. And since the Gillards had a house-party this weekend, he probably had Peter Gillard and Morwenna Poldair as passengers.

'You didn't go for a drive?' he said, feeling that he must say something.

She shook her head. There were tears of hurt and anger in her eyes. 'I don't enjoy automobiling. I've tried to like it for Robert's sake, but it blows you about so, and you get dust in your face, and your clothes are spoiled, and it's forever breaking down and Robert can't mend it, and has to send for a mechanician . . .'

George nodded. He knew exactly what she meant. He had been out for a spin with Robert himself, and it was precisely as Papa had predicted. Robert drove everywhere too fast and too recklessly, so that the motorcar threw up clouds of dust in dry weather, and gallons of mud in the rain. Anyone he passed was likely to be showered with one or the other, and he created pandemonium as he went. Horses started. Chickens scattered. Cats and pigs yelped and ran, and dogs galloped after him barking with all their might. Add to that the constant threat of breaking a wheel, or losing ignition, or running out of petroleum in some out-of-the-way place, and Robert's passengers had to have a thirst for adventure before they could enjoy the drive. Only Morwenna seemed truly to relish the experience, and where she went Gillard went, which was fortunate: his presence in the car avoided scandal.

But only just. It was clear, at least to George, that Robert thought more of Morwenna, and less and less of Caroline. He gave her a friendly smile. 'Well, we'll leave those madcap adventures to the others. We civilised people shall stay at home and have a little music before tea. Won't you play for me?'

She did so, willingly enough, and he listened with as much interest as he could muster, though there was nothing of great merit in her performance. She did, however, recover her spirits, and when she had finished and he was clapping his hands and crying 'Bravo!' she turned to him with a smile.

'You are so kind to me, George. I'm such a little silly, I know, but I can't help feeling low when Robert is so much with Morwenna, and now . . . Oh, never mind. It's altogether too foolish to mention.'

'What is it?' George said, knowing she intended him to ask.

'He's lost his pin, the ruby one I gave him for Christmas. He wore it to Fowey, and he says it slipped out and was lost at the races. I'm sure he didn't intend it, but it pains me a little. Not that he lost it, but that he cares so little for losing it. I asked him about it, and he was quite sharp with me.'

'I see,' George said. He had heard the story of the lost pin, and it was true, Robert was positively secretive about it. He glanced at Caroline. She looked so vulnerable, standing there with her candid blue eyes clouded with tears, that he felt suddenly protective. He longed to comfort her, but could think of nothing to say, except 'But he brought your necklace home when he came from Fowey, didn't he? He was not completely careless of you.'

She brightened at once. 'You are right, George. He took the trouble to take it all the way to Truro and have it mended good as new, and he stopped to fetch it for me, even when he was concerned to buy his motor. Of course he thinks of me, and we are to be married so soon, of course he wishes to spend time now with his other friends. He will not have so much opportunity later.'

She had talked herself into cheerfulness. He couldn't agree with her view of the future. Damn Robert, he thought, could he do nothing but go through life making young women unhappy? He said quickly, to cover the silence, 'Are we to expect your parents for dinner tonight?'

She looked at him, her eyes shining. 'Oh yes, it will be quite an occasion, I believe. My aunt is to be there, and my cousin Gertrude . . .' She prattled on happily.

George gave an inward groan. It was Mama's latest preoccupation, inviting every unmarried lady in the district, and sending him into dinner with them. There had been half a dozen or more already, in the fortnight he had been back from Plymouth. He had a dim recollection of Gertrude at the Selwoods' Christmas ball, a dowdy redheaded girl with teeth, and the prospect of an evening in her company was not exhilarating.

He thought of Kernerwek and her pleasant ways. He thought of a little dark-haired housemaid, and felt his heart constrict. He looked at Caroline. 'Two of a kind,' he thought.

He smiled. 'Well cousin, at least the sun is coming out at last.' He nodded towards the window. 'Shall you and I take another turn in the gardens before tea?'

He offered her his arm, and they went out onto the lawn, keeping in sight of the windows, and that was where Robert found them on his return.

Robert parked the car beside the stables, took off his goggles and driving cap, and hurried down the avenue. He had not intended to be out so long. Caroline would be reproachful, and he was acutely aware that she had cause.

He prepared himself a contrite face, but as he turned the corner of the house he saw her walking on the lawns, leaning on George's arm and laughing. A wave of joyful relief swept over him. Everything was turning out perfectly – luck was running with him.

Take this afternoon, for instance. That little spin in the car, which had turned out to be so much more. He had begun by asking Caroline as he always did.

'I'm taking a drive to Newbridge,' he said casually at lunch, over the cheese and grapes. 'You don't want to come, Caroline?'

She shook her head, and he did not press the point.

'Let's take a turn in the gardens,' he said, and bustled her out, almost before the others were out of the dining-room. A quick turn around the roses and the rock-garden, and then he was able to use the threat of rain as an excuse to shepherd her back into the music-room and take his leave.

He was whistling as he cranked over the car, adjusted the spark and eased the automobile out of the drive and down the lane, keeping his speed to no more than walking pace. It was not until he was well away from the house that he put his foot down and raced along at nineteen or twenty miles an hour. This was how he liked to drive, fast and dangerous, but the smoke and dust and engine noise would have been conspicuous, and he didn't want Papa or George interrupting his afternoon drive, or worse still, offering to join him.

Gillard's house. Gillard's man was watching from the window, and Peter and Morwenna came out almost immediately, as they always did. It saved him from having to stop the engine; it could be tricky to fire up a second time.

Gillard scrambled onto the back, and Morwenna opened the trunk under the seat and took out the goggles, coat and cap which he kept there. He had ordered two sets under the pretext of providing one for Caroline, but she had worn hers only once, and a sorry sight she had looked, drowned in the heavy coat and dwarfed by the little cap and its prominent peak.

Morwenna, however, wore them with stylish grace. His pulse quickened as he looked at her. The mannish cut of the coat made her look even more feminine, and the cap on her beautiful hair was almost jaunty.

'Drive on, coachman,' she said lightly, jumping up beside him on the bench seat.

In the back, Gillard grumbled and fretted, but it was impossible to be out of humour with Morwenna for long, and when she suggested exploring a narrow rutted lane leading down to Lamorna, neither of the men protested.

For the first half-mile it went swimmingly. The lane led down through woodland, where primroses and daffodils were still in bloom in the deep dark shade of the overhanging branches. Morwenna exclaimed over the red squirrels dancing across the branches and the rabbits which popped out of their burrows to see them come, and thudded away with a flash of white powderpuff when the car rattled close.

But there had been too much rain. The road was rough with rocks and pebbles which skittered under the wheels, and sticky with mud in the trenches between. Robert put the brakes on as they came to a particularly steep bend, but the car refused to slow, and it was only with difficulty that he slewed it to a halt by jerking the steering-wheel sideways and sliding it, broadside on, into a gateway.

Morwenna clutched at her cap and gave a little breathy laugh.

'Thrilling!' she said. 'Don't stop, Robert!'

But they had stopped, and not all Robert's heaving at the handle would coax the engine back to life. Gillard glowered.

'I knew I should have brought my motor,' he said. 'This car of yours is all very well, Trevarnon, but you need a more modern automobile for country driving.'

Morwenna smiled at him in a way which made Robert's heart turn over. 'Peter,' she said, in her most beguiling tone. 'What a clever man you are! Of course, your automobile! A piece of rope and it would be easy to pull this one free.'

'My auto?' Gillard said. 'But that's half a dozen miles away, and besides, we should break the axle. No, a horse should be good enough for this. We passed a farm just the other side of the turning.'

'Oh Peter,' Morwenna said, 'how sensible! I'm sure you could get there in no time.'

And Robert found himself alone with Morwenna, as Peter Gillard walked sulkily back up the uneven lane and out of sight.

'Now then,' Morwenna said, turning towards him.

He was not prepared for it. Not all the servant-girls on all the stairs of all the country houses in the duchy had prepared him for this. She took off his cap and held his head in her hands, pressing her lips to his.

He was so surprised he almost protested, but his body knew better. This was what he had dreamed of for months, and he abandoned himself to the kiss as her fingers unloosed his buttons, and then her own, and drew his hands to her breasts.

It was shocking, amazing, but what happened next was even more incredible. She pulled him back into the woods, and he had her, leaning against a tree trunk. It was magnificent, crazy, dangerous, what if anyone should happen by? What if Gillard returned? But she knew that. It was part of the danger, part of the excitement, part of the thrill that took and shook him, and left him panting, exhausted and ill at ease as Gillard reappeared down the hill with a farmer and a pair of stout little horses.

Morwenna took it in her stride. 'You are clever, Peter,' she cooed, smiling at him with a cool self-control which left Robert speechless.

Gillard gave him a swift, triumphant look, and Robert could have laughed aloud. Even the necessity of paying the farmer double what he had reckoned on, and a long ignominious battle with the starting handle when they got back to the road, could not dampen his spirits, or take away from the terrible secret joy in mind and body.

He felt a little guilty, coming back to Trevarnon; doubly guilty, because he was also late. And now here was George, entertaining Caroline, so that she actually smiled at his approach. He felt positively benevolent towards his brother, and as they went in to tea, an idea struck him. He would put a little something George's way, and make a few pounds himself into the bargain. The way his luck was running, he could hardly lose.

It was, after all, an opportunity. Tin was doing well, Gillard was quite right. And the new shaft was under way; they wouldn't be wanting more capital subscriptions for quite a time. If George could be persuaded to buy his share of the mine, it would be a very good deal for them both. He would be glad to get rid of it, George would have an astute investment, and the sale would bring in the money that he needed.

Because he did need money. He had to face that fact. That win at Fowey had barely paid for the motorcar. It had not even covered the expenses of getting it home.

It wasn't altogether his fault, really. He had somehow supposed that driving a car would be very similar to driving a cart, and had not really listened with close enough attention to the instructions the farmer gave him. It was not until the car was his, and he found himself trying to drive it home, that the problems of the situation really struck him.

A horse, after all, did not need to be continually reminded of the shape of the road ahead, and there were some miles of near-misses with trees and gateposts before he became accustomed to the necessity of constant steering. Horses naturally put more effort into walking uphill, and slowed down on the other side, and Robert had been glad that there had been no-one nearby to hear him shouting 'Whoa' and pulling at the steering wheel in his first vain attempt at braking. He was just getting the hang of it, and beginning to enjoy the admiring looks of people at the roadside and of the children who came running out to look, when the engine died, and he had to send a message to Penzance for a man to come up to Crowlas on the train and bring him some more spirit for the engine. Horses eat when they are hungry.

It all had to be paid for. And he must keep up appearances. Selwood must never guess his real financial position. Nor Morwenna either, for that matter. With the Poldair fortunes at her back, and presumably coming to her one day, she was accustomed to the best. She loved automobiling, but she would hardly be impressed if she knew that he was forced to count every shilling. Still, he had the measure of the car now, although it was still an expense. The other problem was more immediate.

He could not leave the tie-pin at the pawnbroker's. It had been an obvious move to pawn it in order to redeem the necklace and pay for the repair, but now he was in an awkward dilemma. Caroline believed he had lost it at the races, so that was not a problem, but he could hardly leave it in Truro. There was always a chance that someone would buy it, if it was not redeemed, and since it was a Selwood pattern, it might easily be recognised and awkward questions might be asked. Besides, it was worth much more than the fifteen guineas he had taken for it. Fifty, at least, with that flawless ruby. Much better to sell it outright, somewhere miles away, like Plymouth or London, where it could never be traced.

But to redeem it he needed money, and what with the car and the motoring clothes, and the mechanician, and expenses like the farmer today, money was in short supply. No, if he could persuade George to buy those stocks, that would solve everything. It would even give him enough money to get married on in comfort. And with the price of tin rising, George would get a good deal, too.

He gave his brother a warm smile across the dinner table. Dear old boring, dependable, George. Thank goodness he had come to the rescue with Caroline. How shocked he would be if he knew about Morwenna.

When George left the party that evening, Robert went up after him.

'George, old man, I was thinking during tea. Suppose you couldn't be persuaded to make a little investment in mining stocks? It should turn you a pretty penny.'

George gave him a wary glance. 'Is this another of your madcap schemes for getting rich overnight? If it is, I don't want any part of it.'

Robert put on an aggrieved face. 'What a cynical fellow you are, George. You might give a man the benefit of the doubt. No, there's no scheme about it. I have a holding in Penvarris mine, you know that, and I want to sell my shares, that's all. It's a good moment. The price of tin has been rising, ever since the start of the African War, and this month's prices are the best for a long time. Couldn't be a better time to buy.'

'Then why are you so anxious to sell?'

Damn the man, why was he so difficult to persuade? Robert tried a disarming smile. 'Tell you the truth, old man,' he said, 'I've been sailing a bit close to the wind where money is concerned. Caroline, you know, and the motor. And the mine has taken a lot of investment lately. That new shaft, new winding gear, new winzes, and then there was that unfortunate accident when one of the surface workers was crushed to death and they had to repair the tin-stamps. So there have been a lot of subscription calls – but it has all been done, now, there shouldn't be any more demands for some time. Anyway, the stocks would be better off in your hands than mine. My heart has never been in it, you know that. Look at it this way . . .'

It took an hour of persuasion, but at last George agreed. He would take the mine stocks, at the prevailing price on the first of June.

Robert went to bed a very happy man.

The time had come.

Lally pulled on her best bonnet and jabbed it into place with a long jet hatpin. It was one of Maggie Warren's pins, typical flibberty-gibbet thing, all shine and sparkle. But Lally had lost her own, and the last few weeks had taught her to be frugal.

The collection from the mine had seen them through till now, by dint of scrimping and saving, and with the money still coming in from the boys in America she had managed to feed the children and still pay the rent, but now there was very little left indeed. She peered at her reflection in the corner of the mirror over the kitchen sink, which Davy had used to shave in. She looked respectable, if a bit tired and drawn.

She set her lips. Well, she wasn't beaten yet. It wasn't really begging, asking for an extension on the rent. She would pay it all back just as soon as she found some work somewhere scrubbing or cleaning. That would be possible now that Rosa was four and old enough to go to school. She'd have to find a penny for that, of course, but that was money well spent. She tried not to think about the little figure walking into the school gates that morning, dwarfed in one of Katie's old dresses cut down, and clinging to Willie's hand for dear life.

Well, that Katie would just have to find a bit to help. She didn't expect anything from Meg and Fanny, with babes to support and only labourers' wages coming in, but Katie was different. With the amount of money in that house you would have thought she'd have sent something without needing to be asked, and that husband of hers had been fair-spoken enough. But what could you expect when folk gave themselves airs?

Lally sniffed. It hadn't been like that when she was a girl! Sherry and hansom cabs and servants fetching and carrying. Whatever next! And as for that underwear!

She smoothed the bodice straight over her own thin body, seized her basket and purse and set off, shutting the door behind her. She went out of the back and up the field.

It was windy, but fine, which was just as well. Penzance, and the estate office, was a long walk, but the bus cost money.

Mrs Goodbody was down the bottom of her garden beating her mats, and called out a cheerful greeting. Lally said 'Morning', gruffly, and hurried on. She could do without people stopping her to ask questions, today of all days.

The road was pitted after the months of rain, and walking was difficult. Once or twice a cart rattled by, or a man on horseback, and Lally was forced to huddle into the wall, among the campions and stinging-nettles, until they had gone by, and even then her boots and skirt were plastered in dirt. Whatever would they think of her in the estate office?

And when one of those newfangled motor-carriages roared past in a cloud of smoke and shower of dust, she went so far as to shake her umbrella after it. Dratted machines! Say what you like, it wasn't natural. No wonder the weather had been so unseasonal all the spring, and half the promenade in Penzance had washed away. And that red-haired baggage in the passenger's seat had positively laughed at her! Typical carriage folk!

She was glad when Penzance came into sight, and she trudged down the long hill into the town. Children playing mumbly-peg in the gutters looked up as she passed, and a herring-woman bustled up offering her wares, which stared up sightlessly from a big basket, full of blood and scales. Lally would have dearly loved a drop of fresh fish, but tonight's tea was bread and scrape, and goodness only knew how they would eat tomorrow.

She found the office at last. It took all her courage to walk in.

Gentlemen in cutaway jackets and pocket watches straining over tight waistcoats were sitting at desks behind a little partition, scratching away at great heavy ledgerbooks, and writing official-looking letters and sealing them with sealing wax.

The oldest and sternest of the gentlemen looked over his glasses and said, 'Yes, Madam?'

'Is this the rent office for the Poldair estate?'

'It is.' He didn't sound friendly.

'I came to ask . . . that is, I wanted to speak about the rent. Mr Warren's house in the Terrace at Penvarris.'

He got down from his stool without another word, and went to consult one of the heavy ledgers stored on the shelf. When he came back he was smiling.

'Yes,' he said, coming up to the partition to speak to her. 'That seems to be in order.'

Dratted man. He must know what she wanted. She licked her lips and said, firmly, 'Can you tell me please, when the next payment is due, and how much?' He was going to do her no favours, that was for certain.

He looked at her mildly. 'The rent is paid up until Christmas, Mrs Warren.'

She said 'Miss', automatically, and almost failed to hear his next words. 'You can tell Mr Olds that the draft for the full amount arrived from Truro yesterday. He will get his receipt in due course. But it has been recorded. There's no need to concern yourself.'

She managed to thank him, and walked out into the pale spring sunshine. Paid until Christmas. Well, that was handsome. Mind, he needn't think she was beholden. She'd find that scrubbing work and pay back every penny.

But she did allow herself to buy some herring, and ride back to Penvarris in the horse-bus.

CHAPTER TWENTY-ONE

Mabel brought the letter in at breakfast. There were always letters for Arthur, three or four of them every day, brought to the table with the newspapers so that he could read them over his porridge and eggs and bacon.

But this was the first time there had been a letter for Katie in the seven weeks of their married life. Mabel propped it up against the cruet and said 'One for you today'.

'Thanks.' Katie gave her a grin. Peabody might grumble and nag, but Mabel never called her 'Mrs Olds' and Katie could not bring herself to say things like 'Thank you Mabel, that will be all'. Some of the callers thought it odd, you could tell, but Arthur didn't seem to notice, and Katie felt much more comfortable this way.

She was learning, with Peabody's help, to oversee the housekeeping – who would have believed there could be so many tradesmen to pay, and such quantities of food and polish? – but on the whole she did not interfere in the kitchen. She still devoted her time to Eva, as before, and accompanied Arthur on walks in the park, or read to him in the evenings by the fire.

She had feared, at first, that she would never fill her time, but she had soon found things to do. Eva was getting stronger every day, and thirsty for lessons, and there were other occupations too. Sewing, for one thing.

As Arthur's wife she seemed to be changing her clothes every five minutes. He expected her to change her dress for dinner, and to put on a tea-gown if they had company at afternoon tea, as they sometimes did. At first she had found this a chore. It was hard to sit still and make conversation with people she did not know, especially important people like the councillors' and landowners' wives who came to drink tea while Arthur discussed building plans with their husbands. She had been mortally afraid of saying the wrong thing, and would much rather have been Peabody or Mabel, handing out the scones and bread and butter or pouring the tea.

But it was important to Arthur, and she learned to smile and nod graciously. She had even managed recently to overcome her nervousness when Aunt Beryl condescended to call. The first two visits had been misery: the old lady's beady eye, queenly manner and immense feathered hats had intimidated Katie so much that she hardly spoke a word. But when she learned from Arthur that Aunt Beryl had commended her as 'an excellent listener', Katie felt a great deal better.

After that she had begun to enjoy the role of hostess, and quite relished the opportunity of putting on a teagown so that she could discard her stays and sit comfortably for once. 'Stays,' she wrote to Carrie privately, 'are the worst things about being Mrs Olds.'

Her old wardrobe, one grey uniform and a skirt and blouse for best, was no longer nearly enough, even with the addition of her wedding outfit, so there were lots of things to be made. She would have preferred to do it all herself – the idea of paying a seamstress or buying ready-made seemed a terrible waste when she had been a sewing-lady herself – but Arthur had other ideas.

'Katie, my dear,' he said gently, 'some poor creature will be glad of the income.'

So now there was Annie, with her work-worn fingers and her skin-and-bone face, sent by Mrs Lomas to sit in the sewing-room at the top of the stairs, doing the coarse sewing and mending, and trying not to look hungry when Peabody brought in her tea-tray of bread and cake. Katie tried to be kind to her, but the poor girl was so frightened by the appearance of 'the mistress' that Katie soon gave up and left her to the mercies of Peabody and Mabel. But she still did the fine sewing herself.

And she read. She was delighted to find books in the house – not a library like Trevarnon, but a score or more of titles which had been given to Arthur when he was a boy, and others that had belonged to the first Mrs Olds. These last were rather poor things, Katie thought, full of feeble girls in grim castles, but Arthur's books were riveting. There were tales of explorers and seafarers, missionaries and knights. Some were stories she had learned at school with Miss Bevan, or heard her father tell, but many were new, and all were printed with wonderful maps and woodcuts which you could turn to and devour again and again. There were even one or two with tinted pictures, carefully protected by pages of tissue paper bound into the book. She could read them for hours, whenever Arthur was out in the evening, or Eva was asleep after her walk.

'You'll wear out those pages,' Arthur said one day, returning home to find her sitting by the fire, with her head full of Richard Lionheart, the book open on her knee and her sewing forgotten. He patted her shoulder. 'There are some paper-books of my mother's somewhere. I'll get Peabody to look them out.'

A whole trunkful of *Household Words* from the attic. All the stories of Mr Dickens, and Mr Wilkie Collins too, told in parts. They became her evening reading, and Arthur enjoyed them too. There were a few issues missing, and she walked the house in a frenzy for days, worrying over poor Smike at Dotheboys Hall, until Arthur came home one day with a tenpenny copy of the book and put her out of her misery.

And all the while, life at Number Twenty-three was filling her body as well as her mind. The mirror told her so. Her face filled out and her skin glowed. Her hair and eyes sparkled. Ungrateful as it seemed, there were times when she could not eat the good food set in front of her. Like this morning.

'I've eaten enough,' she said, pushing her egg away untouched. 'Take that back to the kitchen, Mabel. If you don't want it, Annie might be glad of it.'

Mabel picked up the plate. 'You'll be wanting a paper knife?'

Katie nodded. She had been delaying the moment of opening the envelope addressed in that familiar spiky hand.

'Yes, thank you. It's from my Aunt Lally.' She smiled. 'Goodness knows what she would say to me leaving a perfectly good egg! But I swear, Mabel, I shall be too big for my beautiful new dresses if I eat at this rate. My wedding dress is already too tight around the middle.'

Arthur threw her an enquiring glance as she slit open the envelope. She smiled at him. 'Yes, it is from Lally. Not a deal of news. Fanny is safe in New South Wales – she sends the addresses, and Rosa has begun at school. Miss Bevan wishes to be remembered, she is to retire soon to get married . . .' She broke off, her eyes scanning the spidery lines with increasing wonder. ' "Thank your husband for his kindness in meeting our rent for 1903. Please assure him that I shall repay him at the first opportunity. Your affectionate Aunt, Leila Warren." ' She looked at Arthur, who was pretending to read the financial columns with great interest. '. . . "Our rent"? Oh Arthur, you never said! And here I've been trying to pluck up courage to ask you to do something for Lally for these last six weeks!'

She leapt up from her seat and went round the table to plant a kiss on his forehead. Peabody, coming in with the tea-kettle and toast, withdrew in confusion.

'There, now, Katie, I'm glad you are glad,' Arthur said. 'But it was no more than reasonable – they are your family after all. No need to take on and startle the servants.'

Katie blushed, doubly embarrassed at having embarrassed him. But his eyes were twinkling, and his voice very gentle as he added softly, 'Besides, if your clothes are getting too tight, Katie, perhaps you should not be leaping up and down like that?'

It was a moment before she took his meaning, and when she did she turned more crimson than before. 'Oh, no, Arthur,' she said, scarlet with confusion, 'I'm perfectly well. Besides, seven weeks. There's hardly time. It can't be anything like that.'

But it was.

Robert turned the car into Back Lane, whistling. It was a beautiful morning, the kind of May weather which was made for motoring.

The drive from Trevarnon had been a triumph: not a moment of engine failure, no hint of trouble with the ignition, not a single problem with the suspension or the axles. There had been one anxious moment when the car hit a particularly large boulder and he had feared for the chain-drive or the wheelspokes, but fortune had smiled upon him, and he had made the journey from Penzance in well under four hours. There was time to visit Katie for half an hour, call at the pawnbroker's to redeem that pin, and still be at the Poldairs' for lunch before half past one.

It was a particularly satisfying day to be lunching at Goldmarten. It had struck him forcefully, after that delicious drive, that his wedding date was only ten days distant, and that ever being alone with Morwenna again was something he would have to work very hard to achieve. And then, out of the blue, Caroline herself had suddenly decided to visit Goldmarten by train, since Morwenna was to be bridesmaid, and she wanted a last fitting with the dressmaker. He found an excuse to come to Truro, and contrived to be invited to the luncheon. He was to deliver Caroline back to the station with the seamstress, and then drive Morwenna back to Goldmarten before returning home himself. Already his heart was thumping at the prospect, his senses already aflame.

Perhaps, in a perverse way, that was what had brought him to Back Lane. He was uncomfortable about his last meeting with Katie; he could not pretend that she had welcomed his embraces. But he had promised he would call, he had cash in his pocket, and he could spare half a crown for that child of Fanny's. This time he would not force his advances. He would be charming, irresistible. At least he might make the peace. And if she succumbed . . . what? Perhaps, thinking of the long warm afternoon ahead, he would do nothing, merely turn away with a small, superior smile.

That would be the most satisfying thing of all. Besides, Morwenna made him feel invincible. He went up to the front door and rapped the knocker.

The thin-faced woman opened it, as before. He gave her his most dazzling smile. 'Katie Warren?'

He did not altogether like the look she gave him. 'She's not here.' The woman began to shut the door.

He put his foot in the gap. 'Come now.' He kept his voice sweetly reasonable. 'You know who I am. Has she been telling you untruths about me?' He felt in his pocket. 'A half-crown. A half-crown says you will let me see her.'

She looked at the money for a moment, but then shook her head. 'You don't understand, she isn't here. She married that Mr Olds just after Easter. Hasn't lived here for a month or more.'

Robert stepped back, and she closed the door with a sharp snap. For a moment he was nonplussed. Things had been going so splendidly. But perhaps, after all, it was for the best. It left him free to think about Morwenna – anything else might have been a distraction.

So, Katie was married. That would be something to tell George. Poor old George had always carried a flame for that girl, he was sure of it. Perhaps, if he was honest, that was why he had particularly wanted the conquest himself. Well, they would neither of them have her now. He went back to the car.

After that little setback he would not have been surprised to find that it refused to start, but it fired at the first swing of the handle, and did not die as he climbed into the driver's seat, as it sometimes did. He moved the lever to alter the spark and drove off, his high spirits returning.

The tie-pin, then. It had been remarkably easy to raise the redemption money, in fact. All it had required was a visit to the bank. He had explained about his marriage, about the price of tin, and that he intended to purchase more tin shares and sell them at a profit. It was true, as it happened. He had used some of the advance to buy Gillard's holdings. His contract with George did not specify the number of shares, and George had no way of knowing. The little deal with Gillard ought to turn to a nice profit. And the loan he had specified was a little larger than he needed. Enough to buy the shares, and redeem the tie-pin too. There was even a little to spare, so Fanny could have had her half-crown, had he found her sister in.

He drew the car up on the hill outside the pawnbroker's, chocking the wheels with a convenient stone. He was still whistling as he went into the shop.

The same little man with half-moon spectacles greeted him. 'Good afternoon, sir. Have you something to offer me?'

Robert shook his head. 'I've come to redeem my pin.' He fished in his inner pocket and produced the pawn-ticket.

The old man looked at it. 'But this redemption date was yesterday, sir.'

Robert sighed. So the old man was going to drive a hard bargain. Now he would have to pay a premium to redeem the wretched thing. Just as well he had funds. 'How much?' he said.

The old man shook his head. 'You don't understand, sir.' Everyone was saying that to him today. 'The pin has been sold. A lady came in this morning and purchased it. Said it was a present for her young man.'

'A lady?' Robert's brain was working quickly. It couldn't have been Caroline, that was the main thing. She would have had no opportunity, and in any case, she did not frequent pawn-shops. Well, it could not be helped. If the pin turned up in Caroline's presence he would simply have to stick to his previous story. He had lost it at Fowey races. Whoever found the pin had pawned it. It was a pity, but there it was.

'Thank you,' he said abruptly, and turned out of the shop.

The car was more reluctant to start this time, but he managed it in the end, and limped into Goldmarten just as they were deciding to give him up and go into lunch without him. Caroline scowled, and Mr Poldair looked decidedly displeased. Only the thought of Morwenna's soft, compliant body kept Robert from sulking all through the meal.

George was dining alone with his father. Mama was off at some charity luncheon, and Robert, for once, did not seem to have invited himself.

'Robert not joining us today?' George said, helping himself to the salmon croutes and kidney pancakes from the platters on the spirit-warmer. When Mama was away Mr Trevarnon liked to affect these masculine meals, a simple hearty buffet washed down with a good claret.

His father shot him a look. 'Young scoundrel's wangled himself an invitation to Goldmarten. Some junket of Caroline's, I understand. Arranging attendants' dresses or some such thing. Robert has driven up in that car of his. Damned nonsense if you ask me.'

George said nothing. Papa did occasionally confide his worries like this, but not usually about Robert.

'Spends too much time on that motor altogether,' Papa said. 'Still, keeps him out of mischief.'

George helped himself to wine. 'You think so?'

'You don't?'

'I came across Caroline in the music-room the other weekend,' George said carefully. 'You remember, the day Mama invited that dreadful cousin for me to meet?'

Papa nodded sympathetically.

'The poor girl was feeling positively neglected. She was Robert's guest and he had simply abandoned her to go off in that car. She seemed to think he had gone off to see Morwenna Poldair. Strikes me Robert thinks altogether too much of that girl, and not enough of the one he is supposed to marry.'

He wondered how Papa would react, but he only nodded. 'Tell you the truth, George, I've thought the same thing myself, more than once. And it is getting noticed.' He refilled his glass and pushed the decanter across the table. 'I've even wondered whether we are right to go on with the wedding at all. Few things are more soul-destroying than a loveless marriage.'

George had a sudden vision of beautiful women in a war-ravaged room in the Transvaal, but his father went on without a pause. 'But Caroline has her heart set on it. Anyone can see that. And if Robert tried to call it off at the eleventh hour, I do believe Selwood would sue. He's more than a little concerned by your brother's behaviour as it is.'

'Sue?'

'Breach of promise of matrimony. He'd have a cut and dried case too. The Selwoods have notified half the county and Caroline would look very bad socially if Robert cried off now.'

George took a sip of claret. It was probably excellent, as usual, but it tasted like ashes in his mouth. 'Robert wouldn't do that, surely?'

Papa sighed. 'We can only hope not. Because, I tell you frankly, George, if there was a substantial claim against Robert he would ruin more than himself. If he couldn't find the damages they might make a distraint against me, and that indirectly means Trevarnon itself.'

George paused, his salmon halfway to his lips. 'They could do that?'

'So I believe. I would have to take advice on the subject, and I'm reluctant to do that. I don't believe in meeting trouble halfway. Anyway,' he emptied the last of the decanter into his glass, 'I don't suppose for a minute it will come to that. For one thing he needs Caroline's money – I always suspected that was why he proposed in the first place. And marriage will steady him, no doubt.'

But George was following a train of thought of his own. 'But Morwenna Poldair is worth a pretty penny or two on her account, surely?'

Papa shook his head. 'Poldair, certainly. But not the girl. The Goldmarten estate is entailed, surely you knew that? She'll have an allowance, of course – a handsome one too, her father would deny her nothing – but the house and the land, and all the bloodstock business goes to the male line. Young Gillard, I understand.'

'Does Robert know that?'

'Oh, I imagine so. Poldair makes no secret of it. No, I daresay we are tilting at windmills. Still, I wish he'd pay a bit more attention to that young woman of his. Nice little thing, and besides, I always valued Selwood's friendship.' He looked at George. 'Always imagined you had a soft spot for Caroline yourself.'

George laughed and shook his head. 'The other way round, perhaps, at one time.'

Papa sighed. 'Yes, that may well be so. Pity perhaps, for the girl's sake. By the bye, George, I'd appreciate it if you didn't mention this to your mother. It is only ten days to the wedding, and you know how she frets.'

George laughed. 'At least it diverts her attention from trying to find a woman for me. Just think what I shall have to endure afterwards.'

His father gave a little snort of amusement, but he said more seriously, 'I wish you would think of settling down, George. Some of my estate will come to you, naturally. Perhaps more than you imagine. I'd like to know that its future was assured.'

'Produce an heir?' George said, wryly.

'Not put like that, no. But I would like to think you were happy. I did think, from your letters, that there might have been someone in South Africa . . .'

George sat for a moment in silence, twisting his empty wine-glass in his fingers. He thought of Kernerwek, Anna Brunner, his father.

'I wish you would talk to me sometimes, George,' his father said. 'We might have a good many things in common.'

George looked at his father's face; the years of keeping silence had etched deep lines on it. He nodded. 'Perhaps. But some things are better unsaid.'

A shadow crossed Papa's face. 'So there was someone?'

George got up and pushed back his chair.

'There almost was.'

'And . . . ?'

There was a long pause. George thought of a thousand things he might say, but in the end he murmured, quietly, ' "Almost" is the operative word.'

He took up his stick and limped out of the room.

CHAPTER TWENTY-TWO

Well, Robert thought to himself, this was what he had been waiting for. Caroline was safely on the train, and here he was in the car with Morwenna.

It had been a near thing. Caroline had done everything short of outright rudeness to avoid anything of the kind. She had protested that there was no need for Morwenna to come to the station, suggested that Morwenna took her in the dog-cart, invited other people to come in the car. For one awful moment he had thought she was going to propose that she and the dressmaker might drive home to Penzance with him, but her fearfulness of the car had prevented that.

Morwenna had handled it splendidly, affecting to believe that it was all a good-natured joke and not to be taken seriously. She greeted each new suggestion with a little laugh, clapping her hands and saying, 'You are a tease, Caroline!' until Caroline had abandoned her efforts and allowed herself to be shepherded onto the train as arranged.

He could feel his heart thudding with anticipation as he edged the car away from the station. He had already decided to take the back lanes back to Goldmarten. The road led through a wood, and he had found a spot with a clearing and a stream, where there was a broad flat stone screened from passers-by by a bank of rhododendrons in full flower. He would take Morwenna there. And then . . .

His palms were already sticky with excitement at the prospect of that 'and then', and he could find no words as he turned the car up the lane between the trees.

He found the clearing and nosed the car into it, stopping out of sight, under the shelter of the old wall. He snatched off his goggles and gloves and turned towards her.

'Morwenna!' His voice came thickly.

She turned to face him, her eyes aloof and mocking. 'Yes, Robert? What is it you want? Why are we stopping here?'

'You know what I want.' His hands went out to take her shoulders, but she drew back with a little laugh.

'Mr Trevarnon! How can you be so presumptuous? And you an engaged man too.'

She was teasing him, he realised distantly, and like a goaded bull he lunged, grabbing for her with all the insistence boiling in his blood.

'Robert!' This time there was no mistaking the warning in her voice. 'Lay a hand on me uninvited and I'll have you cried from every street corner in the county.'

He drew back, frowning at her in puzzlement. 'But . . . I was sure you . . . The other week at Lamorna . . .'

She smiled. 'You enjoyed that, did you Robert?' To his amazement she reached out and began to smooth his hair, which was straying from under his driving cap. 'Yes, of course you did. But it is not to be. My silly boy is engaged to Caroline.'

Why, then, had she taken such pains to ensure that Caroline caught that train and left them together? He shook his head, and her hand strayed down to stroke his cheek, his neck.

He understood then. She was playing him like a fish on a line. He knew it and was powerless to resist. She was reeling him in, teasing his desire until he was half-maddened. He reached for her again.

'Remember Caroline,' she said, evading his arms.

'Damn Caroline.'

This time she allowed him to catch her hand, and he kissed it in a kind of frenzy; fingertips, palms, wrists.

She drew it back, and adjusted her hat with it, a tiny feminine gesture of dismissal and self-control. 'This will not serve, Robert, we must go back. You to marry your poor boring Caroline, and I . . . I must make do with Peter Gillard.'

'Gillard!' If Peter had been here, Robert would have choked him. He brought both hands down on the steering-wheel with such force that they smarted and stung.

And then, inexplicably, she was yielding to him. More than that, she came to him of her own accord. She slid into his arms, soft and sudden under his hands, his lips. There was no bank of flowers, no softly-flowing stream – only the car and the wall and a mad burning urgency that left him panting, helpless and drained.

Afterwards, Morwenna watched him languidly as he straightened his clothing. Her eyes were cool and laughing as she said, 'What a bad boy you are, Robert. Whatever would Peter say?'

He caught her arm again, hard enough to bring red weals to the white skin of her wrist. 'You can't go to Gillard. You can't.'

'Don't be absurd, Robert.' She adjusted her hair and hat with a deft little movement. She was so self-possessed, so remote and untouchable that he longed for her again. He wanted to possess her, move her, make her acknowledge him. But she went on looking at him with those casual, unfathomable eyes.

'I'm crazy about you,' he said at last, and knew that it was true. Crazy. Insane. Past rational judgement. 'I'd do anything for you.'

She blew him a light kiss from her fingertips. 'I know. That is what makes you so irresistible. Poor Peter. He is a dear boy, but he is so predictable, and under all that bravado, so desperately conventional.' She laughed, and then added, after a little pause: 'But I am being unkind, and I have bought him such a pretty little trinket, too.'

A vague warning stirred in his brain. 'You have?'

'Such a pretty little tie-pin, not unlike the one Caroline gave you. I found it, you know, in a pawnbroker's shop, quite near where I found you that day in the dog-cart.'

He gazed at her in horror. 'You redeemed it? You bought it, knowing it was mine? Give it back to me, Morwenna, please.'

'Yours? How can it be yours, Robert? You lost your pin at Fowey races. I have heard you say so to Caroline. No, this is my pin. A present for Peter.'

'You wouldn't give it to Gillard?'

She gave him that special, mocking smile which made his pulse race, even now. 'Whyever not? I must find a good occasion for it, mustn't I? Don't you think that would be amusing?'

'Morwenna!' He was in her power now. It filled him with a fear and helplessness that was also part desire.

'Perhaps, if you are a very good boy . . .' Power and danger. They fired her. He could see it in her eyes and in her parted lips.

'Morwenna!' He was desperate. 'I'll do anything.'

She laughed back at him. 'Then you can drive me home.'

He hesitated, and then reluctantly slid out of the car and seized the starting handle. 'I mean it,' he shouted. 'Anything at all.'

'What, for example?'

'Try me,' he shouted, as the engine fired.

He could just make out her answer over the motor's roar.

'I just might do that.' And there was something in her face that might have been triumph.

Katie felt quite the lady as she climbed down from the horse-bus at Chapel Corner. A horse-bus from Penzance station to Penvarris, and it was not even raining! She was glad of the ride though. Her baskets were heavy, and Arthur had made her promise faithfully before she came.

In the fortnight or so since she had begun to suspect her condition he had given her what Mother would have called 'a good spoiling'. She mustn't lift, she mustn't exert herself, and she was forever being invited to sit and put her feet on the little footstool he had brought down from the attic for the purpose.

He was kind and good but, as she protested to Peabody, she wasn't ill. She had never felt better in her life – there would be time enough for all this fuss in another six months or so. But the first Mrs Olds, it seemed, had been a delicate soul, and had taken to her bed as soon as she discovered that Eva was on the way. Well, if Arthur expected her to do the same, he was mistaken.

She thought of her own mother, boiling clothes and scrubbing floors and laying fires to feed a family right up until her babies were born; and that without the benefit of 'building up' with fresh eggs for breakfast, good beef for dinner and 'an apple a day'. She thought again of that cheerful, uncomplaining woman, always with a song on her lips and a smile in her eyes, up to her elbows in baking or washing; and of Jack and the other babies who had died, perhaps for want of doctors. She realised anew her own good fortune.

She left her baskets beside the stile to pick up later, and went down the lane past the chapel to the non-conformist graveyard. She had not brought enough flowers. Instead she bunched the pinks and campions and the big white daisies from the wall as she passed. 'Margaretas' her mother had called them, and loved them as her own.

Her hands were full as she pushed open the little gate and went to the grave.

Lally had been before her. The grass had not yet grown again after Father's burial, but the earth was weeded and tidy, smoothed clean with the little wooden rake propped against a wall for the purpose.

There was a jamjar too, with three lupins from the garden, once as tall and stiff as Lally herself, but now weeping down onto the simple flat gravestone as though their hearts were broken.

Katie looked at the names inscribed there. 'In memory of Jack Warren, aged 6 years, Maggie Warren, 37,' and freshly carved 'and Davy, beloved husband of the above.' She did not often weep openly for them, but she did so now, opening her hands to spread the flowers in a carpet over the turned earth. She had done the same every year since her mother had died, but this was the first time she had strewn her flowers for her father too.

She stood for a long time looking at the warm, sleeping hillside, and remembering. Then she went softly back to the gate, and up to the chapel to collect her baskets.

That was Arthur's idea. 'Take a present for your family,' he had said, thrusting six half-crowns into her hands.

She knew he was thinking of giving the fifteen shillings, or buying food or clothes, but it was not as easy as that. Lally would be mortified by 'charity', especially on top of the rent. Katie had thought for a long time before she had found a solution.

'I shall bring a picnic when I come down to Mother's grave,' she had written. 'We can all have tea down on the cliffs, as Mother used to like.' Really, the number of letters between the Warren family these days was enough to keep the Post Office in business!

So here she was, laden down with picnic: a great cake, a piece of beef, a pound of cheese, and no end of fruit and jam and bread and butter and a bottle of stone ginger with a marble in the top. Willie would have the marble, or take the bottle to Penzance and have a halfpenny or so to spend on humbugs and comfits, so it was two treats in one. There were some dresses too, which Eva had grown out of, and which could be accepted without loss of pride, and the whole was wrapped in two cloths, lengths of cheap striped cotton which could be left behind to become shirts or skirts or bloomers as the need arose. Katie was quite pleased with her 'picnic'.

Lally was ready and waiting when she arrived. She had found a stone jar with a stopper, and when the children arrived from school a minute or two later, she filled it with hot sweet tea, and wrapped it in a towel for Willie to carry carefully upright. Katie walked with him, and Lally followed on with Rosa and a basket of crocks and cutlery.

'Just like old times,' Willie said, but really it wasn't, what with the cups and saucers and plates and Lally dressed up as if she was going to town, and insisting on everyone wearing pinnies. The warm tea was welcome though, and Katie was happy to drink that, and leave the stone ginger (which she was careful to call 'pop' and not 'ginger ale') for the children.

They tucked in heartily. There was news to exchange. Lally had had a letter from Meg in America – she had seen Jimmy and Tom and their families, and everyone was well. Katie had news of Fanny – Nicholas was growing like a tree. Willie told her about school – he was a good scholar, Miss Bevan said, and Rosa was settling in, although there had been a tantrum or two at first.

Katie glanced at Rosa, but the child was on her best behaviour, tucking into cheese and cake with singleminded rapture.

'That Miss Bevan is good with her,' Lally said. 'Though goodness knows how we'll get on when the new teacher comes in August.'

Altogether the picnic was a great success, but they could not stay long. Katie had to get back to catch her train, and Willie was due to go and help Crowdie picking stones behind the plough for an hour before dark.

'He's needing boots,' Lally said, 'and Crowdie was wanting a willing boy.'

Katie had her own ideas about why Crowdie had offered a job to Maggie Warren's boy, but she said nothing, only repacked her baskets which seemed to be as full as ever.

'Well,' she said, in a tone of careful surprise. 'We haven't made much of a hole in this! You'll have to take it off my hands, Lally, I can't be carrying this lot all the way back to Truro on the train.'

And Lally said, 'Well, I don't know, I've done my shopping. But I daresay I can find a use for it, if you don't want to go carrying it about.'

It was not much by way of thanks, but when Katie had emptied the baskets onto the table at the Terrace she reached into the reticule at her belt and gave Lally a florin 'towards Willie's boots'. She caught Lally's eye and added 'It's his birthday soon'.

Lally picked up the florin with a nod. She understood.

Robert brought the car to a halt outside the bank and pulled on the brake. A messenger-boy in a dark-blue suit and peaked hat turned round to look, and almost cycled up the pavement. Robert grinned.

It was still gratifying to see people stare, and although he was fast becoming a familiar sight in the town, he knew he could still count on finding half-a-dozen people crowded around the motor when he came back in half an hour.

He took off his driving-gear, straightened his cravat, and strolled into the bank, whistling.

He was not whistling when he came out. He brushed past the admiring youths without a glance, and shouldered his way to the starting handle. The engine fired almost at once, and he leapt in and pulled away sharply, leaving the young men to jump back and scatter. It gave him a certain grim satisfaction.

He did not pause to pull on his gloves and cap until he was past the station and clear of the town.

Blast and damnation! How could he have been such a fool? The shares had been doing famously, and he had promised himself a fat profit from Gillard's holdings. And now today, of all days – the day which he himself had nominated for the transfer of shares 'at the market price' – there was a sudden slump. If he had only closed with George a week earlier he would have earned himself a handsome sum. As it was he had cut his own profits and lost money on the Gillard deal into the bargain. He thought of taking a small revenge by telling George of Katie Warren's marriage, but even that prospect afforded him very little satisfaction – George thought her married already, so the news would hardly startle him.

He steered the car savagely at a cat sunning itself on the roadway, and was pleased to see it scamper away yowling, with its tail between its legs.

Trust Gillard to get out when the price was high. Trust George to get a good bargain. And trust the bank to have one of those new telephones so that he was forced to sell at today's low prices. Damn, damn and damn.

There was a fat duck sitting on a wall and laughing at him, and he squeezed the rubber bulb of his horn and sounded the klaxon fiercely, so that it fell backwards in surprise with a flurry of feathers. But it was not the cat and the duck that Robert was aiming at, nor even the bank manager; there was still an overall profit from selling his own shares to George. It was Gillard.

Gillard, who always placed the lucky bet. Gillard, who had taught him to wager in the first place. Gillard who talked loftily of his expectations and would never be drawn on what they were, but went on spending money as though he had inherited the Mint. Gillard, with his flashy good looks and his expensive tailors. Gillard and Morwenna.

That was the cruellest part of it. They would be at the Taylors' tomorrow night. Gillard would be squiring Morwenna, while he himself was stuck with Caroline. The enormity of it struck him like a thunderbolt. He did not want his fiancée. He wanted Morwenna.

And there was nothing he could do about it.

CHAPTER TWENTY-THREE

Morwenna was furious. How *dare* her father speak to her like that!
Did he think she was a child to be addressed in that way? She could
recall only one or two occasions, even when she was a child, when he
had spoken so.

She had known that something was amiss as soon as she came into
the drawing room. There was that dangerous flush in his cheeks which
spoke of anger.

'You're late,' he said. He hated unpunctuality of any kind.

She smiled at him. 'I have been out with the horses.'

He softened a little, but his voice was still cold as he said, 'Alone?'

'Yes.'

He rang the bell for the tea-tray. 'You were not with Robert
Trevarnon? That at least is something.'

She was surprised. Her father rarely questioned her actions.
Certainly, she had behaved badly – Robert's simple, primitive passion
made their game of sexual tag-and-run irresistibly exciting – but
surely her father could not have learned of that. She said lightly,
'Robert? He's harmless enough, surely? I find him amusing.' She
flashed him a smile.

He did not answer it. 'Amusing, perhaps. But what do we really
know of him? Father seems a decent enough chap, but the family came
from nowhere.'

'Ah, *mon père*, they might have said the same of grandfather. I
thought you an egalitarian.' She pronounced it in the French fashion.
She had learned to speak a little of the language when they were in
France, and she knew that her father was proud of her

225

accomplishment. Usually it swayed him. But not today.

'Egalitarian or not, do you think your behaviour quite becoming? More than once you have been out with him, alone, unchaperoned, and returned home much later than necessary. It puts out the servants, Morwenna. Besides, it gives rise to comment.'

So that was it. Her father was always extremely sensitive to gossip.

She gave a dismissive little laugh. 'To comment? But surely there can be no cause for comment. The fellow is to be married in a week or so.'

'Exactly so,' Poldair said. 'And his bride-to-be is unhappy about his attentions to you. Her father was here this afternoon and as good as told me so. Trevarnon may have no discretion in his actions, but I expect my daughter to show better breeding.'

She could feel the angry crimson rising to her cheeks. 'How so?'

She did not often defy him, and his voice was dangerous as he said, 'We'll have no more of it, Morwenna. I'll have no daughter of mine driving all over the countryside and disappearing into the woods for an hour at a time with a young man, let alone one who is espoused elsewhere. Is that understood? Besides, Peter Gillard tells me privately that he more than half suspects young Trevarnon of having disgraced himself with some servant girl a year or two back, into the bargain.'

'Rumours!' Morwenna said.

Her father looked at her coldly. 'Well, Morwenna, your reputation may not concern you, but it is my name you bear. You were the same from a child, always wanting the thing you could not have. Well, this time, Morwenna, you must want in vain. I forbid you to speak to Robert Trevarnon again, at least until after his marriage.'

'*Forbid!*'

'Yes, forbid, since polite instruction fails to move you.'

She tossed her head. 'It will be a hard rule to enforce, since I am to go to the Taylors' weekend tomorrow and he is to be of the party. Or would you have me ignore him, and cause a scandal?'

'You could scarcely cause more of a scandal than you have occasioned already. But since you anticipate such a difficult social situation, you might write to the Taylors explaining that you are indisposed, and will be unable to attend. I will have paper and ink sent to your room, and send the footman up later to collect the letter. It would be a pity to embarrass your hostess by failing to warn her of your absence.'

Morwenna caught her breath in fury. He had bested her. She might have said more, but the maid came in with the tray, and they drank their tea in hostile silence.

She had come up to her room to change for dinner and found that there was indeed a writing set on her dressing-table: paper, ink, pens, nibs, blotting paper, envelopes and sealing wax.

It was intolerable. She was to be denied the house-party, forbidden Robert's company, as though she were a child in petticoats and pigtails. It was unlike her father. He was accustomed to indulge her in everything. What could he have heard that had affected him deeply?

Peter! It had to be Peter. She had taunted him gently about her long 'walk' in the woods with Robert. No one else could possibly have known of that. She had never guessed that he would talk to her father about it. Unless . . .

Had he, she wondered, thought of asking for her hand? He had hinted as much once or twice lately, and it would be like Peter to discuss his misgivings with her father.

Well, she would not be talked about in this fashion, bargained over like a piece of farmyard machinery, to be accepted only in good working order. No, if a man wanted her, he would have to take her on her own terms, whoever she chose to see, whatever she chose to do. 'Forbidden', was she? She would see about that.

Robert was a goodlooking man. Wealthy, too – look at the life he led. Too good for that dreary cousin of his. And he loved her. He was her slave. He had said so himself. She thought of him, his eyes dark with desire, his voice hoarse with anxiety, when she told him about the tie-pin. 'I'll do anything,' he had said.

Well, she could put that to the test. Her father was to attend a dinner on Saturday, and if she was not to visit the Taylors . . .

She picked up her pen and began to write.

George was going to the Taylors' reluctantly. They had house-guests, he knew, apparently including Morwenna, which would doubtless please Robert. He himself had been invited to make up numbers, since there was to be a female cousin with no-one to take her in to dinner.

Mama was delighted, of course, but George began to feel more and more like the character in Mr Dickens' book who was likened to a leaf in a dining-room table – added to the party when there was an inconvenient space. He might have enjoyed it had there been someone to whom he could talk of something other than gossip and scandal, but he knew most of the guests and had no hopes at all of finding an agreeable dinner companion.

Papa and Mama, who were also to attend, had ordered the coach for eight, and they were to call at Lower Trevarnon and collect Robert on the way. The night was too dark for motoring, and besides, Robert would be expected to escort Caroline during the evening. Knowing Robert he would contrive to be invited for supper and be sent home with the Selwoods' coachman, thereby saving himself the expense of his own carriage. Really, Robert's manoeuvrings were quite transparent.

George stood in front of the long cheval mirror and wrestled with his collar-studs. Since he had come home from Plymouth he had adopted side-whiskers and they gave him an amusingly weighty air. His dinner partner would doubtless think him tiresomely middle-aged, and turn with relief to the gossip and laughter of his brother, who seemed so much younger. George chuckled at the prospect as he tied his evening tie.

Braces, waistband, waistcoat, coat. He looked dashing enough, although the stiff leg made his trousers hang awkwardly. He studded his cuffs, took his evening cane, and made his way into the hall.

It was one minute to eight, and the coachman was waiting. A minute earlier and Mama would have sent him away, to trot the horses around the house 'until you are wanted'. As it was, she allowed Papa to help her on with her wrap, lifted her dove-grey satin skirts clear of the floor, and consented to be led to the carriage. Papa climbed in after her, and George followed him.

They clattered down the sweep of the drive, the coach-lamps lighting the trunks and branches as they passed. George moved back the curtain and watched their progress, glimpsing the coachman's youngest daughter as she slipped out to open the gates at their approach, and huddled back into the shadows, ready to close them again when the coach had gone.

Down the valley to Lower Trevarnon. Robert had installed a gas light over the entry and it was burning brightly, bathing the front steps in its gentle glow. There was a light in an upstairs bedroom. 'Wretched boy isn't ready yet,' Mama said, fanning herself with her gloves, although the night air was cool. 'Run up and get him for us, George, do.'

George got out of the carriage and went up to the front door. He knocked and rang. There was a long pause. He knocked again.

Somewhere in the basement a door shut, and George heard shuffling feet in the hallway. Robert's cook opened the door.

'Master George? I'm sorry, sir, it's the man's night off. We weren't expecting company.'

'We've come for my brother,' George said. 'I hope he isn't going to keep Mama waiting in the coach. We are expected at the Taylors' within the half-hour.'

The woman stared at him. 'Mr Robert? But he's not here, sir. He got that letter about five o'clock, and he just upped and left. Sent the girl out for a hansom cab and left about two hours ago.'

'Left? He couldn't have gone to the dinner so early.'

'Oh no, sir. I don't think it was a dinner. A weekend of some kind, I should say. He took his cases with him.'

George went back to the carriage, baffled, and they drove on to the Taylors'. Robert was not there, though he had been expected.

'Called away suddenly,' Mama said. 'Though I can't think why he didn't let us know.'

The Taylors were very gracious about it.

'It doesn't signify quite so much,' Mrs Taylor said, 'since we are also a lady short at dinner. Morwenna Poldair writes to say she is indisposed and cannot join us for the weekend. So George, perhaps you will take in Caroline, and Peter Gillard can partner Miss Weston.'

And even then they did not guess the truth.

Dinner was over, and the guests were dancing, when Mr Poldair arrived. George was talking to Caroline.

They had essayed a slow waltz, which he could manage with difficulty, and now they were sitting out by the supper table. Caroline was visibly upset, but George was doing his best to comfort her.

'How could he be so thoughtless?' she said, and there was anger as well as sadness in her tone. 'To embarrass his mother, and his hostess, and me. And for what? Some hare-brained scheme, as we shall hear tomorrow. Or an opportunity to buy something for his precious automobile.'

George had to smile at the justice of this. 'It is possible,' he said. 'Robert sold a good many mining shares a few days ago. The money will be burning a hole in his wallet!'

'Oh, George,' she said, 'what am I to do?'

'You could try some of this excellent supper,' he said lightly, and she allowed him to choose her some of the canapés.

And then Poldair arrived. They heard his thunderous knock, and a startled exclamation from the servants, and then the man himself walked in, unannounced, his face like thunder, and still wearing his cape and gloves.

The musicians stopped and the dancers faltered to a halt. Mrs Taylor took a step forward. 'Mr Poldair, sir, this is an unexpected . . .'

He cut across her. 'Where is my daughter?'

'Your daughter, sir? Why, at home in her room, I suppose. She wrote to say she was unable . . .'

'No!' It was Caroline, her face ashen, dropping her plate and all its contents onto the polished floor. She stepped forward to face Poldair. 'She has gone with Robert Trevarnon, that's where she is!'

She turned and fled from the room. George looked from one face to the other. Poldair crimson with anger. Mama clutching her throat and calling for water. Selwood rigid with fury. And Papa, looking towards him with stricken, frightened eyes.

He turned and went out onto the terrace. Caroline was standing there, leaning against a pillar, her shoulders rising and falling helplessly in time to her racking sobs. She looked up as he put his arm around her.

'He's left me,' she said, and her face was ugly with tears. 'Only a week to the wedding and he's left me – like this, in public. It's so . . . humiliating. Who will ever have me now?'

And he heard himself say, in a voice that was not his own, 'I will, Caroline. If you will have me.'

Katie read the announcement in the *Gazette*. It was a discreet paragraph, tucked away in the social columns, but the name 'Trevarnon' leapt out at her like a banner.

'The marriage of Miss Caroline Anne Millicent Selwood and Mr Robert James Trevarnon, which was to have been solemnised at St Mary's Church on 23 June will not now take place. Instead, Miss Selwood will marry Mr George Edward John Trevarnon at a private ceremony on 1 July.'

She read the notice twice. Miss Selwood, then, was still unable to choose between the two brothers. She wanted to smile at the thought, but there was a painful lump in her throat. She looked at Arthur, dear, dependable Arthur, frowning over his letters at the other side of the table.

He glanced up and caught her eye. Instantly he was all concern.

'Are you all right, Katie my dear? A little tea, perhaps, or a coddled egg?'

His concern did make her smile. 'I'm quite well, Arthur, thank you. Only there is such an odd notice in the paper about the Trevarnons.'

She gave him the passage to read, and he nodded. 'Oh, yes, I heard about that. Quite a nine days' wonder. One of my business colleagues deals with the family – built the new house for the elder son, I believe. Seems he ran off with another woman, and left his brother to marry his fiancée. Just as well, I daresay. It will save the scandal, and all the wedding arrangements are made and paid for.'

Katie had to smile again at this. 'What a mercenary thing you are, Arthur.' Her voice trembled a little as she added, 'I think Caroline was always rather fond of George.'

'Well, there you are then,' Arthur said. 'Best thing all round. Oh, by the bye Katie, that friend I mentioned, the one who built Lower Trevarnon . . .'

'Yes?'

'He is to have a reception in his offices on the fifteenth – the day they are consecrating the cathedral. The firm had some part in the rebuilding, I daresay. In any case, he is inviting people to come for refreshments and to watch the procession. His offices have large windows and they overlook the route. Would you like to go?'

'To see the Prince and Princess of Wales?' Katy dropped the paper in her excitement.

'It is to be a private reception,' Arthur said,' so there is no need to worry about getting jostled in the crowds. We will have a seat high up at the window, so we should have a splendid view. He says there are to be decorations all over the town – a thirty-foot motto arch with garlands and Prince of Wales feathers and all the way up Boscawen Street shields and flags and streamers. What do you say?'

'Prince George and Princess Mary,' Katie said. 'Will we be able to see their faces, I wonder?'

'I should think so, from that window,' Arthur said.

'It's only a pity Eva can't come,' Katie said. 'A Royal visit. Wouldn't she love that?'

'All the schoolchildren are being given flags, and there's going to be a procession,' Arthur said. 'We'll get a flag for Eva, and Peabody and Mabel can take her out to hear the bands and see the floral canopy outside the Town Hall. She'll enjoy that, even if she doesn't see their Highnesses. But you shall go to the reception, if you would like to. It won't be too much for you?'

'I shall be fine,' Katie said, and in answer to the question he did not ask, 'I can wear my new green cape and skirt, and no-one will be any the wiser. It will be months yet before I have to be careful about going out in public.'

The smile that he gave her was so loving and proud that for a moment she did not feel quite so envious of Miss Caroline Anne Millicent Selwood.

CHAPTER TWENTY-FOUR

The wedding was everything Caroline had wished. There were only two attendants, of course, instead of three, and Peter Gillard was chief groomsman instead of George, and the wedding was not at St Mary's but in Trevarnon Chapel, but otherwise everything went off very much as originally planned.

Nobody mentioned Robert, at least in George's hearing. It was astonishing how totally all the guests seemed able to forget that Caroline was marrying the wrong bridegroom. Perhaps there was gossip enough later, on the lawn, when the big marquee was thronged with people sipping Major Selwood's champagne and eating the smoked salmon and strawberries, but George heard none of it. Indeed you might have thought that it was Caroline who had changed her mind at the last moment, and that Robert had fled with Morwenna in chagrin. In any case, people were keeping a discreet silence.

The family had heard from Robert, of course. Poldair had set up a search for him, but by the time he had been located, in the north of Scotland, he and Morwenna were already married. In a blacksmith's shop, so Mama said – George could imagine how that would appeal to Morwenna's sense of the dramatic. Mr Poldair had apparently bowed to the inevitable and agreed that, now they were safely married, he would permit Morwenna home, but Robert had shown enough discretion not to appear until after Caroline's wedding.

George looked around the lawn at the laughing, chattering crowd. He did not know half of them, and did not care for the others. There would be speeches next, and amusing little messages about garters and sleepless nights, and one or two of the younger men would get drunk and noisy, and the older ones would get garrulous. It was, altogether, not a day of his choosing.

He glanced over at the bride, Mrs George Trevarnon. She was looking radiant, in the dress which had been ordered for her marriage to Robert. The toothy cousin was standing by, dressed as a bridesmaid, and smiling hopefully at one of the Taylor boys. George thought of two other women he had known, one blonde and gentle, the other dark and pretty, both now lost to him for ever.

He took Caroline's arm. There were musicians in the marquee, and an attempt at dancing on the lawn. He led Caroline out, but it was hard enough to dance on the grass for the able-bodied, and he soon abandoned the attempt. Then came the speeches, and the drinks, exactly as he had foreseen.

Caroline went upstairs with her attendants and came down in a voile dress printed with pink roses, and a huge picture hat with a veil. The coachman brought the carriage round and they walked over to it, with the women tossing rose-petals from little, long-handled baskets, and some of the men throwing rice. One or two of his old regiment had come, and they drew their swords and made an archway of honour to the carriage door. They paused a moment in the doorway for the photographer, who burrowed under his black cloth, with his flash-maker in his hand, begging them to 'look at the birdie' while he fidgeted with the plates and pulled the camera string.

And then they were off, down the hill to the station and the train which was to take them to Plymouth. Caroline seemed to have enough baggage for a month, although their holiday was to be only a day or two, and it took two porters and the station-master to get her settled comfortably into her carriage. Even then she was restless all the journey, fearful of sitting with her back to the engine lest the motion made her sick, but afraid to face the other way, because she needed to keep the window open and the cinders might blow in and lodge in her eye or the veil.

She got out at every station, to take the air, and more than once the train had to wait because she could not close the heavy compartment door with its leather strap, and George had to do it for her.

But at last they reached Plymouth. George had wired ahead to a hotel he knew overlooking the sea, and their rooms were waiting. He tipped the hotel porter who carried up their bags and looked around him. A suite with two bedrooms interconnected, and a large bathroom between, with a modern geyser offering hot water, and warm fluffy towels. Suddenly, there was nothing he wanted so much as a hot, deep bath.

Caroline preferred to wash in her room, and change for dinner, so he allowed himself the luxury of a soak. He did not lock the door, not knowing quite how to handle the problem, but she did not come in, and he did not see her again until she was dressed and ready. He took her down to dinner, which was excellent, but she ate little. She was nervous and embarrassed, looking at her plate and pushing her food around it with her fork.

Afterwards they went upstairs. She locked herself in the bathroom, and when she came out, in a nightdress flounced and beribboned from neck to hem, she looked stricken. He sat on her bed, and she came towards him unwillingly, her face pale and goosepimples standing on her neck.

'Don't hurt me,' she said in a little whisper.

Suddenly, he was filled with tender pity, and any remnant of desire died in his veins. He went over and took her hands.

'It's all right, Caroline,' he said. 'You needn't be afraid of me. I shan't be much of a husband to you, my dear. My leg pains me too much.'

He saw the relief on her face, saw how she tried to hide it. He leant forward softly and kissed her hair.

'Goodnight, Mrs Trevarnon,' he said softly. 'Sleep well.'

And he went back into his own room, closing the door behind him.

Lally got up a picnic for Willie's birthday. It wasn't a day for it, with a cold, fretful little wind and a hint of rain in the air, for all it was early July. But Willie had set his heart on it, ever since that afternoon with Katie, and Lally had reluctantly promised.

'It won't be a patch on Katie's tea, mind,' she said severely as Willie and Rosa set off in the morning for school. 'We aren't all made of money like some folks I know.'

That was ungrateful and she knew it. They had eaten handsomely for a week on the food Katie had left behind that day. But she wasn't good at frippery, and she had enough to do without turning out picnics.

To start with, there was scrubbing to do up at St Evan. The church, the church hall and the vicarage. She wasn't sure she held with it, but the vicar's money was as good as anyone else's and she was glad of the work. She was used to it now, all that gold and stained glass, and crucifixes everywhere. And the vicar was kind enough, never failed to offer her a cup of tea when she finished, though she always turned it down with a polite 'No thank you, your worship,' which made him smile. Well, let him. You couldn't be too careful with these churchy folk and their queer ways.

It was a long walk back to Penvarris, and she was glad to sit down and have a bit of lunch, bread and dripping as she always had on a Wednesday. It was her treat after a hard morning, and with that bit of wages she could afford it.

Then there was the house to clean. Beds to air and mattresses to turn, rugs to beat and floors to scour. It all took time, without the pile of sewing waiting for her on the settle. Thank goodness for those dresses Katie had brought. There were clothes of Davy's which she could cut down for Willie, but Rosa had become a real problem. She thought back with a little guilty start to the basket of Katie's clothes she had so cheerfully turned to dusters when she had first come to the Terrace. She'd know better another time.

And then it was time for the picnic. There were pasties cooking – meatless ones; they had had enough beef last week to set them up for a while, but they were smelling good. There was a little of Katie's cake; she poured milk over it and toasted it on the griddle and it was as good as tea-scones. A handful of raspberries from the garden, and there you were. A good enough picnic, if it wasn't a feast.

Certainly Willie and Rosa were delighted with it. Willie was set on going down Cape Cornwall way, though Lally grumbled he would never be home in time for Crowdie, and they set off in procession, Lally carrying the tea-bottle, Willie with the basket, and Rosa capering on behind.

The walk was a tiresome one. Rosa had caught the excitement of the occasion and insisted on racing on ahead, clambering up on every stile, and hiding behind bushes and gateposts to leap out and startle Lally – and when she was spoken to sharply, she dawdled behind sulking, which was worse.

It was chilly at the Cape. The wind was biting, and Lally had to find a spot with her back to an old mine-shed to keep the cold from her bones, but they ate their pasties cheerfully enough, and nibbled at the toasted cake, although Rosa spat hers out and fed it to the gulls. Really, the child was becoming a real handful.

'Now then,' Willie said, picking up the empty basket, 'I'll just go down on the rocks and see if I can find any winkles or mussels worth bringing home. We might as well have the makings of a bit of soup while we're down here.'

It was half the attraction of coming, Lally knew. It wasn't so much the soup – the salt, fishy taste of it wasn't nearly so good as other soups she made – but the act of collecting the shellfish appealed to Willie. He loved to stand barefoot in the rockpools, a big stone in his hands, knocking the fish off into his basket. You had to knock them cleanly, first go, or they put out strong suckers and clung to the rock so hard that even a sharp blow would not budge them. Lally nodded, and Willie disappeared down to the sea.

Lally began clearing up, folding Rosa's pinny and shaking the picnic plates so that the crumbs scattered on the springy grass and the seabirds came after it, cawing and crying. Rosa ran after them, waving her arms and shouting with glee when they fluttered off in front of her.

'Mind where you go, Rosa,' Lally called. 'Don't you go climbing on any walls, now. There's mineshafts down there and you could easy fall. You hear me?'

Rosa nodded, and rushed off again after a seagull, laughing and shouting. Well, at least she was enjoying herself, Lally thought. She piled the cups and plates together and walked over to where she could see Willie, busy with his stone.

'You come back here now, Willie Warren,' she called. 'And mind you get those feet dry before you put on those socks! You'll be late for Crowdie.'

He waved back, lifting up the basket for her to see. It was half full of shellfish. She nodded and turned back.

'Rosa!' There was no answer. 'Rosa!'

Drat the child. Where had she gone off to now? Lally glanced back towards the shore, where Willie was carefully wiping his feet on his socks. She gave a deep exasperated sigh and set off up the slope again to look for Rosa.

She saw her, standing on a little stone wall a hundred yards away.

'Rosa! Get down. You're a naughty girl. Those walls are put up to keep you out. It's dangerous. Get down.' She lifted up her skirts and began to run.

Rosa stood on top of the wall, waving her arms. 'I'm a seagull. I'm a seagull. Look Lally, I'm a seagull!'

Lally made a lunge towards her. Rosa gave a little gurgle of laughter, and stepped backwards. And disappeared.

There was a high, terrified scream, and then sobbing.

Lally felt her skin turn cold. She half-ran up the slope and peered over the wall. There was nothing there, only a cluster of grasses and stunted bushes, and, sinister in their midst, a deep black hole.

'Rosa!'

'Lallal!' A cry of terror from somewhere deep below.

Lally was over the wall in an instant. There was no time to think. She crouched by the opening and peered down it. It was wider than it looked – the grasses hid the edge – but below her, perhaps twelve feet down, there was a ledge, and on the ledge was Rosa.

'Lally's coming.' She leaned forward over the hole. The child stretched up her arms, moving dangerously close to that great black hole that gaped beside her. Lally shouted 'No! Stay still.' Suddenly she understood about the ledge.

She had heard Davy talk about this. A 'soller' he called it, a place where a natural ledge had been left, and reinforced with boards, to make a standing-place for the ladders. Beside it the pit went on deep and fathomless, but every few feet there was a soller, so that the men could climb.

They were lucky so far. The first soller could be fifteen, twenty, thirty feet from the surface. This one was shallow, perhaps because the first seam of tin had not been deep. Twelve feet, no more.

She looked up. Willie was walking up the incline, his basket and boots in his hand. He saw her and came running.

'Rosa's fallen,' she said. 'Get help. Men and a rope. And hurry.'

Willie dropped his burdens and ran. Lally turned back to the hole.

'Lallal!' The voice was desperate. There was a movement, a scrabbling. A stone loosed itself from the soller and fell, echoing down the shaft, bouncing off the walls as it fell. It fell for a long long time, and then, far off, there was a splash.

'Lallal!'

If the child moved again she would fall down the shaft like that pebble. Lally took a deep breath.

'Lallal's coming.' She lowered herself over the side and scrabbled with her feet. There was no foothold. 'You keep still.' She looked down to see where Rosa's face gleamed pale in the shadows. 'Mind out now.'

She let go. The stones and soil scratched at her legs and face, as she spread her arms and tried to slow her fall. But the hole was too steep and she slithered quickly. There was a terrifying moment of nothingness and she landed hard, awkwardly, beside Rosa. There was a sharp pain in her leg.

'Lallal's here,' she said.

She tried to move onto her knees and the child came into her arms, sobbing. Lally held her, rocking her in her arms.

'There, there,' she said, awkwardly, over and over. 'Lally's here. Lally loves you.'

The ancient boards under her knees were decayed and splintering. Awkwardly she tried to shift her body. There was a terrible sharp crack, as one of the rotten planks gave way under the sudden weight. The central board had collapsed. Space gaped beneath her, but Lally thrust out her elbows and wedged herself against the stouter timbers of the frame.

They held. She tried to gain some purchase with her legs, her knees, anything to support her dangling body and take the weight from her cracking arms and shoulders, but there was nothing. She was still holding Rosa and the child's weight was almost insupportable, but the slightest movement and Rosa too would have plummeted into that terrible, gaping pit.

Her breath came in tortured gasps. She was tired. Desperately tired. It seemed a lifetime before she heard voices, Willie and Crowdie and Eddie Goodbody and others she did not recognise. There was a movement at the surface and a sudden darkness as someone leant over the hole.

'You there, Leila?'

'The child,' she tried to say, but it was only a groan.

'We're coming.' A man swung over the edge. They had him on a rope and she could dimly see him through the haze of her own blood pounding in her eyes, as they lowered him, inch by inch towards her.

'Give her here, then,' the man said, and lifted Rosa into his arms. She felt him take the child, felt the burden on her lungs and heart ease, saw him rise slowly and surely to the surface, and watched as firm hands carried Rosa to safety. She took great gulping gasps of air.

'Now you,' the man said, and she tried to lift herself towards him, but there was too much pain. 'My chest,' she tried to say, but her heart was cracking.

His hands took her, but she was dying before they reached the surface. Her lips moved and he leant forward to catch her words.

'Say Lally loved her . . .' There was nothing more.

Crowdie stood up, and rubbed his eyes with the back of his hand. 'Reckon she did, too,' he said slowly.

Katie took it very hard. Another visit to the graveyard. Another name on the stone. She went several times with flowers, and stood alone in the wind and rain, weeping tears of unexpected grief for the strange, grim old lady, who had learned to love only once, and paid for it with her life.

Arthur was very good. He never questioned what should become of Willie and Rosa; he simply arranged for Peabody to make up the spare rooms, and suddenly the house was full of children.

'It's good practice,' he said, when she tried awkwardly to thank him.

Eva was delighted by her new company. Willie was much her own age, and delighted to show off for her; bringing her butterflies and birds' eggs and offering to push the invalid-carriage, which she in any case needed less and less. Rosa was better than any doll.

All the same, it wasn't easy. Rosa was a worry: withdrawn, unhappy and subdued, wakening with nightmares night after night. Katie was at a loss what to do with her, until one day she came in and found Eva reading to her. Rosa was sitting rapt, which delighted Katie so much that she tiptoed out again and left them to it.

Something, however, had to be done. A school was found for Willie, but Arthur began to talk of getting a governess in for both the girls. 'You can't go on teaching Eva for ever,' he said. 'And Rosa needs someone. She is wearing you out, and you'll have your own child to see to, before long.'

It was Willie who suggested Miss Bevan. It was such a perfect solution that Katie wondered why she hadn't thought of it herself, and Miss Bevan was delighted to be asked. As soon as she finished at the school in August she would come to Truro, at least until she was married, in a year or so. Until then, Katie could manage, with the help of a nursery nurse.

Suddenly, life was busy. Too busy even to mourn Lally, or to wonder about the new Mrs Trevarnon. So many clothes to buy and meals to order, even though the children mostly ate theirs in the nursery, and only came down for Sunday tea. But already they were looking stockier, and Willie was learning not to eat everything on the table. There would be plenty again tomorrow.

She was so busy, in fact, that she forgot all about the reception party. The papers had been full of the coming Royal Visit, and the town was ablaze with garlands and streamers and flowers in boxes, but somehow when the great day arrived it took her by surprise. It wasn't until Arthur said, at breakfast, 'What time shall you be ready for the reception?' that she remembered about it at all.

Then, of course, there was a great deal to do. She had not been in society before and she was very nervous about it. She did her hair a dozen times, and changed her brooch quite as often. She pinched her cheeks and bit her lips to bring colour to them and 'generally behaved like a girl going to her first ball', as Arthur said.

She had never been to a ball, but the comparison was rather apt.

The occasion though, was everything she had hoped. There was a splendid view of the parades, the bands, and the decorations, and as the Royal couple passed Princess Mary looked up, and waved towards the window, clear as clear, so that Katie felt that Her Highness had waved especially for her. And when the service of dedication was over, they watched the procession move on again, towards Lemon Street and away out of the city. For it was a city now, with its own cathedral, and the people at the reception toasted it in champagne and orange juice.

Katie moved among the gathering on Arthur's arm. He introduced her as 'my wife' so proudly that people smiled. The friend who owned the office came up.

'There's someone here you must meet, Arthur. Family owns a big house and they're thinking of modernising; bringing running water in, gas lamps, that sort of thing. And perhaps building another house in the grounds. Fellow needs a decent architect and I've been telling him about you.'

Arthur smiled down at Katie. 'I'm sorry, Katie. Business before pleasure, as you know. We'd better go and meet this customer.'

'Here you are,' the friend said, appearing at Arthur's shoulder in the company of a fashionable lady in a tippet and a man with whiskers. 'Mr and Mrs Arthur Olds, may I present my clients, Mr and Mrs George Trevarnon.'

'Katie,' George said, and their eyes met.

PART FIVE : 1907

CHAPTER TWENTY-FIVE

After dinner George excused himself and went down to look at the new house, 'Little Manor'. It was almost finished now, and its handsome lines looked well in the golden light of the spring evening.

It was a fine design. The high, pitched roof and lofty bay windows gave it a light, almost airy look in spite of the solid granite of the walls, and it had been designed to sit splendidly in the curve of the hill. The very place, George remembered suddenly, where Robert had once urged Coral into the disastrous leap over the gate.

The gate had vanished now. The whole field had been transformed into a long rolling lawn, and already shrubs and flowers had been planted in some of the borders, while the tall trees at the lower hedge had been retained to form a screen between this house and Trevarnon. Arthur Olds had done a good job: it was a handsome property and George was very proud of it.

Perhaps it was just as well. Without this house, and the Guernsey cows he had introduced on the farm, and his interest in Liberal politics, his life would be very empty. Even his holdings in Penvarris mine, which at one time had commanded a lot of his attention, did not occupy him now. That new shaft which had caused such a run on the subscribers had hit copper just under the surface, and the mine was ticking over nicely, and expected to pay a dividend again soon.

He had rather hoped that the news of the copper find would rouse Papa, who had withdrawn into himself more and more since Mama had gone. But Papa had only said, 'May be tin there yet, copper always lies higher than tin,' and sunk into lethargy again. Blamed himself, perhaps, for Mama's death, but there was nothing anyone could have done.

One moment she had been her usual self, fuming at her milliner. 'The wretched woman has trimmed my new hat with ostrich feathers, although she knows nobody is wearing them now, since Queen Alexandra decided not to wear wild birds' feathers last year. And I simply have not another hat fit to be seen!' And she had gone up to the blue drawing-room with a 'headache'. Nobody had paid much attention.

But by tea-time she was really ill, her face like chalk, and in considerable pain. Appendicitis, the doctor said, and they took her to the hospital to operate, instead of doing it on the kitchen table, as they had done with old Mr Penvarris. But she had died from the effects of the chloroform.

Papa did not forgive himself. 'I should have listened to her, for once,' he said several times, and George hardly saw him these days.

With his brother George had never had much in common, even without the chilly relationship which naturally existed between Robert and Caroline. And as for his marriage . . .

He sighed. Caroline was an agreeable enough companion. Many men who saw them together must envy him his pretty wife, always so smiling and anxious to please. Anxious to please, in all respects but one. He had tried, a dozen or more times, to make her his wife in fact as well as in name, but every time her tears and terror had driven him back. Once, he had almost persisted, but she had stiffened like a corpse at his touch, and her sobs of fright had doused his desire as surely as a cold bath. Since then he had kept his own bed, and his own counsel. For they touched as little in mind as in body. And now Mrs Selwood was pressing to know when she could expect a grandchild.

With an effort he turned his mind back to the house. At least Little Manor would stand when he was gone.

It was taking shape. A fine big kitchen and scullery with two vitreous enamel sinks, running water and a brand new gas oven; deliberately designed to face north to prevent the room becoming too hot in summer. Gas mantles in every room, even upstairs, so that a simple turn of the tap and a lighted match produced more light than twenty candles. Two big reception rooms, facing south to catch the sun, a dining room, a study, a music room, and a big glass conservatory, painted white, which George planned to furnish with *art nouveau* cane furniture.

Upstairs, five fine bedrooms, with a dressing-room each. A bathroom, fitted out in mahogany and brass with rose-stencilled white-ware. Water on tap, a gas-heater over the bath 'guaranteed not to scald', and a little WC in a room of its own, with a wrought-iron cistern that flushed water automatically when you pulled a little handle on a chain.

Yes, Arthur Olds was a fine architect, and a fine man who took pride in his work. George enjoyed his company. He had enjoyed working with Arthur Olds at designing a bathroom and installing light and plumbing into Trevarnon House. He had enjoyed creating this little masterpiece of a house. It would have been the same, he told himself firmly, even if Arthur Olds were not Katie's husband.

Katie's husband. It still gave him a jolt to think of that. He could still remember the earthquake of shock at that reception in Truro, almost four years ago now, when he had stepped forward to be introduced to a prospective architect, and found himself face to face with her.

He had known her at once. She was no longer the girl who haunted his dreams, but a woman, more beautiful than ever. Her wild hair was tamed, and her girlish figure curved now, under the elegant green costume. He knew that his dreams would alter from that day onward. Where the girl had been sharp, shrewd and lively, the woman was graceful and intelligent. Expecting a child, from the way her husband guarded and cosseted her. His stomach knotted with envy. She was altogether lovely, and he had lost her.

He felt that loss more cruelly now, and it was no comfort to read its mirror in her eyes. He cursed himself bitterly for fifty kinds of a fool. Why had he ever allowed himself to be manipulated into going away? Why had he permitted Robert to deceive him, even for a moment? But it was fruitless to think like this. He had been a mere boy, and besides, whatever could have come of it? He should be glad simply to find her again.

It was her first child, as he later learned. He had heard such conflicting accounts of her circumstances that at first he had not known what to believe, but he had heard the truth from her own lips now. The plans for the house had given him an excuse to visit Truro, and he seized it with enthusiasm.

Once or twice he had timed his arrival carefully, so that he 'just missed' Mr Olds, and spent the afternoon 'waiting for Arthur', sipping tea and hearing the story of her life. What a woman she was, he reflected, how different from Caroline. He dragged his thoughts away from that dangerous path.

'I thought you had married and gone to Australia,' he said, and told her about his conversation with Carrie Tremble at Penvarris. 'I especially asked after the second Warren daughter,' he said earnestly.

She laughed. 'Then that explains it, Mr Trevarnon' – she called him that now, though the formality of it twisted a knife in his heart – 'Fanny is the second. I'm the third. We have an older sister, Meg, who lives in America.' She seemed on the point of saying more, but her husband returned at that moment. He did not seem altogether pleased to find George there, and the intimate moment was over.

George had visited again, many times, but since that day she avoided such private conversations with him. He understood why. Arthur Olds had been good to her. But George could not help a secret exultation. Arthur had seen what he himself already knew: she enjoyed his company. He continued to call, finding fresh reasons for consulting his architect, so that at least he could meet her occasionally, although never alone. He was beginning to behave like Robert, he told himself. He despised himself for it, but still he went.

He longed to talk to her now. She would have been interested in this house. She would have discussed with him the telephone he wanted to install, the carpets, the curtains, the electric points in the kitchen which could operate a kettle or a heater, or a kind of electrical suction cleaner. Indeed, she did discuss them – with her husband. Arthur Olds had more than once told him, rather gruffly, of some improvement that 'my wife suggested'.

Caroline suggested nothing. 'Oh, let the servants do that, George. Why do you want to spend your time worrying about the kitchen? Come and look at my watercolours.'

And he would go, and admire them, although she had no great talent. Since that last fiasco in the bedroom he had become like an elder brother to her.

At any rate, he said to himself, glancing around the shell of what was to be the breakfast room, Caroline would like this. She could sit here and sip her tea in her dressing-robe, write her letters, dabble with her paintbox, receive her dressmaker and her friends. Poor harmless Caroline. At least she was not like Morwenna, whose day was not complete without some new extravagance: some gem, some hat, some outing – the latest fad was for a trip to London to visit the theatres and travel in the new electrified 'tube' railway. Poor Robert.

'George! Where the devil are you?'

As if on cue, his brother came into the half-finished hallway.

*

Robert saw his brother turn as he called.

It was no surprise to find him here; this confounded building caper had become a positive obsession. Typical George. Not content with just commissioning a house and letting the builder chappie get on with it, he had to read books and magazines on the subject and plan the whole thing in tedious detail. Why couldn't he just order the best of everything and have done with it? Or simply send away for the latest inventions – there were marvellous opportunities he was missing, a patent massage machine guaranteed to relieve headache, and a wonderfully improved thermal bath cabinet which enveloped you up to your neck and kept the warmth in.

But no, George had to make every decision for himself. He had even bought up half a dozen paintings by that dreadful 'Wild Beast' in Paris. What was he called? Mattress? Matisse – that was it. Frightful garish things, not a bit lifelike. Robert could afford to feel rather smug about that. When he was equipping Lower Trevarnon he had sent an agent to London to buy one or two things from the Royal Academy. Nice solid oil paintings of cathedrals, or children with dogs. The sort of thing that was bound to be a good investment, given time.

Still, this was not a good moment to criticise. He needed George's help tonight, and anyway, he reminded himself, the fellow had a right to spend his own money. Except of course, that by rights it should have been Robert's money, and he and Morwenna would not then have been struggling to keep up social appearances and still make ends meet.

Despite himself his voice was irritable as he said, 'Caroline told me you might be here.'

'Caroline?' George sounded surprised.

'Yes, Caroline.' Confound the fellow. Granted things had been a little difficult when he and Morwenna had first returned from Scotland. Caroline had refused to speak to them for months, and Major Selwood still cut him dead, which could be awkward at family gatherings. But Poldair had more or less accepted them, however grudgingly, so most of the great houses were open to them. The whole adventure was being gradually forgotten as other more interesting people were involved in new scandals, and recently even Caroline had forgiven them sufficiently to be civil. Couldn't George let the matter rest?

'Well,' George was saying, 'you seem to have found me now. To what do we owe the pleasure of an unexpected visit so late?'

Robert knew what he meant; he might as well have said it outright. 'Well yes,' he said, remembering to repair his ill-humour, 'I have come to ask a favour.'

'Money?' George said.

Robert gritted his teeth. He had hoped to put in a word for fifteen guineas or so, but he was damned if he was going to afford George that satisfaction now. 'Well, no, old boy,' he said, arranging his face in an expression of solemn concern. 'Actually it's about the carriage. Old man Poldair has taken a tumble, hunting, and they've tele-graphed Morwenna to come at once. We can't take the motor at this time of night, and we only keep the dog-cart these days.' He guessed the unspoken question in his brother's eyes and said, 'We might have gone by rail, but the last train is not for an hour, and even then we should have to take a hansom cab out to Goldmarten and that would certainly cause extra – delay.' He almost said 'expense', but altered it in time.

George was looking at him with genuine concern. 'A riding accident? Is he badly hurt?'

'A bad fall, clearly, if they sent for us,' Robert said, but even as he spoke he recognised the full force of his brother's remark. A little tingle of excitement ran up under his collar and lifted the hairs on his neck. If Poldair was seriously hurt, or worse, then Goldmarten would surely pass to his heirs. And who else was there but Morwenna? There would be no shortage of money then. He said, with genuine feeling, 'Say you can spare the carriage George, there's a good man. Old Poldair is a decent fellow, and Morwenna would fret if she could not reach his bedside.'

George shot him a look. 'Have the carriage and welcome, for my part, Robert, but you must ask Papa. It's his coachman and horses, when all is said and done.'

'Oh, Papa will contrive,' Robert said. 'He said so. I have told him he may use the dog-cart whenever he wishes. Besides, he doesn't visit like he used to. So if you are sure you can spare it, George?'

George nodded.

'In that case I'll leave you to your house-gazing and make my way back to Morwenna. She'll be getting her maid to put some things into a suitcase. Thank you, old chap.'

He went out, down the long shallow steps and along past the newly planted borders. Goldmarten. Now that would be a reversal of fortune. He felt so benevolent at the prospect that he made a detour on his way home, to call in at Trevarnon House and thank Caroline for her help.

She was sitting in the great drawing-room, when he was shown in, a book open and unread on her lap. She leapt to her feet at his approach.

'All alone, cousin?'

Her cheeks flushed scarlet. 'Mr Trevarnon has gone to his study. And please, you will oblige me if you don't call me cousin.'

He smiled. 'No.' He saw her soften, and he added mischievously, 'I should call you "sister".'

She whirled on him then. 'You will do no such thing!'

He caught her hand. 'I shall then, because that is what you are.' She was colouring now, and the flush was not of anger. He still, then, had the power to please her. It was enough. He let her go, and said with a gentle smile: 'Come Caroline, let us not quarrel. I came past on purpose to thank you. I needed George's counsel tonight – Morwenna's father is dangerously ill after a fall' – strange how the words came so easily to his lips – 'and George says we are to take the carriage and go to him at once. I should have looked all evening and failed to find him, but for you.'

His tone was almost pleading, and she rewarded him with a little smile. 'I am sorry to hear of your misfortune.'

'You were always kind, cousin,' he said, and took his leave. This time, he noticed, she did not object to the title.

She was changed by marriage, he reflected, as he drove the dog-cart back to Lower Trevarnon. The old Caroline would never have had the spirit to confront him like that. What a pretty, gentle, simple girl she was. He thought of Morwenna, awaiting him in a tempest of flashing eyes and headstrong accusations. There were moments when he wondered if George had not had the better bargain, after all.

Katie cast an appraising eye over her reflection in the bedroom mirror.

She had rounded out a little since the children were born, and it suited her. This new gown flattered her figure – no vibrant blue now, but a soft beige silk, trimmed with lace insets and wine-red hoops of braid at hem and waist, and with a high neck and leg-of-mutton sleeves, as befitted a young matron of almost twenty-one.

Katie smiled to herself as she pinned on the wide hat with its festoons of net veiling and wine feathers. She wished George could see her now – but no, she must not think like that. Arthur did not care for that friendship, she could tell.

She bit her lips and applied to her cheeks a touch of the rouge that Arthur had given her for Christmas. It still made her feel a little wicked, but it heightened her colour, and she smiled as she pulled on the long gloves with their score of tiny pearl buttons. Arthur would be proud of her today.

He came in then, dressed in his own finery: frock coat, Piccadilly collar and a grey silk tie with a pin. He was wearing his spats in honour of the occasion, although it was already March and the ground was dry. He looked a little uncomfortable, as he always did in formal wear, as though his waistcoat and trousers were starched as stiff as his collar, and refused to let him bend.

He smiled when he saw her. 'Are we ready, Katie? The cab will be here soon. I told Mabel to order it for ten.'

'Coming!' Katie wiggled a last hat-pin into place, and turned to face him. 'Shall we go and beard the dragon?'

It was strange, this reluctance she felt at venturing into the nursery. Arthur did not feel it at all, and teased her for her fears, and certainly Nurse Mallin, a plump, busy little lady with a waddle, looked more like a duck than a dragon. 'Nurse Mallard', Arthur called her in private, and made Katie laugh, but mallard or not, she made it clear that the nursery was her domain, and little Victoria her special charge. David, who was almost three, doted on her, and was idolised in his turn, but Katie was more than half afraid of 'Nursie' in her blue starched uniform and white pinafore and cuffs.

She often wished for the days of Miss Bevan, when the schoolroom had been the centre of the house, always full of learning and laughter; but the little schoolmistress had married her farrier and gone to live near Redruth. Besides Eva was a young lady now, and well enough to attend a 'finishing school for young ladies of the business classes' in the town, and be taught French, deportment and pianoforte. Rosa too was a pupil at a school nearby, where she excelled at arithmetic and reading and was the despair of the other mistresses.

Willie was to be fifteen in a month or two, and already in the business with Arthur. He worked in the office, and would do well, Arthur said, with his quick mind and his eye for detail. Already he had saved the business scores of pounds by checking the figures and finding out suppliers who delivered a little short and charged a little over, or clients who paid a bill 'all but a few pence'. Arthur, in his easy-going way, had let these things mount up, but the better book-keeping had already made a difference – and it was just as well, Katie thought. With seven mouths to feed and a staff to keep, even a thriving builder-architect could not afford to be careless.

There must be no more babies. She had said so when Victoria was born, but Arthur had only smiled and said that they would wait and see. And indeed to see him bend over, as he was doing now, to swoop little David up onto his shoulder, you would think him a prince lifting his rubies.

Which, perhaps, he was. She felt a little shiver of guilt. It was not only her concern for the family budget which made her wish to limit the family. Life with Arthur would be much sweeter without the occasional duties of the marriage bed. She gave herself a little angry shake. Pull yourself together Katie Olds, she told herself, you are a lucky woman. George Trevarnon can be nothing to you.

She put the thought firmly aside and took Victoria from a glowering Nursie, feeling a little well of tenderness at the child's small puckered face in its froth of white lace and thistledown shawl.

She managed to say 'Thank you, nurse,' and take Victoria down the stairs before the woman protested again. She had been half afraid the 'mallard' would demand to carry the child into the christening herself.

'Too big for her own boots, that one,' Peabody had sniffed more than once. 'Never you mind, Mrs Olds, time'll come when those dear lambs are too big for a nurse, and I know a lovely little girl for a nursery maid.' Katie was already counting the days.

'It is to be hoped the child doesn't cry and disturb the service,' Nurse Mallin said, to no one in particular, as she came into the hall buttoning her cape, and preparing to follow the hansom on foot with Rosa and Willie.

But Victoria didn't cry, not even when the vicar sprinkled her with a cold and watery hand and named her 'Victoria Katherine Leila Olds'. Katie had got used to the church now, but the stained glass and ancient rituals still awed her. Willie, who still went staunchly to chapel, stood behind them fidgeting with his cap.

Then it was back to the house for sandwiches and a cake. Aunt Beryl, looking frail and thin under a great green hat which seemed to have half an ostrich nesting in it, settled herself on an upright chair. She had been standing godmother, to her ill-concealed delight, but turned down all offers of food. 'I can't be expected to eat, after all this excitement,' she said severely, but she did cast longing eyes at the sherry-cabinet until Arthur opened it.

'And this came from Penzance,' Arthur said, adding a silver spoon to the christening gifts displayed on the sideboard. He sounded constrained. 'Very nice of Mr Trevarnon to remember us, I'm sure.'

He didn't look at Katie as he spoke, but she knew what he was thinking. Mr George Trevarnon had not 'remembered' them. He had never for a moment forgotten.

CHAPTER TWENTY-SIX

Morwenna was out of the carriage and up the steps into Goldmarten almost before the coachman had halted the horses.

'My father, where is he?' Robert could hear her voice, and again as he hastened into the hall behind her.

'Where is he, I say? I want to speak to him.'

The butler, holding her cape and bonnet, came forward to take Robert's coat and gloves. 'My dear sir,' he was murmuring awkwardly, 'I don't know how to . . .'

They were interrupted by the appearance of a tall, black-coated figure with a long thin neck and a beaked nose like a vulture. He waved his black arms as he talked, and when he extended a bony claw of a hand in greeting, the illusion was complete.

'Miss Poldair . . .'

'Mrs Trevarnon,' Morwenna said impatiently. 'My husband – Dr Lloyd.' The claw nipped Robert's hand for an instant. 'What have you done with my father?'

The vulture flapped its wings a little, and said in an agitated caw, 'He is in the morning room, Mrs . . .'

'Trevarnon!' Morwenna said.

'Yes, yes. Two of his friends brought him in. Strapped him to a gate. We couldn't take him upstairs. Strain could have killed him. Got the housekeeper to make up a bed. Nasty business. Knocked his head when he fell, and then the horse fell back and trampled him.'

'How did it happen?'

'No-one knows. Tried to jump the gate, it seems. He had fallen when his friends reached him.'

Morwenna fixed him with that look of contempt which Robert knew so well. 'And what does he say?'

The wings flapped more agitatedly than ever. 'But Mrs . . . but my dear lady, he isn't able to say anything!'

She was past him then in an instant, and when Robert followed her into the morning room she was already kneeling beside the chaise-longue which had been made up into a temporary bed. Poldair was lying on it, whiter than his own bolster-case. The bare shoulder, cut free from his riding jacket, was swollen with bruising and lay at an unnatural angle. Morwenna lifted the blanket gently, and at the sight of the purple mass of his ribcage she gave a little shudder and dropped the cover again. A bubble of red spittle formed on Poldair's lips and he breathed with a little moaning rattle.

'What have you done for him?'

'Well, we tried to bring him round . . . Burnt feathers, smelling salts, ammonia even, but we couldn't rouse him. Managed to force some brandy between his lips. When he is a little stronger, we can set that shoulder . . .'

Morwenna turned to Robert. 'The man is an idiot. Take the carriage and get into town. There's a young doctor there who might be able to help us. I went to him once or twice – our coachman knows the address.'

'But my dear,' Robert found himself saying. 'Surely Doctor Lloyd . . .'

'I've tended your father from a boy . . .' the doctor said.

'Precisely,' Morwenna retorted. 'And tended him the same way all those forty-odd years. And my mother too. She would have recovered from that fever if you had not insisted on bleeding her! Well, Robert, what are you waiting for! Offer that doctor twice his fee if he will come at once in the carriage. Can't you see we need the twentieth century here?'

But even the twentieth century, when it came in the person of Dr Marshall, could offer little hope. The shoulder was set and Poldair was supported so that his laboured breathing was easier, but the young doctor still looked grave. 'There may be bleeding inside the skull,' he said, 'and I fear the lung may be punctured. We can hope, and pray, but I think the end will not be long. Two or three days, perhaps, a week at most.'

'Then I shall stay with him,' Morwenna said.

'But the carriage,' Robert protested. 'We cannot keep Papa's carriage for a week.'

Morwenna gave him that look again. 'Well then, take the con-founded carriage home. I'll stay here and nurse my father – our coachman can drive me home when it's over. You can go now and take Doctor Marshall home on your way – oh, and you'd better telephone the Gillards before you leave. Papa has a telephone in the study.'

'The Gillards? Whatever for?'

'Because Peter Gillard is heir to Goldmarten under the entail, of course. That's why. Now are you going to get into that carriage, or stand there gawping all night?'

Peter Gillard? Robert felt a little crawling chill creep up from his calves to his scalp, setting his hairs on end. Peter Gillard? Had he abandoned the Selwood fortune for this?

'Are you quite well, Mr Trevarnon?' Doctor Marshall said, as they got back into the coach. 'You are very pale. Perhaps it is the shock. People often suffer the shock of loss when they face the death of someone dear to them.'

Robert managed to mutter something civil in reply, but he was glad when the coach arrived at the doctor's door and the man got out and left him to his thoughts.

'You should confide in someone,' Doctor Marshall said. 'Suppress-ing your emotion is a dangerous habit. Don't underestimate the shock of loss.'

There was little danger of that, Robert thought bitterly, as the coach bore him back to Penzance along the dark and twisting roads. The shock of loss. That summed it up very well.

'Rosa?' Katie looked up from the letter she was writing. 'What are you doing home at this hour?'

Rosa stood at the doorway, one foot hooked behind her other ankle. 'I've come home,' she said, 'and I'm not going back to that school again. Ever.'

Katie closed the ink-bottle and blotted her letter carefully. Her mind was racing. Rosa was often difficult, but this was something new. 'What happened?' she said, as gently as she could manage.

Rosa said nothing. 'Your copybook?' Katie asked. Rosa's copy-writing was a source of continual heartache, so full of ink-blots, splatters and smudges that Arthur had once joked that she should hand the teacher the blotter to read instead.

'No,' Rosa said. 'Miss Courtney said I was a wicked girl and a liar.

She told me to hold out my hand, but I wouldn't so she caned my legs, but I wouldn't cry, and after that I picked up my books and came home.'

'What lie did you tell?' Katie said. She was surprised. Rosa was often disobedient and spoiled – Lally's doing, so Arthur said – but she was usually transparently truthful.

'It wasn't a lie,' Rosa said. 'It was my story. We had to write about "A Day at the Beach" – and when I wrote it, Miss Courtney said it was well written, but I wasn't to make up such things.'

'What did you write?' Katie said, feeling a little prickle of apprehension.

For answer, Rosa offered her the book. It was all there – the mine, the darkness, the fear, Lally's dying urgent grasp. She read it with tears in her eyes. Never before had she quite imagined the terrible burden of nightmare which Rosa carried. When she had finished reading, she put down the book and pulled her sister close. 'She caned your legs?'

'Yes.' She lifted her skirt and Katie could see the weals – ugly red stripes across the child's calf and thighs.

'My poor Rosa,' Katie said.

'I didn't cry,' Rosa said, but she was crying now, big helpless tears that splashed down her cheeks and onto the copybook on Katie's knee, as if they would wash away the offending pages. Katie let her cry, all the tears which had not been shed for three and a half frightened years. At last the sobbing ceased.

'Miss Courtney didn't know,' Katie said. 'I didn't really know myself.'

Rosa looked up at her with eyes swollen from weeping. 'I only really remembered when I started to write it,' she said. 'I don't know how I ever forgot.'

'We'll go up to the school,' Katie said, but they waited until Arthur returned home.

There had been some constraint between them ever since the incident of the christening spoon, but when he heard the story he was instantly considerate and concerned. All the same, he was adamant. Rosa must go back. It had been harder for her than anyone – a new home, a sister she hardly knew, and a terrible experience which made her feel responsible for Lally's death. But she must go back. She could not run away from her own misdoing.

He took her himself. Katie watched them go – Arthur's solid form, and Rosa, dragging reluctance with every step – and her heart bled. She sat alone in the drawing-room until Arthur returned.

'It's all right, my dear, I have spoken to Miss Courtney and she will know better than to cane Rosa's legs again. I reminded her of her advertisement: "Delicate girls particularly catered for or fees refunded." She understood my meaning.'

'But Rosa isn't delicate.'

Arthur looked at her. 'Not in body perhaps. Anyway, my dear, I think she will be well cared for in future. And she has become quite a heroine among her classmates.'

Katie could not suppress a smile. 'We shall have her turning into an Annie Besant if we're not careful, standing on a stool and demanding votes for women, only in her uniform instead of clogs and shawl.'

'You sound as if you didn't care for the suffragettes, Katie: I should have thought you might have valued the idea of woman's franchise?'

Katie said carefully, 'It would be an advantage, no doubt, given the right women. Miss Bevan now, or Mrs Lomas – Peabody even, they have as much right to say who should run the country as any man. But give the vote to Fanny, or Caroline Trevarnon, and what have you done? Given two votes to their husbands, nothing more.'

'And are men not just as different in their capabilities?'

She thought a moment. 'Perhaps you're right. The difference may be only in education. Perhaps this new Education Act will help. Free, compulsory education for all.' She looked at him thoughtfully. 'I never thought of you as a reformer, Arthur. You've never spoken of this before.'

'You can blame your friend Trevarnon,' Arthur said. 'Made me quite a speech on the subject at one time. Asked me to find a single good reason why your vote would be less intelligent than any man's, and you know, I couldn't find one?'

She could hear the bitterness in his voice, and bent to kiss his receding hair. 'You are biased, Arthur.'

He caught her hand. 'That may be so. But,' he said urgently, meeting her eyes squarely, 'isn't your Mr Trevarnon biased, too?'

She dropped her eyes, unable to prevent a blush. 'It's nothing, Arthur; we're good friends, nothing more. He was good to me when I worked at Trevarnon. I cannot help but think kindly of him.'

Her husband did not release her hand. 'Too kindly, perhaps. Trevarnon is a fine man, and I value his friendship, but I cannot altogether like it when I find him so often here. It is not me, I think, he comes to see.'

Her blush was hotter now, but she replied steadily enough, 'You must not concern yourself, Arthur. I decided long ago that it would not be proper for me to see Mr Trevarnon unless you were present.'

Arthur squeezed her hand. 'You did? Then you must have felt, yourself, that there was something in his friendship that was more than kindness!'

She could not deny it, but she saw the hurt in his face. She said softly, 'I felt there was something in his friendship that you did not care for, Arthur. And I am your wife.'

She would have gone to him, but he held her at arm's length. 'You were my second wife, Katie. Second wife, but never second-best.'

She met his eyes. Like Rosa she squared herself to face her duty. 'And you are my only husband, Arthur. Didn't I promise? Till death do us part?'

And then, at last, he submitted himself to be kissed.

Poldair died on 18 March, without regaining consciousness. Morwenna was with him until the end.

It was a quiet death. No crises. No sudden return to consciousness. No outward sign of suffering. Only the bloodspeckled gasp for breath became steadily weaker until gradually it ceased.

Morwenna looked at the ashen face on the pillow, the broad handsome forehead, the full sensual lips so like her own, smiling a little in death as though they were closed for ever on some private, slightly wicked secret. Perhaps they were. She watched Dr Marshall close the eyes and draw the sheet up over the shattered shoulder that would never now heal. How little she had actually known of her father!

She thanked the doctor mechanically, and went out into the hall. That old fool Lloyd was there, hovering again, although she had asked him more than once to cease his visits.

'Your father sent for me,' he repeated stubbornly. 'It was the last thing he said to his friends before he lost consciousness.' She didn't argue; there was no way now of testing the truth of that statement.

'He was one of my oldest patients,' Lloyd continued. 'This is the least I can do.'

She had to agree with him there. He could hardly have done less. Yet doubtless he would want paying for his attendance, Dr Marshall or no Dr Marshall. Well, that was no longer her problem. A personal allowance for her lifetime, so the family lawyers had said, and her personal jewellery and furniture, but other than that everything went to Peter Gillard. Well, let it. He could worry about paying the doctor's bills, and there was plenty of money to pay with. She had always known that this would happen, and somehow she no longer cared.

Suddenly she felt inexpressibly tired. The strain of the last few days descended on her, a physical weight like five stone of flour. Perhaps Dr Marshall was right, and she should have engaged a nurse and not waited on her father day and night, as she had done. Yet she had needed to do it. Herself. They had never spoken of affection, but that, she supposed, was what it was.

She glanced at her dishevelled figure in the mirror. Her hair had escaped from its pins and tumbled around her face like a waterfall. Her eyes were wild and hollow with lack of sleep, and her gown, which she had thought so daring in its flouting of convention, looked simply eccentric: the flowing 'aesthetic' draperies, and embroidered velvet tunic with its medieval sleeves, hung crumpled and unglamorous after the long sleepless vigil on the chair.

She rang the bell. 'A bath,' she said to the little parlourmaid who appeared, curtseying and smirking. Morwenna turned away without another word. It wasn't the girl's job, and there would be a tedious wait now, while the lady's maid was summoned, water was heated and fetched and carried, and the towels warmed. She began to regret having issued the order, and rang the bell savagely for a drink.

Peter Gillard brought it. She sat up in sudden surprise as he walked in, carrying a brandy in each hand.

'I came across the butler as he was bringing you this,' he said, handing her a glass. 'Thought I would bring it myself and join you, having heard the news about your father.'

She was about to make some retort, but she recollected herself in time. It was, after all, Peter Gillard's own brandy from now on. He had a right to drink it if he chose. She was the interloper now.

He must have read her thoughts. 'How shall you manage – you and Trevarnon? I had thought your father would make Robert an allowance.'

She laughed bitterly. 'Robert? My father always preferred to pretend that Robert did not exist.' Perhaps, she thought, with sudden weariness, her father had not been such a fool at that. If he had chosen her husband, she would not now be faced with a lifetime of debts at

Lower Trevarnon; she would be married to Peter Gillard and still be mistress of Goldmarten. She sighed.

Gillard sat down beside her, his eyes dark. 'I wish he didn't.'

She had not followed his train of thought. 'Who didn't?'

'Trevarnon. I wish he didn't exist. I might have asked you myself, you know, if that cad Trevarnon hadn't whisked you away like that. No doubt you wouldn't have thanked me, but it would have secured Goldmarten for your family.'

In spite of herself, she felt a little flicker of hope, and her spirits lifted. Peter Gillard was an attractive man. Given a little time . . . She lowered her eyes and said carefully, 'I never knew you thought of it.'

He slapped his leg as though irritated and stood up sharply. 'Thought of it? I should say so. Even spoke to your father about it, but since it was obviously useless . . .'

She kept her voice very low. 'You say so?'

He looked at her then. 'You mean you might have consented?'

She raised her head, and met his eyes. They faltered and fell, and she knew the little thrill of triumph. 'How can you have doubted it? All those afternoons driving . . .'

'But dash it all, Morwenna, that was in Trevarnon's car. We hardly ever took mine.'

'You hardly ever offered.'

'And I mean to say, you took enough pains to be alone with the fellow. People were commenting on it openly, don't you know?'

She smiled, running a hand through her tumbling hair. 'Yes, he was clever. I didn't realise how clever until it was too late. And then that day we got stuck with the motor . . .'

'Yes,' Gillard said, downing the rest of his brandy. 'That's just the sort of thing I mean. Half an hour alone on a deserted lane. Anything could have happened.'

She permitted a little silence, drooping her head to let a curtain of hair fall about her face. 'Yes.'

There was a pause, and then Gillard said, 'You don't mean . . . ?'

She was glad of the veil of hair to conceal her smile. It had taken him a long time to grasp her meaning. She said, in the same small voice, 'Why do you think I married him?'

'Good God!' He had seized her brandy now, and was downing it without noticing. She said nothing. 'Wait till I lay my hands on Trevarnon!'

She touched his arm, shaking her wrist so that the sleeve of the tunic hung gracefully, revealing the deep pink silk of the lining against her white skin.

'No, Peter, no. There has been enough unhappiness. And Robert loved me, you know. Really loved me.'

The sullen pink in his cheeks showed that the barb had gone home. 'I loved you!' he muttered. 'If there is ever anything I can do . . .'

She had done it. He had committed himself. She gave a little sigh. 'If only I had known . . .' It was just loud enough for him to hear, then she added, 'But this is no time to be talking like this!'

He was all contrition. 'Morwenna, I'm sorry. I'm a heartless fool. Your poor father lying dead, and I here worrying you like this. Forgive me.'

She squeezed his hand. 'Of course. Peter, you mustn't be angry with Robert . . .' She paused. 'But it would comfort me so much to know I had a real friend.'

He bent to kiss her hair. 'Count on me.' And he was gone.

She gave a deep sigh, and glanced in the mirror. The same dishevelled figure looked back at her, but there was a touch of colour in the cheeks and a certain sparkle in the tired eyes.

'Well, Father,' she said aloud, and somehow it was almost a promise. 'I'll have him one day, and Goldmarten too. We Poldairs are not finished yet!'

CHAPTER TWENTY-SEVEN

Robert walked to Trevarnon in a savage mood. The weather matched his temper. The dense fog of the night before had lifted, and now a snarling wind whipped the early buds from the trees and left brown bruises on the fleshy pink petals of the camellias. He cut a switch from the hedge and used it to behead the daffodils.

What was Morwenna playing at? Ever since she had come home in Peter Gillard's brougham the night before she had been acting suspiciously strangely.

She had taken to calling him 'dear Robert' for one thing, and making a point of acceding to his lightest whim. George had commented on it, and Peter Gillard had obviously noticed. It was rather flattering, in a way, a far cry from her usual tempestuous nature. He had been inclined, at first, to put it down to the loss of her father, the 'shock of loss' as Dr Marshall had said, but as the hours wore on he had been more and more disquieted by it.

She had been more than usually compliant in bed last night, into the bargain; turned to him with something of her old playfulness, pleaded neither headache nor fatigue, and returned his embraces with a passion he had not known since Scotland.

It should have pleased him. Passion was perhaps the only thing they had ever truly shared; and even that had seemed singularly lacking lately. So why was he so obscurely anxious and frustrated this morning? He did not know. Only this behaviour was not in character, and he distrusted it.

The wind seized a branch from a rotten tree in the hedgerow and splintered it at his feet. It was brewing into a solid gale. There had been reports of shipping in trouble in the fog, and this wind would sorely hamper the lifeboats.

He quickened his pace. He was not looking forward to this interview, either. What would George say, he wondered. Surely he would be glad to buy the St Ives farm, wouldn't he? All this messing about with Guernsey cows, he would be delighted to have the extra land. Or perhaps he could even be persuaded to lease the land back to Robert at a moderate rate so that the whole arrangement could be concealed from Papa.

It was a pity he hadn't sold the farm in the first place, Robert thought, rather than the tin shares. Tin had reached an all-time high recently, £200 a ton, to say nothing of the copper, and those shares must have paid a handsome dividend. Trust George to make a profit when a fellow was struggling.

Well, at least his brother would have the capital for this farm purchase, even after building that confounded Little Manor of his. And this time, Robert vowed to himself, he would invest the money. A motor-bus perhaps, like the one that ran out to the Lizard, or a repair shop for automobiles – the sort of thing Gillard was always talking about. There was a good living to be made from either of those, if Morwenna could be persuaded to tolerate trade and give up her passion for hats, and if he himself learned to stay away from the pleasures of horseflesh.

He was glad to turn the corner into the avenue and escape from the biting roar of the wind. He walked quickly up to Trevarnon House.

George's man let him in, and closed the door quickly, against the wind. Robert had expected to find them still at breakfast, but he was shown into the music-room, while the man went to find George and Papa.

Caroline was sitting at the piano, playing.

'Don't stop,' he said, as she half-rose at his approach. 'I like to hear you.'

She sat down again, but said, colouring, 'You never used to care for my playing.'

He smiled at her. 'I've learned to appreciate these things. It's calm and comforting. Go on, play that piece again. I'll turn the pages for you.'

'I can manage, thank you,' she said, but she did consent to play for him. It was soothing and companionable, and when he thanked her it was with a sincerity that made her cheeks blaze.

She was saved from further comment by the arrival of his father.

'You've come, then?' Papa said. 'Sorry business about Poldair.'

'You heard about the inheritance, I suppose.'

Papa looked at him quizzically. 'It's no good applying to me, young Robert. I made my position clear years ago. I don't say I would not make provision if there were grandchildren, but as it stands you've had your share of my estate. Perhaps you should turn your mind to producing an heir.'

'Papa!' he said sharply. 'Not in front of Caroline!'

His father said staunchly, 'Caroline has a right to hear this. She may have her own children to consider, one day.'

'That's enough, Papa. You'll embarrass her.' It was George, tousled and pink-faced from the wind, but his wife was already folding her music away, and retreating with crimson cheeks. She was a pretty woman, Robert reflected.

He could not talk freely about the farm in front of his father, so he was constrained to make general conversation. He was half afraid that Papa would broach the subject of the mine again: the new Trevarnon Shaft was in full production, and Papa had been promised a visit to the mine to see it. He might easily take it into his head to want his sons to come with him. Robert thought of that dismal pit, and shuddered.

Fortunately, though, George had brought news from the town, and the talk readily turned to the weather and the ship even now wedged against the rocks in high winds and mountainous seas off the Lizard.

'Ran aground in the fog, before the wind got up. They managed to take everyone off during the night,' George said. 'Not easy either, carrying infants down rope ladders in those seas. Let them down with a rope under their armpits, and the other end lashed to the deck, so the coachman says. One man fell and broke his collarbone, and a woman near fainted and almost dropped her child into the sea, but it seems that everyone was got off safe and sound. The captain had everyone on the deck for an hour beforehand, and managed to feed them hot coffee and rusks against the cold, by all accounts. I daresay they needed it, poor souls; I hear many of them were in their night attire when they were brought ashore. There were five lifeboats out there, I hear. People being landed for most of the night.'

'What was the ship?' Papa asked.

'The *Seuvic*, so I hear, out of Sydney, bound for Plymouth,' said George. 'A large number of Cornishmen aboard, apparently, coming back from the South African mines.'

'They got home a little sooner than they expected, then,' Robert said, disgruntled. It was obvious George would not give his attention to purchasing farms at present. His mind was with the stricken vessel and her passengers.

'Robert!' His father's voice was sharp. 'How can you speak like that?'

'Well, everyone is safe, so George says. It will be a nine days' wonder, that's all. These things always are. It will give the passengers a story to dine out on, and the curious something to gaze at.'

'They are still trying to salvage the ship,' George said. 'And the cargo. Thousands of crates of meat aboard, apparently. In this wind, too.'

Robert stifled a yawn. 'Well, there you are! They'll rescue their wretched rabbit carcases, the papers will be full of the story for a fortnight, and there will be an end of it. You mark my words.'

But in that he proved to be mistaken.

Breakfast at Number Twenty-three was a noisy affair these days. Eva and Rosa joined the adults, and there was much discussion of their respective schools. Eva was gently enthusiastic, still finding the companionship of other young women a novelty and a delight. Young Rosa was more boisterous, and likely to treat the family to imitations of the teachers unless Arthur checked her.

She had been a much happier child since that incident over her story, and rather to Katie's surprise it had served to create a stronger bond between Arthur and the little girl. Almost eight now, Katie reflected. How swiftly time had flown.

Willie and Arthur were talking about a big house near Truro they had recently finished. Arthur spent much of his time with her brother these days. It was not entirely the demands of business, Katie knew. Ever since that day when Arthur had confronted her over George Trevarnon there had been between them, not a coolness exactly, but a restraint, an embarrassment. They tried to ignore it, but it was there.

It lay between them now, making her say with a false brightness, 'A motorhouse instead of a stable, and no provision for horses at all! What is the world coming to?'

Nurse Mallin came in with David and Vicki, for the children to say 'Good morning', and the moment eased.

Katie encouraged her son to come onto her knee, and planted a kiss on his bouncing curls. She was even permitted to hold Victoria for a moment, before the captives were led away. The nurse didn't like this morning ritual, preferring that the children should stay in the nursery and have their parents come to them, but Katie had insisted.

Mabel came in with fresh scones and tea, and the morning post on a tray, and they could busy themselves with their letters. One from Fanny. Noah had abandoned the minefields and found a job as a 'jackaroo' whatever that might mean. From Fanny's account it seemed to involve a horse and a great many sheep. They were hoping to build a wooden house of their own, Fanny said, and Nicholas and the twins were growing fast and as brown as berries after the Australian summer.

Katie listened to the wind still howling after yesterday's storms. How strange to be away in a foreign country. She herself had never once been as far as Devon!

A letter from Meg next – the eldest boy starting school, and a Christmas meeting with Jimmy and Tom and their wives. Would she recognise her brothers and sister now, she wondered.

'Well, that is good news and no mistake!' Arthur's voice cut into her thoughts.

She looked up. 'What's that, Arthur?'

'A fellow from Shrewsbury, friend of Major Selwood's – you remember Selwood?'

Caroline's father. Father-in-law to George. How could she forget? 'Yes,' she said, keeping her voice equable, 'I've seen him many times.'

'Wants a school built. Latest thing, running water, gas lighting – even talking about installing gas fires for heating. Quite an undertaking.'

'Sounds like Little Manor,' she said, her voice carefully neutral. She did not mention George's name.

Arthur glanced at her sharply, then he nodded. 'Yes, so Selwood thought. Mentioned my name, and here's the fellow applying to offer me the contract.'

She gaped at him. 'Shrewsbury? Arthur, you can't possibly. There must be other builder-architects he could apply to locally.'

He grinned, all constraints forgotten. 'A dozen, I should think. But he spends a lot of time at his club in town, and he was thinking of using a London man, until he came down to see Selwood. Saw Little Manor and was enchanted with the place. It could be the making of us, Katie, a contract like that. Worth thousands of pounds.'

'Thousands?' Most houses cost two or three hundred, Katie knew, and Little Manor had run well into four figures, but thousands? 'Shall you take it, Arthur?'

He looked thoughtful. 'I shall go up and see the man, at least. Willie here can mind the shop.' He smiled. 'And if all goes well, then later on I shall take my beautiful wife to London. I daresay you would like to see the theatres and Buckingham Palace, wouldn't you, Katie?'

She gazed at him in delight. London? The capital of the Empire?

'Can we come?' That was Rosa, looking up from her scones and tea. 'Eva and me, please, Uncle Arthur?' It was the name she had recently chosen for him.

'We shall see,' Arthur said, and the conversation moved to other things. Later, as he was leaving for the office, Katie came to him in the hall.

'Shall you really go to London? What shall I do without you? Can Willie manage at the office?' She handed him his hat and umbrella.

He planted a kiss on her forehead. 'I shan't be away long. A day or two at most. Peabody will look after you, and yes, Willie will do very well. It will be good for the lad. I shall miss you, Katie, more than I thought possible, but I would be foolish to turn down an opportunity for a little inconvenience.'

She sighed. 'If you are sure?'

He looked at her gravely. 'I'm sure – except . . .'

'Except?'

'Don't receive any unexpected visitors while I am gone?'

He meant George Trevarnon. The name was not spoken but it hung between them. She hesitated an instant, then reached up to kiss his cheek.

'No, Arthur,' she said gently. 'I won't.' But he had felt the hesitation, and the kiss that he planted on her forehead was as cold as stone.

It was almost lunchtime before Robert got to the point of his visit. George had known from the outset that his brother had some proposition in mind. Since Mama's death Robert had largely kept away from Trevarnon House, and here he was on his second visit in two days. Also, he was clearly impatient to get George alone.

He made his suggestion at last, over a game of billiards. George put down his cue and gazed at his brother in amazement.

'Sell the St Ives farm? Are you mad? It was Mama's – whatever would she say?'

Robert glowered and looked at his boots, but said equally enough, 'It's all very well to expostulate, old man, but there isn't the money. Morwenna's the devil to keep, and since there is nothing to come from the Poldair direction I have to turn to desperate measures. Besides, it's you I'm offering it to. It's not as though I'm trying to sell it out of the family.'

'But once it's gone,' George said, trying to make Robert realise the enormity of it, 'you have lost it for ever. What income will you have then?'

'I've got some investments in mind,' Robert muttered. He had, too, and George was forced to admit that the prospects for a motor-bus or a repair garage seemed promising.

'Peter Gillard's suggestions,' Robert admitted grudgingly.

'And should you like to work for a living?' George said. He could not imagine Robert doing any such thing.

'Oh, I should have staff, naturally,' Robert said loftily. 'It wouldn't be work, just managing the business. Anyway,' he added, with sudden sincerity, 'I have always enjoyed motoring.'

That at least was certainly true. 'Are you certain about this?' George said. 'I can foresee you regretting the sale in six months or so.' Somehow the story of Esau and Jacob flashed through his mind.

'I don't know how I should contrive without the sale,' Robert said simply. 'You would do me a favour if you would consent to buy it, old man.' There was a little pause and then he added: 'I think I should have to sell it somewhere, and I would rather keep it in the family.'

Perhaps it was that which made George say, 'Well, if you're certain, I'll have my lawyers draw up a contract. Based on the market price, of course; that should bring you in a decent sum. But take my advice, Robert, and try and keep away from the race-track. It seems a poor investment for your inheritance.'

He had taken pains to sound light-hearted, but Robert rounded on him. 'When I want your advice, I'll ask for it!'

George's patience was limited. He said forcefully, 'If you'd taken my advice earlier, you wouldn't be in this position now. And if you are sincere in wishing me to purchase the farm, you can keep a civil tongue in your head. I've signed no contract yet!'

It was a nasty moment, interrupted by George's man tapping on the billiard-room door. 'Someone to see you, Mr Trevarnon.'

They went out together. It was a messenger-boy from a hotel in Penzance, judging by his uniform, out of breath and flushed – from pedalling his bicycle presumably, since he still wore clips on his trouser-legs. 'Which one of you is Mr Trevarnon?'

Robert and George exchanged glances. 'Both,' George said. 'We are brothers. And this is my father's house. We are all "Mr Trevarnon" here. What name?'

'Just Mr Trevarnon, it says here,' the boy said, glancing at a piece of paper in his hand. 'Can Mr Trevarnon contact a lady at the Queen's Hotel. Brought in off the *Seuvic* yesterday, and transferred to Penzance this morning. Lost everything but what she stands up in, poor lady. Said Mr Trevarnon might help her.'

George had a sudden vision of Fanny. Hadn't Katie said she was in New South Wales now with her husband and family? 'Do you know the lady's name?' It would not help him, he realised as soon as he asked. He did not know Fanny's married name.

'Yes,' the boy said, frowning at his paper again. 'Funny name. German by the sound of it. Brunner.'

'Never heard of it.' Robert sounded relieved. It occurred to George that he, too, had been thinking of Fanny.

George took a deep breath. 'I have,' he said. He gave the boy sixpence. 'Tell her I'm coming.'

When the messenger had gone Robert turned to him, a surprised and knowing smile on his lips. 'You old dog! What have you been keeping under your hat?'

George controlled a fierce desire to hit him. Instead he said, through tight lips, 'The family's dishonour. What else have I ever tried to keep under my hat?'

Robert lifted a pair of bewildered hands. 'I've never heard of the woman. It isn't Fanny, if that's what you're thinking. She's called Trembath.'

George looked at him with contempt. 'No, not you for once. Papa, this time. He fathered a child when he was in South Africa, and I met her there. His daughter. Your sister. And before you say anything, he doesn't know of her existence, or she of his. She believes Mr Brunner was her father. I must go to her. In the meantime you will oblige me by not mentioning this to anyone, especially not Papa, at least till I return.'

He jammed on his hat and cloak and went out into the wind. It was still so strong that he had to bend forwards into it. It was appalling to think what might have happened off the Lizard, if all the passengers had not been brought safely ashore.

When he reached Penzance, he gave his name at the hotel desk, and was shown into the lounge.

She was standing at the window, wearing a drab brown woollen gown two sizes too wide and too short for her, and her feet were thrust into a pair of worn black boots. Borrowed from rescuers, obviously. Her hair was a tangle, and her face was salt-stained and weary from her ordeal, but he would have known her anywhere.

But it was not Kernerwek. It was her mother, Anna Brunner.

CHAPTER TWENTY-EIGHT

She was disappointed; he could see it in her face. She had expected to see his father, just as he had expected to see Kernerwek.

All the same, she came forward, gravely extending a hand. 'We meet again, Captain Trevarnon.'

It was strange to hear that title again. He had not been called 'Captain' for years. And of course, he thought, Kernerwek was no longer called Brunner. Married, as he was himself, and Katie too.

'Mrs Brunner.' He had not altogether forgotten the humiliation of that evening when he had learned the truth of Kernerwek's birth. He kept his voice very formal. 'How can I be of service?'

She did not release his hand. 'You have not forgiven me, Captain Trevarnon, and perhaps you have cause. But believe me, I should never have presumed upon your family if it were not for this emergency. It was not my plan to impose myself upon yourself, or your parents.'

'My mother is dead,' George said, and instantly regretted it.

Anna Brunner coloured a little. 'All the more so, in that case.' She dropped his hand and turned away, but something in her manner convinced him that she spoke the truth.

'Then what brings you to England, in that case?'

She laughed, the same laugh. She was still beautiful, he realised, in spite of the ugly gown, the clumsy boots, the matted hair. 'The arrogance of the English! No, my dear Captain, it was not England that drew me. Many of the old mines were being sold up, as I expect you know. Only, my father had a good eye for business. An American company found a rich new seam in land he had owned, and wanted to develop it. I still held his rights – they turned a pretty penny.' He had forgotten the accent, that distinctive lilt. It brought back a thousand memories.

George nodded. There had been American interest in several disused Cornish mines as well. 'So you decided to travel?'

She laughed again, showing her perfect teeth. 'You put it so simply! I helped Kernerwek and her husband, of course. Things for the farm – new stock, new seed, new machinery, that sort of thing. But they no longer needed me, and I received a letter from my husband's niece, to say that his sister had died. I thought how little I knew of his family, his homeland, and of my father's too. I had the means to visit, and so I came.' She smiled. 'And although I cannot altogether swear, Captain Trevarnon, that curiosity would not have brought me to the walls of your father's estate, nothing would have persuaded me to enter them, and make myself known.'

He could picture her, in a hansom perhaps, bowling up to the gates, looking for a moment at the trees and roofs of Trevarnon, and driving on. A woman of spirit. No wonder his father had admired her. To travel, too, halfway around the world, unaccompanied. A remarkable woman.

'Not many ladies would have embarked upon such a journey,' he ventured.

'And perhaps they would have been right,' she said wryly. 'A week ago, I would have pooh-poohed such a notion – I hoped to make a grand tour, except for Russia, of course. The Bolshevik uprising last year put an end to any hope of that. But here I am now, penniless in a strange country, and obliged to ask assistance from old acquaintances.'

She did not say 'friends' George noticed. How humiliating this must be for her. He said with sudden sympathy. 'I'm sure my father would wish me to offer you hospitality . . .'

She cut him short. 'Which I should be obliged to refuse. Can't you see that it would be impossible for me to accept, after all that once passed between us? No, I had intended to ask your father only for a small advance, until I have had time to wire for my own funds in Africa. Just enough to pay my bills at this hotel, and to purchase some more suitable clothing.' She glanced down at the ill-fitting dress.

George coloured. 'Of course. My dear Mrs Brunner, think nothing further of it. I should be pleased to cover the account myself, and I will send for an assistant from the shop to take your order.' He had been going to suggest sending a selection of dresses and boots and shoes, but it occurred to him that other, more intimate items might be necessary, and he corrected himself in time.

'You are very good, Captain Trevarnon.'

'Please, call me George.' The words sealed the new understanding between them. 'In the meantime, with your permission, I will ask Papa. I am sure there are things of Mama's which would be a little more suitable. Or perhaps my wife,' he added, suddenly wondering if she would feel awkward at his first suggestion.

Anna Brunner smiled. 'Your Mama might have had a cape, perhaps? I should be very grateful. And I am happy to hear that you have found a wife.'

He said, understanding her meaning, 'And Kernerwek, is she happy?'

'She is learning to be,' her mother said. 'She has a child now, a little boy, and she adores him. Yes, I think she is happy. And you? Have you any children?'

It was his turn to look away. 'None. Now, I have trespassed on your time too long, Mrs Brunner. I shall speak to the desk on my way out. Please do not concern yourself about the bill. And, forgive me, but you may need some money for immediate expenses.' He laid a pile of silver on the table. 'Please accept this, for old times' sake.'

She closed her hand over the coins. 'I am grateful, Capt . . . George. I shall not forget this. I shall repay it in a week or two, when my own money arrives.'

He hesitated. 'And I shall tell Papa?'

'You must, if you are to lend me your mother's cape. Yes, tell him what you wish. I should have done so myself if he had come in your place.'

As she had hoped he would, George read the meaning in her eyes. He was very thoughtful as he made his way back to Trevarnon.

Poldair's funeral was a very grand affair. Twelve black horses with black plumes pulling the funeral carriage, a funeral band playing the dead march, and the undertaker's men doing the whole thing in old-fashioned style, with half a dozen professional mourners in black hats and tails. The cortège stretched for almost half a mile, and Robert thought wryly that whoever it was in Truro who sold black cloth and veiling must have made a small fortune.

He himself was in deepest black, with a wide armband; sitting in the

275

first coach too, since Gillard could hardly deny him that privilege. He managed to present a decently sober face, too. It wasn't difficult. Looking across at Peter sitting pretty in his funeral suit, and thinking of him as the new owner of Goldmarten was enough to make Robert feel very mournful indeed.

Morwenna, at his side, had managed to contrive an outfit which combined all the trappings of grief with her usual flamboyance. She was dressed in black from collar to hem, but although the bodice and skirt were of silk, the sleeves and yoke were made of a lacy voile so that the whiteness of her skin was clearly visible, and at her throat, and atop her huge wide-brimmed hat with its swatches of veiling, was a single vivid red velvet rose. She had added a little carmine to her lips, under the flimsy net of the veil, and she looked like the personification of Grief from some figurative painting, at once heartbroken and dramatic.

Poor little Caroline, by contrast, following in another carriage with George and Papa, was a martyr to mourning. The black cloth drained every ounce of colour from her pale face, and made her look lost and vulnerable. She was, in any case, overcome by the occasion, and had needed the assistance of smelling-salts, and the support of George's arm, to get into the carriage at all. Robert would not have been astounded if she and George had not attended, but perhaps Papa had insisted. You could never tell what Papa would do these days.

In the days since the wreck of the *Seuvic* Papa had become a different person. There had been a worrying few hours when George first came back from Penzance and went into the study to see him. The news he brought had been a terrible shock, so much so that the Doctor had been sent for, and Papa had retired to bed for the remainder of the day. The next morning, however, had seen a transformation. By the time Robert got to Trevarnon, Papa had already breakfasted, and he was out to the carriage before ten, looking spruce and dapper in his best morning suit and calling for his visiting cards. It had been the same every day since. There was a new spring in the step, an old twinkle in the eye, and Papa was beginning to take the kind of interest in his appearance which Mama had always been begging him to take. He was out for most of the day, and returned only in time for dinner.

Robert had only glimpsed him once or twice, and had to derive his information from George and Caroline. George, in fact, had been very unforthcoming, and had refused to add anything to his earlier remarks, except to say that the woman was not the person he had been expecting, and that it was up to Papa to say anything further. Caroline knew no more than Robert himself, but she had seen Papa's comings and goings, and noticed his uncharacteristic behaviour. Robert had twice taken tea with her, and they had shaken their heads together over the strange behaviour of the rest of the family.

'Robert will have to come back to Truro and ride her home, that's all. Won't you Robert?' Morwenna's voice jerked him back to the present.

'I'm sorry,' he said, 'I didn't quite catch . . .'

'The brown mare,' Morwenna said. 'She's grieving since the bay hunter was destroyed. Peter says we should have her. She used to be my horse, after all. Isn't that good of him?'

'Most kind. We are much obliged,' Robert responded, as civilly as he could manage through clenched teeth. The wretched animal would need feeding and grooming, and there were all the bedding and stabling costs. Still, if Morwenna took to riding it, perhaps she would spend less time running up bills at the milliner's and dressmaker's. Perhaps, he found himself thinking savagely, she could contrive to follow her father's good example and take a hearty tumble. The thought of Morwenna helpless and needing his care brought a little smile to his lips. 'Yes,' he said, more kindly, 'Of course I'll ride her back. Delighted to.'

'Then that's settled,' Morwenna said. She flashed him one of her old-fashioned smiles. She could still make his blood pound. 'And while you are doing that, I will go down and see that the stable is ready for her. There's an empty stall there, but it has never been used except for storing cans of Robert's petroleum spirit. All we need is some oats and hay and things.'

'I've got plenty of oats and hay,' Gillard said, giving Morwenna a little sideways look which made Robert uncomfortable. 'I'll bring some over. I can give you a hand. I know something about setting up a stable.'

Robert was about to protest, but then he reflected that if Gillard was prepared to provide the stuff, at least he would not have to pay for it. And he'd make damned sure that all the harness and gear the horse had at Goldmarten found its way back to Trevarnon, too. 'Oh, very well,' he said ungraciously, and turned his attention to the lane, where all the tenants from the estate were lined up, black bands on their sleeves, to see the cortège pass. The curtains at the estate cottages were drawn, and the men snatched off their caps and bowed their heads as the coffin passed.

Then they were lurching to a stop at the little church as the bell tolled, and passing through the little lych-gate into the dim interior. It smelt of candles and dust and damp, but the weak afternoon sunlight filtering through the stained glass fell directly on the name on the family pew: 'Poldair'.

At the door, a shuffling, and on the shoulders of the pall-bearers the last of the Poldairs began his slow final journey up the aisle.

At Robert's side, Morwenna was weeping.

'Well, I'm proper sorry to have missed your husband,' the woman said, setting down her cup. 'I did want to talk to him about this new gazebo, but he seems always to be away nowadays.' She sat back in her chair with a dissatisfied air.

'He will be back in a few days,' Katie said, 'and I'm sure my brother has taken all the details, Mrs Pritchard.'

The woman sniffed. She was a big, raw-boned woman, married to one of the tanners in the town, and her clothes smelt a little of uncured hide. All the same, they were expensive clothes, and this was not the first time she and her little timid husband had come to Number Twenty-three with a building project. They were good customers and Katie had taken pains to offer her all the hospitality at her disposal, while Willie took the man into the office to discuss the project.

'Your brother!' the woman snorted. 'What does he know about building? Only a slip of a lad, and dragged up in a mine, from what I hear.' She smoothed her skirts and pursed her lips meaningfully. 'No disrespect to you, Mrs Olds, and I daresay you've done very well moving from backstairs to upstairs, but there's some as has breeding and education, and some as don't, and fine feathers don't make fine folks, that's what I say. And I understand even his own aunt doesn't visit any more. Still, I don't hold a man's marriage against him, and no doubt Mr Olds will be back directly, and we can arrange something then.'

Katie put down her cup, her cheeks blazing. She was about to retort that if Mrs Pritchard was going to patronise only the people that Aunt Beryl visited then she was in for a very lean social calendar. Aunt Beryl had taken a fall recently and rarely ventured out of the house. The words were on the tip of her tongue, but she remembered in time that this was a client. She could ill afford to offend the woman, and run the risk of losing her custom altogether. She controlled her anger with an effort, and managed to say, 'It would be better then, to make an appointment when my husband returns.'

It was hardly polite, but it was the best she could manage. The woman's rudeness was unpardonable. To be spoken to in that fashion, and in her own house, too!

But the woman seemed unaware of any offence. 'Yes,' she said. 'Better all round. I knew you'd understand.' She got to her feet, arranging her dainty shawl around her stout shoulders, and went on, as if it were the most natural thing in the world, 'What's keeping the boy? We don't want to be too late home, there's no end of carriages and carry-on. Big funeral this afternoon. Did you see the horses go out?'

Katie shook her head. She did not trust herself to speak.

'Lovely, they looked. All them feathers, and brasses, and hooves polished. I dearly love to see a good funeral. Mind, it was out to St Allen I believe, so we shan't see it come back. Hundreds going to it though, they say. Oh, there you are,' she broke off as Willie and her husband came into the room. 'Well, we'll come and see you again when Mr Olds is back.'

Katie was close to tears of anger as she rang for Mabel to show them out.

'I'm sorry, Willie,' she said, when they had gone, 'I did my best to make her take notice of you. But you should have heard the way she talked – as good as said we were beneath her notice.' She told him about the conversation.

Willie gave his sister a quick hug. 'Don't you worry, Katie. It doesn't matter what she thinks, it's the job that matters. And I think we've managed that. I had a long talk to her husband, and I've persuaded him to a very nice gazebo. A bit bigger than they were planning, too.'

'You talked him into it? She won't be pleased about that!'

Willie grinned. 'Well, it would be truer to say I listened him into it. I just let him talk, and agreed with everything he said, and before I knew it, he'd persuaded himself. I don't think he gets a chance to give his own opinion much.'

Katie had to laugh. 'Well, you may be right,' she said. 'But if she feels that way, how many other people in Truro feel the same?'

Willie squeezed her arm. 'Who cares what they think? Real quality would never talk like that. And there's plenty of real gentlemen and ladies happy enough to know you. Me, for one!'

Katie laughed. 'Arthur will be pleased about the gazebo . . .' she began, but Mabel pushed open the door of the drawing room.

'Excuse me, Mrs Olds, there's someone at the door for you.' She gave a little giggle, and added in a rush. 'It's that Mr Trevarnon, Katie!'

Katie felt the blood rush to her face, so confused by his sudden arrival that she scarcely noticed Mabel's use of her name. Here was a real gentleman, certainly, and glad enough to know her. She had a longing, suddenly, to run to George and pour out her troubles, as she had done when she was a girl fetching water in the barrel. But she remembered her promise to Arthur.

'Show him in,' she said. 'No, Willie, please don't go.'

He stopped doubtfully.

'No, I mean it. I want you to be here. I cannot receive Mr Trevarnon on my own.'

'I thought he was an old friend of yours, Katie.'

She turned to him. 'That's just the trouble, Willie. He's an old friend, and a very dear one. Too old, perhaps, and too dear. I have promised Arthur that I will not receive him, and I want you here to witness me telling him so.'

'Witness? That sounds formal!'

She caught his hand. 'Please Willie, stay. I need your help. I don't trust myself. It would be too easy to ask him to stay for a cup of tea. Just this time. And the next. And the next.'

'A cup of tea?' Willie said. 'There's no harm in a cup of tea, surely?'

'I didn't think so, either,' Katie said. 'But Arthur likes it so little, and I like it so much, that perhaps I was wrong. Please stay?'

'Of course,' Willie said, and George Trevarnon came into the room.

Katie looked at him, thinking how dear he had become. The strong face, a little etched by pain. The clear, intelligent eyes. The fair hair, darkening a little now, and the figure still lithe and graceful despite that disfiguring limp. For a long moment she looked at him, regretting her resolve. And then she spoke.

'Mr Trevarnon, I have something to say to you. I have asked my brother to stay and hear it.'

'What is it, Katie?' But he knew. She could tell by his eyes that he knew.

'You are and have been a good and dear friend.' She tried to keep her words and voice formal, like something in one of Miss Austen's novels. If she spoke from the heart, she knew she would waver. 'A very good, dear friend. But I am becoming too fond of your company, Mr Trevarnon, and that distresses my dear husband. You

280

have known for some time, I think, that I have attempted to avoid seeing you, except in his presence. But it has come to more than this. I must ask you not to call again, unless it is to see him specifically, and even then, I myself shall not feel free to receive you.'

'Katie!' He took a step towards her.

'Please go now, Mr Trevarnon. If you care for me at all, please do not embarrass me by remaining further.' The words sounded so cold, so distant. She longed to say something kind, to take the hurt from his eyes, but she forced the words through cold lips. 'You must see, I can never care for you.' ('Cannot' she thought bitterly, not 'do not'.) 'My husband is away on business, and following a promise I made to him, I am not at liberty to entertain you in his absence.'

'So I am to be banished while you drink tea with creatures like that woman whom I saw at the door!'

There was real anguish in his voice, but she forced herself to answer coolly. 'As you observe, Mr Trevarnon, it was a woman. You are not.'

He looked at her then, and although she tried to avert her eyes, she could not, but gazed tearfully into his. 'Very well,' he said slowly. 'If this is what you wish.'

'This is what I *must*!' she burst out.

He seized her hand and kissed it, and she, grasping his fingers in her turn, lifted them to her own lips.

'Now go.'

He nodded, and left without another word, not waiting even for Mabel to answer the bell.

Katie crossed to the window to watch him go, and saw him stride down the road without a backward glance, brushing past the tanner and his wife who were climbing into a hansom. The woman said something to her husband and looked from George to the house with a knowing nod. Katie turned away, sick at heart. Who knew what she would be saying tomorrow?

'Poor fellow.' She had forgotten Willie, standing silent by the fireplace. Her face coloured at the recollection of what he had witnessed.

'Who's a poor fellow?' Mabel said, appearing at the open door. 'Not that Mr Trevarnon. He's rich as all get out.'

'Been to a funeral though, poor man,' Willie said. It was true, Katie realised. She had been so concerned to deliver her message that she had hardly taken in the mourning dress. 'Katie would like some fresh tea, Mabel. For two.'

'Right away, Mrs Olds,' Mabel said, and went away looking puzzled.

Katie looked at Willie. 'That Mrs Pritchard was outside,' she said, and her voice was barely more than a whisper. 'They will have that visit talked about all over Truro.'

'Then they'll have me to answer to,' Willie said, and began to talk about the gazebo. All the same, from that day onward, she and her brother shared a secret bond.

CHAPTER TWENTY-NINE

Robert went up to Truro at last to collect the mare. Morwenna watched him set off for the train. She had thought he would never go. More than a fortnight had passed since she had extracted his promise, but every day he had found new excuses to stay at Lower Trevarnon.

It was partly her own fault, she realised that. He was enjoying her new treatment of him, and was reluctant to leave it. That was understandable; she had intended him to enjoy it, to be lulled into security. Besides, those long walks she had taken with Peter Gillard while Robert was down at Trevarnon had, perversely, whetted her appetite for her husband.

'Variety and danger are the spice of life.' She had heard her father say that a hundred times, mostly about hunting. But she knew exactly what he meant. There was a particular thrill in lying in Robert's arms when she had spent an afternoon in the woods with Peter Gillard. Not that she had allowed Peter to possess her. Not yet. Only a daring game of touch and tease, until the owner of Goldmarten was stumbling and inarticulate with desire, and then she returned to Lower Trevarnon and her new-found role of adoring wife. It made the role of which she had so quickly tired heady and sweet again, particularly when Peter Gillard could see her play it. Robert was an attractive and charming man, and it had been amusing to have him as her slave, but once he was her husband some of the thrill had palled.

Besides, not only was Robert continually short of money, she had begun to suspect that he was not, after all, even to be heir to Trevarnon House. He had not said so, but there was something in the way his father spoke of the property which caused her disquiet. No amount of charm in a husband could substitute for a solid manor house and a good living. She had snapped at Robert more than once in the past few days, when she had found him unusually tiresome.

So it was not her charms alone which had kept Robert from Truro for so long, she was realist enough to know that. There was some scheme afoot involving George and the farm, that much was evident from the way he scribbled figures about arable acres on pieces of paper and tried to conceal them from her. He hoped to sell it, no doubt. Well, let him try. After this afternoon, if all went well, she could begin to look forward again to a life without penny-pinching. If all went well.

She went back into the house and into her dressing-room. Her boudoir, she called it, but Robert referred to it as the 'glory-hole'. Perhaps he was right. It was stacked high on every side with boxes of dresses and effects, all the things she had left behind at Goldmarten, and which Peter had brought down in his brougham. She had forgotten she owned so many dresses.

Somewhere in here must be the outfit she sought. She began to rummage through the boxes until she found it. It was a Tyrolean costume which she had worn once for a pageant in which she had been supposed to represent Austria. She took it gingerly out of the papers in which it had been packed.

It was perfect. A simple brown skirt finishing a little above the ankle. An embroidered apron, and a matching blouse cut daringly low across the breasts, with a laced brown busk and a loose white cotton kerchief tucked in to cover the décolletage. It was years since she had worn it, but it still fitted perfectly. There was a bonnet too, but she ignored that, and simply wrapped the brown fringed shawl around her shoulders and shook her hair loose. A simple peasant look. Something in the bottom of the box caught her eye. It was a ruby tie-pin, that ridiculous affair of Robert's. With a laugh she pinned it on the shoulder of her shawl, and stood back to admire the effect in the mirror.

Yes, that would do nicely. Not inappropriate for preparing a stable, but much more inviting and revealing than any of her more commonplace garments. And if that kerchief should happen to become displaced . . . She smiled at her own reflection, applied a touch of carmine and rouge, and went downstairs.

The house was already almost empty. Only the cook and parlour-maid remained, and they too had been given an hour or two off once lunch was prepared. The outside staff had also found themselves with an unexpected holiday. If Robert could see her now he would never believe it. Morwenna, who hated physical effort of all kinds, deliberately sending the staff away and choosing to prepare a stable with her own hands! With a little help, of course: Peter had promised to bring the hay over at the end of the morning, and to stay for 'a little refreshment'. Although, she thought merrily, he had probably imagined that she was merely offering lunch.

There was a rattle on the drive. That must be Peter; yes, she could glimpse the brougham through the window–curtains. For one awful moment she imagined that he had brought his coachman, but he climbed down from the driver's seat himself. She composed herself to greet him.

His response to her costume was everything she could have desired: surprise, appreciation, and a faint colouring around the ears and a darkening of the pupils which told her that he was conscious of that kerchief, and what it so narrowly disguised.

'This?' she said, in a tone of light surprise as they were eating the cold collation which had been set for them. 'I found it in one of the boxes you sent from Goldmarten, and thought it would do for setting up the stable. Quite a little farm-maid, am I not? For we shall be obliged to do it all ourselves, Peter. Robert has gone to Truro for the mare, and with one thing and another we have hardly any staff on the place. They all had extra time owing after the funeral, you see, and I had quite forgot. Shall we contrive, do you think?'

A little quickening of the breath told her that the news was not entirely lost on him, but he only said: 'That's a pretty pin. Haven't I seen it before?'

'Perhaps,' she said lightly. 'It was something of Robert's. Now then, since the meal is over, we should make haste with this stable, don't you think?'

He followed her to the yard. He was talking very little but his eyes were bright. Morwenna kept up a constant prattle to cover his silences.

Wasn't it a fine stable block? Robert had designed it on purpose, half for the motor and half for the horses, only of course they had not kept any up till now. The French-style dog-cart was quite sufficient for most purposes, and they could borrow the chaise from Trevarnon whenever they needed it, so Robert said. (With much emphasis on the last three words.)

Here was the empty stall. Quite clean really, except that Robert had two or three cans of spare petroleum spirit here, but once they were moved, and the hay brought in it was as snug a stable as could be, didn't Peter think so?

He did.

There was a hayloft too, and a ladder somewhere, so they could store the extra hay up there. So, if they just got started . . .

It did not take long. Peter seized two of the petroleum cans and carried them into the motorhouse. Morwenna picked up the third. It was lighter than she expected, and she unscrewed the lid and peered inside cautiously, wondering why Robert had stored an empty can. She could see nothing inside it at all, and shook the can a little. A sprinkling of petrol splashed out onto her skirt and kerchief. Really she could not have organised it better!

She gave a little squeal of distress, and removed the kerchief.

'What is it?' Peter wanted to know. She told him.

'It wasn't a great deal,' she said. 'The can was almost empty.'

He came over to look. 'It has been leaking,' he said. 'We must leave the door open. There is quite a strong smell in here; it might affect the mare.'

'I'll cover that patch with hay,' Morwenna said. 'That should help to absorb it. Can you help me, Peter?'

Of course he could. They set to work to move the hay into place, and store the remainder in the hayloft. Peter had brought only a couple of boxfuls and the job was soon finished, but even so Morwenna was exhausted. When there was a full cartload to be shifted, she thought, she was glad there would be a servant to move it, although Robert had fretted and fumed about the necessity of taking on a stableboy. She climbed up the ladder and lay back luxuriously on the hay.

He followed her. Without the kerchief she was aware of the whiteness of her skin, and the division between her breasts. She heard his breathing and knew that he saw it too. He unlaced the busk. 'May I?'

She said nothing, not then, nor later. Only, once, she gave a little moan of pleasure. He was less hasty than Robert, and had a certain skill.

Afterwards, she leaned back with a sigh. 'We must go,' she said, collecting her clothing around her. 'The servants will be back.'

'Morwenna! What are we to do? What shall we tell Robert?'

'Tell him? Why nothing! At least, not now. We need time to think.

Oh, Peter, help me here. I've lost that pin from my shawl. And I can't see in the darkness.'

'Where?' He began exploring playfully with his hands, and she twisted away, laughing.

'No, Peter. Not now. You must help me. I can't leave the pin here, anyone might find it, and how could I explain how I lost it in the hayloft? Come on, help me. Quickly.' She was becoming desperate now.

They searched for a while in silence. 'It must be here somewhere,' Peter said.

'I know!' Morwenna sat up suddenly. 'There's a hurricane lamp next door, in the motorhouse, and matches too. Bring that in and let's have a look.'

Peter went down, and brought it into the stable. It cast a pool of light although the door was open. 'Wonderful,' Morwenna said, bending out of the hayloft and extending her hand for it. 'I'll find it in no time with that.'

He gave her the lamp. She took it. It swung in her hand, and she felt the weight of it. 'Got it,' she called, and made to shuffle backwards away from the ladder.

Something jabbed at the flesh of her knees. Instinctively, she started.

The lamp fell. She watched it with a kind of horror. It seemed to fall in slow motion, shattering against the beam of the hayloft and tumbling down onto the piled hay below. There was a crash, a flash, an explosion. Little flames were already licking around the entry to the loft, and the world was suddenly full of little flying straws of fire.

'Peter!' She stretched a hand for the ladder, but the heat drove her back. He was below her, holding out his hands to her.

'Come on, you must come. Onto the ladder, quick.' Already there was flame all around him, and thick choking curls of smoke that rose up and clawed at her lungs.

She braved the heat that flickered at her skirt, and clawed frantically for the ladder with her feet. Too frantically. Her foot caught the ladder and it clattered down. Through the thickening smoke she saw it fall, saw Peter stagger back under it and drop back against the door, a hand to his head.

A searing pain in her thigh made her draw back. Her skirt was ablaze. She beat at it desperately, backing into the corner away from the blaze which crackled nearer and nearer. She screamed. Again and again, until the scorching fumes silenced her, filling her nose and throat so that she could no longer breathe, no longer feel the pain of the flames that were licking through her gay Tyrolean apron into her flesh and her very bones.

George came back to Trevarnon in a thoughtful mood. The morning at the mine had been interesting, certainly, and Papa was delighted by it, discussing it animatedly all the way home in the carriage.

'Copper! You could smell it! They used to say that at Levant, you know, years ago. Taste it in the water, they said when they were first mining there, though they couldn't find it then.'

George smiled. His father's reluctance to talk about mining had melted away since Anna Brunner had appeared as if he was no longer ashamed of his expertise, but gloried in it.

'Robert will regret having sold you his holding, now they've struck good tin,' Papa went on. 'And just when the price of tin is booming. There'll be a good dinner this year.'

George said nothing. The sale of the Penvarris stock was still a sore point with Papa – not that he resented George's purchase of it, but that Robert had thought so little of his inheritance. But although the investment had proved profitable, there were aspects of the mine which George himself was not happy about. That accounts dinner, for instance, where the best wine flowed like water while the likes of Peter Gillard quibbled over the price of repairs to the pumping engine, or refused to consider providing free candles and dynamite, as some of the other mines were doing.

'Penvarris men have always bought their own,' Gillard had said, last year, when George had proposed it. 'We aren't made of money.' And poured himself another cognac.

But Gillard had always avoided visiting the mine. It was another world, George thought. Men working all day in temperatures which rivalled Africa, and then facing an hour's climb up giddying ladders before they could feel the wind on their backs. No wonder their sinews were like steel, and their faces, under the red dust, as white as chalk. And that, he thought to himself, had been the world of Katie's father. Day in, day out. He shifted the bowler hat he carried on his knee, as though he were mentally lifting it in tribute.

'It's a hard life for a man, facing that every day,' he said.

Papa looked pleased. 'I was younger then,' he said, and George realised with a little start that it had been his own father's world, too, long ago. 'Though I'd sooner be down there than on the surface. Better to be mining tin than shovelling arsenic.'

George nodded. There was a new calciner installed at the Trevarnon Shaft, burning the crude ore from the mine to refine the arsenic to a grey powder. He had watched the men shovel it from the flues, with only a handkerchief to keep the poisonous dust from their lungs. It was not an aspect of the mine which delighted him.

'And there was that poor fellow crushed in the stamps a year or two ago,' his father went on. 'When you were in Africa, that must have been. Father of those girls who used to work at the house – the one who married that architect of yours.'

'Katie Warren?' George said, the words dry in his mouth. He had heard that her father was dead, but the true horror of it he had never known until now. No wonder she wanted no part of a Trevarnon!

'Your mother was fond of her,' Papa said slowly. 'Used to read to her, I believe.' His face clouded for a moment, and then he added, 'Well, what's gone is gone. Shall you be lunching in? I am joining Mrs Brunner in town.'

George shook his head. 'I asked Cook to send something up to my room,' he said. 'I had that saddle sent up yesterday, and I want to try it out.'

Papa said nothing more, but George knew that he understood.

He had been longing for this day, this first serious attempt on horseback. Since Katie had banished him, life had lost much of its savour, but when he came down a little later and climbed painfully into the specially-adapted saddle, he did feel a little glow of exhilaration. He was riding. It was painful and slow, but he was riding. He felt like a prisoner released.

From now on he could ride out, as he was doing now; to escape for his own pleasure. Caroline had been 'at home' this morning, and the house was no doubt still full of ladies, sitting on the edges of their chairs and making polite conversation; or gentlemen, politely clutching their hats and gloves to indicate that this was not a lengthy stay. It would have made little difference to anyone's happiness, George felt, if Caroline had been out, and her visitors had been obliged to leave their engraved calling cards in the little box kept in the hall for the purpose. Secretly, he fancied, many of the gentlemen would prefer to do this. He did himself, timing his visits to coincide with the absence of the hostess whenever possible.

It was good to ride again. He had almost forgotten the thrill of it, the feel of being in the saddle with the horse moving confidently under him. And while he was riding, he could forget Katie.

He made a good ride of it, out as far as Cadgewith Cove to look at the *Seuvic*. There were other sightseers too. The great steamship was still stranded firm on the rocks, although there were men with tugs alongside trying to float her free. The sight sickened him, and so did the appalling stench which rose from the decaying carcases in the ship's hold, and the disintegrating corpses of rabbits and sheep which still lapped in the waters of the bay.

He rode away, as sharply as Blister would take him. The new animal was a good horse, too, willing and affectionate. George had enjoyed his ride more than he had imagined possible.

Then, suddenly, he saw the smoke. He watched it idly for a moment, a great brown plume rising lazily over the trees in the distance, and wondered who had lit a bonfire at this time of year. But it was not a bonfire! The smoke was too heavy for that, too thick, and there was flame now, great yellow pillars of it which leaped in the air crackling and dancing like demented demons. It was a bigger fire, and farther away, than he had thought. It was coming – dear God – it was coming from Lower Trevarnon! Robert might be in there!

He turned Blister towards it, urging the animal to a gallop. But it was hopeless. The lanes were twisting and narrow; the fire was half a mile or more away by that route. He wheeled Blister in the lane, and almost without thinking, set him to the fence. He was still shaky in the saddle, and they had never jumped together, but the animal cleared it, clean as a whistle. George felt his blood quicken. 'Come on, Blister!'

A mad, desperate gallop. Over a wall, across a field, time to shout to a passing farmer to call the firecart, over a hedge and a brook, and then he was hurtling into Lower Trevarnon like a madman.

An appalling scene. The whole stable block ablaze, flames crackling through the blackened roof and showering the courtyard with tiny fragments of burning hay. And next to it, the house. The curtains at an open window had taken fire and the room was an inferno of blazing draperies. Very soon the whole house would be ablaze. George slithered down from the horse and looked around desperately.

'Robert?' His voice was lost in the roar of flames.

From behind the half-open stable door, someone groaned. It was a terrible noise, half moan, half choking. Even as he heard it the car in the motorhouse exploded, filling the air with a thicker acrid smoke and showering down burning fragments of roof.

There was no time to be lost. George stooped for a second to dip his scarf in the rainwater butt, as the army had taught him, and wound it around his mouth, nose and head. Then he dashed forward, hampered by his stiffened leg, but driven by the image of his brother lying somewhere in that blazing building. It crossed his mind that he might be about to die. Well, he thought, it doesn't matter now. Nothing matters. I will never see Katie again.

The thought gave him a kind of freedom, and he lowered his head and ran into the inferno which had been the stables. Flames grasped at his hands with searing fingers. Smoke filled his lungs until his eyes watered and he choked for breath. It was impossible to see. The heat scorched his eyeballs and filled his mouth with acrid ash, but he pressed forward. And then he found it. At his feet something soft and heavy. A body, and still alive, by the laboured breathing. With a last desperate effort he lifted the inert form and struggled out towards the door.

Blessed cool air reached his bursting lungs. He took a great gasping breath and staggered to the water butt. He propped his burden against it, unwound the scarf and plunged in his burning hands and face.

'Mr George?' It was the cook from Lower Trevarnon, hastening across the courtyard towards him. 'I seen the smoke, and somebody's raised the alarm; firecart's on its way. But whoever's this? There wasn't to be nobody in the house this afternoon, so madam said. Whoever it is will be needing an ambulance. Who could it be?'

So it was not Robert. It was difficult to tell. The face was so blackened with smoke and burns that it was almost impossible to recognise, and the clothes were scorched beyond recognition. But there was a ring on the finger which George had seen before.

'It's Peter Gillard,' he said. It was difficult to speak. His chest burned and the world was beginning to spin.

'My life,' the cook said, looking at him keenly. 'Look at your hands and arms. You need an ambulance yourself.'

George looked. 'Blister,' he said faintly. It seemed to him very funny. He felt as if he was falling from a great height. 'Like my horse.'

'Here's the firecart come,' the cook said, and then the stable roof fell in. George's last conscious memory was seeing a ball of flame as the hayloft collapsed inwards and burnt like a torch. They took him to hospital with Peter Gillard.

They did not find what remained of Morwenna for several hours.

★

'Have you seen the paper?' Arthur asked.

He was home again. It was a comfort to have him there, although the distance between them seemed greater than ever. He never turned to her, now, in the night, and more than once she had woken to find him sleepless, staring into the darkness.

She smiled at her husband and shook her head. 'No. Something of interest? Another concert by Clara Butt, perhaps? No, I know. There is to be a white sale this week, isn't there? How like you to remember. Rosa needs a new blouse, and I promised her a jap silk one.' She was talking too much, feeling the need to fill the silence between them.

'No,' Arthur said. 'It seems that an old friend of yours has been acquitting himself rather well.' His voice was almost shaking, and she looked up at him quickly.

'George Trevarnon?' She should not have guessed that so quickly.

She saw the muscles of his face contract, and knew that she had given him pain. 'He has been in hospital, it seems, badly burned around the hands saving a friend of his brother's from a fire. A Lord Poldair. The friend will pull through too, they think, though it is touch and go. Real heroic performance, by all accounts. The cook saw most of it. There's even talk of awarding him a medal. Didn't see the account at the time. Must have happened while I was away.'

'Is he all right?' she said, and heard the urgency in her own voice.

Arthur's face showed her that he heard it too. 'They say he will recover. A slow, painful business though, I've no doubt.' He got to his feet and thrust the paper towards her. 'Here, read about it for yourself. Willie and I have got to go and see about this gazebo.'

She took the paper and stared at it stupidly. Why hadn't she taken the papers in Arthur's absence? George, so desperately hurt, and she had not even known it. Then another thought struck her – the Pritchards! For Willie's sake, she must tell Arthur about what the woman had said.

'Arthur,' she said, 'Mrs Pritchard came while you were gone. She was most unkind about Willie.' She told him the whole story.

She had expected annoyance, but he merely nodded grimly. 'Mrs Pritchard told me she called,' he said. 'And from her account, she was not the only visitor.'

He turned on his heel. Katie stared after him. So that was it! That dreadful woman had been spreading scandal! But it was Willie who spoke.

'Yes, Arthur. We had another caller. Mr Trevarnon. He was here only a few minutes, and I was there too, all the time. Katie asked me to stay, to hear what she had to say.'

Arthur said, without turning around. 'And that was?'

'She asked him not to call again,' Willie said. 'I thought she was foolish to ask me to be a witness, but perhaps she was not as foolish as I thought.'

There was a long silence. Then Arthur turned, and Katie could see the anguish on his face. 'I'm sorry, Katie,' he said softly.

She could think of nothing to say.

He nodded. 'Go to the white sale by all means. Buy something for yourself and Eva at the same time.'

It was meant as a peace offering, a sign that he understood. It was clumsy, they both felt it. He said no more, but looked at her, a mute appeal in his eyes.

She could still find no words, but she managed a shaky smile.

He nodded, and left the room with Willie.

When he had gone, she picked up the paper and began to read. 'Mr George Trevarnon was discharged from Penzance Hospital today . . .'

She was still sitting perfectly motionless, lost in her own thoughts, when Peabody came in half an hour later to clear the table.

CHAPTER THIRTY

Robert cast an eye over the breakfast awaiting him on the buffet. It was excellent, as breakfast at Trevarnon always was, but he had no appetite for any of it. Not even the fresh raspberries and nectarines bought by Cook especially to 'tempt Mr George's appetite'. He felt miserable.

He helped himself to a little oatmeal porridge and cream and went to sit at the table under the big window. Papa and Caroline, it seemed, had breakfasted already, and the papers and the morning post were lying on the tray. He flicked idly through them.

There were one or two letters for him, both from complete strangers. There had been a number of these over the past two months, mostly from elderly ladies, all of them expressing shock and sympathy over the 'terrible events of last April'.

He rather enjoyed these letters. After all, he deserved sympathy. It was a terrible thing for a man to ride into his own courtyard and find half his house a smouldering ruin, his car a heap of twisted metal, and firemen carrying away, on a blanket, something which had once been his wife.

He had relived it in his dreams all night. He always did.

And that was not the worst of it. There was the pin. They had found it, misshapen and discoloured, but still undeniably his ruby pin. Morwenna must have worn it to the hayloft – to that assignation with Gillard.

He was in no doubt about the nature of that assignation. He knew Morwenna's nature – her thirst for excitement, for adventure. But to wear his pin! The pin which had become, in some way unspoken between them, the symbol of Morwenna's power to enslave him, and at the same time, of his own duplicity to Caroline. The taste of betrayal was bitter in his mouth. And yet, to avoid the scandal, he was forced to accept the popular account – that Gillard had gone into the hayloft to save Morwenna. It was hideous, horrible, ironic; the unreality of it sickened him, but it helped to numb the loss.

For he had lost everything. Even now, almost four months later, he could not believe it. That scene of devastation, the scurrying people, smouldering timbers, the smoke, the water, and above all, that blackened lump of flesh on the blanket, visited him every night in his dreams. 'Like a battlefield' Major Selwood had said, and Robert had been forced to wonder, as he tossed wakefully in his bed, how George and his like could ever witness such scenes and sleep like normal men again.

George. Somehow it always came back to George. Trust George to make himself a hero by galloping gallantly to the rescue. Only George would take it into his head to go charging into a burning building to drag a man out of it. 'King' George who had returned from the hospital to hold court in his bedroom as half the neighbourhood came to visit him, bringing flowers and fruit and cake and admiration.

Robert had been forced to witness such an occasion one morning when Gillard's mother had come with grapes and nectarines and a great sheaf of carnations.

She had even included him in her gratitude, grasping both their hands and saying with emotion: 'Poor Peter owes you his life, and Robert and I will never be able to repay you for that, shall we Robert?'

And as Peter's 'best friend', he had been forced to smile and agree, and then go to church on Sunday and listen to sermons on how selfless heroism was a lesson to us all. Really, it was too much.

It was all very well for George, Robert thought sourly. George was a soldier. He was trained to be heroic. Listening to people you would think it was George who deserved the sympathy. Just because he'd ridden across fields and hedges on un untried horse in that headstrong manner. He tried not to remember his own undignified journey home on Morwenna's frisky mare, which had a mind of its own, and had threatened to unseat him several times.

Still, he ought not to be ungrateful. At least George and Papa had offered him a roof. He turned back to his letters, and felt better. Better enough to venture on a couple of rashers of bacon and a few mushrooms. He got up and served himself.

There were letters for George too. Quite a pile of them. Goodwill and get-well messages no doubt. And a bill. Two bills.

Robert picked up the envelope and looked at it. That was odd. It looked like a bill, and yet it carried the name of Penzance Hotel embossed on the envelope. What would George be doing in Penzance Hotel?

He glanced around the room, foolishly, because there was clearly no one to watch him. He took the letter knife and carefully opened the envelope.

It was a bill. Quite a large bill. Intriguing. And even more intriguing was the writing on the invoice. *Mr George Trevarnon: re the provision of sitting-room, bedroom and accommodations for the Lady, as per our written agreement.*

For the Lady? Robert felt a little thrill of victory. He picked up the other envelope, and began to prise it slowly and gently open. It was a bill from a costumier. Caroline never bought ready-made clothes.

'Robert? What are you doing?' It was Caroline herself, coming into the room with a basket of fresh-picked roses from the garden.

He thrust the envelopes hurriedly under the table. 'Reading the mail,' he said, giving her a cheerful smile. 'What lovely flowers. Are they for George?'

She nodded. 'One of the gardeners cut them for me. I hope he will like them.' She sat down heavily. 'He seems to like so little these days.'

Robert looked at her. George liked so little, did he? Damn the man, he didn't know the value of what he had got. He reached out and squeezed her hand. 'He's hurt,' he said encouragingly. 'Of course he's not himself.'

She looked at him with her big sad eyes. 'Oh, it's not only that. He was discontented before the fire. I could tell. For a week or more he just wasn't interested in anything. You know how enthusiastic he was about Little Manor. And then one day, he simply stopped being interested. He never went down there again.'

She had not withdrawn her hand, he noticed. He gave it a little squeeze. When she looked at him again, there were tears in her eyes.

'You don't think, do you, that there is another woman?'

It was so unexpected that he said, almost before he thought, 'George? Good Lord, no! Whatever gave you such a notion?'

She was trembling. 'It's only that, while he has been ill, sometimes when he is asleep he . . . he says a name.' She bowed her head. 'Not my name.'

He had gained control of himself by now. 'When he has a beautiful wife like you? How could he?'

Her head went back then. '*You* could! You were engaged to marry me, and you left me for Morwenna.' She bit her lip. 'I'm sorry. I should not speak ill of the dea . . of your wife.'

He got up and went over to her. Suddenly he felt invincible. 'I was a fool, Caroline. A stupid besotted fool. More than a fool, I think I was a little mad. She had that effect, you know. It was like a spell. I think all men felt it.' It was the truth. He recognised it as he spoke. He looked at Caroline. 'She was in the hayloft, you know, with Gillard. That is how she died.'

She shook her head, wide-eyed. 'I hadn't heard that.'

'We kept it from the papers. The stable, that's all we said. But a lot of people know. George must know.'

She said simply, 'Poor Robert.'

He seized his advantage. 'Poor Peter.' He could almost believe that he felt that. 'And in the meantime, George had you.'

She coloured a little.

'I mean it, Caroline. My first love, my best love. It was hard, you know,' he was working himself into a passion, thinking of Morwenna and Peter, 'seeing you together, seeing your shared looks, knowing that you shared a part of his life, that you shared his bed . . .' He was imagining that hayloft, that look he remembered so well, that soft body, that smile.

She spoke so softly that he almost did not hear. 'No, not that. Never that.'

He stared at her, trying to make sense of the words. 'What did you say?'

Tears now, trickling down her cheeks. She made no effort to stop them. 'I have tried to be a good wife to him, in every other way, but somehow I could not. I was afraid . . . and now I think he has found some other lady. He is a young man, after all.'

He put his arms around her. 'My poor Caroline.'

She twisted away, her face red with crying. 'No, no. I am still George's wife! This may be just imagining.'

It came to him like an inspiration. Suddenly possessing Caroline seemed very important, a kind of culmination of all the events of the past few years. It might take a long time, a long patient courtship. But he was ready for that.

'I am sorry to say this, my dear,' he said softly, 'but I think perhaps you had better read these letters.'

George was sitting up in bed. The burns on his hands and legs had healed, and even the deepest had dwindled to raw red patches which the nurse bathed in cold tea, and dressed with bicarbonate of soda every day. More serious had been the congestion in his lungs, caused, so the doctor said, by inhaling the smoke. George had spent more hours than he cared to count being lifted in bed to inhale balsam, or being rubbed with liniment to ease his breathing. For a time they had even wrapped him, every few hours, in layers of bandages and hot linseed as they did with people who had pneumonia, but the weight and heat of the steaming poultice was agony on his damaged skin, and after a few days they stopped the treatment. His body, left to itself, began slowly to recover.

His scorched throat was easier, and his voice had returned. He was beginning to eat and drink a little more than the sips of water and spoonfuls of cool chicken broth which had kept him alive for the first few weeks. He could sit up for most of the day now, and was even able to take a turn or two around the room, although his leg and back still pained him from his exertions. Altogether, the doctor was beginning to speak of him coming downstairs within the week.

In the meantime, he was bored to tears. His eyes had recovered sufficiently for him to read a little, but the doctor did not encourage it. There were well-wishers, too, who came to visit, and he would never have believed how much he would come to relish the little pieces of gossip that they brought.

'Did you know that Gertrude played tennis last week with the St Aubens?'

'And she went to Brighton. In the bathing machines, no less.'

'Well, we needn't look to Brighton for our fashion. Mr Balfour himself is to visit Newquay!'

Once it would have driven him to distraction. Now it came as a breath of the real world.

Mr and Mrs Gillard came often, embarrassed and embarrassing in their gratitude, with news of Peter, slowly winning the battle against infection, in the hospital. Thank heaven for modern antiseptic. The Selwoods were most attentive, visiting their son-in-law most days and anxious to tend his every need.

At least the incident appeared to have healed the old rift between

Caroline and Robert. Perhaps it was having Robert living in the house while Lower Trevarnon was being rebuilt. Whatever the reason, they often came to see him together these days. Caroline seemed unusually nervous and remote, as though his injuries had cut him off from her in some way. That was a pity, but he did not altogether care.

From Katie he received no word. Had she seen the papers, he wondered? Did she know how ill he had been?

And Papa, coming up the stairs as he did now, every evening without fail, to sit at his bedside and talk as if to make up for the past twenty-six years of silence. He had heard the whole story now – how Papa had met Anna Brunner when he was a young mine captain with his way to make; how he had loved her and left her when he struck gold, promising to return and bring her back to England to a beautiful house, but, when he had bought Trevarnon and returned she had vanished, married and gone, with a child. Papa had returned to England to marry a farmer's daughter with a fine dowry and to raise his sons. He had never known, until now, of his daughter.

Yet he had found her again, this love of his life, and his eyes and conversation sparkled. He had wanted to hear all about Kernerwek, to see the photograph, to chide George for his silence. 'Why ever did you not tell me, my boy?'

And George had said, time after time, 'What good could it have done? It was too late.'

It had created a great bond between them.

This was Papa now; he recognised the tread on the landing. But the man who opened the door was the not the dapper figure he had expected. Papa looked small, sad, defeated. His clothes were as neatly pressed as ever, but he had a crumpled look, as though the joy had been squeezed out of him, like a sucked peach.

'Papa?'

His father looked at him with hollow eyes and sat down heavily in the chair by the window. 'She's gone, George. Gone.'

'Gone where?'

'Who knows? Germany? Holland? Back to South Africa? I wanted to marry her, you know. She said no, but I thought I could persuade her, given time. She had been here for so many weeks and we met every day. I showed her Cornwall. She enjoyed it, I know she did. I couldn't help hoping, whatever she said. I thought she was waiting to know her own mind, and I could not blame her after all that had passed. But she was waiting only for this. It is for you, George.'

It was a banker's draft. Everything she owed him, to the last penny. He put it down on the bedside table.

'She left me a note. She was tempted, she said, but there was no going back.' Papa sounded terribly weary, suddenly. 'I'm an old man, George. I should have swept her away when I had a chance, seized time by the forelock and to hell with the world. You don't know what it's like, my boy, to lose the woman you love like that. Well, I shouldn't be burdening you with all this. I'm very tired. I shall go and lie down.'

He went out of the room, shuffling like a man twice his age. George watched him go. Seize time by the forelock, indeed? What a pretty pickle they had made of things, the Trevarnons. Father, who had been locked into a loveless marriage; Robert married to a shameless flirt who reaped her own rewards; himself in a marriage that was no marriage at all. A sudden wild impatience seized him. He would not lie here like an invalid, and let the world carry him where it would. He would get up and make a battle of it, whatever the doctors said. He could ride, he had proved that now. If he could not have Katie, he would at least make a last effort to have Caroline and have done with this shilly-shallying. And if she would not have him, perhaps he would seek his commission again, or take a grand tour like Mrs Brunner.

He swung his legs out of bed. For a moment he thought that they would not hold him, but he steadied himself against the table. His dressing-gown was on the chair. Three careful steps carried him over to it, another three took him to the door.

His head was spinning and his chest and leg ached, but he gritted his teeth and pressed on across the landing. The stairs loomed before him like a great pit, but he squared his shoulders and placed his hand on the banisters.

'George, my dear fellow, what on earth are you doing?' Selwood, giving his coat and hat to the footman, and bounding up the stairs. 'You will do yourself a mischief. Let me take you back to bed.'

George shook his head. 'I'm getting up,' he said. 'I've been idle long enough. If you wish to assist me, you may help me down the stairs.'

There was something in his tone which made Selwood give him a sharp look, but the arm was offered and George made his way slowly down the stairs.

'The music-room, I think,' George said. 'It catches the afternoon sunlight, and I am less likely to encounter company.'

He pushed open the door.

From the chaise-longue two red-faced figures sprang apart quickly. But not all Caroline's jumping up and covering herself with her crossed arms could disguise that fact that she was stripped to her camisole, nor that the man buttoning his shirt with a feverish hand, and struggling back into his coat and braces, was his brother, Robert Trevarnon.

'George!' Caroline said, in a voice somewhere between a gulp and a sob. 'It isn't . . . I haven't . . .'

He looked at her, and a terrible quiet anger possessed his soul. 'It is to be hoped you haven't,' he found himself saying quietly, 'since I believe an annulment may require a physical examination. Otherwise, my dear, I am afraid it will be a divorce.'

Selwood, standing beside him, was white with rage. 'You young dog,' he snarled. He would have lunged at Robert and sent him sprawling, if George had not leant a little more heavily on the supporting arm, and prevented him. 'Not content with humiliating my daughter when she was engaged to you, you must also dishonour her when she is married to your brother. Well, sir, marry her you shall! George speaks of annulment – if he has grounds, as I imagine from his words that he has, we shall apply for it at once. We shall not have the Selwood name dragged through the divorce courts.'

George looked at his brother and could see the emotions which were flickering across his face. He could read his thoughts, as though they were written in cold print. The Selwood estate and all its thousands.

'Oh, I'm sure Robert would be delighted, sir.'

Robert glowered at him. 'And what of you? What of your bills for "a Lady" in that hotel, and an account for dresses – and more intimate garments too?'

'That requires an answer, sir!' This was from Selwood.

George turned to him. 'For your sake, Mr Selwood, I am prepared to give an account of myself. Those bills were a debt undertaken to assist a Mrs Brunner, an old friend of my father's, who lost everything in the recent shipwreck. I have no doubt my father will confirm it, if you wish. Further, it was a loan only – you will find her repayment in a banker's draft on my bedside table at this moment. But perhaps my brother would care to offer an account of how he came to be aware of the contents of my private correspondence?'

Robert said nothing, and George continued. 'Mr Selwood, I remain your obedient servant. At any time, sir, consider yourself my guest. Caroline, you will go to your room until such time as your father sends a carriage for you.'

Caroline gave a little gasp. 'But I thought . . .' she began, and then hung her head, colouring, and said nothing more.

George turned to Robert, still struggling to readjust his clothing. 'And as for you . . . you are not welcome in this house.'

'But Papa . . .' Robert began.

'I will answer for Papa,' George said. 'You have your own home. Parts of Lower Trevarnon are perfectly habitable. And now if you please, Mr Selwood, you will assist me to my room. I think we have matters to discuss. I am heartily sorry to have subjected you to such unpleasantness.'

Somehow, in spite of everything, he felt a lightening of the spirits. He should have done this long ago.

That night he sat down and wrote a letter to Katie. Not to press his suit, simply to tell her that he was seeking an annulment, and that he was there, if she ever needed him.

David was ill. Very ill. Lying on the great bed upstairs with his face flushed and dry, and his breath coming in short, laboured gasps. He had a raging fever.

It had not seemed so dreadful, at first. Rosa had come from school with a nasty cough, and David had caught it. Katie had done her best to prevent it, rubbing the children's chests with goose-grease and hanging camphor around their necks. Nurse Mallin had pooh-poohed these homely remedies and insisted on spooning malt extract and sulphur-and-black-treacle into everyone, but that had not prevented Eva complaining of a sore throat before she went to bed, and Willie muttering about a headache.

Peabody was a wonder, preparing hot fomentations for Eva's throat, steeping friar's balsam for Willie and Rosa, and bathing David's head with cool water as though he were her own. Poor Mabel did her best, too, even staying awake into the small hours to bring Katie tea and toast while she watched over David in the long, dark, night.

David got iller and iller.

Katie was frantic. If only Arthur were home! She had written him, of course, and was hourly expecting a reply, but she needed his presence. Should she, for instance, send for a doctor? David was sobbing now, declaring there were spiders on the bed and crawling up his face, and although Katie did her best to comfort him he hardly seemed to recognise her. She almost sent Mabel for Dr Marshall there and then. When Nurse Mallin heard of it, she dismissed such an idea and said that a bit of a cold never hurt anyone.

'It'll pass,' she said severely. 'Just leave him alone.'

Katie tried to obey, but she could not sleep. She went into David's room, and found him lying with his eyes rolled back and his face the colour of chalk. Nurse Mallin was sitting in a chair dozing.

Something within Katie snapped. She ordered the woman from the room.

The nurse stood staring at her. 'But the child is ill . . .' she began.

Katie cut her off. 'And he needs his mother. If you must be doing something, take some hot lemon and blackcurrant juice into the nursery, and look after Vicki and the others. But leave David to me.'

'But Mrs Olds . . .'

'Do as I say, if you wish to have a position tomorrow!' For the rest of her life Katie would wonder how she found the courage to speak those words. But it was obvious that she meant them, and Nurse Mallin hurried out.

Katie drew up a chair, and sat close to the little fevered body. First thing tomorrow she would call the doctor, let it cost what it would. For now, she searched her brains to remember what her own mother had done when they were small. Keep a kettle boiling to ease his breathing, and pile him with blankets to draw the fever out.

She tiptoed into the kitchen to fetch a kettle, and found Peabody there before her, unable to sleep. Between them, they stoked the bedroom fire, and contrived a trivet for the kettle, and Katie sat by his bed all night while Peabody brought tea and toast.

But she had no appetite for it. David lay hot and heaving, and she was powerless to help him.

In the morning Mabel found her still sitting there, like a statue, watching the little face, flushed with fever, tossing restlessly on the pillows.

'I've brought you some breakfast,' Mabel whispered, 'and there's a letter for you on the tray.'

Katie picked up the envelope absently. It was not Arthur's hand.

Then, with a little shiver, she recognised the seal. Not many of her acquaintance used sealing wax on their private correspondence, but she had seen it done at Trevarnon. And it was the same seal. Gingerly she lifted the paper knife and prised up the seal.

Her eyes went to the signature, and she felt her heart lurch. Should she read this? She had agreed not to see George Trevarnon. She had said nothing about reading his letters. She scanned the first lines. *My dearest Katie, I cannot help remembering the last time we met . . .*

'Mummy,' a little voice from the bed. She dropped the paper instantly and turned to her son. 'I'm thirsty.'

He was sweating. God be praised, he was sweating. The fever had broken. Katie jumped to her feet.

'Peabody!' She called the name aloud as she rang the bell, and the housekeeper appeared in an instant.

'What is it, Mrs Olds?'

'It's David! It's David! He wants a drink. He knew me. He asked for it.'

'He's awake then? He shall have his drink, the lamb!' And she was gone, while Katie held the boy's hand, sobbing, and rearranged his pillows to make him comfortable.

And when David raised his head and sipped his blackcurrant to the dregs, and asked for more, Katie felt such a wave of relief and tenderness that she had to sit down abruptly.

'He's pulled around, the little angel,' Peabody said, and there were tears of joy in her eyes. 'And it's down to you, Mrs Olds, nobody could have had nursing like that dear lamb has had.' She forgot herself, in her emotion, enough to give Katie a hug as though the years between had vanished and Katie was back in the sewing-room.

It was some time, in fact, before Katie remembered the letter lying unread on the carpet. She picked it up, and hesitated for a moment. Then she folded it carefully and put it into the envelope without glancing at it again. She might love George Trevarnon, but the truly important things were here, in this house. She sent Mabel for pen and paper and thought for a long time before she wrote:

Dear Mr Trevarnon,
I regret I am not able to accept your communications.
Yours very sincerely, Katie Olds.

Her heart lurched with sadness as she addressed the envelope and sent Mabel to the post with it, but a glance at David, tousled now and pale, but peacefully asleep, made her feel better.

And then a noise at the door, a foot on the stairs, and there was Arthur.

'I didn't bother to write, my dear, I came straight home.'

She went into his arms. 'He's much better now, but he has been so poorly, Arthur. I didn't know what to do.'

He looked down at the sleeping form. 'It seems to me you've done the best thing.' He dropped a kiss on her hair.

It had taken the child's illness to seal the truce between them, Katie thought.

And, as if he read her thinking, Arthur said softly, 'My Katie always does the right thing.'

She thought of George Trevarnon and his letter. She would always wonder what it said.

'I hope so, Arthur,' she murmured. 'Oh, I do hope so.'

CHAPTER THIRTY-ONE

January the seventh. It was drizzling again, a cruel, cold drizzle that would soon soak a man's clothes, trickle into his boots and seep into his very soul. A fine day, Robert told his reflection sourly, to have a wedding.

He wrenched his studs into place and adjusted his starched collar. Well, at least this wedding would put an end to the misery of the last eighteen months. It was not so much the gossip, he thought, settling his silk cravat with a neat gold pin; that was only to be expected once the news of the annulment and engagement got about. It was the discreet dropping of his name from the guest-lists of everyone who was anyone. For months he had not been invited anywhere, and it was only the Selwood name, and the patronage of that infernal Gillard, which had recently opened the door to even the most minor of social engagements. Two years ago he would have scorned a charity dinner; now it was the highlight of his social diary.

It had all been deucedly dull.

And so confoundedly unfair! People who might have cut him dead when he eloped with Morwenna, had treated him instead as a kind of romantic desperado, dangerous and delightful to know. He and Morwenna had been positively lionised in some quarters. While now that he was a respectable widower, and due to be married to a lady whose marriage had been declared legally null, he was being shunned by everybody, just on the basis of a few whispers. It was dashed unreasonable.

Caroline did not seem to care. She had been content to creep back into her father's house and avoid the public gaze altogether. Granted there had been all that unpleasant business with lawyers and doctors and affidavits and so on – it must have been very disagreeable for her. He hadn't enquired too closely. All the same, he thought, as he got into the coach with his father, it had been confoundedly difficult for him too.

Well, in an hour's time, it would all be behind him. No one could say he hadn't done things properly. The delay over the annulment had meant there had been a decent period of mourning for his wife, and there was to be a proper church wedding too, even if it was a tiny little church in a village on the Selwood estate. Mrs Selwood had been determined on that, if only to prove that her daughter was entitled to it, and not obliged to marry in the registry office like a little shopworker.

And here was the lane, and the little church with the lych-gate, and the vicar looking miserable and cold under the dripping eaves. He would have to tip him something handsome. Well, this wedding would help matters, financially as well as socially. It was a pity he had been so remiss about the insurance on Lower Trevarnon, but dash it all, a fellow couldn't be expected to foresee calamities of that nature.

The coach came to a halt in a muddy puddle and he picked his way carefully to the more solid path by the gate. Papa followed, under an umbrella which Tibbs was holding for him. It was just as well the repairs on the house had been finished, otherwise the roof would have still been letting water in on their wedding night. He could hardly have expected Caroline to live in half a dozen rooms, as he had been forced to do himself for the better part of six months. He was lucky that George had still consented to buy the farm – that at least had paid for some new clothes and furnishings, and there were only the outhouses and stables to be rebuilt now; that Olds fellow of George's had seen to that. Once he had his hands on Caroline's allowance he would be able to pay it off in full.

He even contrived a smile as he shook hands with the whey-faced vicar, and went into the church. It was half empty. Four or five dozen people, no more, many of them from the Selwood and Trevarnon estates, all huddled up in greatcoats and mufflers against the January weather. Only the women looked a little more festive, with a touch of fur on their muffs and bonnets, or a bunch of early snowdrops pinned to their collars.

Mrs Selwood, plump as an apple dumpling in her unseasonable spring yellow in the front pew opposite, caught his eye and averted her head at once to stare stonily at the carved reredos.

Well, let her scowl – she had chosen the church. It wasn't his fault if the lane which led to it was axle-deep in mud at this time of year, and her boots and hemline bore witness to the fact.

Papa coughed. It was cold in the church and he was only here at all against the advice of his physician, muffled to extinction in a heavy greatcoat. They were whispering about him in the pews. Robert knew what they were saying, but it was not the scandal which had caused the old man's decline. Papa had never been the same since that South African woman went away. All the same, it would be as well if Caroline came soon. Another scandal might be too much for the old man's heart.

He took his own place beside a young Selwood relation with spots, who had been dragooned into acting as best man.

Ah, a commotion at the door. The Wedding March on the squeaky, wheezing harmonium which was all this tiny church boasted by way of an organ. A general rustle among the greatcoats and tippets which indicated that the bride had arrived. And here she was, Caroline herself, not in a wedding gown but wearing a white directoire dress and a white hat with a veil. She carried a spray of white chrysanthemums, which must have been brought on specially in a heated glasshouse, or railed down from London, packed in ice. For the price of that bouquet you could pay a gardener for a fortnight, Robert thought bitterly.

But she was here, and by his side, and whispering the responses in a tiny little voice so that the deaf old clergyman had to lean forward to hear them. There was one terrible moment when the minister asked for any 'just cause or impediment', and there was an unexpected scuffle at the entrance. Robert had a sudden mad fear that George had returned unannounced from his World Tour, and was about to declare that the marriage could not proceed; but it was only the coachman, coming in out of a passing hailstorm. The vows were exchanged and Robert was a married man again.

Then it was back to the Selwoods', and a wedding buffet spread in the drawing room in front of a blazing fire. A good side of beef, salmon mousse, cuts of turkey and ham, hot punch and cold champagne. The cook had made a second plumcake at Christmas, and set it aside to ice for the wedding, and very pretty it looked, with a sugar swan, and a bride and groom under an arch of piped roses. It wasn't much of a feast, and there were not many feasters, but there was music and dancing, and Robert's heart lifted a little. Peter Gillard, still too frail to come to the ceremony, was there, his face and hands a mass of livid scars, being smiled at by the dumpy Selwood cousin with the teeth. Some people, Robert told himself wryly, would marry anyone for money.

It was time then, to repair to Lower Trevarnon in the Selwoods' carriage. Robert now had only the dog-cart, and that only because Morwenna had insisted on keeping the dogs and cart in the coach house, and not in the stables, so that they had been rescued unharmed from the fire.

The house looked warm and welcoming in the evening light: the staff were standing in the entrance to be introduced to their new mistress, each curtseying in turn as the housekeeper called out their name and station. Caroline blushed and smiled prettily and found something amiable to say to each of them, and Robert's heart glowed with pride. She had charm, this new bride of his. Morwenna had flounced past with hardly a glance, and an impatient 'Good. Good. Now get back to work, draw me a bath, and bring tea and sandwiches to my dressing-room in half an hour.'

Not Caroline. All through supper and early evening her modesty and good manners enchanted him.

It was only later, when the housemaid had turned down the bed, and adjusted the new gas heater which he had had fitted in the bathroom, that the problem arose. Caroline had retired to the bathroom and returned in a dressing-gown of *crêpe-de-Chine* trimmed with swansdown. She looked towards him, colouring, and sat at the dressing-table to brush her hair, already shining from the attentions of the maid.

He went over and stood behind her, smiling at her in the glass. 'Caroline. Leave that now, my love.'

She was fresh and sweet, pretty as a freesia with the same air of delicate fragility. He held out his arms to her, and she turned to him, trembling.

He slipped the gown from her shoulder and smoothed the white flesh, as he had done all those months ago in the music room at Trevarnon, and she lifted her face to be kissed.

It was a pleasure. He kissed her, gently at first, and then with increasing urgency. He expected her to respond, but as his passion rose, she stiffened in his arms, pulling away and turning her mouth to escape his own.

'Caroline?'

She gave a little sob and buried her head in his shoulder.

'No, Robert, don't. You're hurting me. Be patient. Give me time.'

He looked at her in amazement. 'Time for what?'

She snatched away from him and went to sit on the bed, hiding her head in her hands. 'Time to . . . become accustomed. My marriage was annulled, you remember.'

He went to sit beside her, his hands insistent. 'This one won't be.'

A sob answered him.

'Oh, for heaven's sake,' he said, his voice rough with desire, 'you're my wife.' He pulled her towards him, stripping off the flimsy nightdress as he spoke. She was very pretty, and he was stronger than she was. It was not difficult to make her his wife indeed.

Afterwards, to his surprise, he found she was crying. He put his arm around her. 'Don't cry,' he said, as gently as he could. 'You'll get used to it.'

'George would never have behaved like that!' she accused, tearfully.

No, he thought, turning back to his own room. Nor Morwenna either. He looked back at the weeping, crumpled form on the bed, and sighed.

This was their bargain, and they must live with it.

It was a beautiful evening on the deck. Warm and still, with hardly a ripple to disturb the huge unbroken expanse of the sea. George leaned on the ship's rail, and for the hundredth time watched the sun go down over the water.

Magnificent. One moment the huge fiery orb was hanging on the horizon, turning the world to crimson and gold – a few moments later it was utterly gone, and there was only the jewelled indigo of the tropical night, and just the glow of stars to light the creaming wake on the dark, dancing surface of the sea. Magnificent.

A married couple from his table came out on the deck and wished him good evening. They were pleasant enough: he a Colonial Army officer, she a good deal younger – pretty and trim in her beige lace dress and a little white fur wrap, which she could hardly require in this climate, George felt, despite her daring décolletage. Charming companions, no doubt, but this evening George wanted no company but his own, unless perhaps it was the little widow with the gentle smile and the tired eyes whom he had spoken to once or twice in the library.

He returned the couple's greeting with a courteous smile and went

back, down the companionway, to his own cabin. It was a comfortable enough room, with fine wooden fitments and its own porthole.
The neatly starched bedlinen had already been turned down and his
nightclothes laid out for him by the cabin steward, but no sooner had
he shut the door than he regretted his impulse. The all-pervading
thrum of the ship's engines and the stifling heat made the cabin less
than inviting.

He sat down on his bunk and smiled at his own discontent. On the
troopship to South Africa he would never have imagined such luxury,
even though he had enjoyed officer's quarters. This spacious cabin to
himself, the deep-piled carpet of the lounges and dining-room, the
mahogany furnishings, the leather desks in the library where he spent
so many hours, the sumptuous meals which the kitchens still managed
to produce, though they had been more than a fortnight out of sight of
land. Not perhaps, the match of the Cunarder on which he had begun
the first part of his tour a few months before, but a fine ship, all the
same.

Was it really only a few short months? It seemed a lifetime. Enough
memories for a lifetime, certainly. A thousand impressions printed on
his brain.

America – landscapes of immense size; thrusting streets where
people of a score of nationalities jostled side by side. The ruins of San
Francisco, already rebuilding after the 'quake of '06. Young Orville
Wright and his amazing heavier-than-air craft, defying gravity in
Virginia. It had seemed almost like magic, and it had been sad to read a
few weeks later that someone had actually died in an aeroplane
accident. The same plane too – young Wright broke a propeller and
crashed, killing his passenger.

But America was mad for motion. Look at Mr Ford's new 'motorcar for the masses' – the Tin Lizzie, as they were calling it – due off the
production lines at any minute. 'Any colour you like as long as it's
black,' Mr Ford was supposed to have said. But colour was the
coming thing. They talked in New York of a new process for colour
photography, and Mr Edison had a method of projecting pictures that
moved. America was truly still a New World.

Europe had seemed very staid by comparison, though he made the
Grand Tour, and goggled at it all – France, Italy, Switzerland,
Germany. He had not liked what he had seen of Germany. The Kaiser
might be the old Queen's son-in-law, but that new imperial navy with
its dreadnoughts could only be a threat. It was a relief to turn to

Greece, hot and arid and airless, where local peasants scratched a living amongst the unregarded ruins of a mighty and ancient civilisation, and offered the visitor strange resinous wine, olives and cheese. There would soon be modern hotels, no doubt. Since the 1906 Olympics, people had begun to discover the beautiful coastline and warm shallow waters.

A return to swarming Naples then, to take ship for Suez and the East, until here he was, halfway across the Indian Ocean bound for Australia, at the beginning of a new year. Hard to believe that at home in England it was winter; that yesterday had been Robert and Caroline's wedding day. And Katie? What was she doing? He would probably never know. Well, it was all half a world away, and he was well out of it.

Through the open porthole he could hear the sounds of music. There would be dancing on the promenade deck, and games, and laughter, since the night was calm. There were a number of people of his own age aboard, including a pair of good-looking sisters and their mother, who thought his limp romantic. He felt a strong disinclination to join them. Still, there was always the chance that the gentle widow from A Deck would be there too. He might ask her to dance; she would be patient with his clumsiness.

He glanced in the mirror set into gimbals over his dressing-chest, and straightened his dress tie. This, after all, was what he had come for – why he had sold Robert's mine shares to the American conglomerate. Well, not entirely why. He remembered that last stormy accounts meeting where he had argued and pleaded for new equipment, for a new safety-cage, for the replacement of the rotten winze; and been voted down by the voices of retrenchment and the prophets of greed.

Well, he had sold, and his father too. What were the mines to him now? Especially when the price of arsenic was rising as the price of tin fell – he had no wish to be part of the sale of poisons. He was well out of it. He had sold at a good price and he was to have the tour of a lifetime, to broaden his mind, to enjoy himself. To forget, he told himself firmly. He straightened his shirt front with a soft sigh, combed some embrocation into his hair, put on his jacket and went out of the cabin to join the dance.

Katie was in the drawing room at Number Twenty-three. The room, with its blazing fire in the hearth, seemed empty now that the

Christmas tree had been taken down, and the house seemed un-naturally quiet, although it was only mid-afternoon.

Vicki was asleep in the nursery, worn out after a hard morning playing with her Christmas toys. Rosa and David were at school, although David had been reluctant to relinquish his hoop. He had been waiting for a week for fine weather, and the chance to try it out in the park.

Eva who had finished school at Christmas, had lost patience with her piano and her books and gone into Truro to spend the two new half-crowns which were burning a hole in the pocket of her new jacket. Willie was at the office (Arthur said they could scarcely spare him now) and Arthur – Katie sighed. Arthur was upstairs overseeing the preparation of his suitcases for yet another of his business journeys.

He was so often away these days. Certainly the business was successful; the Shrewsbury project had paved the way for others, all over the country. But Katie was not altogether sure that she liked the price that the family paid. Since the night of David's illness she hated to risk their new-found understanding by absence. And, she reflected sadly, the tanner's wife had done her work well. There was little company in Truro when Arthur was away.

Oh, she could accompany him – she had done, more than once, and he was always delighted. She had been to London and travelled on the twopenny tube, seen the Houses of Parliament, even been to theatre and dined in a London restaurant. It was all enormous fun, but her heart was with her babies and she did not like to leave them often. Lilly, the little girl whom Peabody had introduced as a nursemaid, was a treasure of course, and would have cared for them like her own. Too much like her own, Katie thought, and she preferred to stay at home.

Still, Arthur would not be gone for long. She set aside the book that he had given her for Christmas, and rang the bell for Peabody and tea. It was an exciting book, one of Mr Conan Doyle's, but she had no heart for it this afternoon. Her mind was full of Arthur and the coming trip.

She was astonished, therefore, when Peabody came to the drawing-room door, not with a tea-tray, but with a message and a startled look.

'Here's Miss Beryl come, Mrs Olds, and Mr Arthur all at sixes and sevens.'

Katie was surprised. It was rare that the old lady ventured into the town these days, since she had been ill, and rarer still for her to visit.

Peabody was still hovering at the door. 'Shall I show her in?'

Katie could not suppress a smile. 'Certainly, Peabody, and you can bring tea for two. I wonder what Aunt Beryl wants.'

She was not left wondering for long. There was a great flurry of capes and gloves and bonnets and shawls and Aunt Beryl came into the room. How thin and tired she looked, Katie thought, for all her fine dresses.

'Such a to-do, my dear Katie,' Aunt Beryl said, as soon as she was fairly seated in the deep armchair by the fire. 'I went into Truro to send a wire and there was such a queue of people waiting to apply for their pensions I quite had to abandon the idea. I thought I should impose on your good nature for a little, and make another attempt later.'

'Pensions? Oh yes, this new Old Age Pension of Mr Asquith's! Started last week, didn't it?' Katie said. 'A lot of people will be grateful for that.' What a difference, she reflected, such a pension would have made to Lally in her old age.

'Five shillings a week,' Aunt Beryl said, 'for nothing else than living to seventy. Handsome, I call it. We shall be paying for that in our taxes by and by, you mark my words. Though the women in the queue were neat and well-mannered, I'll say that for them. Not like the throng that used to wait for outside relief from the workhouse when I was young.'

'Well, it isn't like poor relief, Aunt Beryl,' Katie said, as Peabody poured tea. 'It's for everybody. All except paupers and prisoners.'

Aunt Beryl fixed her with a sharp glance. 'You mean I might be eligible for an Old Age Pension myself!'

'My dear Aunt Beryl,' Katie said, 'what should you want with a pension? You are not in want. Besides, I am sure you would have to appear before a Board, or something.'

'Nevertheless,' the old lady replied, 'I shall be seventy in a month or less. And I'm sure I am quite as deserving as some of those people. I shall get my solicitor to look into it. Indeed, I think I shall see him as soon as ever I have finished my tea. I intend to see him in any case about my will.'

And indeed, nothing would dissuade her, not even the prospect of Arthur's joining them for crumpets, as Katie so pressingly urged. 'No my dear, I shall go while my mind is made up. I have already stayed half an hour. I quite decided to come you know, when I came to town recently and heard some nonsense that one or two people had been deciding not to call. Well, I shall come again, and I shall see that others know it. Now, I must go. I have still that telegraph to send to my cousin, and it gets dark so early at this time of year.'

So that was it. Aunt Beryl had come in a show of solidarity. It was a kind gesture, and not without point. Aunt Beryl might be frail, but she was a force to be reckoned with in respectable society. Her visit would do a great deal to quell rumour.

But Katie knew better than to voice her thanks. Instead she said, 'But look, it has begun to pour with rain. You can't go out now. You will be drenched before you can find a cab. Besides the girls will be home directly, and the babies will be awake soon. Shouldn't you like to see them?'

But it was to no avail. By the time Arthur came downstairs his aunt was already leaving, and even his added entreaties could not detain her, except that she did agree to Mabel's going out for a cab.

'We shall have to think of having a telephone in the house,' he said, after his aunt had been helped painfully into the hansom a few minutes later. 'We could telephone for a cab, then – and it would be possible for me to call you up, too, while I am away. Thousands of people have taken subscriptions.'

'I would like that,' Katie said sincerely. But she felt a little disquieted, when the cab came back by arrangement to take Arthur to the station. Disquieted, without really knowing why.

CHAPTER THIRTY-TWO

Katie was summoned to Aunt Beryl's bedside the following Thursday. It was the maid who came, still in her morning uniform, a tall, thin awkward girl with big clumsy hands and a flushed, stricken face.

'Mrs Olds?' She stood in the entrance hall, twisting her print skirt between her heavy fingers. 'Please, ma'am, it's Miss Beryl, she's been took that bad! Doctor came and said to send for her relatives at once.'

'Aunt Beryl?' Katie was already taking jacket, gloves and bonnet from Mabel's willing hands. 'My husband is away. I'll come with you myself.'

There was a hansom cab waiting. The girl followed Katie's glance. 'Doctor said to take a cab,' she explained hastily. 'I never would have come in it, else. Come quick, Mrs Olds, do – the poor old lady is that poorly I'm afraid to leave her.'

'She's not alone, surely? There's the housekeeper,' Katie said encouragingly as she settled herself into the seat, and drew the cover over her knees against the rain.

'But it's not like me being there, is it?' the girl said. 'Ten years I've been with Miss Olds. Ever since I left school.'

Katie stole a look at the anxious face. The girl could not be much more than her own age. This was what she might have become: graceless, underfed, dressed in cheap washing cotton, her hands swollen with housework, but counting herself lucky to have a 'good situation'. This is what she would have become, without Arthur. What a lot she had to be grateful for!

On an impulse, she leant over and squeezed the roughened hand.

'Don't you worry,' Katie said. 'I'm sure the doctor is doing all he can.'

The girl gave a great gulping sob. 'Oh, I hope so, ma'am. We should have sent for him before, but Miss Beryl wouldn't hear of it. Just a chill, she said, from the soaking she got in all that rain, but she's been getting worse and worse these last few days, and this morning she was that poorly we had to do something.'

'You should have sent for us before,' Katie said gently.

'I would have, Mrs Olds, but she wouldn't let me. Proper set she could be, when she had her mind to something.' Stubborn, the girl meant, but she was too polite to say so. Katie smiled, but the girl hurried on. 'No disrespect, ma'am, but this time we had to do something. Furious, she'll be, when she finds out we sent for Doctor Lloyd, but there was no help for it.'

'She doesn't know now? Though he has been to see her?' Katie felt her heart skip a beat. The old lady was iller than she had realised.

The girl turned a pair of agonised eyes on her. 'She doesn't know anything – thinks she's a girl again and keeps worrying at me to dress her hair for her coming-out party. Oh, Mrs Olds, I'm that scared. Suppose anything should happen to her?'

Katie nodded. She understood. The girl's position was her livelihood. 'What's your name?'

'Alice, ma'am.'

'Well, I should give you a character, Alice, never fear.'

Alice gave her a hesitant smile. 'You're very good, Mrs Olds. All my people are dead, that's how I came to go into service to Miss Beryl in the first place.' No wonder she was anxious, Katie thought. If her employer died, the poor girl would have nowhere to go.

'Never mind,' she said encouragingly. 'It may not come to that.'

But it did. It was clear, even as the hansom drew up at the front of the house, that they were already too late. The curtains were drawn at every window, and the housekeeper was already muffling the front knocker with black ribbon.

'Slipped away quietly, as soon as ever you'd gone,' she said, with a sharp little nod of her head. 'Inflammation of the lungs, the doctor says.' She turned to Katie. 'He's waiting for you in the front parlour, Mrs Olds. I'll send Alice in to you with some tea directly.'

Katie went slowly into the house. The doctor was standing in front of the hearth with his hands under his coat-tails. Not Arthur's doctor, but a much older man, tall and thin with a beaky face.

'Doctor Lloyd, at your service. Sad business. Your aunt, I believe?'

Katie nodded. 'My husband's aunt.'

'Ah!' He began to explain the nature of the illness, a long interminable explanation, and how it should have been treated earlier with hot poultices and quinine.

Katie found herself looking around the little room. She had visited Aunt Beryl once or twice, with Arthur, but this room never failed to fascinate her.

It was a smallish room, musty and dark with mahogany and heavy drapes, but crammed in every part with ornaments and knick-knacks of all kinds. Flower and feather arrangements under glass domes, pictures made of butterfly wings, china shepherdesses with crooked smiles, daguerreotypes in gilt frames, a pottery statue of Queen Victoria as a girl, a pair of ormolu clocks, gilded candlesticks, a stuffed parrot in a cage, watercolours, shell pictures, embroidered texts and samplers – all covering the walls or set on little inlaid tables with frills around them to hide their legs. It always reminded her of the owner's front parlour in the little guest house in Lemon Street, where she had stayed before her wedding. How grand it had all seemed then!

She glanced up. The doctor was looking at her expectantly, as though waiting for a reply. She said, 'And what is to be done now? There must be arrangements to make.'

Doctor Lloyd launched himself on another explanation, offering a dozen suggestions, with a score of reasons for and against each in turn, but she was seized by a sudden impatience.

'Well,' she said firmly, 'I shall contact Aunt Beryl's solicitor and my husband. I am sure you will do everything that is needful here. Now, please excuse me, Doctor Lloyd. This has been a sudden shock, and I have children to attend to.'

She went upstairs to say a last farewell to the little, worn creature which had been Aunt Beryl, sent Alice for a cab, gave her a florin, and returned to Fore Street.

But she did pause on the way to send a wire to Arthur.

Robert looked at the invoice again, and swallowed hastily. The figures simply could not be right.

Caroline glanced up from her coddled eggs and breakfast tea, and asked equably, 'Is there something the matter, Robert?'

He dabbed his mouth with his napkin and got to his feet. 'It's about the fire,' he said. 'You know how it upsets me.' It was true, up to a point. Without the fire these deuced rebuilding costs would never have been incurred. He gave her his martyred little-boy smile. 'Nothing for you to concern your pretty head with. But if you will excuse me, my dear, I must deal with this at once.'

If only it were so simple! He would have patted her hand as he passed, but she withdrew it sharply. She always did if he attempted to touch her, as though afraid it would lead to 'all that', even at this time of the morning. As well it might, Robert reflected bitterly. When a man was married no more than a month, and yet had to insist so hard to achieve his occasional marital rights, 'all that' was bound to be on his mind.

But he had other concerns today. He looked again at the bill. Yes, damn the man, every item was laid out and accounted for. Three thousand pounds. How could he have spent so much? Granted he had told Olds to buy the best and have done with it, but the fellow had no call to take a chap so confoundedly literally. Three thousand pounds. He gazed at the paper for a long time, but no amount of frowning altered that total.

What the devil was a man to do? He might rustle up five hundred. Seven hundred at a pinch, what with the remaining capital from the sale of the farm, but no more. Certainly no more. Perhaps after all it had been a mistake to buy Gillard's brougham and horses, but dash it all, a fellow needed some transport, and the price had been good. He had even resisted the temptation to engage a coachman, and was allowing that fool of a footman to put on the livery and drive him. And he had listened to Caroline's pleas and deferred buying another motor. No one could say he had not been careful.

Except for that little flutter on the cards, of course. That had definitely been a mistake. But it was only once, or twice if you counted that afternoon at Goldmarten, and hang it all he had been sorely provoked. If your wife breaks into floods of tears every time you enter her bedroom, surely a fellow is justified in finding his pleasures elsewhere. Except, of course, he acknowledged to himself, that he had returned emboldened by drink and losses to enjoy her anyway. Well, at least she had got past the crying stage now.

But that was small consolation at the moment. Three thousand pounds. It was no good applying to Papa; management of the estate was in George's hands these days, and George was swanning it somewhere in the South Seas.

It occurred to him that he might apply to Gillard, but he put the thought away impatiently. He had not yet sunk to that. It had been an unspoken condition of his marriage to Caroline that no further scandal should attach to the family name, and publicly he still accepted the story that Gillard had merely been preparing the stable for the mare. The families remained on calling terms. Privately, though, they both knew better, and he would have to be a beggar before he approached Gillard for money.

Which left Selwood. Deuced awkward. He had already had a confrontation with his father-in-law when he had asked for an advance on Caroline's allowance. Selwood had reinstituted it, after her separation from George, and Robert had high hopes of it.

'Shouldn't a married woman have an allowance from her husband?' Selwood had said, and when Robert had pleaded his losses in the fire, 'Very well, then, she shall continue to have it. But into her own hands.' And the confounded man had stuck to that. Caroline had already found that the sacrifice of five guineas would buy his absence from her bed for the night. Really, it was too hard on a fellow.

Well, he would have to tackle Selwood again. He would have to find some way of dressing up the request; there would be the dickens to pay if his father-in-law discovered that he had married, owing a debt like this. He poured himself a whisky from the decanter. That scheme of Gillard's – that was it! A motor-coach business, or a garage. If he showed he meant to buy a business, Selwood might well make him a loan – on favourable terms, too. It might even do him a bit of good in the old man's estimation. And they were going to the Selwoods' for dinner – he would broach the subject that very afternoon.

He drank his second whisky in a much more cheerful frame of mind.

Arthur came back as soon as he received the telegram, and rather to Katie's surprise he did not return to London immediately after the funeral. Instead he stayed in Truro, spending hours closeted with Aunt Beryl's solicitor, and working late in the office with Willie.

Katie wondered about it, but said nothing. Aunt Beryl's estate was his family business after all, and if there was some problem he would tell her in due course.

The moment came one evening in early February. She had gone upstairs to see the babies put to bed and hear David's prayers, and was sitting by the drawing-room fire with the girls. Eva was reading one of Miss Austen's novels, smiling now and then as an apt description caught her fancy. Rosa was curled in an armchair looking at a copy of the *Girls' Own Paper*, occasionally reading aloud from it in her impulsive way.

'Look at this! "Your handwriting lacks character." Indeed, I am glad I don't write to the paper, then. I shouldn't care to be scolded so roundly.'

'Your copybook is much better these days. Mrs Courtney is quite pleased with your progress,' Katie said, putting down her sewing. 'Though she would not be pleased to see you sitting so, Rosa. Your Uncle Arthur will be here directly. Try to comport yourself like a young lady.'

Rosa sighed and moved her legs, which had been tucked up under her. 'It is such a bore being a young lady. I wish I was like Eva, she doesn't mind it. Or like Willie – he doesn't have to mind it.'

Eva looked up and laughed. 'Should you like to have to open doors and carry parcels for the ladies and get up early and go to work for your living?'

'I shouldn't mind,' Rosa said. 'Katie did it. I would a hundred times rather that than be like your poor Great-Aunt Beryl, with nothing to live for but tea and visiting and a stuffed bird in a cage.'

Katie had to smile at the justice of this. 'We shall have you turning into a suffragette, Rosa. Chaining yourself to the railings in Downing Street and throwing stones at cabinet ministers' carriages.'

'Rosa wouldn't care for that,' Eva put in. 'She's too fond of plum duff and chocolate cake to enjoy a spell in Holloway prison. And should you like to wear those horrid coarse clothes with arrows on them instead of your pretty dresses? Mrs Pankhurst had to. It was in the paper.'

Rosa flushed. 'I shouldn't care then! Besides, I should like to wear tweed bloomers and ride a bicycle like a boy! Shouldn't you like to do something exciting, and not just sit about the house all day?'

There was a little pause, and then Eva said quietly: 'I should like to go to training school, and maybe have a school of my own one day.'

'Should you, Eva?' Katie was surprised. 'It might be arranged, I think. I will speak to your father.'

'And be a bluestocking like poor Miss Bevan that was?' Rosa cried. 'I think . . .'

She broke off as Arthur and Willie came into the room.

'What do you think, young Rosa?' Arthur said, crossing the room to kiss Katie's hair and ruffle Eva's as he passed.

'I think it would be fun to ride a bicycle,' Rosa said, stubbornly, though her cheeks were crimson. 'Lots of ladies do.'

'A lot of *females* do,' Arthur said, settling himself in his chair. 'Not many ladies. Not yet. Times may change.'

Katie looked at him gratefully. He had a way of handling Rosa's outbursts which she could only admire. She would speak to him later about Eva.

'In any case,' Arthur continued, 'times may change for us, and quickly too. There is something I should discuss with you, Katie. No – you stay, Rosa, and Eva too. This may affect us all.'

There was something in his tone which made Katie's heart skip a beat, but he looked cheerful enough as he continued.

'Aunt Beryl has left me a tidy sum in her will – two thousand pounds or more. And the house reverts to me anyway, of course.'

'Why "of course"?' Katie put in.

He looked at her, surprised. 'I thought you knew she was the third life. My grandfather built the house, and let it to his sister, at a small rent. It was the usual sort of arrangement at the time – a lease for the duration of three named lives. Aunt Beryl was a baby then. She was the third life. When she died the property automatically reverted to my grandfather, or to his heirs. To me, in fact. It used to be a very common way of writing a lease – almost the whole of Truro was let in that way at one time, but it is dying out now.'

Katie was staring at him. 'So we own two houses now?' Eva might get her school after all, she thought.

He smiled at her. 'Yes. In fact, Katie, we may soon own a good many more. That is what I have been trying to arrange while I have been in Truro. I saw a good piece of land in London. A little farm, just on the outskirts, at Surbiton. I thought at the time, if it was possible to buy that land, and build houses on it – nice houses, for people like us. People with businesses, people who work in offices – they are looking for places to live. A little garden, a good kitchen, an inside bathroom. It is hard to find good modern housing in London. You could even build a motorhouse in the grounds – if this American idea catches on, we shall all have our own motorcars one of these days.'

'But Arthur,' Katie protested, 'we don't want to live in London.'

'We don't,' Willie said, 'but lots of people do. Don't you see – we could buy the land, and build good houses. With the money Aunt Beryl has left us we could build one or two, and when we have sold those . . .'

'You mean,' Katie said, letting the blouse she was trimming fall from her hands, 'build the houses first and find the customers afterwards?'

Arthur said, 'We've looked into it, Katie, and there is a good honest profit to be made. And if we do not do it, less skilful builders will.' He knew how to sway her.

She hesitated. 'Well . . .'

'Truly Katie, it is only like making dresses,' Willie said. 'Once upon a time everyone had dresses made to measure. Now there are ready-made shops everywhere.'

She took up her sewing again. 'I'm sure there's a catch, somewhere.'

Arthur looked at her slowly. 'There is, Katie,' he said gently. 'I shall have to be away for a long time. Months, perhaps, although I shall come home often.'

'Every weekend?' Rosa said. She had been sitting so quietly that Katie had nearly forgotten her presence.

Arthur smiled. 'Perhaps not as often as that, young Rosa, or I shall spend all our profits on the railway, but often enough, I promise. And you shall all come to London too, in the summer, and see the sights – the new stadium where the Olympic Games was held last year. You shall go to concerts, Eva, and Rosa, I shall find you a hack and take you riding in Hyde Park.'

'May I? Really?' Rosa's eyes were aglow, and Eva's too. Katie looked from one eager face to the other. All four of them were looking at her. She knew then that she had lost.

'Well then, it seems to be settled,' she said, keeping her voice cheerful. She picked up the blouse. Magenta. Half-mourning for Aunt Beryl, the same one she had worn for Lally. Strange, she thought, for her own parents she had worn no mourning at all.

She thought of Arthur and the long, lonely months ahead. This time, she felt, as the needle moved deftly to and fro, she was in mourning for more than a dead aunt.

CHAPTER THIRTY-THREE

Robert chose his moment carefully. He waited until the ladies had gone, and he and Selwood were sitting alone over port and cigars. It was good port, he noted with satisfaction, and particularly likely to mellow the Major's mood. Even so, he bided his time.

He was still waiting for a propitious moment when the Major, who was clipping the end of a second cigar, suddenly regarded him thoughtfully and said, 'Young Caroline's looking a trifle tired. Treating her properly, are you?'

Robert was so taken aback that at first he could only stammer, 'I do my best, sir.'

'Hmmph!' From Selwood's tone you might have supposed that he had the gravest doubts about how good Robert's best was likely to be. He lit the cigar and sat for a moment gazing at the glowing tip of it. 'Only, her mother was wondering . . .'

Inspiration came like a dazzling light. So that was what the old buffer was thinking. Hoping, even. A grandchild. He was about to reply grimly that it was his insistence on trying which had robbed the roses from Caroline's cheeks, when common sense intervened.

Of course, if there were a grandchild, old Selwood would be much more likely to come across with a settlement. Securing the child's future and all that. He composed his face into a carefully noncommittal smile.

'It's early days . . .' he said, with just the right amount of hesitation.

He was right. A beam of pleasure replaced the look of irritation which Selwood usually adopted when talking to his son-in-law. 'You mean, there may be . . . ?'

Robert shook his head firmly. It was important not to overplay his hand. 'Far too soon to be certain . . .' He allowed his voice to trail into silence.

'My dear boy,' Selwood said warmly. 'Another glass of port?'

There would never be a better moment. Robert took the glass and said simply, 'Actually, sir, there was something I wanted to discuss with you.'

'Well? Let's hear it.' Selwood's voice was wary, but not actually hostile.

'It's rather a delicate matter,' Robert said, twisting his glass between his fingers. This was even more difficult than he had imagined. 'It is about money. No. . . !' as he saw Selwood about to protest. 'No, I wasn't about to approach you for a loan.'

'I should hope not,' Selwood said, sitting back into his chair and drawing on his cigar. 'Always regarded you as a complete fool with money, young Trevarnon.'

'Perhaps you won't think so when you hear my business proposition, sir. I thought, especially if – if we were right in our guess about Caroline, it is important to start out on a good financial footing. Own a little business, I thought – no shame in being a successful entrepreneur these days, and there is a market in the town for a motorbus, or a garage for mechanical repairs – or an agency for selling motor vehicles. Or all three.'

Selwood nodded, but made no reply, and Robert went on, spelling out the likely markets, the costs, the competition, the overheads. Peter Gillard had had it all mapped out, and he was amazed himself at how plausible it sounded as he spoke. Selwood was obviously impressed.

'You've given this some thought, young man, I can see that. Perhaps family responsibilities will teach you to settle down, after all. Well, and what do you want of me?'

Robert started. He had supposed it was obvious, but he said soberly enough, 'It would need capital. I have a little I could put up' – Why had he said that? He hadn't enough to pay his debts – 'but this confounded fire has cost me more than I bargained for.'

Selwood took a sip of port. 'And how much money are we thinking of?'

Robert took a deep breath. 'Three thousand should cover it. There is a lot of outlay – the motorbus, drivers, stock for the showrooms, engineering equipment, mechanics, a manager . . .'

Selwood was looking at him soberly. 'And how much of this could you put up?'

'Five hundred, perhaps more.' If Selwood came up with twenty-five hundred he could clear his debts to Olds, and even find some premises. And once he had done that, perhaps the bank would stake him. Or maybe he could pay for his motorbus by instalments. 'I am sure there's a market, sir. I have looked into it. There's been a motorbus running to the Lizard for a year or two now, and it seems to be doing nicely. And some of the hotels want buses to meet the trains, and there are school treats, and works' outings all wanting charabancs . . .'

Selwood drained his glass. 'It is an interesting proposition. A lot of money, but not impossible.'

'So you will consider it?'

His father-in-law looked at him for a moment or two. 'Consider it, yes. I shall look into the sales figures and running costs you have suggested, and discuss it with my bank manager. And then, if it seems promising, perhaps we can work something out.' He ground his cigar stub into the heavy ashtray. 'I'll let you know in a month or so. By that time we should be more certain how the wind sits in other directions, too. I tell you frankly, young Trevarnon, I would consider this only if you are correct in your guess. There is some hope, it seems, that fatherhood would sober you. In the meantime, you take care of Caroline, you hear me? Now, shall we join the ladies?'

After that, all Caroline's offers of five guineas were of no avail.

Perth, Adelaide, and now Melbourne. A warm summer day with the wind winking off the water. George was glad to get ashore, down the rickety gangplank and onto solid land again. A freak southerly across the Australian Bight had given them a rougher few days than any of the tossing storms of the Indian Ocean.

It had been a frightful storm. China flung from the dining-tables. Suitcases skittering dangerously from wardrobes and lockers. Anything left on a cabin surface became a flying missile, and was likely to strike you sharply on the shins. More than once George had sat with a cup of beef-tea in his hand, ready to raise it to his lips, when a lurch of the ship sent the contents flying into the air, covering his clothes with liquid.

He was a better sailor than most, but standing on the heaving deck, clutching the stanchions for support, even he felt his stomach churning, and cursed himself for ever venturing to sea. There was hardly anyone else on deck. Most of the other passengers had taken, moaning, to their beds, or leant over the rails on the lee side retching. Only the crew seemed undeterred, keeping their feet as if by magic, and even managing to make and offer trays of that beef-tea which became so wilful when he took it into his own hands.

Oddly, now that he stood again on solid land, his legs betrayed him, and he rose and fell in time to an imaginary motion. It was high time he stayed ashore for a little, he decided. Time for a hotel and a wide bed, and a bath of fresh water, in which the soap would lather, and a man could wash without feeling sticky for an hour after.

There was a grimy train to take passengers into town, and he climbed aboard it. It was a long way, much longer than he had imagined, across a salty marsh and sandhills, and along beside the slow, wide waters of the Yarra, until they crossed the bridge and edged into Flinders Street.

There were cabs waiting to take visitors to their hotels, but he sent his cases on and elected to walk around for a bit. He turned away from the bustle of the station, and walked, lost in his own thoughts.

A little later he began to regret his decision. The sun was very warm away from the sea breeze, and the road was dusty. There was not much shade either, the tall grey-green trees which he had learned to recognise as eucalyptus gums, gave off a faint warm aromatic smell, their trunks white and ghostly even in the midday sun.

He was, simply, much too hot. He looked around for somewhere to sit, but there was nowhere. He was out of the centre now, row after row of little wooden houses, each in its own garden, each neatly painted, with a corrugated iron roof, and wrought-ironwork on the shady verandahs.

A woman trotted by on a horse, laden with parcels. She rode casually, astride, as if it came easily to her. She looked at him without curiosity as he called to her.

'Oh, yes,' she said, in answer to his enquiry. She pronounced it 'yis', as though a hundred years, and not thirty, separated her from the land of her birth. 'There'll be a horse-tram along. You can catch it up there.' She nodded to another road which crossed their own. 'About ten minutes. Drop you right at the door.'

She trotted on. He watched her go, her cotton dress and bonnet sober against the brilliant blue of the sky. From a nearby tree, hung with blossom bluer than wisteria, a mocking cackle of laughter startled him.

He whirled around. A squat, malevolent bird gazed back at him, opened its beak in another mocking caw and flew off, scattering a dozen scarlet parrots as it flew.

George laughed to himself. Kookaburras. He had heard of them, and of the koalas, kangaroos and snakes which still, apparently, lived in and around this up-and-coming little city.

He was still smiling when the clattering horse-tram took him back to the centre of the town. This was a modern, thrusting little metropolis. A new electric tramway being constructed. Fine new shops and imposing municipal buildings. A little network of straight roads which interlaced methodically. Not like Penzance, or London, he thought to himself, which had just grown, haphazard.

He found his hotel without difficulty. Comfortable too, with a big fan stirring the flies on the ceiling, and a bathroom where the geyser produced warm, clear water. He lay in it for a long time before going down to the lounge to order a drink, a gin sling. The colonial's drink, they called it. He sat back to sip it, and to watch the crowds that came and went.

'Trevarnon, as I live and breathe!'

George looked up, astonished. Who did he know here, among these sunburned men in coarse jackets and wide-brimmed hats? But there was no mistaking the face which smiled down at him, leathery and brown as the polished boots he wore. It was a face he had last seen in a blockhouse in the Transvaal.

'Harry Leadbetter! What brings you here?'

'Sale of some good breeding stock. I've got a station – a farm – sixty miles or so north of here, and I heard of a fellow who's selling up. Fancied trying my hand at breeding horses.' He looked at George shrewdly. 'But I might ask the same question of you! What brings you here? Travelling? Alone or with your family?'

'I have no family,' George said, and then, more lightly: 'But travelling, yes. And enchanted with this little city of yours.'

'Well,' Leadbetter said, 'if you're alone, you might join me for dinner tonight. Or do you have other plans?'

George shook his head. He did have the address of the little widow in his pocketbook, but that was in New South Wales, a thousand miles from here. Perhaps, in a week or two, he might find his way to Sydney. 'No other plans,' he said.

'Then it's settled,' Leadbetter said. 'I do have a family, but I've left them all back on the sheep-station. And tomorrow, if you have nothing better to do, you might help me look at these mares. I never knew a better judge of horseflesh.'

It was irresistible. The meal, the sale, the inevitable invitation to 'the station' – although he was a little taken aback when he discovered that Leadbetter proposed to ride the fifty miles home with his stockmen, driving the horses.

'The train passes close,' Harry said. 'You can meet us there.'

But George had other ideas. 'I might ride too,' he said, 'if we can adapt a saddle.'

It took the saddler an hour to improvise something suitable, and George found himself one of the party. It brought back the Transvaal: Leadbetter, the long hot days, the wide open spaces. George greeted it all with joy, even the inevitable discomfort of hours in the saddle for a man unaccustomed to it.

'You have a good life,' he said to Leadbetter as they reined in together on top of the rise, and looked back across the parched hillsides shimmering in the sun.

'Why not you too, George? It's a hard life. You work with the men, but it's a fine existence. A new continent. A new beginning. That farm that was selling up. The land will be on the market in a few weeks. Very small place, maybe five hundred acres . . .'

'*How* many?'

Leadbetter laughed at his surprise. 'Out here that's tiny. I have almost a thousand acres, and I'm a pigmy in this business.'

George whistled.

'Think about it,' Leadbetter said. 'I know you have your father to consider, but you say your brother is nearby. Let him pull his weight for once.'

George said slowly, 'I would have to go back to England and sort out a few matters first. That land will be sold by then.'

Leadbetter laughed. 'There is always land. Great empty continent like this – land is one thing we're not short of.'

'They say that any man who is prepared to work can make a living here,' George said, thinking of Fanny and her husband. Katie had said they were building a home of their own.

Leadbetter nodded. 'Times have been tight, mind you, for some, these past few years.'

George said thoughtfully, 'I know a young family that emigrated here a few years ago – at least, I knew the wife. She worked at the house. I wonder how they are faring.'

'It's a big country,' Leadbetter said. 'You might trace someone through the Governor's office, if you'd a mind too, but it wouldn't be easy.'

George shook his head. 'No, no. It was a passing thought, that's all. Thinking of people who had started a new life here.'

Leadbetter smiled. 'Well, as I say, think about it yourself. And now come in and meet my family.'

George laughed doubtfully. But in the days that followed, as he rode with Leadbetter and baked to a berry in the sun, George found that he was thinking about it more and more.

It was March, one of those sharp blue spring days when the wind billows the clouds like washing and the daffodils toss their golden trumpets with the sheer joy of being alive.

Katie came into the hall, her cheeks warm with walking, and pulled off her bonnet and cape. 'Now, Vicki, you run along with Lilly,' she said, swinging her daughter off her feet and handing her to the little nurserymaid. 'Mummy is going to ring the bell for Mabel and have a cup of tea. Wasn't that a lovely walk?'

The child smiled up at her, dark curls shining under the childish bonnet, chubby face aglow. 'Mummy read story?'

Katie laughed. 'Later perhaps. When David comes home from school. Mummy will come up and see you eat your egg, and perhaps we will have a story then. And Daddy's coming home tonight. He shall come up and see you when you are in bed.' She watched the little figure walk determinedly up the stairs, clinging to Lilly's hand.

She smiled fondly and went into the drawing room. 'Oh, thank you Mabel,' she said, when the girl came in with the tea-tray. 'Is Eva home yet?'

'Not yet.' Mabel, setting down the teapot, gave Katie one of her huge, pleased grins. 'She's some enjoying her training college, isn't she, Mrs Olds?'

'Yes,' Katie said. 'Her father was concerned that it might be too much for her health, but I think it has been a great success.' She took the cup that Mabel offered. 'He will be pleased when he comes home. I wanted to do that, myself, when I was a girl.'

Mabel grinned again. 'You'd have to go a long way to find a better teacher than you, anyhow, Mrs Olds, training college or no training college. Look what you did for Eva.' She picked up the tray again. 'Shall you be wanting scones?'

'Not for me, Mabel, but Rosa will be home directly, and I expect Eva will when she comes in. So yes, ask Peabody to send some up in half an hour. Ah! The front door, that will be Eva now.'

But it was not Eva. Mabel returned a moment later looking shaken. 'It seems to be a policeman, Katie,' she said.

Katie looked up sharply. The use of her name told her at once that Mabel was alarmed. 'A policeman? What does a policeman want here?'

Mabel shook her head. 'I don't know. He won't say. But he's asking for you. Shall I show him in?'

'Yes,' Katie said quietly. 'I think you'd better.' She set down her cup and plate and composed herself a moment. Whatever could a policeman want at this time of the day? Rosa hadn't got mixed up with that meeting of the suffragettes, surely? She'd threatened to go to a rally in Victoria Square once before, just after Christmas, but it had turned out to be a hoax, and instead of Annie Besant nobody turned up in a coach but a rather bewildered woman with a child, who had come to buy nightdresses in the emporium.

But there was no joke today. The man whom Mabel ushered into the room looked grim. He was a big man, in his middle years, tall, solid, broadshouldered, and in his dark uniform with its shining buttons and broad leather belt, with his helmet under his arm, he seemed to fill the room.

Katie felt her heart quake. In all her life she had hardly ever spoken to a policeman, not since she was a very small girl and her brother Tom had gone scrumping for apples from the vicar's tree up at St Evan. He'd been lucky to get off with a caution – the boys with him had been birched. Katie had learned to be very cautious of policemen.

She felt like a child again now, but she managed to say, 'Is something the matter, officer?'

'Mrs Olds?' His voice was not unkindly, but something in his manner made her blood run cold.

'Yes.'

'Mrs Arthur Olds? Wife of the builder and architect?'

'Yes. But if you are looking for my husband, I am afraid he is not here at present. He has been in London on a business matter. I am expecting him home this evening . . .'

He raised a hand to stop her. 'Sit down, Mrs Olds, I am afraid I have bad news for you.'

'Bad news?' She sat down, obediently, in the chair she had just vacated. 'What bad news?'

He coughed uncomfortably. Katie stared at him, not daring to think, as if time had slowed down and she was caught in a moment that would never end.

But he was speaking again. 'It's your husband, Mrs Olds. I'm afraid there has been an accident.'

CHAPTER THIRTY-FOUR

They brought Arthur's body home in a coffin. Willie arranged it, everything from the laying out of the body to the 'quiet' and dignified funeral service, for which the little church was packed and flowing over.

Katie herself was too shocked to act. The account of the accident haunted her. Every time she shut her eyes, she dreamed it – Arthur, smiling, talking, leaning against the door of the railway carriage and then the shocked face as the door opened and he fell. A moment of voiceless screaming, and he was gone, under the remorseless wheels of the up train coming in the other direction. She had never seen that poor mangled body – Willie had spared her that – but the reality could be no worse than her imaginings.

For weeks she lived in a kind of daze. She ate, slept, walked, talked, so that people said she was coping wonderfully, but in truth she was coping not at all. More than once she found herself in the street engaged upon some errand, without the slightest recollection of how she got there, or what she had left the house to do. It was Willie that she turned to; Willie, at rising seventeen, so like her own father that it almost made her weep anew.

The provisions of Arthur's will were simple. Aunt Beryl's house was to be Eva's as soon as she was twenty-one, and until then could be used 'as Mrs Olds sees fit'. The business was left in Willie's hands, in trust for David. And for Rosa there was a small cash legacy. Everything else was Katie's absolutely, to pass to Vicki on her death. He had done his best to provide for them all.

But Katie cared nothing for money or possessions. She missed

Arthur more than she would have believed possible. He had been away so much of recent months that she half-supposed it would make the loss more supportable, as everyone said, but it was not so. Instead it seemed to make it worse. She found herself half listening for his foot on the stairs, waiting with bated breath for a letter in the breakfast mail, and having to learn each day anew, with a sad lurch of the heart, that he was truly gone for ever.

It was David who brought her to herself. She was in the hallway, needlessly rearranging the flowers which Peabody had set in the ornamental vase beside the mirror. David was in the drawing room, come in to say goodnight, but she made no effort to go to him as she would once have done.

She heard his voice, a clear childish treble. 'Eva, will you come and hear me and Vicki say our prayers tonight?'

She could see Eva through the open doorway, putting down her book in surprise, and heard her say gently, 'Won't Mummy be doing that, David?'

Katie stopped, a sprig of blossom in her hand, as David replied, 'Oh, she comes, but she doesn't listen. She comes, but she isn't there inside any more.'

'She's thinking about Daddy,' Eva said softly.

And David's voice, very low, with a little tremble in it. 'I know. But he was my Daddy, too.'

The words stung Katie like a whip. What had she been thinking of? Those poor children, Eva especially – their loss was as great as hers, and instead of being there to support and comfort them, she had withdrawn into herself, just when they needed her most. She met her own eyes in the mirror, and was surprised to find them full of tears. She had been too dazed to weep.

She straightened her shoulders, lifted her chin, and went into the drawing room. Eva looked up, obviously alarmed lest Katie had heard the child's words.

'Eva and I will both hear your prayers tonight,' she said, holding out her arms to her son. He ran into them, and she lifted him up, and carried him upstairs. Eva followed, and together they knelt beside the little beds and heard the soft murmured childish phrases whispered into the dark.

As they came downstairs Eva turned to Katie. 'Thank you.'

It was too much. The tears of those weeks welled up, and tumbled down her cheeks. She could not check them and she did not try. She let

Eva lead her to the drawing room and into a chair, and sat there sobbing helplessly with Eva's arm around her, until Peabody came in, unsummoned, with the supper tray.

'Now Miss Eva, there's hot milk, honey and nutmeg by your bed, and I'll send up some sandwiches by and by. You run on upstairs and leave Mrs Olds to me, or you'll never be ready for your lessons in the morning.'

Eva bent and kissed Katie's forehead. 'Goodnight Katie.'

'Goodnight,' Katie managed. She squeezed the girl's hand in parting. 'I'm sorry, Peabody,' Katie continued, as the door closed behind Eva. 'I don't know what came over me.'

'Don't you worry, Mrs Olds,' Peabody said. 'You've been needing a good old cry – we've all of us said so, and it does my heart good to see you. You're looking more yourself already. Here, I've put a drop of the best brandy in this. You drink that up, it will help you to sleep.'

Katie smiled a little to find herself being mothered so, and took a sip of the hot milk that Peabody offered. The rich, unaccustomed taste of the alcohol took her by surprise. She put the cup down, hesitantly. Whatever would Lally have said to this?

Peabody seemed to read her thoughts. 'Medicinal uses, that is. Dr Marshall says it's the best thing out. So you drink it up, and don't give it another thought.'

Katie took another sip. It was comforting and warming. 'I upset the children,' she said, after a little pause. 'I didn't mean to. I was upset.'

'No wonder.' Peabody said. 'He was a fine man.'

'I loved him,' she said.

'Course you did,' Peabody said comfortably. 'He knew that. Everybody knew that.' She picked up the tray. 'Now you finish that up and try to get some rest.'

But Katie had no need of brandy now. The realisation had come to her like a balm. She had loved him, and he had known himself to be loved. It was only that she had not recognised the fact herself.

Robert was in high spirits. That week or two of concentrated effort had had the desired effect, and now it was beyond doubt. Caroline was expecting a happy event. Happier than she knew, Robert thought triumphantly.

Strangely enough, Caroline herself seemed almost pleased, however unwilling she had been to join in the endeavour. Perhaps she hoped the news would keep him from her bed for a while. Well, no matter if it did. It was oddly pleasing to think that a fellow had fathered an heir, supposing it was an heir. He was conscious of holding his head a little higher and his chest a little broader, and was quite proud to squire Caroline to her parents' house, and hear their solicitous enquiries.

It was true what they said, he thought to himself. Marriage did alter a man. He had never felt like this when Fanny had sprung her news upon him.

Papa was delighted. A handsome present of a hundred guineas 'for the nursery expenses'. He'd given it to Caroline, of course, but there was sure to be some way of laying hands on it. In any case, Robert thought, his son deserved the best. Perhaps, after all, he would let Caroline lay it out on whatever she thought was necessary for herself and the child. He felt quite a little glow at his own generosity.

And then there was that little matter of Selwood's. The Major wanted to talk about it, he had made that obvious – and it was clear that Robert's proposition had not fallen on deaf ears. 'A word with you after dinner, Trevarnon. Might hear something to your advantage.'

Pot au volaille had never tasted so sweet.

And after dinner, when Caroline and her mother had gone into the drawing room to cluck over nursery furniture, and baby linen, and other womanly intimacies, Selwood sent for the best vintage port and Havana cigars, and then dismissed the butler for the evening. Robert felt his heart thump.

'Well then, young fellow, I think we have things to discuss.' Selwood leant back in his chair and held his glass to the light so that the ruby liquid glowed with a warmth that you could almost feel. 'That business proposition you made to me.'

'Yes?' Robert said, and added for good measure, 'Sir?'

'I've looked into it. It seems the idea is as promising as you say. Well . . . .,' He seemed to be trying to read the future in the glowing wine glass, as if it were a crystal ball. He put the glass down suddenly. 'I think I am prepared to help you.'

'You mean you'll lend me the capital? Help me set it up?'

Selwood looked at him shrewdly. 'No, Trevarnon, not quite that. This idea may be a sound one, but I've seen the way capital can disappear in your hands. Why, the way you've rebuilt that house alone must have cost you a fortune, and Caroline tells me that you are constantly in want of money.'

Damn Caroline, why couldn't she have kept her own counsel? He said dully: 'So you won't put up the money?'

'That's not what I said.' Selwood took a long sip of his port. 'I said I wouldn't lend it to you. No, tell you what, Trevarnon – I propose to set this business up myself.'

'And leave me in the cold?' The words were out before Robert had time to call them back.

Selwood regarded him mildly. 'My dear young fellow, you do jump to conclusions. I propose nothing of the kind. Of course you are welcome to put in your own capital – five hundred pounds I think you said – and own a portion of the company. About a sixth, if our calculations are correct.'

Robert swallowed. His plans were falling in ruins around his ears. 'A sixth? But that's nothing – I mean to say, there would be very little profit from one-sixth of the company.' He stopped, realising that he was betraying his ambitions. 'Very little in the first year or so,' he amended, 'when my family needs are likely to be greatest.'

Selwood beamed at him. 'Nonsense, Trevarnon, the plan as you outlined it to me has a great deal of potential. The company would be profitable in no time, especially with the right kind of committed and enthusiastic manager to oversee the day-to-day running of it.'

Robert nodded unwillingly. Perhaps, after all, something could be salvaged. 'Who did you have in mind?' His mind was searching all Selwood's known agents and managers for a likely candidate.

'Why, you, of course, my dear fellow,' Selwood said. 'Can you think of anyone more suitable? You would naturally have a real interest in protecting your investment, and therefore mine – and the salary would help you through those family commitments you were complaining of.'

'Me?' Robert had given up any attempt to disguise his astonishment. 'But that would mean . . .' He trailed off.

'Yes,' Selwood said, 'it would mean seeing a little less of your family than you might have envisaged, but I am sure that you can see where your interest lies. In any case, Trevarnon, that is my proposition. I would be glad of a reply within the week. I have found some premises which I think may be very suitable for our purpose.'

'Thank you, sir, I shall give it my consideration,' Robert said, but he knew in his heart that he was beaten. What choice did he have? And what was he to do now about that wretched Olds fellow and his three-thousand-pound bills? The best he could do was to send him two or three hundred and leave him whistling for the rest. It was to be hoped the fellow didn't sue. How was he to find it, he wondered glumly, with only a salary to rely on?

Salary. The word sent shivers down his spine. Good God, had it come to this? Geting up at the crack of dawn, summer and winter, to sit in some dingy office and worry about the comings and goings of motorbuses?

He could feel Selwood's eyes on him. He forced his lips into a smile. 'A splendid idea, sir. Of course, I shall have to talk to Caroline about it.'

His father-in-law poured himself another glass of port. 'I'm sure she will think it a fair arrangement. My wife discussed it with her earlier in the week.'

So they were all conspiring against him! Robert refused the decanter, and at the earliest opportunity excused himself, on the pretext of Caroline's delicate health. As he left he could have sworn Selwood was laughing.

It was Willie who brought it to her attention. He had been looking worried for days, and she had said nothing, supposing that the responsibility of the business was weighing on him.

But when he came late to dinner for the third time in a week, and sat abstractedly through it with a furrowed brow, she knew something must be done. When they were repairing to the drawing room she said softly, so that only he could hear, 'Willie, what is it? Something is bothering you. Can't you tell me? A troubled shared is a trouble halved.'

He turned to her with such relief that she realised he had been waiting for such an approach, and when the others had gone to bed, he poured his heart out. The business, it seemed, was in trouble.

'This land purchase in London, and the houses we're building there – they have been a great drain on our resources. They're fine houses, and if they were fairly finished we could sell them for a good price. But they're not finished – it's been such wretched weather for May: snow storms and hail and a proper blizzard most of last week, no weather for building. If we sell the houses unfinished we shall make a loss, yet we have no money for the building costs.'

Katie stared at the ledgers which he had fetched and spread on the table. 'But I don't understand. There was no such problem when Arthur was alive.'

He looked at her sadly. 'No, nor would there be if he was still with us, Katie. The trouble is with the men who sell us the stones and brick and plaster. The man they know has gone, and suddenly they're anxious for their money – they would have trusted Arthur six months or more.'

'But you're as honest a man as he was. Why should they not trust you? Surely if you told them about the London houses . . .'

Willie pushed a hand through his hair. 'They don't know me, Katie. It's like that Mrs Pritchard said – they think I'm just a miner's boy. In a year or two, I know, they would have come to trust me for their money, but as it as, they hear the news and they are foreclosing.'

'You mean, Arthur has bought these materials without the means to pay for them?'

The weariness on his face touched her heart, and she almost wished that she had not pressed him.

'It should not be so, Katie – it would not be so if our creditors had paid *their* bills. Pritchard himself owes us nearly fifty pounds, and there are one or two customers with really large sums outstanding. I've written to them several times, but I've had no reply. They *are* large sums, Katie – if those debts were paid, we should have not the slightest difficulty in meeting our own.'

She met his eyes. 'How did this happen?' She would go herself, she told herself, and confront that tanner over his gazebo. 'I thought that you were making sure that we collected all that was owing.'

He shifted his gaze. 'I tried. But these – one man is dead, and there is a quarrel now about his estate; another has lost his business and will pay only so much in the pound – and the third . . .' He closed the ledger with a little jerk. 'The third family were old customers. They have always paid their debts fully and on time. It's my fault, Katie – this was a different man, and I allowed the sum to accumulate. That payment alone would see us out of our difficulties.'

'An old customer?' Katie asked. 'Surely if they knew of our difficulties . . . Let me see the account.'

Willie looked uncomfortable. 'Don't concern yourself, Katie. I'll write to them again.'

She looked at him, aware that he was hiding something. 'Do I know them, Willie?' He made no reply, and she said more urgently, 'Willie, show me.'

He opened the ledger unwillingly. 'Arthur never told you of this commission, Katie,' he said slowly. 'He didn't want to mention the name in your presence – and I haven't done so either.'

The words danced before her eyes. *Outstanding from Mr R. Trevarnon, the sum of three thousand pounds.*

CHAPTER THIRTY-FIVE

Lower Trevarnon. Katie looked at the house. How handsome it was, with the banks of rhododendrons in full flower, and the roses and honeysuckle springing in the hedges. It had been scarcely more than a shell when she had seen it last – when she and Fanny had been maids up at Trevarnon. How long ago it all seemed, and yet her heart was thudding as though she were a servant again.

The house was different, of course, rebuilt after the fire. Much more handsome now – the lofty lines and large windows showed Arthur's hand as surely as his signature. It had been an imposing place – he had made it a beautiful one. She squared her shoulders. Well, Mr Robert Trevarnon need not suppose that such skills were his for nothing. She was come to demand the money that he owed.

She had already been to the Pritchards', and it had been, in a strange way, satisfying. Her resolve had almost deserted her as she knocked at the door, but she persevered, and was shown by a frightened little maid into a front room of enormous proportions.

The tanner's wife rose to meet her.

'Mrs Olds. What brings you here? Do please take a chair.'

The memory of how this woman had turned the town against Willie and almost come between herself and Arthur drove Katie's carefully prepared speech from her mind. She was suddenly furiously angry.

She did not sit politely, but confronted the woman, hands on hips, as though she were thirteen again, and confronting Lally. 'What brings me here? Money, Mrs Pritchard. Money that you owed my husband and have not paid. It is not a great sum, less than fifty pounds, but I'm sure a woman in your position' – she said the words with emphasis – 'would not care to have it bruited among the tradesmen that you did not pay your debts.'

It was not at all what she intended to say, and as soon as the words were out she would have called them back, but the effect was dramatic. For a moment the woman puffed herself up like a turkey-cock, and then, as if someone had let the air out of her, she deflated like an empty air-balloon, sat down in her chair, and rang for the parlourmaid.

'My dear Mrs Olds, an oversight. Of course, an oversight. Of course you shall have your money by the week's end. I was so sorry to hear that dear Mr Olds had passed over, and his poor aunt too. I hear that she had quite taken you up, before she died? Do, please, stop and have a muffin.'

The woman was so transparent that it was all Katie could do not to laugh. The money was on Willie's desk the next morning.

But today was different. She could not quite decide, even in her own mind, why she had resolved to come here. Some feeling perhaps that Robert Trevarnon, too, would be shamed by her presence? The memory of how he had cheated poor Fanny, refusing to pay her even the one guinea that he owed? An unwomanly desire for justice and revenge? It could not, could it, be the realisation that a visit to Lower Trevarnon took her very close to another house, and to its owner?

She had made a promise to Arthur not to seek George's company. That promise had been faithfully kept, a little voice inside her prompted secretly. 'As long as we both shall live.' And in any case, what harm could it do? Wasn't George Trevarnon himself married, to Caroline Anne Millicent Selwood? If she did see him, which was not likely, it would only be to exchange pleasantries, and to tell him, perhaps, of Arthur's death. He could not know of it, she was certain, or he would have sent his formal respects. Perhaps the news had not reached the papers in Penzance.

Did he, she wondered, know of this debt of Robert's? Probably not. It would be tempting to tell him – George would do all in his power to ensure that it was paid – but something inside her rebelled at the notion. Let Robert at least attempt to regularise matters himself first.

But however long she hovered and hesitated no George appeared – although she loitered all along the lane that skirted Trevarnon, and stood on tiptoe to peep over the wall. There was the new manor house which Arthur had designed and built for George and his new wife, nestling serenely among the sweep of the trees. There was Trevarnon House itself, four-square and forbidding behind the glossy leaves of camellias and magnolia. There was the avenue, the drive, the steps. But there was not a soul in sight.

There was nothing for it. She marched firmly on down the lane, up the front steps of Lower Trevarnon, and rang the bell.

There was a long silence before the door was opened by a man in footman's livery. He looked at Katie enquiringly.

'I wish to see Mr Robert Trevarnon,' Katie said stoutly. 'I am Mrs Olds, the wife of the architect of this house, and I wish to see him most particularly on an urgent business matter.'

The footman inclined his head. 'I am afraid neither Mr nor Mrs Trevarnon is at home,' he said. 'He is in Penzance on business, and the mistress has gone to Trevarnon House to be with her father-in-law, who is in failing health. Do you wish to leave your card?'

She had not thought of a card. She had imagined a thousand outcomes in her mind, but the possibility of failing to find the Trevarnons at home had simply not occurred to her.

'Thank you, no. But you may say that I called.' And she beat a retreat, flustered and confused.

Her route back to the station took her past Trevarnon House again. It made her heart turn over to see it. Should she go in? It was tempting. She might say that she was looking for Mrs Trevarnon – but in her heart of hearts she knew that she would do no such thing. All the same, she stood for a moment, gazing up towards the house.

A large plump woman with a flustered face bustled by in a shawl and apron. Katie nodded to her absently, and the woman said 'Afternoon to you, ma'am.'

She walked on by, a dozen paces, and then to Katie's amazement, she suddenly stopped and turned.

'Katie Warren! It is you, isn't it? Well, I'll be blowed!'

Cook. A little older, a little fatter, her mild blue eyes as kind as ever, dropping her parcels in her surprise.

'Cook!' Katie ran forward in greeting and enfolded the older woman in her arms.

'Well, let me look at you,' Cook exclaimed, holding Katie at arm's length and regarding her from top to toe, taking in the elegant black Liberty silk of her dress – fashioned on the sheath pattern so popular in the London magazines – and the smart gloves, hat and boots. 'My life, Katie, you look like a fashion plate! Fell on your feet, I can see.'

Katie smiled. The woman's directness was somehow comforting. 'Well yes,' she said, 'I was lucky. Found a good, hardworking man. It was my husband rebuilt Lower Trevarnon. That's why I came today – my husband died recently, and he had some unfinished business with Mr Robert.'

Cook snorted. 'Well you won't find him at home in daylight. Mr Selwood has made him junior partner in a garage business in the town – motorbuses and all, they're planning to have. Got him as manager, working all the hours God sends!' She gave a little wry laugh. 'You can't help feeling sorry for Mr Robert in a way. Wasn't brought up to it like we were, and he's taking it very hard.' She chuckled. 'Do him the world of good, mind you.'

Katie said, hardly daring to, 'And Mr George?'

Cook sighed. 'Poor Mr George. We've missed him terrible. Always a pleasure to work for, he was – never above giving you a kind word, or stopping to pass the time of day. No he's in Australia. Thinking of stopping there, too, so rumour says. Ruby had it from Mr Trevarnon's man. Going to buy a farm or something, by all accounts.'

Katie's mouth was dry. She said, 'And what does Miss Caroline think about it – Mrs Trevarnon, I should say?'

Cook laughed again. 'Poor lady. If there is anyone I feel sorry for, it's her. Never did anyone any harm that I can see. But she seems happy enough with this baby coming.'

Katie said, greatly daring, 'Doesn't she miss her husband?'

'Glad to see the back of him, I shouldn't wonder, if the truth be known,' Cook said. 'Are you coming up to the house yourself?'

But Katie shook her head. The idea of Caroline Trevarnon with a baby was almost more than she could bear.

'I have a train to catch,' she said. 'I've finished all my business here.'

It was, she reflected, nothing more than the truth.

Damn, damn and damn. What did that confounded woman want to come knocking at the door for, leaving messages with the footman so that there was no disguising it from Caroline?

'Mrs Olds?' she said, when the message was delivered. 'Whatever was she doing here, Robert?'

He did his best to hide his own surprise. 'Some unfinished business about the house, no doubt. Her husband, who was head of the firm, is recently dead, I hear.'

She looked at him steadily. 'Do we owe them, Robert?'

He would have denied it, but he could feel the tell-tale colour in his face. 'A little,' he said tetchily. 'It's nothing to concern yourself about, Caroline.'

'It may seem a little to you,' she said, 'but to that poor woman it is obviously an important sum, or she would not have come in person to claim it. She has too much sensibility for that.'

He looked at his wife sharply. How did she know that? If she knew who Katie was, matters were even more dangerous than he thought. 'You know her?'

'I met her once, with George, at a reception for the opening of the cathedral in Truro. A pleasant woman, I thought her.' She frowned a little. 'She reminded me of someone, though I cannot think who. I seem to have seen the face.'

'Some other function, possibly?' he said carefully, settling himself at table. Under cover of taking up his napkin, he watched her face, but she said casually enough, 'Perhaps,' and the moment passed.

Later, though, as they sat together in the drawing room, she with the baby's bonnet she was embroidering in white silk, he with his copy of the sporting papers, she said suddenly: 'There is no help for it, Robert. We shall have to pay that poor woman. We cannot leave debts outstanding – it will ruin our credit, and diminish our standing with the tradespeople. I had meant to keep it from you – I know how you love the gaming tables – but I have a little money put by from my allowance and from what your Papa gave me for the baby. Tell me how much it is, and I will pay it and have done. This once, Robert, and no more. And oblige me by not mentioning this to my father. He has threatened to cut off my allowance altogether if I allow you to squander it.'

He shook his head. 'It is too big a sum,' he said. In fact, confronted by Caroline's goodnatured generosity, he suddenly recognised how big a sum it was. 'How much do you have? Two hundred pounds?'

She dropped her work in agitation. 'As much as that? Robert, this is insupportable – a debt of that size unpaid! Papa was right, you are not to be trusted with capital. No, I have a hundred and forty guineas. We must send that at once, and then we shall have to be truly diligent and make economies on your salary. I wish you had spoken to me of this before, Robert. I should have been more frugal with the house-keeping.'

He gazed at her, suddenly appalled by the enormity of it. Even with the two hundred pounds he could lay his own hands on, Caroline's hundred and forty guineas gave him very little – three hundred and forty-seven pounds. Say three hundred – a man needed a little reserve for an emergency. That would make a very small dent in the sum he owed to Arthur Olds. How could he tell Caroline that the debt was for thousands, and no amount of buying pork instead of chicken would account for the shortfall?

He said, with genuine emotion, 'You are very good, Caroline.'

'In the meantime,' Caroline went on severely, 'you must write to Mrs Olds and explain that it will take some time to release the rest of the money.' She sighed. 'And we must keep this from our parents. Papa already suspects you of a poor head for money, and a matter of this kind might make him cut you out of the business altogether. He might even send for me to come home.'

'Caroline, no!' He would starve, with a house to keep and nothing whatever coming in.

She flashed him a smile. 'Then from here on, Robert, we shall manage all the bills in this house together. That way I can prevent another difficulty of this kind. Two hundred pounds outstanding, and the work finished for months!'

He could not tell her. Not then, and not later. He did send the money, together with a carefully-worded letter which did not mention the size of the sum outstanding. Caroline read it. It gave him a little time to think.

But there was only one possible solution. Selwood would not help him; Papa could not. Applying to Gillard was as good as having his debt cried from the rooftops. The next Monday, in the privacy of his office in Penzance, he wrote a long letter to George.

He read it twice before he sealed it. Finely judged, he felt. The problems of providing for the baby, the unexpected expenses of the rebuilding, the necessity for setting up a business, and, as a final touch, the distress the debt must be causing to the newly widowed Mrs Olds. If that didn't bring George up to scratch with the money, he thought with grim satisfaction, then nothing would.

He took the letter to the mail with his own hands.

Katie was delighted. 'Three hundred pounds? I misjudged the man. I thought we should have to sue him before we saw a penny. My visit to Penzance must have done some good, at least.' She looked at Willie. 'Though I have no doubt it will come to court yet. He says he will send the rest "as soon as he can release the funds" – but goodness alone knows when that will be, if ever. In the meantime, our creditors want paying.'

But Willie was looking thoughtful. 'I don't know,' he said slowly. 'It might be enough for something to be made of it. We could do what he has done – make a small payment to each of our suppliers. There would be almost enough, I think – with the other small amounts we have collected – to do that, and to finish the first of the houses in London. Just one – and then if we sell that, we could finance the second . . .'

He scribbled some figures on the corner of the blotter, and sat for a moment lost in thought. Then he looked up at Katie with shining eyes. 'Yes,' he said, 'I think we might. At least it would stave off catastrophe for a while.'

'Catastrophe?' It was Eva, coming into the room, so softly that they had not heard her approach. 'Are we expecting catastrophe?'

'It's nothing . . .' Katie began, but Willie forestalled her.

'We must tell her, Katie. It will affect her as much as any of us. And the news is not as black as it was.'

Katie took a deep breath. 'It's like this . . .' she began.

Eva listened a long time in silence. Then she said gently, 'I think Willie is right. The company might be saved. And I must help. Aunt Beryl's house is standing idle. With Willie's help, it might be turned to rooms and bring in a little income. And downstairs, perhaps . . .' She coloured. 'The woman Annie sews for on Monday has a child who wants to learn the pianoforte. Aunt Beryl has a piano. I might teach her, don't you think? I should like that above anything.'

Katie gazed at her step-daughter in admiration. 'You could manage that?'

'Miss Bevan might help, if we need her,' Eva said. 'Or Mrs Russell, I should call her now. She has no children, and she might be glad to come for an afternoon and teach a little.'

Katie wondered about suggesting that she would help, too, but Willie said firmly, 'Katie, you will have to mind the books if I am to go to London and see to the building. But I think, with Eva's help, we might manage for a month or two, while this Robert Trevarnon tries to release his money. If he doesn't, we shall have to call on the lawyers, but at least this way we can keep the company afloat.'

And so it was arranged. Willie drafted a sharp note to Lower Trevarnon acknowledging receipt of the three hundred pounds, and threatening legal action if the remainder was not paid before Quarter

Day. Katie signed it, and smiled when she read it through. 'Your obedient servant'. Not any more, Mr Robert Trevarnon. Not any more.

That summer it was a struggle, there was no denying it. Not the grinding life-and-death struggle that Katie had known when she first came to Truro, but a struggle nonetheless. And the more difficult perhaps, because their creditors and clients must never guess that times were hard.

But they were hard, although it was not want they faced, but a lessening of luxuries. No more training school for Eva, no more silk dresses and hansom cabs. Eva was uncomplaining, but it was hard for her, walking everywhere in all weathers, and retrimming an old hat or skirt instead of choosing a new one. The younger children were contented enough; the school fees were already paid, there was good plain food on the table, and good clothes on their backs, so there was little change for them. Willie had known struggle before, like Katie herself, and in any case they had the demands of the business to occupy their minds. Once again, it was hardest on Rosa, forced to let down last season's skirts and let out last season's blouses when all her schoolfellows were wearing new, but she had taken to modelling herself on Mrs Pankhurst and being resilient and uncomplaining, which was a mercy.

The staff were an unsupportable expense. Poor Lilly was found another position as a nursery maid, and departed weeping. Even so, finding the wages was a real problem, and Katie could see no solution. She could afford one and a half members of staff, but no more.

With a lump in her throat she called Peabody and Mabel together to discuss the matter. 'As things stand,' she said, sadly, 'I cannot afford to pay your wages, and I can hardly ask you to work for less.'

Mabel and Peabody exchanged glances, and Katie had the sudden conviction that they had known what was coming, and had talked about it between themselves. 'My dear Mrs Olds,' Peabody said, 'whatever do you think we are? Of course we must stay, and if there are a few pennies less in the pay-packet, well – you'll make it up to us again if you can, I daresay, when times look up. There's more than threepence a week makes a good position. This is my home, and you'll break my heart if you turn me off, and the same goes for Mabel too.'

Katie looked at Mabel, her round face nodding until her cap shook, and found that her heart was too full for speech.

'That's settled then,' Peabody said, and that was that. She and

Mabel threw their souls into the household effort. They were wonderful, creating miracles of good food from the cheapest seasonal ingredients. Cauliflower cheese and apple dumplings instead of roast beef and caramels – and Katie was astonished to remember how once these simple foods would have seemed a feast.

The help in the house was a boon, besides, because Katie was needed in the office. Even Annie was kept on somehow – her needle working overtime, and her work was more necessary than ever – but by hook or by crook they contrived. A casual visitor to the house during the day might never have noticed the change in their circumstances, but in the evenings it was a different story. More sitting up by lamplight to write letters, turn hems, or pore over bills, and less lounging by the fireside in teagowns with Mr Conan Doyle.

And there were casual visitors to the house, these days. When she had been a lonely wife, alone in the house, they had avoided her whenever her husband was away. Now that he was gone for ever, and she was a busy woman with a business to supervise and a family to keep, people were leaving cards. Whether it was the confrontation with Mrs Pritchard, or Aunt Beryl's patronage, or just neighbourliness to a young widow with a large family, Katie did not have time to consider. The important thing was that the family was being accepted, and with that acceptance came the first two or three small jobs in the locality for Willie and the business.

Katie began to breathe again. Aunt Beryl's house was scrubbed and papered, and three respectable lady-clerks were taken as upstairs lodgers, dinner provided. Little Alice came back to keep the place clean, and Eva kept the front room for her piano and found a second pupil, and a third. It was not a fortune she earned, but it paid for coals and light and servants, and when, by the end of July, Willie wrote from London to say that by working all the hours of daylight, the men had the first house almost finished, and a buyer was already found, Katie knew that the worst was over.

Almost, she had enjoyed it. She was no stranger to hard work, and what with running the office, and the house, and hearing Rosa say her catechism, and listening to Davy read, and telling stories to Vicki, she had no time to feel the loss of Arthur, or grieve for a young laughing man she had once known. She was, in a strange way, content.

Until one day the doorbell rang.

Mabel answered it, and came into the drawing room in such a fluster that Katie set down her pen and blotter and got to her feet at once.

'Whatever is it, Mabel?'

The girl looked at her. 'It's Mr Trevarnon, Mrs Olds. Says he has come to see you about some money.'

Of course! Katie felt her heart sink. It was almost Quarter Day. Come to beg an extension no doubt. Well, he should not have it. They would manage somehow to pay lawyers, and wait for their money if they had to. She folded her arms, and set her face in what Rosa called her 'Lally look'. She would show Mr Robert Trevarnon.

'You may show him in only if he has come to make a payment,' she said. 'If he has come here to ask for time, then the answer is no.' She turned to the window. That should get rid of him. She lifted the drape, expecting to see him walk disconsolately away.

'That's a pity, Katie, because time is what he wants.' A dear, familiar voice behind her.

She whirled round. 'George . . . ! Mr Trevarnon!'

'I prefer "George",' he said. He held out his hands to her and she walked to him and seized them warmly. How brown he looked. How bronzed. How beautiful.

Her heart was thumping treacherously as she said, 'I thought you in Australia.'

He laughed. 'And I thought you married, until I received my brother's letter. I am presumptuous, Katie – I came at once.'

She dropped his hands then. 'And what of your wife?'

'My wife?' He sounded astonished.

'Caroline. And . . . and the child.'

'But Caroline is married to Robert.' His words seemed to come from a dream. Was she hearing correctly? 'Did you never read my letter?'

She shook her head.

'You returned it, but it was opened.'

She nodded, almost unable to speak. 'Davy was ill. I opened it – but I never read it. I didn't know . . . You must have thought . . .'

He was smiling. 'I thought you had sent it back because my marriage was annulled. Because I was a free man, and might have been a threat. It *was* annulled, Katie, and I *am* free.' He looked down at her gravely. 'Was I wrong? Was I never a threat at all? Should I have stayed in Australia and raised horses, after all?'

She regarded him helplessly, still almost unable to believe her eyes. He was there, beside her, when she had thought him lost for ever. No words came.

He said softly, 'Answer me one question, Katie. If the answer is no, I will give you the money my family owes, and walk out of this house for ever.' He took her hands again. 'Do you love me?'

She still could not speak, but stood there, tears of wonder standing in her eyes, nodding as though she would never stop.

CHAPTER THIRTY-SIX

It was a small wedding. It made no more than a tiny paragraph in the daily newspapers, and there were no titled guests at the registry office. Only the children, and the staff from Number Twenty-three, come down for the day, and Cook and Ruby, and Cissie Tremble wearing the same hat she had worn to Meg's wedding but with a new ribbon, and poor old Mr Trevarnon, thin as a ghost but smiling all the same. No Robert. A very small wedding.

There was no marquee on the lawns, though the September day was fine enough, just a simple wedding supper spread on the big dining table in the blue drawing room, among the vase upon vase of massed red roses which George had plundered from the gardens with his own hands. A simple supper, but splendid: salmon, capons, salad, trifles, profiteroles, bowls of fresh grapes and apricots and, crowning it all, a cake on which Cook had lavished all her skill and hours of love.

No honeymoon. Only a drive in the carriage with George himself at the reins. Out to the moors and the cliffs, where the mine chimneys raised their smoky heads against the deepening blue of the sky, and the sea rose and fell with a gentle, contented sigh.

And then back to the house, and in. Not the backstairs this time, cold and draughty and peopled with shadows, but up the wide main staircase, the warm red carpet welcoming underfoot, and into the master bedroom. And there . . .

It was a revelation, a joy she had not imagined. She had known, always, that her pulse stirred beside him, but she had never guessed to what purpose they stirred. She lay in the moonlight and loved him, blessing the world that so much happiness was possible.

And in the morning, they loved again, and went down to breakfast with Rosa and Vicki and David, and wrote a letter to Willie and Eva, and walked out to see Little Manor and the sun twinkling on the water. They held hands and laughed, and stood under the trees at Trevaylor and watched the first leaves of autumn float gently away in the stream.

That was all. Not a remarkable event, in the annals of mankind.

EPILOGUE

It was another summer's day, the sky as deep as infinity and the little wind frisking the waves along the river, and whisking the skirts of the ladies who walked along the water's edge, and watched the little boats come and go across Plymouth water.

He had brought her here more then once since they were married, to the South Hams and Batten beach. Vicki and David loved it, attacking the sand with great wooden-handled spades and dangling crabs from their fingers, to the great detriment of their summer clothes. David nearly lost his sailor hat with the ribbons in the gusting wind, and it was only saved by the elastic. Vicki trailed her petticoats in the tide and had to be carried in by her stepfather, with her flounced hems all damp and sandy. Rosa, at thirteen, was too much of a lady to bounce on the sands, but she sat and read her book under her parasol with a good grace, and only occasionally made meaningful remarks about bathing machines at other, more fashionable resorts.

Katie sat on the deckchair rocking the twins in their perambulator-carriage. She might have had the nursemaid do it, but it always gave her pleasure, minding the children herself. She smiled down at the sleeping faces in their broderie anglaise sunbonnets under the heavy fringed hood of the baby-carriage. Katherine Margaret Anne and Edward George Frederick. What a big mouthful for two such little people.

What sturdy, contented babies they were too – the pride of their grandfather's heart. Not a bit like that sickly, sulky son of Robert's. Caroline doted on the boy, of course, but Robert was already finding the child's tantrums tedious. You could see that he was almost glad to

357

get away to his office, these days, much as he disliked working! And to think she had once been envious of Caroline Selwood!

She looked up and smiled as George and Vicki came and sat beside her.

'What a beautiful day,' she said. 'You feel you could see for miles.'

He gestured out across the blue expanse of sea. 'Go far enough across that water, and you will get to Europe. France, Spain. Fascinating. When the children are older, I'll take you there, Katie. We could do what I did, perhaps – tour Europe, see America and Australia. You could visit that family of yours which seems to be doing so well in all those far-flung places. We could see Fanny, and I could meet Meg and those two brothers of yours. Even you have relatives you've never seen – all those nephews and nieces. Would you like that, Katie? Would that make you happy?'

She smiled at him again. 'Of course it would be lovely. But I'm happy already. Sitting here, surrounded by our children. You and me together. Even Willie and Eva in Truro, in Number Twenty-three. I should have guessed the way the wind was sitting! And what a good job they made of the company, and that little school, even before we sorted out that debt of Robert's. No, I am a very lucky woman.' She gave a little sigh of contentment. 'What could possibly spoil our happiness now?'

She looked around at the sparkling sea, the milling people, the tall blue vault of the sky. Behind her, far out over the sea, in the direction of the Continent, a small dark cloud was forming.

It was nineteen hundred and twelve.

also available from
THE ORION PUBLISHING GROUP

All Orion/Phoenix titles are available at your local bookshop or from the following address:

Littlehampton Book Services
Cash Sales Department L
14 Eldon Way, Lineside Industrial Estate
Littlehampton
West Sussex BN17 7HE
telephone 01903 721596, *facsimile* 01903 730914

Payment can either be made by credit card (Visa and Mastercard accepted) or by sending a cheque or postal order made payable to *Littlehampton Book Services*.
DO NOT SEND CASH OR CURRENCY.

Please add the following to cover postage and packing

UK and BFPO:
£1.50 for the first book, and 50P for each additional book to a maximum of £3.50

Overseas and Eire:
£2.50 for the first book plus £1.00 for the second book and 50p for each additional book ordered

----

BLOCK CAPITALS PLEASE

name of cardholder ....   *delivery address*
....   *(if different from cardholder)*
address of cardholder ....
....
....
....
postcode ....   *postcode* ....

☐ I enclose my remittance for £.............................

☐ please debit my Mastercard/Visa (delete as appropriate)

card number ☐☐☐☐☐☐☐☐☐☐☐☐☐☐☐☐☐☐

expiry date ☐☐☐☐

signature ....

prices and availability are subject to change without notice